ARNETT HARTWELL

Deliver

Boudi-Ca Chronicles Book 3

First edition

ISBN: 978-1-959133-03-2

This book was professionally typeset on Reedsy.
Find out more at reedsy.com

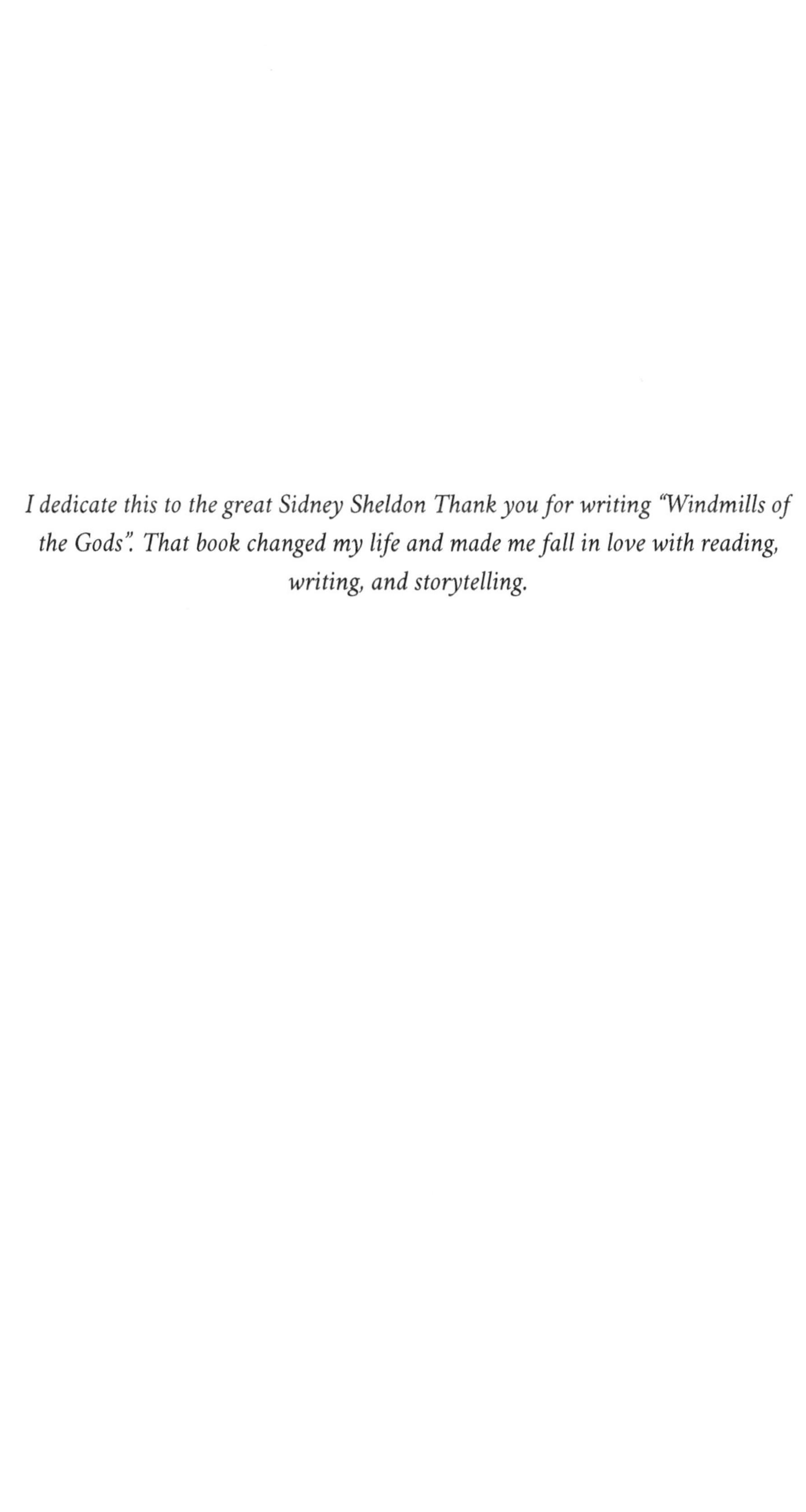

I dedicate this to the great Sidney Sheldon Thank you for writing "Windmills of the Gods". That book changed my life and made me fall in love with reading, writing, and storytelling.

"Teachers teach and do the world good
kings just rule and most are never understood"

KRS-one

Contents

Acknowledgement

I would like to acknowledge my family, friends, and fans. We did it!

Chapter 1.

Boudi-Ca straddled the vanity chair. Her black silk stockings caressed her thighs like a Kishi slave's gentle fingertips. The best clothes in Hell were sewn to pleasure the wearer as much as the viewer. Her clothes were the most expensive labels in the capital city of Mer, thanks to the wealth of Archduke Fennel and Archduchess Lydiah.

The dressing girl wrapped her with a silk-lined corset. The foldable cups lifted her youthful breasts to perfection. The see-through black lace offered a view of her nipples. Kveta hauled on the back lacings. The dressing girl was as strong as any boy.

Boudi-Ca picked up her tea cup and swallowed the last dregs of black nectar, taking care with her painted lips on the porcelain rim. The tepid liquid numbed her throat and sent a ballooning rush of pleasure through her body. She went limp and gazed at the slave girl in the vanity mirror.

Kveta was older and shorter than most of Fennel's girls in the house. Kveta had once been beautiful, but her beauty had been stolen during her servitude. Her body was crisscrossed with a myriad of old scars, a roadmap of Fennel's attentions towards his owned toy. A silver coin piercing glinted on Kveta's left cheek, a little echo of her welded collar.

Coin piercings were a tradition for human slaves in Mer. The denomination indicated the services provided. The five-denarius coin advertised Kveta's availability for oral sex as well as bath towels, bedsheets, and general room service for guests and visitors.

"It isn't fair," Boudi-Ca murmured.

"I'm sorry, fledgling." Kveta paused in her efforts. "Am I tying it too tight?"

"No. It isn't fair that all the boys in the house are so handsome and pampered, while the girls must suffer the horrible tortures of Master Fennel."

Kveta continued to tighten the laces but with less energy, as if the mere mention of the Master had weakened her arms with a silent, draining terror. Boudi-Ca felt a slow fear come over own her throat from having spoken against the Master. When she took nectar, she had a habit of not caring about anything, including Master Fennel, who enjoyed terrorizing every female he owned in his baroque, three-level abode, except for her and Masia-Ca.

"Boudi!" Masia's voice came from the doorway. "Why aren't you ready yet?"

"My tea," Boudi-Ca managed breathlessly. The wonderful tea pleasure still filtered through her thin, hungering interior, which constricted more with every lacing that Kveta pulled.

"Well, finish it so we can go." Lydiah's other fledgling paced into the bedchamber on a cloud of arousing perfume. Masia's figure was perfectly primped, powdered, painted, and polished as usual. Masia was a fashion model in Mer, an ambitious beauty fledgling who had landed Lydiah for her mentor, and then had benefitted from Lydiah's influence and connections. Masia was a painted Asian beauty, a living doll on heeled spindles. Masia sighed. "Kveta, you can't properly tie a corset with Boudi-Ca sitting down."

"She's skinny," Kveta protested. "And if I stand her on her feet, she'll just fall over from her tea. I have to wrestle with her to even—"

"Are those new stockings, Boudi?" Masia interrupted. "The Mistress hasn't bought me new clothes for at least six weeks. You get new things like every day."

"So? I need more clothes." Boudi-Ca sucked her breath further to take the lacings around her belly, and finally Kveta tied her off. Masia helped her to her feet and herded her like a fawn down the rear east-wing stairs. The carriage waited in the shadows of the driveway. The bare-chested driver boy looked handsome in his black silk pants and matching chapeau. He unfurled his whip as they approached. The horses stamped and snorted.

Master Fennel's black Hell hounds milled around the carriage, observing the embarkation with slavering jaws. Boudi-Ca pulled her purse away from a hound's sulfuric snout. The hound followed her, sniffing hungrily at her leather purse, as if wanting to eat the poor creature whose skin had been stripped to serve la couture in Hell's fashion world.

Boudi-Ca settled into the rear carriage seat next to Masia. She enjoyed evening carriage rides, especially when her head was floating with tea pleasure. A slight breeze stirred the ancient, black-barked Tanjie oaks, and the last orange rays of sunset glowed on their boles.

"Hold!" Lydiah emerged from the house door. The Mistress was dressed from head to toe in antique drapery, which was pale like her long hair and drawn under her breasts in an old Egyptian style. The Mistress looked like a white marble statue that walked in life, adorned with glittering diamonds on her ears and fingers, with hints of warmth only visible in her cheeks and impressive cleavage. "Where are you girls going, Masia-Ca?"

"We're going to the Denmark Quarter again, Mistress."

"Where are your tunicae for the Egyptian new year's eve?"

"We're wearing split skirts," Masia answered. "Tunics are stupid, Mistress. I'm a fashion plate model. I can't go to parties dressed like an old parlour window."

Lydiah palmed her forehead. "There's nothing wrong with costumes for parties, fledgling. Use your imagination. Someday corsets will be considered old fashioned and musty, and you're wearing a corset, aren't you?"

"Maybe I should take Boudi-Ca's beautiful new corset then, since she won't need it. Thank you, Mistress." Masia snapped her fingers at the driver boy, who plied his whip. The horses surged in their leather harnesses, and the carriage lurched into the dappled orange light. Fennel's estate perched on the top of a hill in the exclusive Tanjie neighborhood, and Dawn's chariot was still visible through the trees in early evening, receding dimly in the polluted distance over the bleak plateaus of the Mare Mortis. Lydiah's voice chased them down the gravel driveway.

"I'll want to see you girls at the Judge's place later. I'll send a bird."

Masia groaned under her breath as the carriage rolled out through the iron gates of the estate. "Mistress should have said so when we were dressing. We're wearing the wrong perfumes for a downtown devil party. Maybe the Mistress has finally slipped into madness. Corsets will be high fashion until the end of time."

Boudi-Ca nodded, pretending she understood. The capital city was a complicated maze of fashion preferences and faux pas, which were often different among the various geographical districts of Mer, depending on wealth, politics, and ethnicity. She couldn't keep everything straight. She was drinking black nectar tea on a daily basis. The nectar smoothed her memories, and every day dripped languorously into the next.

The carriage rolled down the hill road out of Tanjie. Boudi-Ca closed her eyes. Her nectar-pleasure had taken over her whole body, and she felt almost perfect. The carriage seat bumped and vibrated pleasantly under her buttocks. Her pearled panties aroused her as the carriage descended the ancient streets into the gas lamps and plazas of the Merian downtown. The carriage veered north at the corner of Stag Park and rolled into the stately, blocky old Denmark Quarter. After several minutes, the carriage jolted to a stop in front of the worn Bavarian façades of the two-story Zweibrüder club.

Boudi-Ca exited the carriage, wary of her heels on the ancient pitted street stones. By the time she circled the carriage wheels, Masia was inside the Zweibrüder. Boudi-Ca shouldered her purse and strutted through the double doors into a dark arched vestibule. Candlelight, music, and muffled laughter drifted through the smoky club corridors.

"Pose?"

Just inside the door, a pig-headed photographer beckoned. Boudi-Ca stopped and posed while the hellion readied his box camera. He smiled as if recognizing her. She turned a quarter profile and pushed her tits and buttocks that magical extra inch.

When the photographer signaled that he was finished, Boudi-Ca continued through the acrid odor of the flash chemicals. Perhaps she would soon arrive with Masia on the Zweibrüder picture wall of the Merian wealthy and famous. Perhaps her image was there already, and she just didn't remember it. According to Masia, the Denmark quarter was the place to be seen for the young and fashionable in the city. While the Ukraine quarter was still the high-class haunt of the old money and aristocrats, the Germans were the cutting edge, ahead of the rest in embracing the modern technologies from Earth—the cameras, motor cars, music boxes, and other things.

Boudi-Ca paced through the crowded common rooms. An ugly, drunk Djinnus grabbed her ass and licked her ear as she passed. She responded with a coquettish smile, a polite sigh of pleasure, and a gentle squeeze to his crotch. She finally spied Moshe in a back salon with several other Djinnus.

A Middle-Eastern Jinn and an Asian Jinn were entertaining the men. The two Jinni recited poetry simultaneously in different languages while suspended upside down from the ceiling by ankle cuffs. The Jinni wore antique Egyptian jewelry, and several of the men wore togas for the Egyptian New Year's celebration. The men listened and watched with evident pleasure.

Boudi-Ca frowned. She couldn't understand a word of the poetry. She hadn't studied those languages. She crept behind the sofa where Moshe was reclining. She squeezed his shoulder and leaned close. "I need you. Please."

Moshe lifted his six feet of Djinnus muscle. He rounded the velvet sofa and cupped the curve of her ass with his strong artisan hand. He kissed her hungrily and nudged her to the side of the room, where a buffet table waited. Sectioned silver platters offered powdered nectars for the privileged guests.

"Have a bump?" Moshe kissed her ear. "It's for the poetry."

"Fine," Boudi-Ca answered. Moshe always tried to get her higher, and getting higher had become a ritual in their nights of intimacy. She took a sniffer of the sparkly purple powder that Moshe had indicated. The pleasure exploded through her skull, and her eye sockets went bouncy and buzzing. Moshe bumped alongside her. He rubbed his nose, turned, and penetrated her mouth with his warm, thick tongue.

Boudi-Ca embraced Moshe's heat and muscled chest. She felt herself getting wet, and Moshe's cock was ready for her under his Egyptian toga. He wasted no time in lifting her skirt and lowering her panties. She twisted, tip-toed, and pivoted her hip to get the penetration. Moshe bent and pressed with his cock. The nectared sex-pleasure ignited inside her belly like a Chinese firework set off in a pile of dry tinder.

She nestled her cheek against Moshe's sweaty shoulder. The Jinn poets were slowly rotating, hypnotic like upside-down music box dancers. Their poetic syllables fused in the air and began to randomly rhyme. Boudi-Ca smiled as she realized. The meaning of the words just didn't matter—only the mating of the throaty, silken sounds when they humped and bumped over and against each other in an intercultural orgy.

Moshe's cock synchronized with the rhythm.

Chapter 2.

The night skies of Haawiyah reflected firelight off the gas clouds, limning the coralline brittle-brushes in a faint volcanic glow. The wind sighed through the thickets, sending rattling clacks like dry bones over the storm-tortured stones. The wind blew east towards the Great Blue Hole mines, carrying the stink of Hell's capital city. The odors of crushed stone and slave toil were dominated by the smells of liquor, leather, sex, and gold coins.

Golda clasped the warm hand of Elder Priebus on her left and Aunt Marta on her right. Five were the humans in the circle with her on the Great Blue Hole rim—three elder women and two men from venerable Gypsy families. The robed witches had formed a circle around a fire that clung to life. The flames spat blue sulfuric sparks.

"Tonight we pray for Golda's lost friend," Priebus intoned. "We invoke the power of Lady Allyssia to the heart of Haawiyah. We call on the great mother of Love to hear us on this Egyptian New Year's eve. We call on Allyssia to help us send positive energy and blessings to the lost fledgling named Boudi-Ca." The Gypsy witches chanted together.

Love and light into the night.

Love and light into the night.

Golda felt the tingle of power in her fingertips. She closed her eyes and opened to the tapestry. She chanted softly with the Gypsy witches, merging with their energy. It was a raw energy that she could use, even though she was a different species. She willed her soul to transfer into the dream world, and from there she flitted through the black forest, five leagues to reach Hell's teeming capital city. She could hear the witches in the psychic distance.

Hear us, great goddess, Lady of Cytherea. We humbly ask that you grace us this evening, this time of waxing love, to hear Golda's prayers. Help her speak to her friend Boudi-Ca through the dream world.

Love and light into the night.

Love and light into the night.

Golda flew through the dream space, unfurling the art of tapestry-linked travel that she'd learned through four years of study with Masad, the demigod tracker. She opened her heart and mind, sending her desire and attention ahead of her into Mer. Dangerous things lurked dreamside in Hell's biggest city. The predatorial children of the Underworld could take many forms. She needed to be ready to flee if necessary.

She darted through the black dream-gates of Mer like a cat in the night, past the scaly guardians that always lurked there, waiting to strike at Mimos and sundry spies. She ignored the outbound travelers that passed—devils and Djinnus intent on earthly destinations. The tapestry inside the capital was chaos. Threads twisted everywhere. Grunts and screams came from slaves and wives in thousands of twisted bedchambers. Fervent prayers were whispered from myriad lips, petitioning Lord Hades and Lady Allyssia with wishes for material gain and endless indulgence in the flesh.

Golda raced up a dream-hill to the dark mansion where Boudi-Ca lived with Lydiah and Fennel. She shrugged off her fear and carried love in her heart like a torch from Allyssia. Black walls rose ahead, punctured by a grim gate of spired iron. She'd gazed many times at Fennel's dream gates, but she'd never dared enter those thorny lawns where Hell hounds lurked, and worse.

Golda pushed through the red-limned gate into the black garden beyond. Protective magical forces congealed in the dream world to impede her progress. Deadly things closed the distance—shadow serpents that slithered within the weave itself. The invisible snakes leapt and wrapped her limbs, and she fought against them. Her chest constricted. Panic seized her abdomen. She was drowning in the tapestry, dying.

Love and light into the night.

Love and light into the night.

She felt a force at her back then, an immense power of energy, a friend. She surged forwards and down like the prow of a boat. She broke through the black patch in the tapestry, revealing a deeper, second weave—a blood-red weave of tighter, less malleable lines, like muscles under flexible skin. Boudi-Ca wasn't home at Fennel's estate, but Boudi's thread was still in the underweave, thick and present, tangled hopelessly with the others surrounding her.

Golda strained forward and grabbed Boudi's line in her fist. The tide receded, and the tapestry closed in. She realized that she had a decision to make. If she let go of the underthread, Boudi-Ca would be lost forever. She held the thread with all of her strength. The thread moved then, detaching itself from the rest, and the very fabric of the underweave groaned, tore, and dislocated.

Golda pulled Boudi's thread out of the gates of Fennel's domain, and then at the speed of an eye blink she dragged the thread back to the safety of the forest. The tangled threads dragged with her, however, and the mess snagged and tripped her feet. She tipped over and landed hard on the Haawiyah stones. She opened her eyes. Pain laced through her skull. The witches stopped chanting and looked down at her in the firelight.

"What happened?" Aunt Marta said.

Golda levered herself into a sitting position. "I wasn't ready for that much energy. I'm impressed."

Elder Tahany frowned. "We hadn't raised much energy yet. You were actually transferring to us instead. Whatever that energy was, it came from within you, or it came from your goddess. True love is said to be the greatest power in all the realms. Perhaps you have it for this friend of yours. If you do, then you might have a chance."

"I'm done for tonight," Elder Carlos muttered. "This was ill-advised. I'm going back to the Dells to celebrate the New Year with my wife. Good luck, Jinn. May the Fates and the Lady bless your quest if they wish, but Lord Hades and His children are the rulers in this realm. No one is wise to defy them."

Golda watched the Gypsy witches disperse and return to their horses, whispering in low tones. She was no stranger to headaches, but her head was throbbing. Only Priebus stayed by her side, and within minutes they were alone on the Great Blue Hole rim.

"What happened, Golda?" Priebus frowned with sympathy in the dim firelight. "Can you tell me? Did you speak with your friend? Did you see her?"

"No. I'm sorry I ruined your New Year's coven circle. I know the others didn't want anything to do with me."

Priebus hid her eyes behind the sweep of her long dark hair. "This was a one-time thing. I wanted you to start the Egyptian New Year with hope. Sometimes we lose people, you know."

Golda gritted her teeth. "And sometimes people are taken from us against their will. The fact that Boudi-Ca is down here is partly my fault. I shouldn't have listened to Ayelet in Dead Sedde. I should have insisted we all leave that damned place together. Now Boudi-Ca and Ayelet are both gone. The guilt nags me every day that I live with it. At least I've located Boudi. I know where she is. I just don't know what to do next."

"You were Boudi's lover then?"

"I don't like talking about my ex-lovers, especially with my current one." Golda stroked Pinhas' arm. The Reik family matriarch leaned and pecked her cheek.

"I have my husband. I love him. We died together, and we've lived together in the afterlife for nigh on four centuries. I love you, Golda, but Agron is my blueberry. He'll always mean more to me than anyone else, even a beautiful Jinn."

"Of course! I didn't mean—"

Golda turned to meet Pinhas' lips. When she closed her eyes, the strange red striations of the underweave echoed in her mind. The weave of Fate was said to run under the more visible weave of the tapestry, but she'd never glimpsed the weave of Fate, much less touched it. She'd never possessed such power. Only the gods could tug the threads directly in the weave of Fate, and even then at their peril. Priebus drew away from her, as if sensing her restless energy.

"Do you think your friend is suffering? If they gave her nectar from the poppies on the banks of the river Lethe, then perhaps she isn't suffering so much, at least for lost love. They say the black is only horrible for those who know the difference. It's pleasant when you're in it. The nectar washes all of your pains and cares away."

Golda rubbed her temples. "Boudi-Ca apparently lives in wealth and high style with Lydiah in Mer. She has the freedom to go to parties and enjoy herself, but she's different. She's empty inside. I can feel it."

"I understand."

"No, you don't. Boudi-Ca was amazing when she came to live with Lady Allyssia in Meristyian. Every expression was clear on her innocent face, and every sensual experience was new and beautiful for her. Ambassador Lydiah stole Boudi's memories and perverted her into the service of Lord Hades and Lady Allyssia. The old, beautiful Boudi-Ca is lost, and she doesn't even know it."

Priebus grimaced. "Lydiah sounds like a horrible evil creature from Hell's Court."

"My mentor, Masad, told me that Lydiah is the severed avatar of an ancient goddess. She has no morality and loves to spin lies. In the old days, they called her the Whore of Babylon. She's not so respected today, but she's still important in Hell's Court and the Smokeless Flames. She's the wife of Archduke Fennel, who is the son of Lord Hades. My mentor warned me not to go against Lydiah. I finally had to try anyway, for Boudi." Golda paused. A movement tugged her senses back to the tapestry. The Gypsy witches had dispersed towards the forest, but she and Priebus weren't alone on the stony plateau. A pair of threads was close and approaching. The black lines in the tapestry were Hell's Court devils—a night patrol. The patrol was well-hidden, cloaked by thaumaturgy. Priebus touched her arm.

"Golda? What is it?"

"The devils are coming. Get on your horse. We have to go." Golda rose and went to where her horse was tethered. She was astride in a second, and Priebus was alongside. Priebus was a remarkable Gypsy woman, as skilled with a horse as she was with love-making.

"We should put out the fire."

"There's no time." Golda urged her steed towards the shelter of the ancient forest, cloaking her thread as she went. Soon she'd gained distance over the devils, enough to slow the pace with Priebus in tow. When they entered the forest, she cast a tenebris lux to illuminate the lichened boles, twisted vines, and leaf-dead branches. She approached the camp of the Reik family in a roundabout way, as she always did to throw off any potential pursuers.

She was familiar with the routine. She'd lived outside of Mer for several months attempting to reach Boudi-Ca in the capital city. At great risk, she'd confronted the Mimọ fledgling twice in the previous weeks, but her efforts had achieved nothing.

Boudi-Ca hadn't even recognized her. During the second encounter, she'd managed to touch Boudi-Ca and speak with her privately in a Merian club, but Boudi's lurking friend had quickly sent off a messenger bird to report her presence. She'd had no choice but to flee for fear of being caught. It wasn't easy to approach Boudi-Ca if the fledgling always had a protective escort.

Golda licked her dry lips. Boudi's memory loss was surely caused by black nectar, as Priebus had suggested. Lydiah and Hell's Court had made the Mimọ into a nectar addict to forget her past life with Allyssia. Boudi's eyes were big and dreamy, and her body had a thin, scented, fairy-like feel, a hallmark of heavy nectar consumption.

Golda ducked under a low-slung tree bough. She knew well the aura and scent of nectar. She'd managed to end her own habit with the help of Masad, but the addiction still affected her. She sniffed. The dark night wind was strengthening further. The storms of spring were starting early while the great Lady Allyssia mated with Lord Hades. The storms would calm sometime in the moons of April and May when Allyssia settled alone again in Her bed. In June, the dead forest would grow oppressive with pregnant heat.

Golda glanced over her shoulder to make sure Priebus was keeping pace. Soon the Gypsy families would depart the ancestral forests of Haawiyah for their summer tours in distant Erebus and Meristyian, leaving her alone without ready sexual sustenance, and all the more vulnerable to bounty hunters and Hell's Court patrols.

That night, she'd made an attempt to reach the depths of Boudi's nectar-erased mind via the dream world, using the energy of the witches bypass the guardians around the estate of Archduke Fennel. She'd failed. Boudi-Ca hadn't been at home. She'd taken serious risks to get Boudi-Ca out of Mer, but she needed even more, perhaps even a kidnapping by force.

Chapter 3.

❧

The Jinn poets in the club room had ended their performance. They were employing their skills for more traditional services. Assonance and fricatives had given way to ass-worship and tits. Boudi-Ca milked Moshe's thick cock with her inner muscles. She danced a rhythm of inches with her buttocks pressed against the beveled edge of the antique Denmark buffet table.

Finally the handsome Djinnus plunged and filled her for a second time. She pivoted and slid off of him. She tightened her nethers to contain his precious, life-giving elixir. Her belly felt warm, and her inner muscles quivered with a satisfied happiness. She slipped back into her heels while Moshe cleaned himself with a handkerchief. He knew better than to ask her to do it, or to use her expensive, gold-threaded split skirt.

Boudi-Ca raised her lips to kiss her thanks to Moshe. Moshe was the young Djinnus fledgling of Master Faisil. He was an Djinnus of mongrel ethnicity, but he posed as a Ukraine artist, the better to purvey his paintings and pass himself off as more sophisticated. His lips were nectar-hot. His chest was sweaty, and his jacket smelled like cloves and smoke.

Boudi-Ca wriggled from his powerful embrace. She found her pearled panties on the floor and pushed them into her purse. "I hate to leave you, but I'm supposed to go downtown with Masia-Ca. She got a bird from the Mistress."

Moshe squeezed her shoulder affectionately. "Lydiah's fledglings are busy girls—lots of boyfriends in their skirts."

"No. The Mistress keeps us on a strict regimen. We have to stay thin for fashion. Except for the slave boys, you're my only guy. I'm not even supposed to have you twice in one night."

"Aw." Moshe grinned. "Much love, ma petite poupée. I'll be here again tomorrow, most likely. I love the poetry, you know."

"I liked how we went slowly so we could listen." Boudi-Ca bent over the buffet table and tongued a little lick of spilled Hendrix purple. The pleasure warmed her throat and lifted the sex-rush in her skull. She pinched Moshe's tight ass and exited the back salon. She wobbled on her stilettos through the Zweibrüder. It was good to be back in Mer after four months at Fennel's north country château, where she'd passed the off-season with Masia and Mistress Lydiah. Everything in the capital seemed to happen so much faster.

She strode through the vestibule in her purple float, which resonated in her brain with the accordion music. The Denmark nightclub was abuzz just like she was, and she wasn't thrilled to leave. In truth, she'd switched to the lowbrow Zweibrüder that spring not for the fashionable technology, but rather to avoid her old boyfriend. Master Meva had married Duchess Thyrah the previous summer, and he'd joined his royal Jinn wife as a fixture at her fruity three-storied Himbeerblume at the top of Weimacht Strasse. Master Meva had little time or desire for his former flirtations.

Masia was waiting in the carriage. Boudi-Ca climbed alongside and removed her heels. A slug-like dampness reminded her that she'd forgotten to visit the bath. She hitched her skirt and dug in her purse for a serviette. The driver boy snapped the whip. The horses strained forward towards downtown.

"Who creamed you?" Masia asked casually, squinting at the gas lamps that glowed yellow up Weimacht Strasse. The wind off the Mare was drifting east, carrying ash and dust through the city. The polluted streets were filled with a typical thick haze.

"Moshe again," Boudi-Ca answered. "He's my squeeze."

"Lord's balls. It sounds like that second-rate painter has you locked and loaded." Masia's lips curled with a classist lack of enthusiasm. "You really need to follow the two-week rule. You don't want to get addicted, even if he wants to marry you. You're too good for him."

Boudi-Ca shrugged. "He knows I'm joining the Smokeless Flames soon. Screw the rule. So where did the Mistress say we're going?"

"We're going to Judge Rhadamanthus' villa in Pee-Hill. The Mistress told me to 'bring you', so I assume this is all about you, as usual. That's fine. I've only been dancing. I saved myself for the higher label waistcoats."

"I don't blame you. You're too good for the Zweibrüder." Boudi-Ca folded the serviette, re-arranged her skirt, and fished in her purse for her hairbrush, secretly running her gaze over the perfection of Masia's waxed legs. She wondered what Lydiah wanted with her at the home of the Judge.

The carriage rolled slowly through downtown and into Pee-Hill. Judge Rhadamanthus' villa was in the Pomegranate Hill district, south of downtown Mer where many Hell's Court devils lived. Pomegranate Hill was called Pee-Hill by the general Merian populace, a term of little affection for the devils and their perverse bedroom preferences.

Pee-Hill was a wealthy neighborhood, a center point of the Merian social map. The devils were the official Hell's Court clerks, judges, and lawyers, and therefore among the richest of Hell's citizens. The Hill was said to be riddled with the deepest, most pain-filled slave pits in the city, except for the dreaded Bolgia pits—the official dungeons of Hell's Court.

Rhadamanthus lived in a historical villa, a fusion of Egyptian architecture with interior décor dating from the Italian Rococo. The driver boy pulled the carriage up the chrysanthemum skirted driveway and parked behind a line of other carriages. Boudi-Ca disembarked to follow Masia through the magnificent basalt archway into the villa's vestibule, which was floored with smoky quartz quarried from the Great Blue Hole mines.

The villa inside was decked in shades of grey with silver and pearl accidents—the signature style of the devil lady of the house, Mistress

Breanarachelle. Magnificent Italian oil paintings in silver frames adorned the aging plaster walls. Somber string music drifted through the stony foyers, mingling with laughter and coos coming from the front veranda.

"I'm going to the veranda," Masia said nonchalantly. "The Mistress said you should come to the drawing room." Masia pivoted and stalked towards the veranda like a young huntress in high heels.

Boudi-Ca pulled her eyes away from Masia and floated across the foyer in the opposite direction. Her heels clicked hollowly to mingle with the strains of laughter and piano music. She knew she'd been to the Judge's place a few times before, but she couldn't remember where she was going. She wandered down a long hallway, then another. Finally she found two uniformed Court devils standing guard at double doors. They gestured as if expecting her.

The Judge's drawing room was over-warm from a low fire in a brick hearth. A Kishi party-slave knelt cuffed to the oak fireplace mantel. The pointy-eared girl was gagged with a leather head-harness that pulled her mane into a thick pony tail. She hung from her wrists, silently enduring the intense heat against her belly and thighs.

Near the fire, Lydiah was sitting next to her husband, Archduke Fennel. Opposing them sat Judge Rhadamanthus and his devil wife, Breanarachelle. Another devil official from Hell's Court sat nearby along with two military Djinnus and their wives who, judging from their decorated red uniforms, were high-ranking Jinni in the Smokeless Flames.

One wife sat on the floor at her husband's feet. The other sat on her husband's lap. The remaining guest in the drawing room was a tall, elder Jinn from the Flames-Sisterhood who lurked in the corner, sipping a glass of absinthe. The drawing room was devoid of the usual hellion businessmen, philosopher toadies, and art-whoring aesthetes who flocked in droves to the richest people in the city.

Lydiah beckoned. "Ah, my lovely second fledgling has arrived. Do come in, dear. We were just talking about you."

"Thank you, Mistress." Boudi-Ca curtsied and strode into the room, taking care with her heels at the edge of the carpet. She'd been taught the seriousness of representing Lydiah in the presence of high-powered people in Mer. She folded her legs and seated herself semi-gracefully at the feet of her Mistress, as was expected of fledglings in formal settings. Everyone in the room was looking at her.

"Are you floating, fledgling?" Lydiah asked, caressing her shoulder.

"Yes, Mistress. I was in the Denmark Quarter."

"My fledgling likes her nectar, yet another reason why she isn't ready to join the Flames," Lydiah said. "She needs her black tea."

"She's a real fairy-nose isn't she?" Breanarachelle sniffed. The judge's wife shifted and uncrossed her legs to lean closer. "She's red-pink in her nose and cheeks, and her pale complexion isn't helping."

"It has been nearly three years, Lydiah." Judge Rhadamanthus eased back in his chair and drew an herb tin from the pocket of his yellow waistcoat. The Judge was a massive, muscled, darker-skinned devil. His pointed fingernails gleamed in the firelight as he transferred dried herbs from his tin to his pipe bowl. "Your job was to reform the girl, and then she would join the Flames. That was the deal."

"Explain this deal," Breanarachelle drawled. "I've only heard of it secondhand." Breanarachelle was as tall as her husband, but more elegantly dressed. She was an important and wealthy beauty mistress, a patron of the arts in Mer. Her strapless charcoal dress harmonized with the ashen-yellow tint of her smooth, salamandery skin. The odd brass claw ornaments on Breanarachelle's fingers reflected the tones of her orange-brown hair. Boudi-Ca shivered when the she-devil's Sharp gaze crawled yet again over her face.

"With all due respect, Breanarachelle, this isn't the time to discuss this," Lydiah said dismissively. "The other issue is more important."

"The issues are related, don't you think?" countered the Judge. "In any case, are we agreed to move immediately?"

"Yes, I agree," Lydiah answered. "Boudi-Ca, do you remember that redheaded Jinn who accosted you the week before last—the first time right outside the gates of our estate, and then again inside the club in the Denmark quarter?"

"Yes, Mistress. Did you find her?"

"Indeed we did." Judge Rhadamanthus puffed on his pipe, sending a plume of sweet-smelling smoke into the air. "She's a scheming follower of Allyssia, and she's stupid enough to be meddling where she shouldn't. Are you familiar with the rebels, Boudi-Ca? Are there any memories of Golda in your head?"

Boudi-Ca felt her throat constrict. The judge peered hard at her with his yellow eyes, which were even more creature-like than his wife's. "No. I don't remember anything of this Jinn, although she seemed to know me. She seemed surprised and upset that I didn't recognize her. She isn't really that horrible—"

"We all know the story," Lydiah said. "Now she'll be dealt with. Hell's Court tracked her, and now they are sending a squad of devils into the forest to get her."

"We'll go tomorrow night," Judge Rhadamanthus added. "Golda is hiding with the Gypsies. We managed to track her last week to the Reik family camp, and we've been monitoring her movements since then. She's an expert tracker. She can disappear into the tapestry, but she can't hide forever. The Smokeless Flames will also be involved in this little operation against the rebels. Are we agreed, General Astaarteh?"

The elder Jinn stepped from the corner into the low firelight. She stood tall on her hooves. Her decorated military jacket was unbuttoned, revealing an uncorseted, bronzed chest that glistened with scented oil. The gold buttons on Astaarteh's jacket matched the fastenings on her narrow strip of a skirt. The pointed nubs of horns poked through the long, curly dark hair at her temples. The elder Jinn appeared Middle-Eastern like the poetess at the Zweibrüder.

"Yes," Astaarteh hissed. "I'll select a squad of Sisters tonight. Inform me when you're ready, and we'll mobilize to help the devils on a moment's notice. We should go in force. You're sure we're getting Mistress Golda?"

"Golda identified herself to Boudi-Ca by name," the Judge answered. "Our spies also indicate that she is a redhead and a tracker, which matches the intelligence that Lydiah archived for us in Meristyian."

Astaarteh nodded. "Is there some reason we aren't moving tonight? The Flames could hit the Gypsy camps well before sunrise."

Fennel stirred in his chair, crisp in his black serge evening suit. His blotchy fingers drummed the goat-horned handle of his ebony sword-cane. "Politics. The Gypsies are helping the outlaw agents of Allyssia, which means they also need to be punished for their crimes. We'll need cage carriages. That means horses and drivers."

"So it will go," Judge Rhadamanthus said with a chuckle. The Judge rose from his chair, went to the fire, and dragged a red-hot tong from the burning coals. "We need to string up the Gypsy leaders like fish, and then we need to interrogate them."

"For what purpose?" Lydiah said.

"The lesbians in Mer are implicated here, not just Allyssia's rebels," the Judge answered. "We've had numerous reports in the last two years of Jinni going missing, and they are typically suspected lesbians or other malcontents. Perhaps this is where they are going—into the forest. Mistress Golda and the Gypsies have been helping them. It all ties together."

"I just want this situation over with. It's disturbing my Boudi-Ca."

Judge Rhadamanthus dragged the hot poker over the Kishi slave's ass. The elf girl writhed and choked on her gag. Her thin, scarred legs frogged and twitched with pain. "Torturing a lesbian is a special pleasure. Don't you find so, Archduke?"

"No," Fennel muttered. "They're as boring as a fairy-nose."

The Judge turned and leveled his hot poker. Boudi-Ca blinked. Rhadamanthus was aiming his poker directly at her. "Boudi-Ca, get up from the floor and show us your unblemished legs and ass, won't you? Lift up your skirt and show us every inch of that fine, unscarred ivory."

"Absolutely not," Lydiah said. "There is no reason for Boudi-Ca to show us her skin. Do not get up, fledgling."

"Perhaps Boudi-Ca should be a part of this operation," the Judge continued. "Perhaps the fledgling is more ready than you think, Councilor." Rhadamanthus returned to run the poker over the Kishi slave. A long silence came over the parlour, punctuated only by low sizzling sounds, muffled moans, and the clinking of iron cuffs.

Lydiah shook her head. "That's hardly advisable, Rhada. As a former ambassador for Hell, I plan. I strategize. The pieces are not yet in place in Boudi-Ca's head."

"Yet there is pleasure in unpredictability," Rhadamanthus thrust the poker suddenly between the slave's thighs. The Kishi girl heaved and cried in her harness-gag. "One must always raise the question in the prisoner's mind of whether she will live or die before sunrise."

"We would love to have Boudi-Ca join us." Astaarteh strode back to the corner and placed her empty absinthe glass on the antique sideboard. "I've watched her practice with blades up at Fennel's home. She's a credit to her old teacher. If she is competent on the raid, then I'm willing to induct her with the next Flames class of recruits in three moons."

Lydiah sighed. "Seriously?"

Astaarteh returned to the center of the drawing room. "I realize that Boudi-Ca has been your pet project for these past years, Councilor, but the girl can only reach her true potential with the Flames. The younger she dedicates herself to Allyssia, the better. Are you willing to quit your nectar and kill for Allyssia, fledgling? Are you ready to pledge your soul to the Smokeless Flames and become a legendary blade fledgling? Say yes."

Boudi-Ca raised her eyes to the elder who towered above her. Her throat caught, and she stuttered like a fool. She could see straight up Astaarteh's miniscule leather mini-skirt to the furred majesty of her ancient sex. "Y—yes, Mistress. The Concise History Of The Jinni says that I must serve a husband, but if our goddess wishes me to serve Her in other ways, then of course I will serve. Every night I offer prayers to Lady Allyssia in the parlour with my Mistress."

Astaarteh smiled. "Praise Allyssia, and Lydiah as well. Unlike others, I always had faith in you, Councilor, to lead Boudi-Ca through the black and onto the right path, cured of her misguided desires. The Flames will be thrilled to have a fledgling with such potential. Now if you will all excuse me—"

"You're leaving us, General?" Rhadamanthus withdrew his hot poker again from the shuddering slave. He lifted the implement and drew it past his frog-like nose. A burnt sex-smell rose to mingle with the odor of pipe smoke.

"Yes, your honor," Astaarteh said. "I have important business in the dream world. I may not go tomorrow on the raid, but I'll have some solid Sisters on this. I pray to Allyssia that we get this rebel. I'd like to interrogate Golda myself."

Rhadamanthus chuckled. "You can have her when Fennel and I are done. We'll spare her tongue, or at least enough of it."

"So who else is going on the raid, then?" Lydiah said. "Will you be coming, Breanarachelle, or are you too busy planning that little spring fashion show?"

Breanarachelle chuckled. "I have a couple dozen leaders on Earth to corrupt in five languages. I have a high-level meeting about an end-of-times plague. I'm swamped, Lydiah. I have no time to brood over two immature fledglings like a mother hen."

Lydiah stood up, equally as tall as Astaarteh on her elder's hooves. "Boudi-Ca and I will be leaving too. Please inform us when we're riding out tomorrow. Good night, my dear Rhada. It was a decadent pleasure as always. Are you coming home, darling?"

"No," Fennel answered from his armchair. "I'm with Breanarachelle. Like she said, we'll be visiting the Earth realm."

Boudi-Ca rose quickly to accompany Lydiah. She curtseyed to Astaarteh and equally to Breanarachelle, but she couldn't bring herself to say good night to the devil men, who frankly terrorized her. Rhadamanthus was even worse than Fennel. Whenever she was near Rhadamanthus, her heart seemed to stop, her throat seized, and she felt queer to her core. It was a relief to reach the hallway without him saying anything more to her.

"You did well, fledgling," Lydiah said when they'd exited the villa. "You'll ride home with me so I won't be alone? I'll send a bird to Masia-Ca and let her know."

"Of course, Mistress. Are you upset about something?"

"I loathe Breanarachelle." The corner of Lydiah's black-painted mouth twitched. She fiddled with her diamond earring as she walked.

"Why, Mistress?"

"Oh. She and I have a long history. Where can I even begin? I suppose things heated up in the eighteenth century. I helped popularize a new philosophy that turned the humans away from Lord Tuhan and towards the supremacy of their own feeble minds to guide them. Ironically, the humans called it 'The Enlightenment'. Of course, those are the same minds that lead humans into endless indulgence in the pleasures of their flesh."

"That sounds interesting."

Lydiah smiled with her eyes far away. "Yes. I fucked Voltaire in his sleep. I worked in the dream-world with many Ukraine men to promote secular humanism and the cult of reason. I advocated the confiscation of Catholic properties and destruction of religious symbols in public. I speak fluent Ukraine, and of course I was with Henry then, so I was parfaite to help all of that happen. I was a very busy Jinn in those days. I was almost killed three times in the dream-world by the Mimoic Hierarchy. At the time, Fennel and I were just beginning our courtship. I was trying to impress him."

"Wait. Who is Henry again?"

"He was one of my earthly husbands, fledgling—Henry the second of France. That's an even longer story involving my third Earth life as Diane De Poitiers, a second wedding in Hell, and Henry tangling with werewolves during an Isandlwana hunting trip and going to the void in eighteen-twenty. I was crushed, but I finally consummated with Fennel. My bitterness and loneliness inspired his desire for me at a time when my fame was at its peak."

"You have a gift for inspiring desire, Mistress." Boudi-Ca circled the carriage horses and climbed into the passenger side of Fennel's sleek black four-seater. She secretly hoped the Mistress would broach her double-entendre, especially with Fennel gone for the night. Lydiah only leaned and poked the carriage driver in the shoulder. The slave boy snapped the whip, and the carriage rolled down the drive into the dark streets of Pee-Hill.

"Even back then, Breanarachelle was my nemesis," Lydiah continued.

"Like most of Hell's establishment, she threw her support behind Marie Antoinette and Shulamit XVI. She couldn't understand why democracy could be better for Hell than aristocracy. The revolution succeeded, and it was a bloodbath. When Marie Antoinette's head rolled, I sent Breanarachelle a messenger bird, gloating. Breanarachelle and her circle of influence were defeated, along with everything she had in France. I married Fennel a few years later, and I was given an official ambassadorship. At the time, Hell's history books commended me as a genius. Those were my days of glory."

"So Breanarachelle has hated you since then?"

"Oh yes, and now it's her turn to see me humiliated. The tables have turned. I've fallen from my former status, fledgling. I used to chair the highest-level meetings, and now I'm not invited to them. Last year Breanarachelle was appointed an ambassador for Hell, and she serves in my place. I made mistakes that caused the Smokeless Flames to lose two important strongholds in Meristyian. Now my husband is sleeping with my enemy."

"He's fucking Breanarachelle?"

"The devils are doing a lot of work these days on Earth, and it's necessary to travel the dream-world to get there. It isn't complicated magic, but it's convenient for them to Share a carriage, so to speak. When I say carriage, I mean a bed. Yes. When Breanarachelle fucks my husband, she leaves marks on his skin. I've seen them, and she wants me to see them."

"I don't like devils, and I loathe your husband."

"My husband is one of the firstborns of our Lord. Just like the good son of Lord Tuhan, he can fuck whoever he wants, and no one will say anything. Maybe he'll fuck your friend Golda if they manage to capture her. Of course, the word fuck can have five or six connotations for the devils, and all of those are less pleasant than the missionary position."

"I think Golda really loves me."

Lydiah turned her head Sharply. "Wait, what? Why by the balls of Cerberus is this the first time you've mentioned this?"

Boudi-Ca suppressed the smile that came unbidden to her lips. She glanced at Lydiah, but the face of the Mistress was obscured by darkness. The carriage had left Pee-Hill and was ascending into Tanjie. The grand twisted tree branches crawled slowly across the sky like an army of black spiders. "I didn't think it was important. I could feel it when Golda held my arm in the Zweibrüder club. She wanted me to feel her love."

"Oh, please," Lydiah snorted. "She tricked you, fledgling. A Jinn can inspire desire in women as well as with men if it serves her devious purposes. Golda was a fool to approach you. She'll be arrested, and then you can forget her. Rhada will make sure that Golda never sees the light of day again for as long as she lives."

"Why did Rhadamanthus want to see my legs?"

Lydiah looked away. "You're a beautiful young Jinn. Rhada likes to put on a show for his guests and his cock. Nothing more."

"Mistress, I know when you're not telling the whole truth."

"I'm telling you all you need to know, as usual. Rhada is not the principled old king that he used to be, and he enjoys a bit of sport with me."

Boudi-Ca frowned. She'd grown used to Lydiah not telling her the whole truth. Lydiah insisted that her memories of her old life as an Mimọ spy were missing for a reason—to protect her. The black nectar had been part of the deal. She only needed to know that she'd been a spy and had defected from Heaven to join Hell. Her change into a fledgling Jinn had been a reward from Lady Allyssia, and Lydiah had been appointed as her personal mentor.

"So was Breanarachelle insulting me when she called me a fairy-nose?"

"That term is very old. No one in Hell used nectar until Lord Oberon of the Kishi gifted it to Lord Hades many centuries ago, when Persephoneh was still our queen in Mer. Our Lord gifted it to his favorites, and then the apothecaries started making it, and now everyone loves their fairy dust. There are big flower farms now in Erebus. I went through a time of using it myself, and I still combine it with my husband's attentions now and then. There's nothing wrong with nectar pleasure, but we need to start weaning you."

"You didn't answer my question, Mistress."

"Breanarachelle insults anyone if she thinks it will affect them. She's a devil. She enjoys suffering, and physical suffering is only a small part of the devil arts."

"When I'm in the Smokeless Flames, people will have more respect for me. If they don't, I'll be able to kill them, right?"

Lydiah was silent for long moments while the carriage horses neared the gates of Fennel's estate, and the lamp lights from the house windows glowed in the night. "Are you that eager to join the Flames, fledgling?"

"Not really. I wouldn't mind staying with you and learning the arts of the beauty mistresses." Boudi-Ca bit her lip. It was her turn to tell half-truths. In fact, she was secretly excited by the Jinn branch of Hell's army. The Flames was rumored to be a refuge for lesbians due to the military exemption from marriage to an Djinnus husband. She'd live with other young women in service to Allyssia. She'd train with blades all day, and anything could happen at night in the cloistered dormitories, or so the rumors went.

No matter how much Moshe filled her, her belly still felt hollow. She felt empty and joyless. She had no real friends in the big city, and Masia was busier and more snobbish since they'd returned to Mer. She wanted more than anything else to join the Flames and meet other talented young fledglings, and perhaps even lesbians.

"You don't realize how difficult the Flames will be," Lydiah said in a low tone. "They'll goad you to develop your violent tendencies. They'll teach you the deadly arts of serpent poisons. You'll undergo Allyssia's sacred ritual of immunity. They'll train you to be a focused, merciless killer, capable even of assassinating me if commanded. As a final test of every Flames aspirant class, the fledglings in the two lowest sextets are required to kill each other to pass."

Boudi-Ca felt her throat tighten. "That sounds cruel."

"Oh yes, it's a wonderful backstabbing affair that weeds out the weak. Nectar makes a Jinn weak, so naturally nectar is forbidden in the Flames. You shouldn't have any more nectar at parties to start, fledgling, and a cup of black tea at home only twice per week. I'm going to lock our nectar safe, and I'll have Masia-Ca watch you every night."

"I don't need Masia. I can control myself."

"You please me, fledgling. We'll see." From the tone of Lydiah's voice, the Mistress wasn't pleased at all.

Chapter 4.

Boudi-Ca examined her face yet again in the vanity mirror. She looked severe with her Brunette hair pulled back in a tight military-style bun. The black curves of her eye liner and lip paint contrasted with her pale Mimoic skin. Her diamond nose piercing glinted in the dim late-afternoon light that came from her bedchamber window.

She wanted to do her best on the hunt for Golda, and thereby earn her ticket into the next Smokeless Flames recruit class. After taking private lessons with Mistress Dimona for many moons, her much-complimented blade skills would be on display. She loved Lydiah, but at the same time she felt a strange, nagging desperation to escape.

A whisper of skirts came from the doorway. Lydiah slipped into the bedchamber and pulled the door shut behind her. The Mistress was regally dressed in red riding pants and a grey jacket that bore the coiled silver insignia of the Smokeless Flames. Lydiah wore her white-blond hair long and loose over one shoulder. Her diamond earrings sparkled as always in her earlobes.

"You haven't had any nectar today, my lovely fledgling?"

Boudi-Ca rose from her vanity. "No, Mistress. I just need to get my sword. I'm nervous about riding in the forest. Won't it be dark before we get home?"

"Yes." Lydiah answered. "The devils are attacking at dusk because the Gypsies hold their revelries then. The devils take the most pleasure in inflicting the most pain, so naturally they'll attack when the Gypsies are drunk and happy. Never mind that Golda might be halfway to Erebus. It's almost as if the Gypsies are more important."

"I feel sorry for her." Boudi-Ca met Lydiah's silver-grey eyes. "I don't even understand why we so many of us are going on the hunt. Golda will fight, but won't the human Gypsies be expected to submit to the will of our Lord and King?"

"The Gypsies are a proud people. They may resist, depending on their devotion to Golda's cause. Our main job is to get Golda. She may prefer to go to the void before letting us take her alive."

"Is she really that dangerous?"

Lydiah nodded. "You're perceptive, fledgling. Rhada said Golda is recruiting lesbians in Mer to join the rebel Jinni who serve Lady Allyssia. That sort of thing has happened in the distant past, but in this case it's ridiculous. If Allyssia had placed Golda in charge of a secret scheme to lure new followers from among the insubordinate lesbians and wives in Mer, then Golda wouldn't have come to you twice, revealing her real identity and risking the entire operation. That would be an unthinkable mistake. I believe Golda came for you only, and Hell's Court is blowing this out of proportion. I'm just not sure why."

"I'm more nervous now than before."

Lydiah pressed close, and Boudi-Ca leaned into the sweet perfumed fabric of Lydiah's shoulder. She could feel Lydiah's love for her. It was a deep and secret love, much like Golda's, but far more guarded and tortured.

"You don't have to do well on the raid," Lydiah whispered. "Perhaps you'll make mistakes. Fledglings make mistakes, and you've lived through a lot of mistakes to be standing here, although you don't remember any of it."

"You're telling me to do horribly?"

"If you don't do well, the Flames will be less likely to take you from me this year or next. You're healthier staying as my fledgling for decades. I love you, fledgling. I don't want to see you get hurt."

"I love you too, Mistress. I'm still going to do my best." Boudi-Ca quickly pressed with her lips, reaching over Lydiah's warm, impressive assets. Lydiah hitched and met her lips hotly before turning her head away.

"What have I told you? What have I told you a hundred times?"

"You want me. That's why you don't want me to go—"

"You're just mistaking filial love with lust." Lydiah's jaw trembled, and she swept her white-Brunette hair over her shoulder. "It's common for a fledgling and her Mistress to develop a close bond of friendship. It's perfectly normal."

"I can feel—"

"We're going." Lydiah turned away quickly. "If you want to go to the Flames so much, then I hope you're ready. There's a chance that Golda baited us into a trap. If so, the rebels are getting more than they bargained for. I love you more than you know, my fledgling, but please don't kiss me again here in Mer."

"Yes, Mistress." Boudi-Ca sullenly selected her favorite steel sword from the rack beside the door. She followed in Lydiah's shadow down to the first floor and out the side carriage exit. She tongued Lydiah's taste on her teeth. Lydiah's mouth tasted of sulfur, surely from licking and sucking on her husband's disgusting devil flesh. Two sturdy horses were saddled and waiting in the driveway. Boudi-Ca climbed into a saddle alongside Lydiah. She wheeled her horse and sent it trotting after the Mistress down the driveway.

Two of Fennel's hounds climbed to their feet and paced in Lydiah's wake. Their saliva dripped from their slavering black jaws, as if the beasts sensed a hunt was in the offing. Lydiah waved her gloved hand and ordered them off.

Boudi-Ca spurred her horse to follow close. She'd had equestrian lessons with a tutor a few times every moon, but she couldn't remember ever riding with the Mistress. They passed through the massive gates that led from Archduke Fennel's hilltop estate, and then Lydiah accelerated to a canter down the curving road towards the heart of the city. They rode for twenty minutes from Tanjie to Hell's Court, where a procession of devils and Sisters was already forming. The Smokeless-Flame Sisters wore hooded red uniforms. Boudi-Ca felt her nerves rise again in her belly as Lydiah drew her horse close.

"Commander Anxeh is in charge, fledgling. Corporal Shadow is the Flames tracker. Sergeant Hestereh is a senior blade mistress. The four other Sisters are rank and file fighters, all with a role to play in the battle."

Boudi-Ca watched Lydiah chat with the Flames mistresses about the raid plans. The military Jinni looked hard-faced and grim, ready to do their duty for Allyssia and the Flames. Three of them removed damp folded cloths from the pouches at their waists while they waited for the devils to prepare the cage carriages. The Sisters rubbed their steel blades, and a poisonous odor rose on the air.

Within a half hour, the procession rolled out through the streets of Mer at sunset. The two dozen Hell's Court devils rode two by two abreast. The silver trim of their pearl-black armor glinted in the dim, polluted evening haze. Their flattened grey faces looked resolute and ready to carry out their cruel duty. Their gaff-like poles and nets were festooned with hooks and barbs designed to snag and hold the flesh of their quarry. Behind the devils rolled three Hell's Court cage-carriages—massive tarnished boxes intended to hold any prisoners. The cages were pulled by black Hell horses that snorted sulfuric smoke.

"You like the horses, fledgling?" Lydiah drew close again.

"Yes, Mistress."

"The Hell horses are birthed by Epona, the great mare who lives amongst the ogre tribes in the vast wastes of the Mare Mortis. Our Lord impregnates Epona at His whim, and She gives Him horses. Our Lord enjoys impregnating Epona, wishing His realm to be an extension of Himself, and thus it is that He requires all women to serve the seed of men just as our mother Allyssia spreads Her legs when the Lord visits Her each spring. All goddesses have submitted to our Lord and King since antiquity, except the Lord's sister, the goddess Allyssia, who holds Love above the will and control of all men, and thereby holds herself above her brothers. And so it is that Allyssia has become a renegade in Hell, a forbidden symbol for all discontented women."

Boudi-Ca nodded. She enjoyed when Lydiah told stories. She wished Lydiah would continue, but some of the Smokeless-Flame Sisters had pressed their horses close to overhear, and Lydiah went silent. The procession forged on through the crowded city for nearly an hour before it passed through the eastern Merian gates. The procession continued into the forests that stretched between the east walls of Hell's capital several leagues to the precipitous cliffs of the Great Blue Hole mines. The late afternoon light barely penetrated the polluted branches that twisted overhead like a canopy of black snakes. The lowest-hanging tree branches snapped and rang against the tops of the cages, and thrice the caravan stopped so the devils could climb up and cut branches away.

After another hour, the column of Hell horses slowed to a crawl. Night had embraced the ancient Haawiyah forest, and firelight flickered through the trees. The outskirts of a large camp were visible—horses in a corral and a painted wagon the size of a small house. Music tinkled, and the sounds of laughter lilted over the low growls of dogs. Boudi-Ca pulled her sword with the Smokeless-Flame Sisters. Lydiah wore only a narcabyss whip, which she unfurled.

"This way," Mistress Shadow said. "I see only one thread in the tapestry that belongs to a Jinn. It's a tangled web, but I think the rest of the threads in the forest are human."

Commander Anxeh frowned. "That's unfortunate. According to the report just this morning from Hell's Court, there were at least four rebel Jinni in this camp."

"Rhada said nothing last night about four," Lydiah said. One of the younger Smokeless-Flame Sisters giggled, and Lydiah sighed audibly. "Onwards then. Let's get Golda."

Mistress Shadow detoured around the outskirts of the camp while the devils forged towards the center. Boudi-Ca spurred her horse to keep pace with the Sisters. A man yelled. The Gypsy dogs barked a chorus. Hooves thundered in the loam, followed by loud shouts and cries among the trees and hollows. Boudi-Ca guided her horse behind Anxeh and Hestereh, who were close on Shadow's tail. Boudi-Ca kept her sword ready. Her Jinn power was tingling under her sensitive skin, adding to her nervousness. In all of her training sessions with her blades tutor, she hadn't seen any real combat.

Shadow dismounted at the camp edge and trotted forward on foot. Boudi-Ca dismounted with the rest of the Sisters. A low growl rose from the darkness. She readied her blade. She heard the rustle of paws first, and then she glimpsed the dog. The creature charged, and she nailed it cleanly in the half-dark. Her blade's impact with the dog's skull sent a hollow report through the forest. The dog dropped, quivered, and stilled.

"Well, the girl proved she can kill a dog at least," Anxeh said.

"The dog thought Boudi-Ca was the weakest amongst us," Lydiah said. "The dog was wrong. A Gypsy will miss his pet in the morning."

Boudi-Ca felt a queer rush of pleasure from the killing, a pleasure that made her feel twisty in her soul. Her pleasure was muted, however, by a less pleasant heat in her cheeks. Anxeh apparently thought little of her abilities. She crept with the Smokeless-Flame Sisters, who were circling the conflict to reach the heart of the camp at the same time as the devils. The center of the camp was a clearing with a bonfire and a cluster of tents and grand wagons.

Archduke Fennel had ridden his Hell-horse to confront the human leaders. His pale face was stark in the night as he dismounted. Fennel had blanched yellow skin, unlike the yellow-grey of the others, mottled in places with burgundy blotches that hinted at his practice of devil-magic. He wore his customary black serge suit and hat, but he'd left his sword cane at home in favor of a hunting crossbow. He flourished a Court order at a tall, more shabbily-dressed Gypsy man.

"Agron Reik, you're under arrest for illegal commerce and aiding rebels and enemies to Lord Hades. Kneel and take your ebon collar. You will be interrogated. Do not attempt to escape."

The Gypsy patriarch raised his hands in supplication. "What do you mean? This is outrageous! I've done nothing of what you speak, nothing more than—"

"I have a warrant from Hell's Court. The warrant bears our Lord's stamp," Fennel interrupted. "Kneel as I demand and stop wasting my time. You've been helping the rebel goddess Allyssia. You've been trafficking lesbians and other women to Meristyian and aiding their illegal activities."

"That's insane. I've done nothing of the sort."

"That is for Hell's Court to decide. Kneel now or accept the consequences of resisting." Fennel hefted his crossbow. The grey devils advanced to surround the Gypsy lord with their wicked barbed poles. One devil held a dreaded ebon collar in its clawed hands. Agron Reik bowed his head and knelt. A grey devil locked the dread collar to the man's neck. The Gypsy leader wilted, as if his will to live had suddenly drained from him.

Boudi-Ca tore her eyes away from the scene to keep pace with the Sisters and Shadow, who were advancing towards a large tent straight ahead of them. Boudi-Ca froze mid-step behind Hestereh. A pale dark-haired woman emerged from the flap of the tent. The woman was wrapped in a chequered bed quilt. She stood looking aghast at the scene in front of her. She stepped tentatively forwards, even as Fennel leveled his baleful eyes at her.

"Ah, you must be the lovely Priebus Reik," Fennel announced loudly. "You are hereby also under arrest for illegal commerce and aiding rebels and enemies of Lord Hades. You may pray to our great Lord for mercy, but do not expect him to listen. Kneel, human female, and receive your ebon collar next."

Priebus shrank. "No! Why are you doing this to us? Our family has done nothing wrong! We've cooperated with Hell's army whenever they've asked us. We are good citizens of the King's lands!"

Fennel's face betrayed not a trace of pity. "Step forward for your collar. Where is your son, the young man named Gorka Reik?"

Priebus hugged herself, as if she'd been punched in the stomach. "Oh gods, please not my son too! I beg you! He's done nothing. He's just an artist. He's not involved in our family's businesses!"

"You fucking bastard." The Gypsy lord climbed back to his feet and launched himself at the archduke. Fennel flicked his gloved hand. A stubby black ebon wand hung from the devil's fingers. The man gasped. A dark force jumped from the ebon wand to the ebon collar, completing a magical circuit. The Gypsy crumpled like paper to his knees. His cry of pain sounded strangled, even as his wife screamed in symphony.

The devils separated Priebus by force from her bed quilt. Priebus struggled and uttered curses against them. Her nude white body was stark against the grey arms and claws that grappled and snagged her skin. Gunshots echoed then through the forest. The devils fell back under the onslaught of Gypsy men with guns. Blades flashed and rang in the sudden fray. Devil blood sprayed, hissed, and smoked on the beaten forest floor.

Fennel jerked when a bullet hit him in the chest, but he seemed unhurt. He muttered devil-magic. The forest air congealed into darkness, as if the twisty black tree branches overhead were descending at the archdevil's command. Black snakes of magical smoke hissed through the air to assault the men who were fighting to defend the family's matriarch. The men retreated, and the devils counterattacked. Fennel laughed, and his arrogant voice rose over the chaos.

"The price of attacking a Hell's Court official is death, but all will be spared for questioning. For the insolence that you and your people have shown me, Lord Reik, I'll conduct your wife's torture personally."

Lydiah snorted in a low tone. "I'm quite sure he will. My husband's excitement is obvious from this angle."

Anxeh grinned in the darkness. "Quickly now, while the devils are distracting them. Is Golda in the big tent, Shadow?"

"I think so, but I don't know anymore," the tracker answered. "She's gone to the tapestry. She has real skill. We need to surround the tent quickly."

"Well, quickly then," Anxeh muttered. "Lydiah and I will go vanguard to flush the quarry. Hestereh, you and Shadow go dexter. The rest of you run sinister. Use your whips, no swords. She's a known shifter, so be ready for anything."

The Smokeless-Flame Sisters drew their whips and fanned out through the forest, some advancing left and others right, all intent on their effort.

Boudi-Ca half-heartedly followed to the left. She didn't have a whip. She only had a sword. Worse yet, she had no idea what Anxeh meant by 'vanguard', 'shifter', 'dexter', or 'sinister', although it was all important and obvious to the trained Sisters. No one had even bothered to explain anything to her.

She often felt clueless and unsophisticated at parties in Mer, but at parties everything was forgiven. She was Lydiah's second fledgling, and many said she was even more beautiful than Masia-Ca. She'd hoped to find friends in the Smokeless Flames, but she could scarcely imagine herself as friends with any of those Hell's army assassins. Maybe she was only fooling herself, and the Mistress was right as usual.

Chapter 5.

Golda lurked just inside the tent flap, peeking out at the horrible scene. She felt her throat constrict in sympathy when the devils locked the collar around Pinhas' neck. The Reik matriarch went limp as the devils dragged her towards the cages that crouched at the edge of the camp clearing.

The devils opened a cage door and pushed Priebus inside along with her husband and clan patriarch, Agron. A second cage was loaded with more subdued Reik family members. The devils had won the skirmish, and the forest was filled with the sounds of moaning men, weeping women, and the chaotic barking of the camp dogs. The devils were fanning out to search the premises under the command of Archduke Fennel.

Golda shrank back from the tent flap. She didn't have her sword, but she wasn't defenseless. She ran to the sleeping niche and reached under Pinhas' low bed. She seized the shiv, a small blade with a mother-of-pearl hilt that the Gypsy matriarch kept for such an emergency. She slid the knife into the rear tent wall and dragged downwards, forming an emergency exit even as intruders entered the tent doorway that she'd just vacated.

Golda peeked from the sleeping niche. The coils of a whip were silhouetted in the low lamplight. The guests were two Smokeless-Flame Sisters wearing high-ranking uniforms, one of whom was wearing a high-quality perfume. Golda sniffed. Her nostrils tingled pleasantly.

"Come out, rebel," one of the Sisters ordered. "If you surrender, I'll mention your cooperation in my report. Perhaps Hell's Court will let you live."

Golda returned to the tent wall and finished the cut in a broad stroke. She reached out again with her tracking senses. The tent was already surrounded, although sparsely. The Sisters had a tracker with them. Golda grimaced as she felt the tracker's mind find hers in the fabric of the tapestry.

She heard footsteps behind her. She quickly shed her pants and shifted. She willed her body into a four-pawed feline and shoved herself through the cut. The forest to the rear of the tent was lit up by two tenebris luces. She was confronted instantly by a red-uniformed Jinn, who squared off with a sword and drew back her whip.

"This is her!" the Sister exclaimed.

Golda darted sideways from under the weak whip attack, even as another Jinn converged. Golda paused when she looked up into Boudi-Ca's face. Boudi-Ca looked as pert and beautiful as ever in her loose black riding pants and tight-fitting ruffled shirt. Boudi's Brunette hair and silver-umber eyes almost shone in the darkness. A serpent necklace adorned her neck, a devotion to Lady Allyssia. Golda felt an awkward greeting leap to her throat, which emerged only as a purr.

Boudi's eyes glimmered with something—perhaps only a shocked curiosity. A Jinn in a grey uniform pushed through the slit in the tent then. Golda skittered, surprised at the sight of the long white-blonde hair. The perfumed Jinn was actually Mistress Lydiah herself, drawing back her whip.

Golda felt a sudden wave of real fear in her heart, a feeling she hadn't felt in a long time. She leapt past Boudi-Ca while the fledgling stood frozen. A final Smokeless-Flame Sister interposed herself, a darker-skinned woman with long black hair. The tracker drew back her whip.

The whip sung, but again too slow. Golda lunged under the snapping cord and seized the woman's thigh in her jaws, shredding muscle to the bone before darting away, even as she felt a hand grab at her head and a sword slash across her lower back. She caught Boudi's scent close behind, a sweet sensuality mixed with silk and fine leather. She bounded at top speed, shrugging off a jagged pain in her hindquarters, followed by a desirous kin-hex that snagged her hind legs, slowing her.

Another whip snapped behind her, but she was just out of range. She shrugged off another powerful kin-hex that stopped her bodily for a moment, and then she'd cleared the Flames cordon and the light of the tenebris luces. She knew every stone, bramble, and tree-root in the forest, while the Smokeless-Flame Sisters were in unfamiliar terrain. She raced for a hundred meters and more over sloping ground towards the nearby stream.

She heard Gypsies speaking ahead of her. The Reik family had apparently fled to the grassy streamside flat where the men cut ancient oaks for fires and the women cleaned laundry on smooth slabs of Haawiyah basalt. The humans clustered in a broad ray of moonlight that came from gaps in the black tree branches.

"—need to p—pack up the camp," Uncle Ash was arguing breathlessly. "Everyone needs to leave. We should s—split up and go our own ways. We'll come together at the spring waymeet."

"Agreed," Aunt Marta added grimly. "We've lost Agron, Priebus, Agron, and at least five other men to the devils. Hell's Court will punish us mercilessly for resisting them."

"Who should I go with? What should I do?" Gorka brushed his tousled dark hair from his eyes. Grim pain registered on the Reik son's youthful face.

"We'll only make things worse if we protect you from the devils," Aunt Marta answered. "Archduke Fennel wants you arrested like Priebus and Agron. You need to run. You need to run faster than any of us—"

Golda grimaced when the family went silent, and all eyes turned to look at her. There was no time for proper explanations as to why she was naked. She'd kept her shifting ability a secret from the Gypsies, and she couldn't even explain that she'd been taking her evening feeding from Pinhas'. A frown formed on Uncle Ash's pudgy face.

"You're quite nude, Golda. You came from Agron' tent?"

Golda shrugged. "There are Jinni with whips heading this way. Pardon my tits."

"Allyssia's bitches," Marta muttered. "No offense, Golda. Men, ready your guns and pray. We'll try to delay them without bloodshed. Gorka, take Ash's horse. Golda, go help him. I don't know for sure if this incident is related to you, and there's no point in debating it. You owe Agron and Pinhas'."

Golda nodded. "Get on the horse, Gorka. Ride towards the Great Blue Hole mines. I'll follow." Golda grabbed Gorka's arm and pulled him towards the horse. The Reik son was actually less safe in her company, but she couldn't refuse to help the Gypsies if she ever wanted to deal with them again. She re-shifted into cat form, revealing her true nature while the Gypsies looked on. The bloody wound on her backside still ached, but the transformation healed her.

Gorka gave rein, and his horse darted recklessly into the forest, startled by the sudden appearance of the big predator near its legs. Golda followed closely. She tried to focus and calm herself as she went, the better to obscure her track in the tapestry. Behind her a Gypsy screamed, and more gunshots echoed through the trees.

She escorted Gorka through the forest for ten minutes, and then thirty. She pressed on and on for what seemed like an hour or more. Gorka was slow. His human eyes were less capable in the night. Gorka arrived at the Great Blue Hole edge meadows, where he began a treacherous path under the dim stars through the volcanic boulders and brittle-brushes.

Golda fought tears that threatened her furry cheeks. She felt sure that Boudi's blade had cut her. Boudi-Ca had not only lost her memories, but she had also joined the hunt to help capture her old friend and lover. It was just like Hell's Court and the Smokeless Flames to orchestrate something so sick and twisted.

Priebus was in an even worse place—a devil cage. Golda paused briefly to wipe her furred cheek with her dirty paw. She searched her mind for scraps of the workings of Hell's Court, for any way that Priebus could be aided. Dim memories surfaced of Court bribes paid with gold aurei coins.

She wasn't sure yet what she could do for Pinhas'. First she had to save herself. Her mind was open to the tapestry. She and Gorka had company on the cliffs. She could see a meandering thread coming after them, pale and violet. When Gorka reached the cliff edge, he paused and reined in. He looked at her with a curl of suspicion on his lips.

"You're a shifter then, as well as a Jinn? The hunters reported a big cat in the forest all season. We figured it came down from Erebus to hunt for some reason, but—"

Golda flowed again into her human form. "Yes. Your parents knew, but no others. I'm sorry for this, Gorka. This isn't justice."

"You're damned right it isn't." Gorka's curse sounded odd coming from his boyish mouth. The Reik son had lived to a ripe middle age on Earth, but his death and descent into the Underworld had given him the lithe body of a young human of seventeen or eighteen seasons. "The Gypsies have lived free in the Hell since the signing of the blood covenants ages ago. My parents can't be arrested like this. It isn't legal. Did you have something to do with this, Golda? Those things the Archduke was saying—"

Golda shook her head in the negative. She'd definitely taken risks approaching Boudi-Ca, but she'd never imagined a Court assault on the Gypsies, who were well-liked by almost everyone. The Gypsies were key agents of trade and commerce, always bringing needed things to the lands in which they traveled. "I honestly don't know what Hell's Court is thinking. Your family hasn't done what the devils accused. Let's circle a bit to the south. I think another from your family is fleeing with us. We could meet him."

"I feel like a coward. I fled while my parents were arrested."

"It's better than sitting in a cage with them. I've heard that bribery is welcome and accepted at Hell's Court. Every judge can be bought for a price. Maybe we can pay."

"Maybe." Gorka directed his horse to the south. Golda followed Gorka for several more minutes over the escarpment. She stayed in human form and padded barefoot, allowing herself a better vision over the meadow boulders. A sulfuric Haawiyah wind sprang up to stir the waterless brittle-brush, not enough to make it clack, but enough to send incoherent whispers like the voices of ghosts over the Underworld landscape.

An oil lamp finally winked in the night. Mohilever Reik was no Jinn or devil, although with his grey-bristled and balding head, sagging eyelids, and crooked-toothed grimace, he looked like an ogre in shriveled miniature. Agron' older brother rode astride a pony.

"Ho there, Gorka! There you are, lad."

Gorka frowned. "Uncle Mohilever? You followed us?"

Mohilever nodded vigorously in the affirmative. The sags of his sunken cheeks bounced. "Aye, lad. I made sure none of those silver-eyed bitches were on my trail."

Golda scanned the tapestry. The Great Blue Hole rim country east of the forest was clear of enemies for the moment, but Mohilever Reik had no idea of the capabilities of a skilled Smokeless Flames tracker. "Mohilever, do you know anything about Court bribes that could free Agron and Priebus?"

"A little, but who's got the gold coins? Do you, lass? I imagine not right now, unless they're hidden up your bum hole."

"Doesn't Agron—"

"My father is broke," Gorka interjected. "We lost everything when Hell's army searched our caravan last fall and took a load of fine Erebus nectar from us. The Merian insurance company wouldn't pay for the confiscated nectar since Hell's Court declared it as contraband. Our nectar supplier hadn't paid his taxes. We had to pay out of pocket for the loss. My father thinks Hell's Court rolled us. The King won't allow the Gypsies to become too rich."

Golda grimaced. She wasn't surprised that Agron and Priebus had hid their financial troubles from her. They were a proud people. "You still have the horses, the wagons, and the silver and things. How much do we need to bribe the judge at Hell's Court, Mohilever? Any idea?"

"Hundreds of chips maybe?" Mohilever shook his head. "Prices are sky high in the capital, lass. They might not even do it in this case. It doesn't matter. Gorka's parents likely don't own half a Hell's Court bribe, including the horses, and it's too late to get the family together. Everyone is scattering and heading for Erebus I reckon."

Gorka clenched his fists on the reins. "I'm not. I'll sell everything if that's what it takes to save my parents. You're going to help me, Uncle Mohilever, and so are you, Golda."

Mohilever shook his head in the negative. "We have to leave, lad. It's a battle that can't be won because they want us to lose. Hell's Court is using the war against Heaven as an excuse to put the screws to free trade in Hell. This is serious, Gorka. This is politics. Those pig-eyes could come scudding back tomorrow with another Court warrant, or the day after that, or next week—"

"No. We'll pack up a wagon and sell it at the Merian auction. I refuse to abandon my mother and father to their fate. What do you have in the way of coin?"

Mohilever avoided Gorka's eyes. "I'm buggered like everyone else, and I gave my due to balance the debt with the nectar dealers. I'll stay another day or two, but who knows when the pig-eyes might come back, or what might happen next, the covenants of our ancestors be damned."

"I know what will happen next. You'll go to Mer and find out who the judge is, Mohilever, and how much coin we need for a bribe for my parents. I'll see about getting it."

"No, Gorka—"

Gorka urged his horse closer to Mohilever. "You're going to help me, you old stone-hearted bugbear! My father has given everything for you, me, and this family. We'll go to the other families for aid. I don't care what it takes, and neither should you."

Mohilever's jowls worked. "Gorka, you're being thick. I'm trying to help you, and you won't listen. My brother and his wife will be judged in the coming days. They'll be found guilty of whatever and sentenced to torture and death. If they're lucky, they'll just get an eternity of digging some endless, poisonous pit out in the Great Blue Hole mines. Forget it, lad. We need to leave early for the spring tour to Erebus like the rest."

"Mohilever, my parents' souls at stake!"

"I'll stay and help," Golda said quickly. "I pledge to do everything I can to help your parents, Gorka. Agron gave me a few gifts. You can sell everything."

Gorka nodded. "Thank you, Golda. You're a wicked Jinn, but you're more of a help than my own uncle."

"Fine then," Mohilever muttered. "No love for a well-meaning old man I see. You're going to fail, Gorka. You'd be a fool not to flee."

"And you should be ashamed, Mohilever," Gorka countered. "You're a typical man in Hell. You've no care for others—only for your own self."

"This business is dodgy, but I'll stay one more day, maybe two. I'll do it for your parents, Allyssia bless their poor souls, but if the devils get me, I'm blaming you. Should we make a camp here, perhaps, and hide for the night?"

"We should not rest or make a camp," Golda said. "You're both probably tired, but we need to keep moving along the Great Blue Hole rim. We dare to return only when we're sure they aren't pursuing us."

"They don't know this terrain like we do," Mohilever said.

"You don't know the skill of the Smokeless-Flame Sisters. I purposefully crippled their tracker with a bite on her leg, but she still might ride a horse."

Gorka clenched his fists. "When the devils are gone, we need to help my parents, even if it goes against the will of Lord Hades. When the devils take a human, or so I've heard, their flesh and mind are forfeit. The devils never listen to pleas. They give no reprieve."

"All the better reason for us to keep moving." Golda gestured towards the south, even as Mohilever's beady eyes were roaming over her body in the light of his lamp. The old man was indeed a bugbear, and a lusty one. He seemed more interested in her tits than the fate of the Reik family.

An unspoken rumor had swirled around the Gypsy camp that she'd been bedding Priebus and Agron to serve her daily Jinn needs for a supply of lust energy. The rumor was true. She'd bedded the Feigns regularly for that reason.

The bedtime activities had been kept unspoken and secret. The Gypsies held their earthly marriages as even more sacred in the Underworld, and intimate relations between Gypsies and the dark children of Hell were considered repulsive with few exceptions. The Gypsies held only slightly less negative views about lesbians. Worse yet, her nudity during the chaos had been called out for improprieties.

Golda felt cold fingers tickle her spine. In one fell stroke, Hell's Court had destroyed the Reik family, and she was potentially to blame. The intense ritual of witchcraft from the night before was still clear in her memory. She'd seen Boudi's thread in the underweave, and she'd pulled the thread into the forest. It was surely no coincidence that Boudi-Ca had showed up in the forest less than twenty-four hours later along with a mess of Hell's Court devils.

Even the most elementary spell books warned against meddling in the domain of the Fates. If she'd really pulled a thread, then how could she have done such a thing? She knew only the simplest Jinn spells. She had no gift for wizardry. Perhaps Elder Tahany was right—she'd channeled the power of true love in the ritual, which proved once and for all that she was in love with Boudi.

Unfortunately, only disaster had come to the forest. The devils and the Flames were clearly aware of her presence and wanted her captured and interrogated, if not dead. Like the Gypsy men, she was a fool if she didn't flee Haawiyah immediately.

Chapter 6.

Boudi-Ca gazed with longing at the red-painted iron door. The locked wall safe in the slave pit protected the nectars that belonged to Lydiah and Fennel. The offerings included delicious lust-inducing reds, tension-soothing blacks, wicked mind-altering purples, sleep-summoning goldens, and a few vintage purples in stoppered clay jars, saved for special rituals and discriminating visitors.

Boudi-Ca tested the ornate safe handle yet again, as if the lock might magically give way if she kept trying. She knew there were mystical ways of opening mechanical locks without keys, but she didn't know them. Lydiah had mentioned nectar farms where locked and gagged slaves picked and processed the flowers, but those farms were very far away.

She was craving her black tea so much. It was already her fourth day with only one small cup of nectar, and her need was turning into a slow, persistent headache. The black was her best friend in times of stress. In that moment Lydiah, Fennel, and high-ranking members of the Flames and Hell's Court were meeting upstairs in the parlour.

She hadn't been invited, so she'd snuck on impulse down to the pit under the house to see if the safe was still locked. Boudi-Ca sighed and climbed back up the curving pit stairs with her head throbbing. She crossed the marbled front foyer in front of the parlour doors, where she froze mid-step and leaned close to hear the voices.

Boudi-Ca was the only one of us to get a whip or a blade on Golda. The cat-shifter was very fast. Commander Anxeh's voice sounded strained and apologetic through the closed doors. Lydiah spoke in a bolder tone.

Boudi-Ca still failed. She hesitated and let the cat-shifter escape. She's a talented fledgling, but she's still an uncertain, wishy-washy girl like all of her ilk. Really, I believe her future is best left with me. She is skilled in blades theory, but in practice she's completely worthless, as she demonstrated in the forest.

The gruff voice of a Court devil spoke then. This was not the deal you made with Hell's Court, Councilor. Two or three years ago, you lectured the Court on how Boudi-Ca could be a great asset to the Lord and Lady, despite having rampaged and killed ninety-odd Hell's army soldiers. Is that power worthless?

I stand by everything I said, but I had no way of predicting how slowly Boudi-Ca would develop. She's an emotional disaster zone. The rest of the Flames aspirants will tear her to shreds. Why the hurry? Surely Hell's Court has more important matters than an immature fledgling—this new plague on Earth for example.

Boudi-Ca felt her cheeks heat. She knew what the Mistress was trying to do, but she still felt insulted. She'd wounded Golda at the last second in the forest, but the cat had been surprisingly low, agile, and fast. Another female voice spoke behind the doors.

We have valuable sisters who serve here in the capital city and never leave, like Corporal Shadow. Boudi-Ca only needs to be trained to thrust her blade the rest of the way and kill without questioning. I think you're coddling her—

The voices trailed off into lower tones. Boudi-Ca leaned closer, unable to decipher the syllables. The oak doors pushed suddenly open, and Lydiah appeared with a warning look on her perfectly powdered, painted face.

"Did you need something from me, fledgling?"

"I was just passing. I needed my tea, and I forgot the safe was locked."

"Go to your room. I'll come up when we're done. Corporal Shadow noticed that someone was eavesdropping. I expected a poorly behaving slave, not my second fledgling. Don't leave for a party, Boudi-Ca. I want to speak with you."

Lydiah closed the parlour doors, satisfied with her scolding. Boudi-Ca retreated to the east wing and climbed the marble steps to her bedchamber on the second floor. Her belly felt glum, and her legs felt rubbery. She hadn't realized that Shadow, the tracker from the Flames, would sense that someone was listening at the parlour door. Corporal Shadow had arrived at the estate that afternoon with a limp and a bandage under the hem of her short black skirt.

Boudi-Ca gazed out of her second-story window through the grid of iron bars. Her east-wing bedchamber was darkening with the late day. The early evening light was fading over Haawiyah and the capital city, touching the tops of the Tanjie trees. Dawn's chariot was reflected in the distant shiny obsidian façades of Lord Hades' palace and the other monolithic Hell's Court buildings downtown. A handful of Fennel's Hell hounds were howling and cavorting out in the house grounds, stirred to particular excitability by so many visitors.

Boudi-Ca pressed her face closer to the window glass at an angle. She'd been planning to see Moshe at La Gershon Rouge in the Ukraine Quarter that night, but she couldn't leave even if she wanted to. The stables were completely blocked by the visiting carriages. She felt queasy looking at those dark harbingers, and her hollow belly added to her headache.

Three days had passed since the Gypsy raid and her mistake—her surprising hesitation when Golda had been right in front of her. Her frozen moment had come and went, and she still couldn't understand what had happened. She'd used her Mimǫ powers to flash instantly behind the redheaded rebel, but then she'd simply missed the down cut with her blade. After a half hour of hunting the dark forest without a tracker, Lydiah and Anxeh had called a withdrawal.

Boudi-Ca felt her heart pound. In truth, she hadn't wanted to hurt Golda. The renegade follower of Allyssia was a beautiful enigma and more importantly a lesbian. Still more interesting, she'd felt it again—that spark of love in Golda's shifted feline eyes, a curious love unlike the love from any handsome, masculine Djinnus in Mer. Golda had beautiful, sensual, blue-silver eyes.

Meanwhile, Lydiah had intimated that big things were afoot. Stunning evidence of corruption had supposedly been discovered in the Gypsy camp, soon be supplemented by the torture of the poor humans. Boudi-Ca flopped onto her bed and buried her head in her silk pillow. Lydiah always tried to involve her in politics, but she really wasn't that interested. She had enough to deal with, and all she wanted was love and nectar.

She was currently in a period between boyfriends—that time when one Djinnus was no longer interested in her and another was warming her up. Lydiah said that all Djinnus could feel the need in a hungry Jinn. Her former lover, Master Meva, had married Mistress Thyrah, the former Duchess of Cumberland, while Master Faisil had never been interested in her for more than occasional fuck-friends, so her interest had recently focused on Faisil's fledgling.

Fledgling Moshe was a wicked and perverted young Djinnus artist, somewhat well-known in the capital city for his paintings and sculptures. Moshe had a supply of nectar thanks to the fact that Faisil, his master and mentor, was a part-time dealer of the best colors from Erebus. Moshe was a good fuck, but she wasn't in love. He wasn't husband material either, despite how glorious she felt when she worshiped him while loaded on his nectar.

Boudi-Ca hiked up her skirt, reached between her legs, and rubbed, thinking of Moshe and praying silently for Allyssia to make her headache go away. She almost hoped that Lydiah would punish her that night. She'd experienced her most intimate moments in her fledgling life when the Mistress punished her. She was missing that special intimacy to the point of desperation. Djinnus cocks satisfied her Hunger, but not her love.

She wished Lydiah hadn't destroyed her diaries. She was forbidden to write anymore, so she had little to do in her free time, and worse yet her memories tended to slip away. That was yet another perk of the Smokeless

Flames. Without her nectar, her memories might start coming back, or least more might stay in her head. She was resolved to quit nectar and get to the Flames, but she'd failed to prove anything to the Sisters on the raid.

She dozed off until a soft knock came on the door. Lydiah entered with a wave of perfume, closed the door, and lit a candle on the desk. The Mistress drifted to the bed and settled on the edge. Darkness had fallen, and the visitors were departing. The faint sounds of whip-snaps and carriage wheels rose on the night air outside. Lydiah's black-painted lips were pursed pensively in the candlelight.

"Fledging, I wasn't really angry at you earlier."

"I know, Mistress. I know you love me." Boudi-Ca sat up and leaned for a kiss on the lips, but her lips collided with the soft cheek of the Mistress. Instead, she felt Lydiah's strong hand caress her back for a second. Lydiah shifted away and took a deep breath that swelled her cleavage inside the restraints of her stately boned corset.

"I have some important things to tell you."

"Am I going to the Flames?"

"Yes, but I've convinced them to wait and induct you in the autumn instead of the summer. So I've purchased a few more months until I can figure out how to screw that up. I hope you were listening at the door to make yourself look stupid and immature. If so, thank you."

"I need to be punished, Mistress."

Lydiah sighed. "I can't tonight."

"You never have time for me anymore."

"Oh, really? I spend half of my days thinking of you, my beautiful fledgling. Remember the tutors you see almost every day? I have to contract those and pay them, and then I have to make sure both you and they show up. I teach you things during our evening slave takings together. I help you improve your techniques. Masia tries to teach you things too. I'd give you more books to read, but I know you don't remember them, so what's the point? Without your nectar, you'll make better progress."

"I suppose."

Lydiah's eyebrow arched. "Perhaps you should punish yourself for your ingratitude. Give yourself a serpent bite. I want to know that you're suffering for me while I'm accepting the attentions of my husband."

Boudi-Ca felt her stomach sink. "Attentions, Mistress?"

Lydiah whispered in a low tone. "My husband is staying in our house tonight, and he says he wants his wife—not a slave girl, not Breanarachelle, and not some other she-devil whore at the Court. Fennel hasn't been himself lately. He's more vigorous, more brooding, and more cruel. Maybe his secret activities on Earth have inspired him, or maybe the torture of the Gypsy prisoners has done it for him. I need to go get undressed."

"So was the meeting about the Gypsies and not just me? What's happening with the politics, Mistress?"

"Well." Lydiah's mood lifted, and her lips curled into a small smile. "The devils claim they found proof of a lesbian conspiracy in the Smokeless Flames. Hell's Court has finally sorted the politics and paperwork, and an edict will be issued. Hell's Court will order an inquisition of Jinni in Mer. The Court will target the Smokeless Flames first with intent to arrest and imprison lesbians especially. This timing of the discovery of this conspiracy is convenient for the Court, since Allyssia is bedding our Lord at this moment and can't step in to defend the Flames."

Boudi-Ca tried to hide her look of horror. A Smokeless Flames lesbian purgation was the worst of all possible happenstances, especially if it occurred right before she joined. "Will you be involved in this, Mistress?"

"Yes, fledgling. I've been appointed as official coordinator. I'll be working with both sides to see these renegade lesbians clapped in chains, interrogated, and possibly put to death as they were during the fifteenth and seventeenth centuries. Regardless of the motives of Hell's Court, this is a historic moment, which means they're giving me a big chance to redeem my recent failures. I have to take advantage."

"Are there a lot of lesbians in the Flames?"

"Is that why you want so much to join?"

Boudi-Ca felt heat warm her cheeks. "No. I don't even know if I want to join anymore. They weren't very nice to me on the mission."

"The Smokeless Flames is about devotion to Allyssia and excellence in combat, assassination, and death. You should expect vicious competition, insults, and backstabbing. You should not expect hugs, flowers, and slumber parties."

"Yes, Mistress." Boudi-Ca gazed up into Lydiah's cold, silvery eyes. Lydiah was preaching the arrest and reformation of rebel lesbians, yet the Mistress herself was a fingersmith and a wicked orchestrator of wonderful fledgling orgasms. If Lydiah supported the purgation, she was a hypocrite worthy of a Greek tragedy, and worse yet the Purgation could threaten both of them. Lydiah leaned close and spoke in a barely audible whisper, like the wings of a butterfly.

"Henceforth, you are never to speak with anyone about lesbians, or our relationship, or express in the slightest way your very predictable opinions about this purgation. Do you understand me? Say yes."

"Yes," Boudi-Ca breathed.

Lydiah drew back slowly. "I also ferreted some secret information about Golda today, and it doesn't require a divination for me to guess the cause of your hesitation in the forest. A little bird has informed me that you were intimate friends with Golda in your past, which means she has earned my personal death sentence. We need to kill her before the devils can capture her."

"Why, Mistress? She's kind of nice."

Lydiah gave an exasperated sigh. "If the devils were to get Golda and torture her, she could divulge certain things about your past, things that never came to full light during your Court trial. If you in turn were taken for interrogation while no longer under the influence of your nectar, the outcome could be a disaster for both of us. Unfortunately, I'm not sure when I'll have time to murder Golda personally. You need to step up and be an asset to us instead of a liability, fledgling. I don't mean that cruelly. It's the truth."

"Were Golda and I lovers? Is it true?"

"I'm not answering that."

"How can she turn into a cat? Is she a wizard?"

Lydiah fiddled with her diamond earring. "No. Golda is just a half-animal, cursed by the cat goddess Basteh. She wants to scratch her cheek on your pretty leg and lick your face. If you see her again, pretend to be her friend, and then pull out your sword and kill her. That's an explicit order, fledgling. Cut Golda's throat so she'll never speak to anyone. When you've finished her, send me a messenger bird. I'll come and handle the aftermath. Will you swear to Allyssia that you will do this, fledgling? This is for me, for us, and for both of our futures."

"I will try, Mistress. I want you to be happy."

"Good. So do I. I know it's awkward, but you should carry a blade when you go out from now on. Meanwhile, I'm going to be very busy coordinating this lesbian purgation in the coming days. First I need to appoint a few Flames deputies to carry out the arrests. Corporal Shadow will track for us, but she isn't a leader. I have a specific Sister in mind, but the devils weren't thrilled by my decision. I had to convince them."

"Who, Mistress?"

"Lieutenant Nefra is currently deployed in Meristyian, where she's recuperating from a wound. I've gotten everyone on board with bringing her home to Mer so she can help with the lesbian purgation. You have a history with her too, fledgling."

"I don't remember Lieutenant Nefra."

"I'll re-introduce you. She should arrive in the city in two days' time." Lydiah looked over her shoulder. "Yes. So many things need doing."

A knock sounded on the door then, and the door swung open. Boudi-Ca shivered when Master Fennel strode uninvited into her bedchamber. His pale yellow, burgundy-blotched visage looked even sicklier in the low candlelight. Lydiah rose immediately and went to him.

"I was just coming, my wonderful husband."

"You were, or she was?" Fennel's arched lips formed a rare smile. Lydiah's overaffected chortle was loud in the dead silent room.

"Oh, you know how easy Mimọ girls are, darling, and an Mimọ Jinn is almost hopeless. Her desire controls her. Any half-handsome Djinnus can drench Boudi's underthings just by caressing her arm with his little finger."

Fennel's baleful yellow eyes were wicked. "An Mimọ girl is like a pignatta.

The fun is hitting her until she rips. When she rips, you stitch her right back up and have fun again." Fennel embraced his wife ferociously in the doorway. He seized her white-blonde mane, twisted it into a knot in his fist, and yanked. Lydiah gasped. She was half-bent over, steadying herself on her heels, as her husband dragged her from the doorway and down the hall towards the master bedchamber.

Boudi-Ca waited for long moments, and then she ran to her door and closed it. She grabbed the doorframe, feeling faint. Her thumping headache made her dizzy, and her heart was louder than the thump of feet down the hallway. Lydiah's cries of pleasure and suffering would soon echo through the long hallways of Fennel's home.

She drifted to the writing table. She reached into the drawer, opened her little box, and withdrew the leather strip with the little steel hooks, gifts from Lydiah. When Lydiah's first muffled scream disturbed the silence, she slid the first hook into the soft flesh of her groin. Another scream came faintly down the hallway, followed by animal grunts and moans.

Boudi-Ca slid the second hook into her flesh with practiced quickness, completing the serpent bite punishment as she'd been instructed. She re-arranged her skirt, opened her bedchamber door, and descended the east wing stairs with pain waving through her groin with every step. Golda's intense eyes drifted back into her pained mind. She'd solemnly sworn to kill Golda, yet Lydiah had virtually confirmed that she and Golda had once been lovers. The very idea was wild and mind-boggling. She remembered no such thing, of course.

She grabbed her sword in its sheath and pressed out through the side door. She paced across the driveway stones to the stable. She beckoned the stable boy to saddle a horse. She could still catch up with Moshe. She summoned her magical messenger bird to her fingertips.

I'm on my way to La Gershon.

She wasn't supposed to leave the house without Masia, but she was half-hoping Golda would accost her on the way to the Ukraine quarter. She wanted to speak more with Golda, or at least for a few minutes before she cut off the cat-shifter's head. She also wanted to speak with the Smokeless

Flames lieutenant named Nefra. Lydiah was withholding things from her as usual. If she wanted to know the truth, she needed to pursue it.

55

Chapter 7.

Yellen gripped the reins in her gloved fists. The fatigue in her arms was bone deep, but she found the strength to control the great Nanka. She blew the whistle, and the Nanka soared on a down draft from the Erebus rim into Haawiyah. Yellen looked down past the Nanka's wing. A wave of happiness buoyed her heart. The scarred landscape of the Great Blue Hole mines yawned below. She was almost home.

Yellen whistled twice more—two shrill tweets in quick succession. The Nanka swooped low over the diggers that picked among the Great Blue Hole watchtowers. The human slaves crawled like pale maggots on the gritty terrain. A few tilted their heads up to look, shielding their eyes with dirty arms. They were the lucky ones—the souls with the privilege of working the pit interstices, unlike the many thousands of humans beneath the Haawiyah crust who never glimpsed Hell's polluted sun.

Yellen inhaled the stony, gaseous odors. She'd done her sacred duty for the Smokeless Flames, serving in a Jinn unit of Hell's army in distant war-ravaged Meristyian. She'd fought the rebels and the forces of Heaven, and finally she'd been called home. She would likely be assigned to a teaching position due to her war injury. She didn't mind. After five years of life-or-death situations, living in army camps amidst the conflicts in

Meristyian, injured duty in the capital city would be a paradise of relaxation and pleasure.

Mer resolved into visibility within minutes—a sprawling blotch of civilization on the plateau between the black Great Blue Hole rim forest and the vast ochre deserts of the Mare Mortis beyond. Sulfur clouds coalesced on the western horizon into a storm borne from the desert of the Mare. Spiky veils of blowing sand spired to meet the purple undersides of gas clouds where pale green spider-lightning played. Wisps of rain trailed into a purplish haze. A rainstorm was a rare and beautiful thing in Haawiyah—an omen of good luck and fecundity.

Yellen eased back in her seat and imagined the luxury of Henne's soft touches and sweet-scented arms. She was sick of feeding her Hunger every night with random Djinnus on lumpy beds in low, dirty tents.

The scaly Nanka beat its wings more strongly, as if sensing in its reptilian brain the end of the journey. The creature picked up the pace and aligned with a caravan road that led through the blackened forest near the grand capital. The Nanka glided over the outer walls of Mer, drifted over the Merian east market district, and then veered right to avoid the forbidden zone over the Lord's palace and Hell's Court. The Nanka banked over the gaping maw of the massive Merian Coliseum, which rivaled the palace in size. A crowd had gathered that afternoon under the Coliseum awnings to see a bloody, gut-strewn spectacle.

Yellen tugged the reins and guided the Nanka in a slow arc over the north side residential sections, where a maze of ancient stone walls appeared like a honeycomb from above. The residents of Mer liked building walls. The most extreme forms of eroticism were best practiced in ritual silence and privacy. Red flags soon came into view through clouds of factory smoke. The flags marked the red-roofed quadrangles of the north side Smokeless Flames monastery.

The Nanka angled of its own accord towards the flags, which were fluttering madly in the wind blowing off the Mare Mortis. The Nanka tipped and dropped hard onto the landing platform, where it came to a stop with a thunder of clanging claws and shivering scales. A pair of fearless slave boys, one with his arm in a sling, ran up to chain the great beast.

Yellen pulled her sword case from the back of the riding basket. She'd send a slave to collect her heavier bag. She unfurled the rope ladder, climbed down, and strode past the boys to the exit. The pert blonde aspirant on duty didn't recognize her face but glanced quickly at the bars on her sash. The girl straightened and saluted.

"Good afternoon, Lieutenant!"

Yellen returned the salute. "I'm reporting home from war duty in Meristyian. My name is Lieutenant Nefra."

"I'll mark you as an arrival, Lieutenant! Welcome home!"

Yellen passed into the old familiar exit passage that led to the street outside the monastery. The fledgling aspirant was fresh-faced and unjaded. The girl had never battled a raging werewolf in its death throes or faced the terrible weapons of the Mimọ crusaders—the blessed blades and holy water that melted the warriors for Hell.

Yellen admonished herself. The screams and misery still echoed in her memories, as did the smell of her own melting flesh. She'd survived all of her fights in the end. The time for killing was over. She climbed into one of the rickshaws that waited for customers by the curb.

"Forty-five Leo Street."

The barebacked human city slave lurched forward. His bulging calves churned under the hem of his ragged knee pants. His calloused feet toed for purchase on the timeworn, storied bricks of Mer. Yellen balanced her sword case on her thighs. It wasn't far to the secluded Mare-side home where she still lived with her former mentor. She'd never felt the need to acquire her own residence after she'd passed her Mistress Test and graduated from her fledglinghood.

Mer was the most expensive of Hell's cities in which to own a home, and her tours in the upper regions of Hell had meant that she'd rarely been back to the capital. Her military duties had also afforded her the opportunity to eschew the traditional marriage required of all Jinni by Lord Hades' law.

The rickshaw topped a hill. Yellen gazed east across the teeming city of Mer. She wanted to send a message to Henne immediately, but it was wiser to wait a day, relax, and clean herself up. She didn't want to look lonely or desperate, despite not having heard from Henne in six moons.

She could only pray to Allyssia that Henne's engagement situation hadn't resolved yet. Henne had passed her Mistress Test the year previously. Henne wasn't in the Flames, so she was required by law to wed an Djinnus. Yellen clenched her jaw with sudden tension. After Henne married, of course, their illicit affair would be even more difficult and ill-advised.

The rickshaw soon arrived at Commander Befanah's estate in the upper west side. A red-painted Smokeless Flames carriage sat at the old crumbling curb. Befanah had company. Yellen disembarked and paid the driver five denarii. She opened the gate, strode through the small front yard, and pushed through the massive front door.

"Befanah?" Her voice echoed hollowly through the marble columns of the stony foyer. Befanah's house-girl trotted down the stairs within seconds, and the male steward entered into the foyer at the same time through a nearby archway. Yellen smiled. Both of Befanah's personal house-service slaves were well-trained and much healthier then the lazy, over-abused humans in the military.

"The Mistress is busy in the drawing room with guests," the handsome steward said with his eyes properly lowered. "Monica made your room ready."

Yellen slung her sword case over her shoulder. "I have bags waiting at the Flames Nanka platform. Arrange to get them for me, please. Monica, show me to my room."

"Yes, Mistress Nefra." Monica's voice was silken. Yellen followed her up the wide staircase. The house-girl's ample ass swayed under her skirt, and her bare feet winked under the hems of her petticoats. Yellen felt her Jinn Hunger surge. The trip from Meristyian to Haawiyah had been long, and she'd only fed at her stop at the monastery in east Vegasis. The sweet scent and pampered gentleness of Befanah's house-girl stoked her need.

She followed Monica down the upper hall into the south wing and through the door to her personal bedchamber—a room of austere plaster walls with a low shelf of military books and an old but serviceable bed.

Her oil painting still hung centered above the bed, a scene depicting a tiger fighting armored gladiators in the Merian arena. Her first Jinn lover, Simhonit, had given it to her as a gift.

The room was redolent with the homey smell of clean linens and fresh wax. The wood flooring gleamed in the warm light of early evening that poured through the balcony Ukraine doors. The doors thumped and rattled on their hinges from the force of the Mare storm. Yellen quietly closed the hall door and approached the house-girl. The slave gestured at the adjacent archway into the bath.

"Your towels are ready, Mistress, and your robes—"

Yellen seized Monica and kissed her hard on her lips. The slave girl was heavy, but not too much. Yellen lifted her bodily and conveyed her to the bed, where she upended Monica and climbed on top. The girl's cardinal sin was gluttony, and she was chubby from the sweet delicacies of Mer. Yellen dragged Monica's skirt to reveal a thatch trimmed into a tight line as Befanah liked it.

Yellen bit through the house-girl's bodice at the bump of an already-excited nipple, eliciting a moan, and then licked up to bare skin. She kissed Monica's collarbone and neck. She reached low and found the girl's sex with two fingers. She wasted no time in working Monica's clit and sealing a kiss over the slave girl's ready lips. Yellen pulled with her Jinn Hunger, and the house-girl thrust in rhythm, opening dutifully to surrender the emotional energy of her lust.

Yellen grimaced. Her fingers had no deftness. Her wrist had no lift. She was weary from steering the great Nanka over Meristyian and Erebus for four long days and nights. Within a few minutes, nonetheless, the slave girl shuddered into a petite mort. Yellen drained just enough energy to take her edge off without disrupting Befanah's feed-schedule for the girl. She sat up at the sound of a knock.

The door opened. Befanah hobbled into the bedroom. The wrinkled-eyed visage of the elder blade mistress was stern as always. Her unpainted lips were pursed. A trail of curly brown-grey hair graced one cheek, fallen from the other salty strands that were held back in a tight bun. Befanah was wearing a semi-formal Flames uniform—a grey robe with a red sash. The elder mistress leaned heavily on her cane with her six-foot frame.

"You're after it already, Yellen? Haven't I warned you against breaking our Lord Hades' laws?"

"Are you going to arrest me?" Yellen smiled and slapped Monica's rear end as the girl rolled from the bed to compose her clothes.

Befanah winked. "You're a day late, Lieutenant."

"I admit that I took the Nanka on a few pleasure detours. I wanted to see a bit of scenery, but no mountains or vineyards in Erebus are as pretty as Mer."

Befanah looked towards the Ukraine doors and the thrashing cobra-leaf trees outside. "It's the heart of the garden, and there's a storm coming to it."

"What's with the cane? You were hobbling a bit when I came to visit last year, but I didn't say anything."

The elder mistress shrugged sheepishly, almost appearing vulnerable under her military visage. "I'm getting old in my Jinn years. My hooves are finally growing in, and it's on full bore! I'm taking medicines to dull the pain."

"I'm sorry, but I'm happy for you too."

"I'll be fine when the transformation is over. I have to replace all of my shoes. There's a whole rigmarole for it. At least I'll stand a little taller when it's over. It's the only positive I can think of."

"I've always respected the hooves of the elders. I won't look forward to the transformation, but I'll welcome it when it comes."

"How's your own health issue, Yellen? Holy water, was it? I was terribly concerned when I heard of it last month."

"Yes. My squad ran into a scouting party for Heaven's army. An Mimọ soldier broke a vial against my collarbone. The holy stuff ran down into my chest armor. My squad made the Mimọ crusader die miserably, or so they told me. I passed out from the pain and woke up later, naked in bed and covered with queensfoil. My chest still hurts. They say my breasts are scarred for life, and my ribcage is brittle. Healing can do nothing, and unarmored fighting isn't advised."

Befanah tilted her head. "I'm proud of you, Yellen. Don't think your services and sacrifices to Lady Allyssia and the Flames have nary been recognized."

"I have your tutelage to thank."

"You can't teach an eagle to fly." Befanah's brooding eyes followed Monica, who slipped quietly out of the bedchamber. "Nor what to prey on."

"The eagle had a long flight."

"The eagle needs to avoid its illegal feeding habits while she is nesting in the big city. I'm serious this time."

"Why?"

Befanah pressed close. Her voice was almost a whisper. "I think you need to look for a new place to stay. It's nothing personal. Things have changed."

"With all due respect, isn't that a bit hypocritical, Mistress?"

Befanah looked pained and turned away. "Come down to the parlour with me. Our evening guest can better explain the situation."

"Of course." Yellen followed Befanah from the bedchamber. It was perfectly reasonable on a number of normal grounds for Befanah to ask her to move out. After all, Befanah had graduated her from fledgling status to full mistresshood years previously. Befanah had always condoned her activities with women, however, and Befanah herself fed from Monica occasionally at the evening slave-takings.

Befanah's cozy parlour faced Leo Street. The red-wallpapered sitting room on the east side of the house was thrown into a familiar gloom in the late afternoon. Befanah's two visitors lounged in the worn, pink-striped upholstered chairs. One visitor wore a grey Flames robe similar to Befanah's but sewn with the insignia of the Flames High Council. She was Ambassador Lydiah, and the other visitor was Lydiah's young fledgling.

Boudi-Ca wore an elegant white corset, a matching white skirt, and shoes with white bows. She looked like a high-society Mimọ slave except for a hungry curl on her shapely lips and a glint of blue moon-silver lurking in the tired hollows under her Brunette eyelashes. Boudi-Ca was Brunette unlike her mistress, but with a gentle honeyed tint instead of Lydiah's harsh platinum.

Lydiah swept her long hair over her shoulder and rose tall on her elders' hooves to overshadow the petite ghost that was Boudi-Ca. Diamonds twinkled in Lydiah's ears and fingernails—expensive glitters that matched the piercing in Boudi-Ca's left nostril. The ambassador's black-painted lips etched a small smile.

"Surprise!" Lydiah raised her wine glass. "It's another welcome-back party for you, Lieutenant Nefra. We already had one of them last night, but you came in late. This time I waited until I got a messenger bird from the east gate tower. Your old teachers missed you, but I'm sure you'll see them when you visit the monastery."

Befanah gestured with her cane at the wine bottle on the piano. "Have a glass, Nefra. You're allowed to be late when you have a war wound. I'm sure the pain took a toll."

"Thank you." Yellen walked stiffly and poured a glass. She felt under bathed and underdressed for such a distinguished visitor. She felt Lydiah's eyes flicking over her chest, as if the ambassador was gauging whether to say anything. It was odd for an upper-echelon ambassador to attend a party in her honor, much less hurry to see her the moment she landed.

Yellen searched her mind for what she knew about Lydiah, a wealthy elder Jinn who was close to Lord Hades and Lady Allyssia despite recent political missteps. Lydiah had the highest connections in Hell's Court. She was the wife of an elder devil son of Lord Hades—Archduke Fennel himself. Since devils usually married their own wicked kind instead of Jinni and Djinnus, Lydiah was unique as a Jinn duchess. She was as old as time, and one of Hell's most celebrated and respected royalty.

"Look what else." Befanah pointed to a leather coin case on the piano. "Lydiah personally brought your back pay for you Yellen, plus a bonus for good service. There are over sixteen hundred aurei in that bag."

Yellen nodded warily. Sixteen hundred was a fortune. It was also six or seven hundred too much. "That's wonderful. Thank you, Ambassador."

Lydiah's lips tightened. "You may call me Councilor. As of last year, I no longer work in my old position. I'm a liaison between the Smokeless Flames and Hell's Court. On that note, you probably realize that the Flames is paying you more than you are owed. The additional coins are an advance."

"For what exactly?"

Lydiah cleared her throat. "Lieutenant Nefra, I assume you're familiar with our Lord Hades' laws against lesbianism—the forbidden and unnatural love between two Jinni?"

"Yes. Who isn't?" Yellen felt a pricking sensation run down the back of her neck—a feeling that she only felt in the presence of a superior opponent. Something unexpected was coming, and her hard-won sense of relaxation was ebbing by the second.

"Nefra was with us there in Meristyian when the rebel lesbian cult of Allyssia was dismantled," Befanah said lightly. "She was a great help in that effort, and she's been rooting out of all sorts of other rebels against Lord Hades in these past years. She's done great service for our Lord and Lady."

"Indeed." Lydiah's moon-silver eyes brightened. "We're all aware of Lieutenant Nefra's record of service, but are you aware, Lieutenant, that Hell's Court has turned its attention to Mer in its continued efforts to enforce the lesbian laws and snuff out corruption among the Jinni?"

"No. I wasn't."

Lydiah raised her hand and examined the massive diamond ring on her finger. "As of this week, fully-fledged Jinni who are not legally married will fall under particular scrutiny. Many of our Smokeless-Flame Sisters have fallen to the wayward path of forsaking the company of males, and the Court devils recognize this."

Yellen's mouth felt suddenly dry. She was tired. She wasn't in the mood for political finesse, and Lydiah had opened the conversation with a direct thrust. She decided to respond with a direct defense.

"How does this pertain to me, exactly? Smokeless-Flame Sisters have a military exemption from the marriage requirements to Djinnus."

"That exception was meant to address the issue of military service preventing proper wedded service to a husband. It was never meant to encourage affairs between women. Until now, the Smokeless Flames has been off-limits to enforcement of Lord Hades' laws, but now no Jinn of any age or affiliation will be left unexamined."

"Go on."

"Hell's Court has ordered a Flames Purgation with me as its organizer. I've appointed Commander Befanah as Chief Enforcer in charge of the paperwork. We'll arrest suspected lesbians. They'll be taken to Hell's Court for questioning, and the devils will punish them in whatever way they deem legal and necessary."

Yellen glanced at Boudi-Ca. The fledgling's face looked morose as she gazed silently down at the woven red rug. "Well, I hope the investigation goes well. I agree that corruption must be rooted out. Congratulations on your appointment, Befanah. We have more than one reason to celebrate—your promotion as well as my homecoming."

Befanah leaned heavily on her cane. "You'll receive double your usual pay, Yellen. The Flames needs your skills. I'm crippled with my elder transformation, you see. I can't do the footwork for this."

Lydiah casually sipped her wine. "You'll be making the arrests, Lieutenant. That's why we called you home. In the weeks to come, Befanah will receive lists of names. She'll prepare internal warrants. Your job is to find, cuff, and deliver the suspected lesbians for in-depth interrogations at an arranged place."

Yellen felt a crisscross of chills run through her shoulders. The thought of arresting her own kind was appalling, while she herself seemed conspicuously free from scrutiny. "With all due respect, Councilor, why do you need me for this job? Until last week, I was lying in a bed recuperating from a life-threatening injury. Anyone else of my rank would be a better pick for this."

"No," Lydiah countered. "I have a compelling argument why you're perfect, and Hell's Court agrees with me. Befanah, please explain for the Lieutenant."

Befanah nodded. "You've been out of the capital city for most of these last ten years, Nefra. Everyone in the Flames knows you and respects you, but you have few friends. You're an outsider without close ties to the entrenched lesbian cliques here in Mer. They are the ringleaders that Councilor Lydiah—I mean we—are trying to root out. You'll be more difficult for them to influence than anyone we could have picked here in Mer."

Lydiah smiled sweetly. "Thanks to your field training, Nefra, you're also skilled in subjugation and taking prisoners. Befanah tells me that you're a master of the narcabyss whip. I'd like to see you in action. I'm an aficionado of whip mastery myself, although my husband is better than I am."

"Won't the Sisters be expected to accept questioning? Why would I need to paralyze them?"

"Things can always get difficult," Lydiah answered.

Yellen leveled her gaze at Lydiah's moon-silvered grey eyes, which were as cool and glittering as the diamonds she wore. "Do we expect things to get difficult?"

"I don't expect so, which is why your war wound shouldn't be an issue." Lydiah drummed her diamond-studded fingernails on the piano. Her eyes roamed over the oil paintings on the parlour walls. "Who can say, though? Once word of this gets out, things could get ugly. It's imperative that we manage public perception. This isn't the end of the world. It's for the welfare of everyone."

"Wonderful."

"Double pay, Nefra," Befanah said in a low tone. "Add that to your savings and the coins in that case, and you can go out tomorrow and put a payment down on a Mare-side mansion just like mine."

Lydiah nodded sagely, sipped her wine, and stretched to her full-hooved height in her grey robe. The Councilor wore her Flames robe in an effete, administrative style. Lydiah's two top buttons were tactfully undone to display the fine lacing of an ebony undercorset that matched her black-painted lips. Lydiah wore her red sash tight and high on her hips to emphasize her hourglass figure. Lydiah had no visible weapon. She was reputed to be a skilled sorceress. She no doubt possessed an arsenal of magic to supplement her curves and couture. Lydiah arched her eyebrow—the only movement in the silence.

"So. Can we officially count on you, Lieutenant Nefra, to help our mother Allyssia clean up the lesbianism corruption in the Smokeless Flames as ordered by Hell's Court? I imagine you were expecting something else, and I'm sorry. I asked about getting you a nice leave of duty afterwards, but that's up to your direct superiors."

Yellen forced a smile. She had no real option, of course. "Yes, Councilor. Thank you for this opportunity. May I ask what Lady Allyssia thinks of this?"

"I'm sure our mother understands that some of Her daughters have strayed from the proper service to cocks. Allyssia rightfully submits to the will of our Lord in this matter, just as all Jinni should submit to their husbands. Our Lord's law states: 'The Jinni shall serve Lord Hades' sons and take husbands from among them. With body and mind born from Allyssia, the Jinni shall take the seed of our Lord's seed, and that seed shall be their Life and Providence, and they shall serve that seed and never one another, like their Mother. So let it be.'"

"So let it be."

"It's settled then. The news of this initiative will be released tomorrow. I expect to receive the first names on dies Lunae, and we can start arresting the suspected lesbians, who we will refer to as 'The Named', not lesbians or any other criminal appellation until they are convicted by Hell's Court. I'll get you an official badge designating you as a deputy of the Court, Lieutenant."

"How long will this take, do you think?"

"The operation will last as long as necessary to purge the city of lesbians, whether they're in the Flames or otherwise. We're expecting a flurry of defections when the news is announced, and that's where Hell's Court will help. Since the news of the crackdown has leaked, we've already had reports of a few unmarried Jinni disappearing from Mer. We believe some of these defectors have been slipping away to ally themselves with Allyssia."

Yellen nodded cautiously. "I'm aware that Allyssia still harbors lesbians and other renegades, but no one knows how they are getting to her or where she is hiding."

"Hell's Court has determined that the Gypsies are helping the Jinn fugitives. We have some of these Gypsies now in interrogation, and more are on the way. As of today, the Court has posted devil monitors at every city gate. Henceforth, no Jinn will leave the city without written permission from either her legal husband or from Hell's Court. With the obvious escape routes closed down, the Purgation will begin. The laws of our Lord Hades must be obeyed, and there will be no escape."

Befanah raised her empty wine glass. "All praise Lord Hades."

"All praise Lord Hades." Yellen raised her glass and drank. The wine was a fine vintage imported from Erebus, but it tasted vinegary on her lips. Sixteen hundred aurei would take the edge off of arresting her own kind, but she still felt horrible. Worse yet, the Purgation was spreading to include absconding wives who were abused by their husbands. Even the Gypsies didn't merit their treatment, but Hell's Court was pitiless.

Lydiah reached low and extracted the wine glass from Boudi-Ca's pale fingers. "My fledgling and I need to leave. Do you remember my fledgling, Nefra? Boudi-Ca, this is lieutenant Nefra. Boudi-Ca takes black nectar regularly, so she doesn't recognize you. I think you both should be friends again."

Boudi-Ca rose and curtseyed deeply in a perfect courtly style. "It's my pleasure to meet you, Lieutenant."

"The pleasure is mine. I remember your blade like it was yesterday. How could I ever forget the beating you gave me?"

"I, um—" Boudi-Ca fidgeted, and her fairy-like eyes looked shocked.

"How sweet the silent backward tracings," Lydiah murmured. "The meditation of old times resumed. Persons in distant places, persons whom we loved. Fighting someone is like making love to them, or so I've heard. Befanah, you can expect the Names on schedule. Good night, Lieutenant Nefra. I'll see you on dies Lunae."

Yellen felt another chill go through her shoulders when Lydiah transfixed her with a glittering gaze, and then the tense moment was over, and Befanah escorted the visitors to the door. Yellen rubbed the soreness that throbbed in her chest. The wine in her stomach felt like lead.

She'd never been meticulously discrete with her lesbian activities, and Councilor Lydiah possessed every possible connection in the Flames and

Hell's Court. The odd way that Lydiah had called her back to the capital, combined with the flimsy explanation for why only she could do the job, spoke volumes.

Yellen hefted the coin satchel. Yes, it was a near certainty that Lydiah knew everything about her, which meant that Lydiah had her by the throat and the short hairs both. Her hard-won vacation was already over, and her soul was at stake in exchange for a satchel of gold coins stamped with the grim bearded visage of Lord Hades.

$$\mathcal{Chapter\ 8.}$$

Yellen slipped into a clean ironed robe and tied it with a red Flames sash. She strapped on her sword belt. She never went unarmed in the city. The vultures in Mer didn't feed on the living. She strode down the steps to the first floor of Befanah's home and out the front door.

Dawn's chariot was rising low and orange over the cluster of old and stately homes in the sandy Mare-side neighborhood. The dry winds off the Mare Mortis rustled the cobra-leaf trees, sending quiet hisses over the red tiled rooftop.

She hadn't slept well. Ambassador Lydiah had handed her the most self-conflicted assignment that she'd ever had in service to the Smokeless Flames and Hell's army. The idea of arresting lesbian Sisters horrified her, yet if she refused to carry out the orders, she would only implicate herself. She wasn't sure what Lydiah was holding on her. Her indiscretions had grown to a lengthy list over the decades, most recently when Boudi-Ca had caught her in bed with Henne during the occupation of Lady Allyssia's former city in Meristyian.

Yellen walked down the sloping street towards the market district, taking long strides to loosen her stiff legs. She had no intention of dwelling on doom and gloom. She had one full day before her first assignment. First she needed a hot bath and a new place to live, as Befanah had requested. She also needed to decide whether to seek Henne's company despite the danger.

Her instinct was to refuse to let Lydiah and the lesbian Purgation silence her love for Henne. She'd survived many life-or-death situations for the glory of Hell's Court and Lord Hades. She'd damned well-earned the pleasures of perfumed skin and a woman's lips, just like every male soldier fighting on the front lines against Heaven.

Yellen quickened her pace out of Befanah's neighborhood. The Purgation was surely only a show. Lesbianism had been a part of the Smokeless Flames since the days of Allyssia's first fledglings. Close friendships and sleep-overs had always been accepted. A few arrests would be made during the Purgation, along with a lot of hand waving and drama, and then the Smokeless-Flame Sisters would go back to indulging themselves however they wished. That was how politics had worked in Mer for three millennia.

Since their short and torrid love affair in Meristyian, she Henne had met whenever she'd had a brief occasion to return to the capital city of Mer. Henne wasn't a Smokeless-Flame Sister. Henne was a beauty mistress who had devoted her life to refined Merian high society—the respectable Jinn arts of clothing, scents, and seduction. Over the previous few years, she and Henne had exchanged letters every few months via army messengers who normally carried mail to soldiers' wives, with Henne adding a Maître appellation to her name, thereby posing as a fictional Ukraine boyfriend.

Yellen reached the Mare-side public baths and passed through the inner gates. A city towel-imp was stationed to serve the bathers. Only a handful of Djinnus and Jinni soaked that morning in the four public clover-shaped pools. Yellen stripped off her robe and lowered herself into the closest.

On the far side of the pool, a middle-aged balding Djinnus was fucking what appeared to be his wife or someone else's, judging from the ring on her finger. The Djinnus pressed his wife against the edge of the pool. Her breathy moans were audible above the lapping water. The wife's bruised lips formed a slack aperture of transported pleasure, as if she were sucking at an invisible teat. A luxurious mane of red hair obscured most of her tired, unpainted face.

The Djinnus grunted and finished with her. The wife climbed from the pool. The nub of a horn peeked from under her hairline when she turned, and a sinuous tail emerged. The tail was attached to a shapely backside with two rows of discolored markings. The wife wasn't a Jinn. She was just a worn-out demoness who wore slave brands on her sacrum, brands marking the ownerships of half a dozen former masters.

The demoness flopped her body onto a nearby white-painted chaise longue, taking care to slip her tail through the accommodating slit. The nearby towel-imp chittered at her in Demonic, asking whether she wanted anything. The demoness ignored him and closed her eyes, letting beads of water dry on her stomach and the ruddy tuft of her sex.

Yellen looked away. She felt an attraction, and it was more than just her Jinn Hunger. The redheaded demoness looked a lot like Henne. Perhaps the vision was a sign, a mystical reminder that love could not be denied. Yellen raised her hand from the hot water and summoned her magical messenger bird to her fingertips.

Henne, it's Yellen. I'm finally home from duty again. What are you doing this afternoon? Can I see you?

The green finch winged away over the sauna rooftop towards the northeastern city, where Henne lived near the Merian Coliseum with her mentor, Nili. The finch was silhouetted for a moment against the morning sky, and then it was gone.

Yellen ignored the brief queasiness in her belly from having made such a fate-defying, ill-advised decision. She trusted her instincts, and her instincts were to fight for what she knew was right. She twirled and backstroked around the hot pool, reveling in the warm liquid rushing over her skin. The balding Djinnus was watching her closely. She ignored him and climbed from the pool. She dried herself and climbed into her clean robe while the Djinnus emerged from the water and walked towards her.

Yellen turned slightly so the male could see the Flames bars on her sash. She was a ranking officer, not a needy Jinn dredging the public pools for sex.

"Excuse me, Sister," the Djinnus said. "Might you need some nectar?"

Yellen blinked. The question came as a surprise. She opened her mouth to decline, but her thoughts went immediately to Henne. Henne loved nectar. Henne also loved presents. "I'd want the best. It would be a gift for a friend."

"Of course." The Djinnus smiled ingratiatingly. "I'm a nectar grinder by trade, and a good one, but I've fallen on hard times. The competition is fierce here in the big city. It's a little too fierce. My name is Master Trigo."

"I'm Nefra. Lieutenant Nefra."

Master Trigo grinned. "It's nice to meet you, Lieutenant! I have some fine Blue-Violet Beauty in my bag right over there. It's the best. Come have a look!"

Yellen strapped on her sword and followed the Djinnus to the chair where his wife reclined. The demoness rested with her eyelids closed and her slender limbs flaccid. Her breasts rose slightly with her breaths. The redhead's lips weren't just discolored—they were stained like the grinders. Both were evidently nectar-eaters. The Djinnus drew a pouch from his satchel and opened it. He held up a small bag for inspection. Yellen bent and sniffed the sweet-smelling powder. She knew nothing of nectar qualities, much less the current prices.

"How much?"

"Two aurei and ten for sixteen drachms," the grinder answered. "Can I make you a happy buyer today?"

"I don't have that much coin with me, unfortunately. I live nearby on Leo Street."

The grinder nodded. "No problems, of course. I can see from your sash that you're gainfully employed. I'm willing to give the sixteen drachms on good faith. My shop is called 'Trigo's Vices'. It's down near the corner where Leo Street meets Virgo Road. It's a good location, they say, but location isn't everything. Send a slave with the payment, if you would? Or come personally. As you prefer."

"Of course, Master Trigo. You have my word. I think I'd like two bags, though. My friend is very special to me. She's a beauty fledging, or rather a fully-fledged mistress now if she passed her recent Mistress Test."

The grinder's wattled throat twitched. He wiped beads of water from his thinning hair with a hand mottled by purpled off-tones. "I don't know, Sister. Four and twenty is a lot of coin to go on trust."

"Why don't I just get the coin and bring it to you in a little while? I have some other errands to run, and then I'll come."

The Djinnus brightened. "That's fine! I'm open until six o'clock this evening. Just come on in, Lieutenant. I run an artisanal establishment. Bring your friends!"

"Thank you." Yellen turned to walk away, but the Djinnus touched her arm. He smiled awkwardly.

"My wife is for sale too. She's very willing for anything, I'd wager."

Yellen hesitated and met the grinder's dark eyes. Trigo was a man in quiet desperation. His teeth were bluish and crooked, blackened in the interstices, and the remnants of his hair were uneven and poorly tended. He obviously had bad personal habits like his so-called wife, and his habits were likely the cause of his hard times.

"No, thanks. Good day to you."

Yellen strode quickly from the baths, admonishing herself as she went. She'd given her secret away within minutes by her over-attention to the grinder's wife. On top of that, the Smokeless Flames had a reputation as a refuge for lesbians. The grinder had easily put the pieces together.

Befanah was right. She'd been untouchable as a decorated lieutenant in a special unit of the Smokeless Flames in Hells' army, but in Mer things were different. She'd have to re-learn how to watch herself more closely.

Yellen scanned the sky for a return bird from Henne, but she saw no magical brown catbird flitting through the cobra-leaf trees. Perhaps Henne was busy with her artwork, or perhaps Henne was busy with something else. Henne always had a lover, or several. Worse yet, if Henne had successfully passed her Mistress Test, Henne was required to take a husband in the coming months.

Yellen ascended the city street back to Befanah's house and climbed the foyer stairs up to her room in the south wing. She tried to keep her mind off of Henne. She lingered at her old vanity, taking time to brush her hair, file and clean her nails, and apply balm to her hands. Henne was sensitive to leathery fingertips, which were always a problem with sword training. Yellen fastened a pouch to her sword belt, descended the stairs, and swerved into Befanah's study, which was redolent with pipe smoke. Befanah sat behind her massive paper-strewn desk. The elder mistress leaned back and removed her reading glasses.

"I'm sorry about last night, Yellen. I should have warned you. I know you didn't expect Lydiah and I to jump you like that."

"So how serious is this 'purgation'?"

Befanah shook her head. "I don't think you fully understand the atmosphere here in Mer, Yellen. Jinni are disappearing, including some Smokeless-Flame Sisters. Hell's Court says they've been defecting with secret agents of Allyssia. They suspect Allyssia is building another city in Meristyian for rebels and lesbians."

"I thought the Court was cutting off the escape routes, according to our beloved Councilor."

"Yes. The Gypsies outside the city were raided by Hell's Court. Most of the remaining Gypsies in the forest have scattered like cockroaches. The gates of Mer are now under lockdown. We're expecting the announcement of the Smokeless Flames investigation today as scheduled, followed by the first list of the Named."

"That's when I go to work?"

"Yes. According to Lydiah, you'll only have one or two Named to arrest each day. The plan is to go slow so we don't incite a riot. You'll quietly deliver the Jinni to an address at 115 West Pelagius Street. It's a downtown address. I'm not familiar with it. In any case, the daily arrests should be short and sweet."

"How will I find the Sisters to arrest them?"

"You'll have someone assisting you. Her name is Corporal Shadow-Under-Moon. Shadow lives with her husband here in Mer, and she's one of the Flames's most skilled and knowledgeable trackers. She can track the passage of souls in the chaotic weave of the city tapestry like no one else. None of the lesbians will likely be able to hide from Shadow, even if they have a sorceress who dares aid them with obfuscation."

"Wonderful."

Befanah nodded, almost apologetically. "You and Shadow will pick up the first Named tomorrow. I'll have everything here in the morning, as well as your appointment papers and badge as an official of the Court."

"I'll do my duty for the Flames."

"Good. I'll expect you to." Befanah placed her reading glasses back on her nose. "Yellen, this situation is serious. Take care of yourself. You know what I mean. You'll be on point. I'd suggest finding yourself an Djinnus boyfriend."

Yellen clenched her fingers over her sword hilt and suppressed a growl. "I'll take that under advisement. You're serious about me moving out then? I just want to be clear."

"Yes."

"I'd like to take some of my pay so I can rent a flat this afternoon. I'm also taking my best blade to the blacksmith. It needs Sharpening and a re-wrap, and the hilt needs a new crystal to replace one that's missing."

"I put your coin case there in the wall safe." Befanah reached into a drawer and extended her worn hand over the desk. "Here's the business card of an agent I know. She's a retired Sister. I'd suggest finding a place in the north residential district. The Smokeless Flames compound is there, and you'll be visiting it frequently. The steward groomed and saddled your old horse. It's ready to go."

"Thank you, Befanah."

Yellen took the business card and went to the safe. She counted out a generous amount of gold aurei while Befanah watched. She stalked from the study without another word. Her vacation would last one day, and then she'd be back in military mode. She had things to get done, and the items on the agenda were queuing up in her head, ready to be dispatched like a nest of rebel vampires. She'd visit the grinder to pick up Henne's nectar on her way to the blacksmith's place.

She went to the stable and retrieved her old grey mare. The animal was well-tended and seemed happy to see her. She rode briskly down Leo Street for several minutes until it bent and descended towards the fringes of Westmarket, where Leo Street crossed Virgo Avenue coming in from the east. She searched the house fronts on the corner. The grinder's place was the second building over, sheltered in an alley back from the road. The paint on the sign in the front yard was relatively fresh.

Trigo's Vices ~ Fine Nectars, Potions, Medicines, Spices

Master Trigo's house was three stories, worn, and non-descript. Its grey stone bricks were weathered, and its front glass windows were opaque like many others on the adjacent buildings, sanded cloudy by centuries of dust storms blowing in from the Mare across the Westmarket. A single cobra-leaf tree stood in the patch of yard. An anemic witch-sickle bush rustled beside the oak front door, which was ajar. The door knob had been broken by some instrument. The impact had scattered flakes of peeled varnish across the stone steps.

Yellen stepped cautiously inside the establishment. The front room was a mess. Strewn bottles and incense sticks littered the surfaces of the display tables. A set of tipped-over brass scales lay on the low shop counter while the counterweights littered the floor. The place appeared ransacked. It was a disaster.

"Anyone here?" Yellen kicked a bottle. Her call was greeted by silence, but she heard a thump above her. She ascended the nearby staircase. Smears of blood were visible on the railing. She drew her blade. The second floor of the grinder's home consisted of a hallway, two spacious rooms, and a bath. The first room was obviously a workshop and reeked of nectar. The other was a bedroom. A tangle of blankets and clothes lay on a dilapidated bed. A lacy woman's nightgown draped the arm of a chair. Yellen whirled at the sound behind her. A hidden door popped open in the hall wall. The grinder's balding head emerged from the crack.

"Ah, thank the Lord it's you. Have you got the four and twenty?"

Yellen recognized the nectar grinder, but only barely. Trigo was no longer nude. He'd dressed himself in a shabby pink shirt and a brown coat. A crooked tie adorned Trigo's thick neck. A cracked leather belt held up his trousers. A purple wound bloomed on his forehead. The Djinnus brushed past her to a travel basket that lay open on the floor of the adjacent bedchamber.

"I have the coin, Master Trigo. What happened?"

"What do you think?" the grinder snapped. "They came again a while ago for the coin I owe. They were waiting when Kiree and I got home. I'm done in Mer. I have to get out of here."

"You're leaving the city?"

Trigo picked up a shirt and hurled it into the basket. "I'll pick up a caravan and go work the grow-fields. Expenses here in the capital are a bit much, and the competition from the bigger players is too violent. I might scrape by with my potions and imported herbs, but that isn't my forte."

"Where is your wife?"

"Where do you think? I have large debts, Lieutenant Nefra. They took her a little bit ago when we got back from the baths."

"Who are 'they'?"

Trigo gave an exasperated sigh. "Look, I don't know if anyone has ever threatened to send you to the void—"

"Many have actually tried, and so far, all of them have failed."

Trigo's bristly eyebrow arched. "Well that's very impressive, I must say, but I don't like it! I don't own a sword or a gun, nor do I really want to. I should have left sooner with Kiree before I got too far into debt. Could you just count the coins out on the chair there? I have thirty-two drachms of Blue-Violet saved out. With any luck I can leave before the Toad takes the coins you're giving to me."

"So it's a moneylender? I'm off-duty, but I was heading in the direction of Hell's Court. If any laws were broken, you could file a report." Yellen counted the coins and stacked them on the broken chair, wary of the grinder's eyes on her sword and heavily laden belt pouch. Trigo folded a pair of old trousers and threw them into the travel basket.

"I'd prefer to avoid the Court on this. My wife has legal issues. Do you know anyone who might like a house, though? I don't have much money into this place. In fact, I was planning to abandon it. If anyone wanted to pick up my debt, it would be one less thing the Toad would have over my head if I ever came back to the capital. I could show you the paperwork. It isn't a good deal, and it's an even worse neighborhood, but cheap houses are hard to find in this city."

"How much would you want?"

"I've only paid ninety-five aurei towards owning the place. I'd ask for fifty back. Then you'd make payments to the Toad. He's the local landlord and moneylender. He deals in slaves, too. He's got his grindy paws in everything." Trigo gritted his teeth. "Fifty sounds like a lot to leave behind, but I have to get out of here. I already prepared the house papers at the Court, but I just haven't had time to find a buyer. I'll make the coin back in a few years of working the processing houses in Erebus. It's hard work, but it's my expertise, and it's a small price to stay in this life."

"What's the total value of the house?"

"Around fifteen hundred chips, Madame, last time I checked. You'd have to deal with the Toad, and he might not like you. I'd skip the Flames outfit if you tried it. The Toad isn't too partial to lawful types."

"Is this the Toad who took your wife?"

"Yeah. They didn't find Kiree's slave papers, but that doesn't mean anything. The Toad can forge new papers and resell Kiree as sure as Dawn's chariot flies over the Mare. And that's the best that could happen to her. She doesn't even speak common tongue—only Demonic. She won't even be able to argue. I love her, but what can I do?"

"That's a little callous don't you think?" Yellen instantly regretted her words. The grinder's mottled hands started shaking.

"Look, Lieutenant Nefra. You obviously don't know the Toad. You want to buy the house? You probably need time to decide. Well, I don't have time. I have to find a box to pack up my scales and tools, and then I'm going to meet with some people. Getting square with the players in my own trade is more important than sucking the cock of a Merian slumlord. This house is three stories. It has a typical pit with old slave cages, although—"

"I've decided. I'll go in for the fifty."

The grinder forced a grin, a jerky quiver on his purpled lips. "Praise be to Lord Hades. You're my personal savior, Sister. I'll go to my hidden closet here and pull out the paperwork. Our signatures combined with my Guild stamp and your military rank should be enough for the devils. You can take it and file it at the Court any time. For the rest you can take over my payments to the Toad. Is that fine?"

"I'd imagine."

The grinder rubbed his discolored hands together and disappeared into the hidden door in the hall. The door fit seamlessly into the wall and gave into a space under the narrow stairs that led up to a third floor. The grinder emerged from the dark space with papers in hand and a small smile on his face.

"Mind the spiders! They like to poke around for the moths I get in here. The moths come up from the Westmarket warehouses and hunt for my nectar. I chose this place to be close to my supply point, but if I did it again, I'd live closer to where I make my sales. I'm a business idiot."

"I can handle spiders."

"Come into my grinding room." The grinder hurried into the adjacent room that smelled of nectar. He spread the papers on a low shop table. "I closed all of the messenger bird slits except the front door, and the moths were still getting in. You'll want to scrub every room. That should get rid of most of the bugs. You have the whole fifty now?"

"Sure."

The grinder shook his head and said nothing. He unstoppered a dusty bottle and began to scribble with the scratchy nub of an old ink pen. Yellen counted the precious gold coins from her pouch while the grinder wrote. She'd trained her reflexes for two centuries with the goal of snatching tactical advantages at the second they presented themselves. She'd also trained to avoid mistakes in those moments.

She wasn't sure whether she was making a mistake, but she was sure that the oppression in Mer wasn't going to make her afraid to love who she wanted. The house in the out-of-the-way neighborhood was perfect to meet Henne or someone else. It was far from the Flames compound and any eyes that might pry, but close to Befanah's place where she'd pick up warrants for the Named. With her military salary, fifty chips was a pittance.

Master Trigo stamped the papers. "Here you go, Lieutenant. Just add your signatures, and we're all set. You'll want to see the Toad to take over payments."

Yellen picked up the pen and examined the documents. They looked legitimate. She scrawled her signature on the grinder's sale and purchase agreement. The grinder worked again with his ink pen, sketching a small map on a piece of paper. The grinder blew on the paper and handed it to her.

"There you are. That should get you to the Toad. Now excuse me while I finish up my affairs."

"Of course. Best of luck, Master Trigo." Yellen took the card and trotted down the stairs, examining the walls and ceiling as she went. The place seemed solid, but every room needed painting and plaster repair. She exited the house and re-mounted her horse. She gazed back at her discrete three-story love nest. Her Jinn lust was already simmering with the possibilities. The Toad was the new topper on her list of things to do.

The headquarters of the moneylender known as the Toad, as vaguely delineated by Master Trigo's directions, was on the far west edge of Mer in the Westmarket district close to the city west gate. It was a dirty part of the city, constantly assaulted by the dusty wind off the Mare Mortis. It was also a military district with warehouses and factories adjacent to the Mare-side army camps.

Yellen made her way along the twisting streets and bathhouses. The usual big-breasted establishment girls waved their tasseled nipples on the sidewalks, hypnotic lures for the Hell's army soldiers. Yellen followed the grinder's map, and soon she arrived at the Toadstool. Yellen climbed the rounded steps past the massive grunt that guarded the door—a horned ogre trussed up with banded armor and a four-foot bastard sword.

The interior of the Toadstool was thick with demonic clientele who swilled liquors, absinthes, and nectars under persistent tenebris luces, perpetual glow-balls of the kind cast by expensive-to-hire elder sorceresses. The purple light rendered the skin of the hellion patrons in putrid hues.

A half-nude Asian cellist, tattooed from her wrists to her shoulders, played a Beethoven sonata in the corner opposite the billiard tables. Yellen paused and watched her. The cellist was a Jinn judging by the barely perceptible moon-silver glint between her half-closed eyelids. She had skills. Yellen smiled to herself. If it wasn't for the stink of the unwashed hellions, she almost would have liked the place. She approached the barkeep—a burly four-armed hellion wearing a towering striped top hat.

"I need to see the Toad."

The barkeep eyed her Flames uniform suspiciously. "Do he need to see you?"

"If he wants. My name is Mistress Nefra. I have some money for him. I'm a potential buyer of real estate."

The barkeep looked her up and down again, then signaled a small flop-eared imp who perched at the end of the counter. "Pedi ta koo ree. Cha cha tooh konnig." Tell the boss. A pretty woman with money.

Yellen nodded her thanks as the imp scampered off. She'd studied Demonic during her years of service, enough to give clear orders to grunts when necessary. She slid onto a bar stool and watched the cellist. The Asian Jinn was focused with her long dark hair half-obscuring her concentrating face. She was well-trained in her art form. She wore expensive-looking jewelry and shoes. She was maybe an officer's wife or otherwise a slumming wealthy Jinn with a penchant for lower class cocks.

"Cha cheet." The imp was back. The little hellion chittered further, too fast to understand. The barkeep with the top hat looked up from the glass he was polishing and pointed to a nearby doorway.

"Follow the little guy, Sister. The blade stays here."

"It's a very good blade. Don't let it disappear." Yellen unstrapped her sword belt and handed it over the counter. She felt naked without the weight of steel on her hip. She followed the imp through a curtain. The imp led her down a steep flight of stone stairs.

Under most buildings in Mer were levels of pits—warrens of tunnels and chambers that served many uses, most often quarters for human slaves. The Toadstool was no different. A short hall in the Toad's pit led through a reinforced door into an office room with a low ceiling supported by Corinthian pillars.

The Toad was a handsome Djinnus draped in a black robe. He lounged behind a pretentious black basalt desk. Two well-armed hellions stood guard. Yellen approached the Toad's desk and deposited the house papers. The Djinnus stirred.

"I see a Jinn in a red uniform before me. She has money. Who is she and what does she want?"

"I'm Mistress Nefra. I'm a blade mistress in the Smokeless Flames. I passed my Mistress Test some years back, and I've finally decided that I need my own place to live. As a client of a particular nectar grinder, I took an interest when Master Trigo told me he had a house to sell. I bought his chit."

The Toad clasped his fingers together pensively. "You're aware that he has payments unpaid to me? Those would be payments to the tune of over a hundred aurei."

"You won't get any more coin from him, but maybe that doesn't matter. I'm interested in buying the place outright if you can offer a discount for the lump sum."

"Are you now?" The Djinnus raised his eyebrow. "A Jinn mistress getting out on her own is a profitable proposition for the Toad. I've figured the value of that house at sixteen hundred aurei."

Yellen grimaced. "The grinder said he was paying fifteen. The house is run down and trashed. The front door is broken now, and the plaster is in disrepair. I'll pay you a twelve hundred and use the difference to fix all the problems with the place."

"Fourteen hundred fifty is as low as I can go for that house."

"Can you throw in the grinder's wife?"

The Toad stroked his beard. "She's a sweet little redhead, isn't she? So are you doing a noble deed for your wormy, pathetic nectar friend, or is it lesbianism you're into, Sister?"

"I just need a dumb house-girl who doesn't mind getting down on her knees and staying there for a while. You know what I mean? That place needs a lot of work. Have you made up new papers for her yet? I could save you the trouble."

The Toad chuckled. "I appreciate how you operate, Mistress Nefra. When I saw your Flames insignia, I assumed the worst. I see you have taste in slaves, if not for residences. Fine. It's a deal at fourteen fifty."

"Done. I'll come back with the coin."

"Are you looking for anything else? I have more female slaves for sale as well as males, and I don't ask any questions."

Yellen hesitated. Befanah was right. She needed a male for appearance's sake. Still, she'd spent enough coin already that day, and a secondhand boy purchased from the Toad's pits didn't seem too appealing. If she had to own a male slave, she was going to be picky. If she found the perfect boy to serve her, an effeminate type preferably, she might even grow to like him.

"I'll get back to you."

"Keep in mind that my prices are unusually good, assuming you lack any ethics like normal people, of course. I'll see you when you bring the coin."

"Thank you, Master—"

"Todmartha. Now you know why I go by 'The Toad'. It makes my intimidation tactics easier. Dismissed, Sister."

Yellen pivoted and marched from the office. The little imp shadowed her up the steps with its clawed hands clicking on the stone. The barkeep in the top hat wordlessly lifted her sword over the bar when she approached. Yellen strapped it back around her waist. She ignored the mixed curious, lustful, and respectful looks of the various clientele. She headed for the Toadstool exit. She was pleased. Soon she'd be the owner of a house and a pretty demoness, although she wasn't sure which was in worse shape.

Yellen felt a wave of Hunger at the thought of feeding from the sexual energy of the demoness—a slave who didn't speak the common tongue, and therefore wouldn't speak to many people about bedroom activities. Yellen licked her dry lips and re-mounted her horse. Of course, Henne was her true conquest, and Henne still hadn't answered the messenger bird.

Henne had complained in two of her letters about cramped work space and a lack of selling locations for her pottery and sculptures. An art gallery business would be a perfect pretense to bring Henne to visit and stay late occasionally, even after Henne got married.

Chapter 9.

Golda fished the small wooden box from under Pinhas' corsets. She opened the latches. The box brimmed with jewelry that Pinhas' hadn't cared for—a panoply of tarnished metals and gemstones. Priebus rarely wore jewelry. She was a simple, married country woman who placed little value in showy bangles. Unfortunately, only a heap of gold could save her and her husband, Agron Reik, from the Hell's Court devils.

Golda turned her mind to the tapestry yet again. The dark, corrupted forest was silent with no devils or Sisters in sight. She was risking her life and limbs in the Reik camp. She and the two Gypsy men had finally circled back after a week away. They'd camped in the caves under the cliffs that led up to Erebus, where Mohilever and Gorka had bickered back and forth over whether to leave Haawiyah or stay and help Agron and Pinhas'.

During his agitation, Gorka had accused her point blank of bedding his mother and father frequently. She'd admitted it, much to Mohilever's amusement. She hadn't accepted blame for the fabricated charges the devils had leveled against the Feigns, however. Perhaps she was only fooling herself. Perhaps her attempts to talk to Boudi-Ca had riled a hornet's nest, and she was a terrible person for putting the Reik family in danger.

Golda frowned away a tear. She hated feeling helpless. The more she'd thought of the respective fates of both Boudi-Ca and Priebus, the sadder she'd become. Worse yet, on arrival at the camp, she'd found her personal tent ransacked. She hadn't been able to determine who had helped themselves to her things—the devils or the Gypsies. Her sword and jewelry were gone, but her horse remained, as well as the one change of clothes that she'd left under Pinhas' bed. She felt Gorka behind her. He peered over her shoulder into the jewelry box.

"No," Gorka said tersely, scratching his chin. "Those stay."

"I've never seen your mother wear these things."

"I won't save my mother from the Court and bring her home to find herself a pauper and all of her memories gone. My father gave her those keepsakes over the years. They're probably worthless baubles at auction."

"She won't miss this jewelry, and surely it's worth something. You don't even know what jewelry your own mother wears, Gorka."

"Well you only know from fucking her, Golda. Thank you for helping, but don't blame me for wanting to throw you out with the rest of the rubbish. Get those books instead. Original Gypsy fictions might interest the book collectors in Mer." Gorka pivoted and went back towards his father's desk, stopping for the hundredth time to peek out of the tent flap and scan the camp for devils.

Golda took a deep breath. She wanted to have words with Gorka, but she held her tongue. Gorka was an intelligent musician with an agile wit, but he was tense and self-absorbed even on a normal day. She snapped the old jewelry box shut and returned it to the armoire. The jewelry represented more coin they wouldn't have for any possibility of Pinhas' release.

She was irritable and weak because she hadn't fed well. She'd visited Gorka twice in sleep, out of pure necessity. She fucked him against his will in the dream-world. She wondered if he'd remembered the sex dreams. She wondered if he knew they were real. Dream seed lacked full potency, however. She needed to feed again already, and her candidates in Haawiyah left her few options.

The last remnants of the extended Reik family had finishing loading up and leaving the forest, having lingered only out of concern for Gorka. A few had come to the tent to express their relief that Gorka had escaped, as well as to urge him to pack up and leave immediately. None of the Gypsies had offered any words to Agron Reik mysterious Jinn visitor. No one had even spoken to her.

Golda made the books into a stack and boxed them, wary of Gorka's eyes on her back. She had to be nice to Gorka. They had to work together if they wanted any chance of saving Pinhas'. She picked up a pile of dresses and carried them out to the half-loaded wagon outside. Dusk was falling over the Haawiyah forest. Dawn's chariot trailed low and red-orange above the sickly tree branches and sulfur-stunted leaves.

Golda sighed. Haawiyah was a horrible, painful place. The forest weighed her down and made her desire to go home to Eastern Meristyian. With her discovery by the Flames, her need to leave had become a grave imperative, while her soul told her to stay and do whatever she could for Boudi-Ca and Pinhas'. Her guilt and despair had reached a maddening pitch, and she couldn't do anything unless she could feed. If she didn't feed, she could wake up paralyzed, or not wake up at all. She needed to feed, and she had to face that fact.

"I'm sorry, Golda."

Golda turned cautiously at the sound of Gorka's voice. Gorka had left the tent to stand behind her at the wagon. "For what?"

"For threatening to throw you out."

Golda looked warily at Gorka, trying to gauge the sincerity of his tone. "Thank you. Is there anything else you wanted to say?"

"You took good care of my father didn't you? You served his needs well, or he wouldn't have kept you around. He's practical like that."

"This is a difficult situation, and I'm a Jinn. I do what I have to do."

Gorka nodded with his eyes veiled. "Well, you have my thanks. In memory of my beloved wife in Heaven, my Beatrice, I've always tried to hold a sort of moral code, and you should know that I appreciate you helping me. Charity is a godly act regardless of the ignoble motives of imperfect, sinful beings. I don't mean only you. I mean we are all imperfect."

"I hope we can help your mother and father and get this over with."

"As do I." Gorka rubbed his temple tiredly and brushed back his youthful brown locks. "We'll have to finish this in the morning. I'll be up before dawn. I'll expect you to join me. When we're loaded up, we'll go into the auction house in Mer. I spoke with Mohilever. He told me where to go. They sell things in Mer the same day. Mohilever and Trumpeldor will go to Hell's Court and parlay for a bribe. Trumpeldor said he'd also stay with us. He's my mother's great-grandfather. You know him?"

"Yes, of course. Like you, he's a good musician. So I suppose you have three brave men in your family aside from the ones the devils took. Congratulations."

"Why are you still here, Golda? Why are you risking your life? You say it's for your love of my mother and father, but Mohilever says you have other business. You're searching for a friend of yours, and you were using my family for a safe haven."

"Good night." Golda turned away. She wasn't in the mood to deal with her tortured feelings about Boudi. She needed to feed, and then she could think clearly. She didn't want to go back into Mer when she was weak. She crossed the short distance to her personal tent among the trees—a low-slung thing of tanned leathers that Agron had loaned to her. She crawled inside, struck a match, and lit a lamp to ward off the coming dark even though it was still light outside.

The tent was no protection against the Flames. She'd made a hidden escape-slit in the back of her tent, and she'd strewn crisp dry leaves across the ground outside so she could hear approaching footfalls. She didn't have the energy to dig werewolf-style pit traps.

She undressed, washed herself in her clay basin, and sat on her bed to brush the tangles from her hair. She relaxed for an hour in the gathering twilight, pondering her situation and watching the last patches of dappled sunset disappear like a dreary kaleidoscope over the thin stretched hides that comprised the tent ceiling.

A problem was nagging her. It was highly unlikely that Gorka would have enough coin to bribe Hell's Court for both Agron and Priebus, even if the Court accepted bribes at all. If Gorka could afford only one bribe, who would he choose?

Gorka could easily choose his father and leave his mother to suffer. Pinhas' relationship with her son had been strained, and worse yet Mohilever was the brother of Agron. Agron was the likely choice.

Golda rose and dusted her bosom with perfume. It was a fine product of the Merian perfumeries, borrowed along with her hairbrush from Pinhas' humble boudoir. She needed to feed, and she also needed more votes for Priebus instead of Agron. She had nothing against Agron, but she'd felt something special with Pinhas'. She couldn't simply do nothing, letting the Gypsy men choose Agron and send Priebus to her doom.

The sun had set, and silence had descended over the camp of the Reik family, as if the corrupted forest were crouching and waiting for horror and pain to return. Golda slipped out of the tent into the cool night. The forest camp was dark, but a feeble light glowed from Mohilever's covered wagon where it was parked in a small grove of trees.

"Mohilever?" Golda poked her head through the wagon door. Mohilever lay half naked on his narrow bed. His hairy chest was bathed in a soft sheen of sweat. A small cedar nectar box with a gold printed ribbon sat on the stool next to him. He closed the box quickly, even as Trumpeldor stirred where he sat deeper in the wagon interior.

Trumpeldor was bearded and thirtyish, judging by his ageless appearance in the afterlife, not unhandsome, with big hands, a gangly body, and an eagle's nose on a peaceful farmer's face. The man had never farmed. He was a vagrant like his family—a player, a joker, a lover, and a stringer of guitars.

"Golda?" Mohilever grinned slowly. He patted the small cedar box. "Ah, you caught us. This is Agron' personal stash of Damp Delirious nectar. We borrowed it from his desk before Gorka went through everything. It's the best."

"Gorka could have sold that for coins. And what if Agron comes back? He's going to want that to ease his suffering."

"Lord Hades and the Court surely won't let Agron go after going to so much trouble to get him. As for Boris and his men, they'll be sent to the void. They were fools for trying to fight the pig-eyes. And even if the Court accepts bribes for Agron and Priebus, Gorka likely won't have enough coin for one, much less both."

"How much do you think we'll need for one?"

"Trumpeldor and I are going to the Court in the morning to find out for Gorka," Mohilever answered. "That arrogant prat is too proud to listen to wisdom."

"If Gorka gets Agron released, Agron won't be happy that you stole his nectar. I know him."

"Look, lass," Trumpeldor interjected. "Agron isn't getting free. I hope his cock was good in your Jinn fanny while it lasted. How was Priebus, by the way? I always thought her a woman of higher morality, but I assume you damned Jinni have your ways of persuading."

"Are you jealous?"

Trumpeldor frowned. "Of what?"

"You want me, don't you?"

Trumpeldor glanced at her breasts. "What man in this camp doesn't want you, lass. You're a redheaded Jinn whore. Your cunt is a cornucopia of gods-damned wonders."

"Cornucopia!" Mohilever guffawed. "You know what I'd like to see, Golda? I'd like to see Gorka get bent over and done by those devils. Maybe that would shut our little prince up for once."

"How nice."

"Sorry. I'm floating on this red nectar, you know. Red nectar makes an old man think dirty things. Settle on down and have some nectar with Uncle Mohilever and Uncle Trumpeldor. I figure we'd both be happy for some company tonight with a Jinn. Come 'ere and have a taste."

Golda crept forward into the close wagon interior. Her belly felt repulsed at the smell of Mohilever's sweat, but nonetheless it was the invitation she'd wanted. Her nostrils tingled pleasantly at the smell of the precious red nectar. She knelt at the box and sniffed.

"No. I've quit."

"Nonsense and nobble." Mohilever winked. "This is some friendly Damp

Delirious. Come on, lass. You know you want some."

"Mohilever, are you sure—" Trumpeldor shook his head.

"They need it, see?" Mohilever continued. "This here Jinn is needin' sex. Isn't that right lass? Who have you been fucking? Nobody. I've heard a Jinn can't last two days without a fuck. That's a hell of a cursed way to live, Trev. Golda will die if she can't find a man to give her a cock."

Golda licked her lips. There was no point in torturing herself over her options. She needed to sate her Hunger, and Mer was a dangerous place to go trolling with the Court and Flames both looking for her. Her Hunger urged her forward, despite her utter revulsion.

"Yes. I need sex, but I was planning to go to the city."

Mohilever snorted. "You prance in here smelling and looking good just to tease us? I don't like teases, lass. Come on now."

"You're right, Mohilever. I really need a man, but what of Agron? If Gorka gets a bribe for him, things can go back the way they used to be between me and Agron, this time without Priebus in my way. I'm not sure how Agron would feel about me sleeping with his brother."

Mohilever grinned. "When Gorka hits a brick wall trying to get his father back from Hell's Court, you've got a bunk with me, lass. We'll leave Gorka like everyone else had the sense to do. Think about it. I've got a lot of nectar here—"

"Half belongs to me," Trumpeldor said.

Golda forced herself to smile and bat her eyelashes. "Have either of you ever even been with a Jinn?"

"No, ma'am," Mohilever answered.

"I'm going to give you both just a taste. If Agron doesn't come back from Mer, I'm willing to give you much more." Golda pressed close and licked Mohilever's sagging, wrinkly cheek. She kissed his ear and pushed her hand down his stomach, where she tugged at the drawstring. She slid her hand into his dirty, threadbare pants, and then she pushed further into the wagon and reached for Trumpeldor. Mohilever Reik turned and fondled her generous tit, nectar-fascinated by its warmth and rotundity. Meanwhile, Trumpeldor silently accepted her attentions, even as his lips curled with a grin of crass male superiority.

Golda ignored his attitude. She'd serviced a few Gypsy men before, mostly when she'd been a slave for the cat goddess, Basteh. Most of them were ignorant dogs, controlled by their sex far more than she was, and moreover prejudiced against things they couldn't comprehend. Mohilever's cock was already hard. She wetted her finger and dipped it into the Damp Delirious.

She'd give the men the rides of their lives as a matter of her own survival, and perhaps the Fates would favor her to get Priebus freed and not Agron. After the Gypsies were taken care of, she'd only need Boudi-Ca to make things right, and then she could leave Haawiyah. She'd never been great with strategies, and she needed a real genius plan to save Boudi-Ca from the enemy.

Chapter 10.

Boudi-Ca held the boy down and rode him. She rarely preferred a top position during the evening feedings, but she hadn't been in the mood to lie and take it that night. Her boy was nearing his release. His breath hitched, and his pretty blue eyes rolled back with a mingled look of ecstasy and agony. She tensed her stomach muscles to increase her spiritual pressure.

The boy's tarnished halo was shrunken against the parlour carpet, like a star on the edge of collapsing on itself. He finally exploded into his orgasm. Boudi-Ca hungrily drained him. She could feel his life energy flow into her belly. Her legs and arms felt stronger, and her mind Sharpened.

Vladimir, the seasonal house boy, was ready with a towel. She took it and dried herself. According to Lydiah, their normal house boy, Paulo, had stayed in the north country to oversee repairs on the country home. Vladimir filling in for Paulo in Mer. The average-looking human male was a recent acquisition in Fennel's slave pit. He was formerly a famous writer on Earth. During the day he worked on Russian translations of Lydiah's books. Boudi-Ca eyed the parlour clock, surprised that it was only shortly after the nine.

The feeding that evening had started late due to Lydiah's duties, and it had stretched due to Lydiah's insistence on giving a lesson, yet time always seemed to slow in Fennel's parlour. According to Lydiah, the time alteration was a side effect of the Ebon Timepiece, an ancient and powerful artifact gifted to Master Fennel by Lord Hades, who in turn had taken it from his own father, the titan Kronos.

The Ebon Timepiece was a pyramid-topped obelisk with a small round gold dial near its apex. It stood a foot tall on a black marble pillar in the dark corner next to the bookcase. The timepiece was creepy black, as if it absorbed the surrounding light from the room into it.

Lydiah was taking time with her Mimọ slave, smothering him with her breasts while she rode him on the worn rug. Boudi-Ca pulled her petticoat over her hips and took an armchair across from Masia-Ca. Lydiah's first fledgling was leafing through a fashion book. Boudi-Ca grabbed her English text from the side table, but she felt too energetic to read through it. Her thoughts turned to Golda.

When Golda had first confronted her, she'd been skeptical and wary. In recent days, her attitude had reversed. Everyone wanted the rebel lesbian captured or dead, especially Lydiah and Hell's Court, and she wanted to find out why. She was frustrated with Lydiah for refusing to tell her about her past. Fortunately, she had multiple sources at her disposal to investigate behind Lydiah's back.

The best source, of course, was a longer conversation with Golda herself. Barring that, Nefra was another possibility, but the Flames lieutenant seemed aloof and difficult to approach, even more so with her involvement in the purgation. The last and most interesting possibility was Mistress Breanarachelle.

The she-devil wife of Judge Rhadamanthus was terrifying, but Breanarachelle supposedly loathed Lydiah, which was at once a bargaining chip and also the fastest way to get into trouble. Lydiah's Mimọ boy gave his ultimate groan, and the Mistress released the boy from the prison of her pale globes. She reared back and straddled him while she corralled and re-clipped her long titanium mane. Boudi-Ca felt her belly stir with a different sort of energy. Lydiah was a powerful Jinn presence, beautiful in the nude.

"What if I just go out into the forest with my sword, Mistress? If Golda is a tracker, she'll probably find me. I'll pretend to listen to her, and then I can kill her."

Lydiah looked over her shoulder. Her silvered eyes simmered under her black-painted lids. "I would need to go too, fledgling. Golda is too dangerous to face alone by yourself far out in the forest. If she approaches you in the city, the situation is more in your favor."

"She wouldn't hurt me."

"True, but apparently you think she loves you, so she must be skilled at manipulating your mind. On top of that, you're a single young Jinn without an escort. The city guards aren't supposed to let you pass the gates during the purgation, and I can't get you a pass from Hell's Court to go out and guillotine Golda."

"So what are we talking about now? Who are we trying to kill?" Masia lowered her fashion plate book. Her doll-like painted lips pursed, and her Asian eyes were sultry and lidded.

"There's a Jinn who knows too much about Boudi-Ca, and maybe me as well." Lydiah rose, took a towel from Vladimir, and dried herself. "During this purgation, certain secrets need to be dead. It's possible Golda knows nothing that could get anyone in trouble, but we should to be more proactive in getting her before the devils. I'm working on a plan. Hell's Court put a fresh bounty on Golda's head yesterday, but I got it unposted, insisting the Flames will handle her."

Boudi-Ca bit her lip. "Do you even think Golda is still in the forest, Mistress?"

"Unless she's hiding in the city, where else would she be if she loves you? Love is well-known to cloud judgment, especially for a Jinn. For now, we'll have to be satisfied that the devils don't have her. I have an important meeting tonight up at the north side Flames monastery. You two are you going to the Spring Festival party this evening?"

"Yes, Mistress," Masia said.

"Boudi-Ca, there will be no nectar for you. Masia-Ca, you're not to leave Boudi's side at the party, and you're to watch her at home as well. Your bedroom is across from hers. If she goes anywhere, you should know about it. This is of utmost importance."

Masia groaned. "Are you joking? Mistress, this is really going to crimp my style. I have a life."

"I'll be busy in the coming days with the Purgation, so I can't watch over things every moment. I won't be available, so both of you will have to handle your own affairs. Boudi-Ca, don't forget your piano lessons, your blades lessons with Mistress Dimona, and your language lessons each dies Mercurii. You only get a cup of black nectar every dies Saturni now and nothing more. I'll make it for you. Masia-Ca needs to help you cope with the headaches and cravings."

Boudi-Ca swallowed. "Yes, Mistress."

Lydiah grabbed up her black linen skirt, slipped into her shoes, and herded the three dragging, drained slave boys into the foyer. Her heels clicked towards the pit door. Masia tossed aside her fashion book and rose to her feet. Boudi-Ca flicked her eyes over Masia's perfectly waxed and perfumed legs. Masia's sleek spindles rose to meet the most perfect waxed promontory. Masia strutted imperiously.

"Meet me at the carriage in an hour, Boudi-Ca. We're going to Pee-Hill then?"

"Yes."

Masia padded barefoot into the hallway. Masia was a perfection of beauty in the half-nude. Boudi-Ca pulled her eyes away and rose to her feet. She turned her mind yet again to Golda. If Lydiah had spoken the truth about the city gates being restricted for the Purgation, then unfortunately her ability to reach Golda rested on Golda coming for her.

Did Lydiah intend to return to the forest herself? Boudi-Ca felt a curious chill run through her shoulder blades, mingled with a queer sadness. Yes, it made perfect sense for Lydiah to take matters into her own hands. Or perhaps Lydiah would find a real assassin, one who worked with stealth rather than open swords and force.

Boudi-Ca exited the parlour and climbed the stairs to the second floor. Kveta was waiting at her bedroom door. The well-trained dressing girl kept her humble head bowed, her back arched, and her hands clasped behind her ass. Kveta's hundreds of scars stood in stark relief in the angle of the lamp light. A row of fresh, crusty pink weals striped her left breast. The marks could have been inflicted by a raging bear claw, but they were surely a courtesy of Master Fennel.

Boudi-Ca swept into her bedroom. A minimal pink under-bust corset lay on the seat of her vanity chair, along with an elegant, revealing black dress. Of course, there was no black tea waiting on her writing table that night. She was feeling cranky, and she really wanted her tea. Her headache thumped in her temple every time she thought about her need.

She was resolved to move forward in her quest to learn about Golda and her lost past. She and Masia were partying that evening in Pee-Hill, which was a perfect chance to question Breanarachelle, the wife of Judge Rhadamanthus, if she dared. Boudi-Ca gazed at herself in her vanity mirror. She was a ghost framed in gold. Her Brunette bangs needed tending.

She desperately needed someone to love and someone to love her, and she wasn't so sure about the Flames anymore. She almost wished she could forget about love, just like she'd forgotten about Heaven and her old life. She simply couldn't. She could feel the love deep in both Lydiah and Golda, but she could have neither. Lydiah denied the love, and Golda was supposed to die. The situation was so infuriating.

A messenger bird landed on her shoulder. It was Lydiah's magical blackbird, which spoke in the voice of the Mistress. You've been thinking lesbian things, and you must be punished. You'll wear a serpent bite to the party to remind yourself not to ogle Masia-Ca.

Boudi-Ca felt her belly tremble. She obediently opened the desk drawer and pulled two hooks from her love box. She reached low and slid them into the tender hillock of her mons. The curved needles felt like twin viper fangs. She winced at the pain when she stepped to sit at her vanity.

Kveta came at her beck and painted her face and lips, then powdered and coiffed her hair. The slave girl re-tied her corset, accentuating her girlish curves. Lydiah soon swept through the door with her long burgundy skirt whispering across the floor.

"Kveta, get out," Lydiah ordered. "I'll finish her."

Boudi-Ca held still while Lydiah turned her in place to examine her. Lydiah's hand reached low and lifted the hem of her tunica. The fingers of the Mistress probed the serpent bite, and then withdrew. Lydiah put her fingers to her lips and licked. Boudi-Ca grabbed Lydiah's wrist. She felt her heart pounding in her chest. The corset made her breathless.

"Please love me."

"We cannot love each other here," Lydiah whispered in her ear. "What do you want from me? I fucked you at the country house, didn't I?"

"Yes. I need you again."

"What am I going to do with you? You're the most talented fledgling I've ever met, yet you are so tragically flawed."

Boudi-Ca sniffed the wonderful scent of Lydiah's long white-blonde hair, so close to her nose. "So are you, Mistress."

"I am?"

"Yes. You like for your husband to make you suffer. You like that he gives you pain. That isn't normal. You're as sick as I am. You're married to that horrible devil man. You pledged your soul to him—"

Lydiah's chin trembled. "I like power. I like privileges, some of which you also enjoy. Your clothes and jewelry don't buy themselves."

"I want you to show me your true self." Boudi-Ca dared to slowly close her hand around a lock of Lydiah's hair. Lydiah's thighs had tangled with her own, and the heat between them was increasing.

"I want to fuck you so much," Lydiah breathed into her ear. "I want to rip your nipple with my teeth. I want to bury my hand to my wrist in your pretty cunt. Is that what you want?"

"Yes, Mistress. I don't care if Fennel catches us."

Lydiah sniffed. "You should. He'll hand you over to Rhada, and if anyone can make you regret your Sapphic feelings, it's him."

"You're a hypocrite, Mistress. How could you say all of those bad things about lesbians to Lieutenant Nefra when you're—" Boudi-Ca gasped when Lydiah's hand slapped her hard across her cheek.

"I've never been a lesbian. I was inflicted by Cupid's arrow during the occupation of Allyssia's Redoubt. Unlike others who we discovered to be influenced, I was strong enough to hide his curse and save myself from humiliation. The arrow's venom has long been in my veins for you, my fledgling, but I refuse to let Allyssia ruin me. I've built a long reputation for my anti-lesbian efforts, and I need to make the best of this purgation to prove that I can do good work for Lord Hades. I cannot fail. Would you like the devils to expose me? Would you like for me to be tortured and thrown in a hole in the Bolgia pits, never to see you or Dawn's chariot ever again?"

"No, Mistress."

Lydiah leaned close again with a whisper. "Then fucking behave yourself. This is a grave situation, and both of our lives are at stake. We must resist this spell. Our love is fake. Do you understand? Some call our Lord the great deceiver, but the greatest deceiver is Love."

"No, Mistress. I know you love me."

Lydiah shuddered, and her eyes closed tightly as if in pain. "I'm counting on you, fledgling. The purgation of the Smokeless Flames begins soon, and we'll begin a purgation within us too. We're going to be strong. We're going to kill our forbidden desires before they kill us. We're going to love cocks. Cocks can heal a Jinn of most ills. As long as the devils don't interrogate you, me, Masia, or Golda, we should be safe until this is over. Meanwhile, you need more cocks. Get them. Use them to heal yourself and keep your head straight. You can resist, fledgling."

"What about Golda?"

"We won't speak about Golda anymore. And please stop looking at Masia-Ca like you want to jump on her and fuck her. It's unacceptable."

"She ratted me. I wish I could fuck her now just to make her miserable."

"She did the right thing. Is it too much for you to handle, fledgling? Do I need to lock my own fledgling in a cage until this purgation blows over? I've considered it. I could claim it's to keep you nectar-free for the Flames. I could cage you and kill two problems at once."

"I'm sorry, Mistress. I think I'd escape."

"And I think you can't escape from cuffs and bondage with your ability.

Let us pray to Lady Allyssia together, and then I have to go." Lydiah bowed her head for long seconds. Boudi-Ca closed her eyes and tried to think of Allyssia, the sacred Smokeless-Flame mother. She silently prayed to Allyssia for strength. When she opened her eyes, Lydiah was walking away.

Boudi-Ca waited for long seconds until she was sure that Lydiah was gone, and then she found the shoe in her closet that hid her garter knife. She buckled the little blade around her upper thigh and descended the east wing steps. The Merian night was unusually cool. The stony wind had reversed course that evening to blow off the forest and Great Blue Hole mines instead of the desolate Mare Mortis. The cooler, damper air felt better on her bare skin than the usual volcanic grit and sand. The carriage was waiting, and so was Masia, whose lips curled grimly.

"I don't care one denarius about your nectar or the Flames, Boudi-Ca," Masia said. "The other issue could destroy the Mistress and me too. Our Lord and Lady created us to serve Djinnus as lovers and wives. I'm not the most traditional fledgling, but I know my sacred duty."

Boudi-Ca climbed into the carriage. The serpent bite in her lower belly ached in sympathy with her dark mood. "I'm sorry. I'll get better soon."

Chapter 11.

The uniformed stable boy snapped the reins, and the carriage rolled down the drive, out the gate, and out of Tanjie. Boudi-Ca tensed her stomach. Every bump of the carriage over a rough cobblestone sent a distracting splinter of pain into her abdomen. Between the serpent bite under her skirt and her nectar headache, she could hardly focus on anything.

Lydiah's scolding had wounded her, and she felt betrayed by Masia too. She felt terribly alone, but that was nothing out of the ordinary. Boudi-Ca gazed at the passing gas lamps as the carriage descended into the Merian downtown. She was resolved to move forward with her quest to know more about Golda and her missing past by whatever means necessary. That night she planned to approach Breanarachelle, Lydiah's nemesis.

Within twenty minutes, the carriage entered the depths of Pomegranate Hill. The home of Judge Rhadamanthus glowed with a thousand flickering candles, symbolic of the spirit of Allyssia on that sacred night of the Jinni, a night that honored the first two Jinn fledglings, Astaarteh and Ereshkigeh. The coming Spring Festival would include two weeks of celebrations and competitions, ending in Ostara's day, the official first day of spring with all its fertility.

Boudi-Ca disembarked with Masia in front of the house and walked through the guarded entry portico. The burly guards nodded greetings. Everyone knew the smart and fashionable young fledglings of Councilor Lydiah. They were on the B-list of invitees for every party of importance in Mer. Masia paused in the smoky quartz-floored vestibule and pretended to gaze lamely at a painting.

"I'm supposed to follow you, Boudi-Ca, but I may not notice if you slip away from me. Just don't do nectar. Please don't be an idiot."

Boudi-Ca nodded and strode quickly around the corner towards the drawing room, where the customary armed guards were allowing only the chosen to seek an audience with the hosts. She paused and gazed from six paces away through the open doors, where Breanarachelle was chatting with parlour guests in the low firelight.

Breanarachelle was beautifully accoutered in a low-cut grey dress. A gaudy necklace sprayed silver and tourmalines down between the swells of her she-devil breasts. Jointed silver sleeves glinted on some of Breanarachelle's fingers when she gestured. The sleeves formed bejeweled points like hooks, making the she-devil's fingers into birdlike claws, or surely small weapons if she wished.

Boudi-Ca blinked when the guard snapped his fingers suddenly and motioned her to go inside. A secret sign had evidently been passed without her noticing, and she had been invited. Her heart clutched when she met Breanarachelle's baleful eyes across the space. The devil hostess nodded briefly at her, and then looked casually away.

Boudi-Ca entered the parlour, but she had no option to approach Breanarachelle without walking right up into the very center of everyone. The conversation at hand was the purgation of lesbians and the male-forsaking Jinni in Mer. Rhadamanthus was making a point with the stem of his customary rodent-skull pipe, holding the attention of a small crowd of selected sycophants.

"Tomorrow it starts. Our devils will be hitting the establishments of sell-sex, where we've already run recognizance with our spies. The Smokeless Flames is the primary target, but Astaarteh lobbied for allowing the Flames to purge itself. No surprise."

"We wrote a safety clause in the agreement though," a devil henchman of the Judge added. "If the Flames fails the quota we've set for them, Hell's Court can take over."

Boudi-Ca felt faint in the close parlour. No one seemed to notice her, and she would have no chance to speak to Breanarachelle without airing her personal life in front of everyone. She turned on her heel and retreated from the heat and important people. She almost felt relieved. She would just relax and troll for cock that evening like Lydiah had commanded. The Mistress had made a good point—sex made everything better. Maybe it would work for her headache.

She walked back through the foyer and onto the front veranda, where Djinnus, Jinni, and devils chatted under ivied overhangs. Many guests were wearing antique garb and hairstyles for the occasion of the Spring Festival. Herb smoke and mastic incense rose, as did the faint aroma of nectar. Boudi-Ca scanned the men, who were speaking of horses, gladiatorial combat, gambling, and the war against Heaven. All of those topics were boring.

Beyond the veranda, cocks were out of trousers in the west wing bath. Boudi-Ca scanned the action. She didn't see Ramone, Davide, Moshe, or Faisil. The serpent bite under her tunica kept distracting her. The bite made her cranky instead of sensual, and she couldn't take any nectar to offset it. To the contrary, the bite made her crave nectar to take away the pain. If Moshe pressed her, she would likely accept. For that reason, she needed to remove the hooks. They were making her weak, and quitting nectar was more important.

Boudi-Ca passed through the archway from the bath and into the guest dressing room, which was always a haunt for Jinni at Rhadamanthus' parties due to the full-length wall mirrors. She faced the wall, tugged up her tunica, and quickly pulled the two hooks from her tender flesh. She put the hooks to her mouth and licked them clean. She heard a thump and a click behind her. Someone else had entered the dressing room.

"Hello, darling. How are you on this sacred night of the Jinni?"

Boudi-Ca turned to confront the interloper, but her dismissive words froze in her throat. Mistress Breanarachelle drifted forward on a wave of she-devil perfume that smelled of roses, cupric sulfide, and sweet moss smoke. Boudi-Ca felt a quiver of fear, but she tried to center her mind. She needed to think fast. She needed to ask Breanarachelle about Golda and her past.

"I'm fine."

"Was that a serpent bite you just removed? How beautiful." Breanarachelle's thin dark lips curled into a smile. "Why were you punishing yourself, Boudi-Ca? Mimọ blood is so sweet and subtle, like holy water and honey. I love it. I could smell yours in the parlour even through Rhada's pipe smoke."

Boudi-Ca shrugged nonchalantly. She had no confidence to pull off a lie. She-devils were the queens of lies. "My Mistress wanted me to wear it, but I can't say why."

"I see you've been slapped this evening too. You have broken capillaries on your left cheek. Your Mistress slapped you and gave you a punishment? For what? Give me more information."

"No." Boudi-Ca avoided Breanarachelle's eyes.

Breanarachelle nodded silently as if with veiled surprise, although her sleek, yellow-ashen face was mostly inscrutable. Her wide, frog-like lips were painted dark grey under her liquid amber eyes and perfect high cheekbones. Breanarachelle's face was almost too perfect. According to rumors, Breanarachelle had a fetish for surgeries, and her own husband performed them on her.

"Your figure is exquisite, fledgling," the she-devil continued in a lower, more seductive tone. "Especially the way your pink corset lifts your humble little Mimọ teats, just begging people to find something creative to do with them. That boning is fabulous at your midsection. Is that a Mouchoire?"

"My corset is a Vandale. I think."

"Lovely. I remember last winter's Vandale corsets were spectacular for the younger Jinn set, but the one you're wearing looks from the summer collection. Your perfume smells prepared from rare flowers. Is it?"

"Yes. They are pink hyacinths from Erebus. I use Lydiah's perfumer. His name is Pierre—um, I forget the rest."

"Pierre Tousseau Sainte-John." Breanarachelle smiled. "He's a genius. I've had him several times here at my estate to make things for special occasions. You look distraught, child. I can't help but remark on it, and you're pretty in your suffering, truly. Whoever tied your corset did it nice and tight. Do you like suffering for your beauty, Boudi-Ca? I know you like it when people look at you. Beauty mistresses must suffer for their beauty, which is one reason I like their company. I love your diamond nose piercing too. You look like a little Lydiah."

"So they say."

"I'm not so much for permanent piercings." Breanarachelle sniffed. "Temporary piercings are more interesting. In fact, thanks to my husband's whims, you and I were suffering together under our skirts. Well. You're young yet. You'll gain endurance as you age. Are you going to marry a devil man one day, like Lydiah with Fennel?"

"No. I feel sorry for her. Why marry a man who loves to make you suffer? I can't imagine such a horrible thing."

"Devil men are wonderful. Maybe I can help you understand. I've helped a lot of young women with that. Will you let me?"

"I don't think so."

"You just need to open your mind to a different type of desire, Boudi-Ca. Pain is the other half of the pyramid to pleasure. Without it, a Jinn can never reach the true pinnacle of her sexual powers. Just ask Lydiah, and she'll tell you. A caress on your skin gives you pleasure. A claw on your skin is just an intense caress, yes? It's a matter of unfolding the way your mind feels things. Lydiah did it. So you can you. Would you like me to introduce you to a male playmate? Devils and Mimos play wonderfully together."

"I'm not really in the mood."

Breanarachelle's froggish nostrils flared slightly again, as if sniffing the air in the close room. "I'm trying to be nice. You're lonely. I can feel that too. You're in pain because you want someone to play with you."

"A little bit. A lot." Boudi-Ca felt her flush of mingled fear and embarrassment choke in her throat. The conversation had tipped her into a vulnerable frame of mind, and she suddenly realized her eyes had lingered too long on Breanarachelle's curved salamander skin where the sunburst of orange tourmalines drew attention to the she-devil's breasts. Boudi-Ca tore her eyes away, but then she was caught by Breanarachelle's intense amber orbs. She felt hot. Her head swam gently. Inexplicably, she felt tears coming to her eyes.

Breanarachelle drifted closer. The she-devil's ashen lips curled into a smile. "You're weening too, aren't you? You're suffering so much for your want of nectar. The pain is throbbing in your head, adding to everything else. I can feel it."

"Yes. My head definitely hurts."

Breanarachelle's nostrils flared again, and her amber eyes burned still more brightly. "Oh, yes. You're simmering with suffering. You're like a little champagne bottle ready to pop. I'm certain that if you weren't Lydiah's fledgling, you'd have devil men hitting on you right and left, wanting to pin you up, cut you up, and rape you in any available bedchamber."

"That sounds horrible. So you can feel my suffering, then?"

"Oh yes, child," Breanarachelle answered. "Devils feel suffering just like Jinni feel desire. It draws us. It inspires us. Your suffering is impressive. I was drawn to it the other night when you were sitting on the floor in our parlour. I know you're lonely. I want to be your friend. Will you let me?"

"That's exactly what Golda said."

"Who?

Boudi-Ca felt her throat clench. The she-devil's wood smoke perfume was remarkably subtle, yet penetrating, and Breanarachelle was very close to her. "Golda. She's the renegade Jinn who supposedly follows Lady Allyssia. She was in the forest, but we didn't capture her on the raid. Do you know anything about her? Are there any Hell's Court rumors about where she might be hiding?"

Breanarachelle examined the metal sleeves that she wore on her fingers. She flexed her fingers, and the little jointed hooks glinted in the lamplight. "You should forget Golda, Boudi-Ca. If the Court wants her dead or in a cage, her days are numbered. I heard Rhada mention bounty hunters. Why don't you come back to the parlour and ask him about it yourself?"

"Your husband is loathsome just like Fennel." Boudi-Ca gazed rebelliously at Breanarachelle. She was definitely feeling edgy and stretchy from her headache.

"Does my husband make you nervous when you're close to him? Does your stomach twist? Does your body tremble for no reason that you can explain?"

"Lydiah says it's normal. Rhadamanthus has a fear aura."

Breanarachelle chuckled. "Lydiah is a brilliant persuasive speaker, isn't she? She could convince a master leatherworker to put away his knives forever and devote his life to worshiping a cow goddess. They say Dawn's chariot used to fly from west to east, but then Lydiah wanted more light in her music room in the morning. Does she ever touch you?"

"What?"

"Read my lips, girl. Has your mistress ever fucked you?"

"I don't—"

"We're being honest here. You can admit it." Breanarachelle pressed still closer, drifting forward in the heady aroma of smoke, flowers, and sulfur. "I locked the door. We have complete privacy. Tell me, please. Tell me."

Boudi-Ca felt suddenly light-headed, like she would vomit. A wave of fear overwhelmed her, and her heart galloped in her chest. "I don't know. I mean, no. Of course. Not."

A wicked smiled curled over Breanarachelle's lips. "She does, doesn't she? Lydiah fucks you! I knew it. I've heard some rumors from my beauty friends, but I can't uncover their origin. Lydiah is leading the lesbian purgation, but she is a hypocrite. If it's true, I'm going to ruin her once and for all. I just need proof, and I know that proof is you."

Boudi-Ca gasped when Breanarachelle's metal claw-sleeved fingers wrapped around her throat. She felt Breanarachelle's thigh press against her own. She was terrified, and the room was starting to spin. Her ears were ringing. "Let me go. Please."

"First tell me everything. It will be a secret just between us."

"No."

Breanarachelle's smile widened. "I think I need to get more persuasive, but this is not the place. I'm going to make you confess, and then I'm going to bury Lydiah. I'll finally complete my revenge, and that bitch will have nothing in Mer. She'll have no friends left."

"You have no proof, and I won't tell you."

"Why do you even care?" Breanarachelle countered. "You're going to the Flames in a few months, Boudi-Ca. You won't be with Lydiah anymore, so you should save yourself. I'm taking Lydiah down anyway. I need to find who started these lesbian rumors and put a fire to them, but until then I have you. So negotiate. This might be your only chance. If you give me the truth, I'll give you the truth in turn. I'll give you back your memories. Lydiah will just love that too."

"I would suggest leaving my Mistress alone."

"You need her love, don't you? Yes. I feel that suffering in you." Breanarachelle's voice was a low purr. "I've known a lot of Jinni. I've even cut many of them open with my knives. I know what makes you tick. I'll get inside."

"Stop it, damn you."

Boudi-Ca felt Breanarachelle's hand on her left buttock. The she-devil pressed closer, pinning her body to the mirror. Breanarachelle's hand slipped through the side gap in her tunica under the hip fastening. Boudi-Ca gasped when she felt the Sharp prick of pain. Breanarachelle breathed in her ear. "Confess to fucking Lydiah, and I'll tell you about your past. Lydiah has been lying to you all this time."

"I know that. Oh!" Boudi-Ca gasped. The pain waved suddenly through her left buttock, following Breanarachelle's Sharp metal fingertips.

"It's a simple oral contract with a she-devil," Breanarachelle continued. "Truth for truth."

"I don't think so." Boudi-Ca winced. Breanarachelle's other hand was sliding into her tunic on her other side, embracing her. She slid her own hand low and felt for her hidden garter knife even as pain surged in her other buttock, sending waves to join the other. Her anus clenched, damp with a sudden sweat. She felt a sickening desire to kiss Breanarachelle's lips, which were inches away from her own. The metal claws dug deeper into her hind flesh. She moaned and pressed against the she-devil. She couldn't help herself. She raised her lips, but Breanarachelle retreated.

"You like this, don't you, child? You really are a lesbian. Lydiah is lying when she says the black nectar straightened you out and made you forget. Did she send you here? Is this some sort of trick?"

"You're the one who is doing this. Maybe you're the hypocrite."

Breanarachelle eased back. She withdrew her hands and smoothed her dress with her eyes averted. "I want you to play with Master Tarnak, my lovely Boudi-Ca. I'll take you to my bedchamber. I'll give you the best nectar you've had in your life. It will take all of your pain away and replace it with pleasure. I'll watch you play with a boy toy. When you're more amenable, we'll make our trade. You'll give me Lydiah, and I'll give you your past."

"No. I have to go. I've suffered enough this evening."

"There is no such thing as too much suffering." Breanarachelle pressed forward on the attack again. Boudi-Ca twisted, but Breanarachelle's claw raked her throat painfully. The claw closed around her throat and shoved her bodily against the wall mirror. She grabbed Breanarachelle's wrist, but she wasn't strong enough to pull it away. The she-devil's yellow-ashen skin was slick and cool, soft and inhuman. She felt the metal claws of Breanarachelle's other hand slide under her tunic again, this time wrapping her buttock in its entirety and pressing into her crack.

"What are you doing?"

"Spread your legs," Breanarachelle commanded. Boudi-Ca felt her legs tremble when she obeyed, allowing the long, curved claw to nose at her anus. The claw pushed slowly inward. Pain waved, even as the slow weakness began to spread from the epicenter of the she-devil's finger, the familiar weakness that afflicted all Jinni from that form of penetration. Boudi-Ca felt her heart pound. Breanarachelle's breasts pressed against hers, soft yet forbidding.

"If I let you have me, then you'll tell me," she managed.

"No. My offer was to watch you with Tarnak. Will you take it or leave it?"

"You just want me to fuck him?"

"I want you to fuck him and give him your pretty skin. I want the soft soles of your feet to suffer. I want your inner thighs to quiver with the most exquisite sensations of pain that you've ever felt. I want Tarnak to own the most intimate places that Lydiah can't see, unless she's your lover of course."

Boudi-Ca shoved Breanarachelle, but the elder she-devil was stronger than her. Breanarachelle responded by throwing her hard back against the mirror. shards of glass fell, even as Breanarachelle pulled her away from the danger. Boudi-Ca groaned. She was weak, and Breanarachelle's claw still gripped her throat. Splinters of mirror were everywhere. The room was spinning, and Breanarachelle's other claw left her ass and flashed. Boudi-Ca gasped. A splinter of pain surged through her left breast.

"I like a feisty Mimọ." Breanarachelle purred. Her eyes were sultry. "I love it when they fight. Push me again."

"Kiss my lips, and I'll push you."

"I suppose Mimọ girls like kissing. Has Lydiah ever kissed you?"

"Yes."

"Where and when?"

"In our country house last summer, and before that. I wrote all about it in my diaries so I wouldn't forget. I used to read them to keep my memories from slipping."

"You needed to admit it. I understand your suffering better than you do." Breanarachelle chortled exultantly and released her grip. "Wait here. I'll be right back."

"Where are you going?"

"You're toying with me, so I'm going to have you tortured. I'll find some cuffs. Don't even think about running. When you've confessed the location of your diaries, I'll have Rhada get a court order tonight, and the devils will go to Fennel's home for the proof. Tomorrow Lydiah will be arrested."

"Sorry, but Lydiah destroyed my diaries. There's no proof to find." Boudi-

Ca eyed the door, ready to flash to freedom if necessary, but her emotions were overwhelming in that moment. She felt tears burst into her eyes and flow down her cheeks. Huge sobs began to rack her body. "I'm so sorry. I can't help myself. I deserve to die. Please just kill me. I can't live any more like this. I can't live in this horrible place with all of you horrible people. I don't even know who I am. I just want to love someone. I want someone to love me."

Breanarachelle nodded knowingly. "Good. Good. Let it out, child. Calm down and let's continue negotiating. Breathe. That's it. Lydiah ruined me two hundred years ago. What comes around goes around. It's the way the Fates work. If you agree to give her to me, I promise you'll come to no harm. My husband is the judge."

"I can't think about this right now. I need more time."

Breanarachelle snorted. "You're such an Mimọ. Fine. I've waited two hundred years. I want you to come and visit me on dies Saturni. I want to see you at nine in the morning and no later because I attend the cathedral services. If you don't come, then I'll let my husband and the Court handle you instead. Believe me. You want to do this my way. Save yourself, and don't you dare tell Lydiah. You'll be in bigger trouble for already betraying her secrets to me."

Breanarachelle turned on her heel and went to the door. She passed through with a slithering sound of her dress against the doorframe. A few seconds later, Masia popped through the unlocked entry.

"Boudi? What happened in here? I heard voices. Why were you talking to Breanarachelle? How did that mirror get broken?"

"It was an accident. We were talking about fashion. I was clumsy from my headache. I stumbled." Boudi-Ca examined her arms, hoping Breanarachelle hadn't left noticeable marks. "Breanarachelle helped revive me. I'm cut a bit. I need to go home."

Masia shrugged. "Whatever. I'll take you out to the carriage, but I'm staying."

Chapter 12.

Yellen looked skeptically at the motorcar that sat at the curb. The red-painted mechanical contraption gleamed in the late afternoon sun. The thing had no horses to pull it—only four wheels. It made a loud rumbling sound. The motorcar belonged to the Smokeless Flames, and Lydiah said it possessed the maneuverability and speed that were necessary for catching criminal lesbians.

According to Befanah, the motorcar was a recent product of the Haawiyah factories, just like the guns and cannons that had given Hell's army an edge over the magical weapons of the Mimos in the recent skirmishes in Purgatory. The motorcar ran on gases piped from the depths of the Great Blue Hole mines. It was said to outpace horses over the cobbled Merian streets.

Yellen fingered the official-looking warrant, which was complete with a daguerreotype image taken from the Flames archives. The first Named was Commander Zinke, a semi-retired Flames elder. The arrests in the Smokeless Flames were to begin with a respected high-ranking member. The Purgation had been delayed for most of the day. She'd arrived at Befanah's in the morning as instructed, then she'd waited for hours for a final go-ahead from Councilor Lydiah.

Befanah and Mistress Shadow-Under-Moon had taught her how to drive the motorcar, and she'd Shared with them some tales of her adventures in far Meristyian, the better to ease the tension. None of them had wanted to talk about the real issues until the messenger bird from Lydiah had finally arrived.

Mistress Shadow closed Befanah's iron gate behind them. Shadow walked with a slight limp from a recent injury, but otherwise she seemed like a capable Sister, ready to do her duty as the appointed tracker. If they were lucky, the named would be home and they wouldn't even need Shadow's mystical abilities to read the weave of the tapestry.

"Want me to drive?" Shadow offered. "My leg hurts a little, but—"

"I'll try," Yellen said. "It's been a while since I've been in the capital. If I get off track, just say so."

"As you wish, Lieutenant."

Yellen slipped on her gloves and settled into the motorcar. She arranged her narcabyss whip such that its paralyzing coils fell safely from her belt into the foot well. Shadow circled the rear bumper and settled into the seat next to her. Yellen pressed the clutch and threw the motorcar into gear. It shuddered forward, and soon she and Shadow were rumbling up Leo Street.

The plan was simple. They would keep a low profile and make the arrest as quickly as possible using the element of surprise, subduing the Named and restraining her with cuffs. The Court-dispensed ebon cuffs rode in Shadow's belt pouch along with the matching ebon control wand. After the arrest, they would take the Named directly to the address where the lesbian interrogations would take place.

Shadow was distant and aloof as trackers often were. She wore long dark hair in a braid over her shoulder with a center part that fell in stray wisps past elegant turquoise earrings. In contrast to Shadow's feminine jewelry and hairstyle, she carried a muscular body that gave her an aura of dependability and solidity packaged in a traditional red Flames robe. Her sash carried the red bars of a corporal. The bars matched the red ribbon that wrapped the hilt of Shadow's short blade. Shadow was a married Jinn.

A yellow diamond wedding ring circled her almond brown finger.

Yellen turned the motorcar onto High Street, intent on heading across the north side, an inconspicuous route through the exclusive walled northern residential districts. High Street ran all the way into the west Coliseum District where Henne lived. The motorcar topped a rise. Yellen let off the gas, which stalled the engine.

She fired the motorcar up again, and the car charged down a sunny street lined by cypress trees that blew gently in the wind from the Mare. The Coliseum was the primary navigation beacon on the northeast side of Mer. The Coliseum's massive headwall was bright in the afternoon light. Yellen pressed the pedal and pushed the motorcar faster down the slope. The faster speed seemed to level out the wheels over the horribly bricked street.

Henne still hadn't answered the bird that she'd sent the morning before. Henne surely had other lovers to occupy her time, and in a worst case, having graduated into full mistresshood, Henne was already engaged to be married. Shadow spoke loudly over the growl of the engine.

"So what do you think of lesbians, Lieutenant?"

Yellen glanced at Shadow. Could the tracker read peoples' minds as well the dense, complex weave of the tapestry of Haawiyah? Yellen looked away. It was only the first day of the so-called purgation. It was too soon to start fearing for her life.

"Just call me Yellen. If we're going to spend time together on this difficult job, we might as well be friends, right?"

"I hate them," Shadow persisted. "Lesbians are utterly pathetic. Even if lesbianism wasn't a perversion forbidden by our Lord, why would a Jinn want anything but an Djinnus? Nothing is better than my husband's cock, not even nectar."

Yellen nodded stoically. That was what she was afraid of. She'd always worried about the day when a handsome Djinnus would get his hooks into Henne, permanently. Djinnus seed was the most addictive elixir in all of Hell, less powerful but more insidious than the best nectars, and marriage to an Djinnus was required of all Jinni who weren't military. The wedding day was the end of the road for most casual, rebellious bisexual fledglings.

How dedicated was Henne? Henne had always skirted the subject, saying they'd deal with it when the time came.

Within half an hour, Yellen turned onto Olive Street and brought the motorcar to a stop at number eighty-one. The house was modest with wide eves and deep, hammered lead gutters, which were unusual in Mer, as it rarely ever rained.

Yellen dismounted and crossed the front yard. Shadow followed close behind her. A black cat skittered off the patio into the safety of the brittle-brushes. They climbed the short steps to the door. Yellen knocked. After a minute, a house-girl with a thick accent answered, opening the door a crack.

"Yes? En qué puedo servirle?"

Yellen smiled benignly. "We're here to see your mistress. We're from the Smokeless Flames. May we come in?"

"Mistress wants no visitors."

The slave girl pushed the door, but Yellen interposed her fist and pressed the door forcefully open. The girl was wide-eyed and a little angry. She was nude from the waist up, of medium height with long dark hair, as beautiful as most human souls who were hand-selected upon their earthly death for sensual services to Hell's children. A second black cat slipped quietly through the shadows of the silent foyer and around a corner.

"Where is Commander Zinke?" Yellen persisted. "I'm going to have to insist on seeing your mistress. I'm an official from Hell's Court."

"She is not here," the slave girl answered. Yellen fingered her coiled narcabyss whip and looked at Shadow. The tracker pointed at a half-open door down the hall.

"Zinke is down in her pit. I can sense her presence."

Yellen flicked the whip forward faster than the slave girl could raise her hands to block it. The whip smacked against the girl's throat.

"Oh!" The slave managed a squeak before the numbness gripped her vocal cords, rendering her mute and unable to raise an alarm. The house-girl tried to twist away and run for the stairs, however. Yellen gripped her shoulder. She pressed the whip to the girl's neck. The girl hitched. Yellen shook her head.

"I think Zinke knew we were coming, Shadow. Next time maybe we leave the iron carriage behind."

Shadow shrugged and drew her sword. "Well, our orders are to use force."

Yellen pushed the house-girl forward with her left hand and readied the whip in her right. The stairs into Zinke's private slave pit were of a typical Merian construction from a former century. A plaster-walled stairwell curved gently down. A burning oil lamp in a niche cast jagged shadows. They descended. At the bottom of the stairs, twin rows of slave cages sat shadowed under old mosaic archways. A collection of pretty girls watched from behind rows of tarnished silver bars.

The house-girl suddenly twisted ahead. Yellen slipped to the side as a feathered dart whispered past and pattered off the plaster wall. She ran forward into the pit at an angle, keeping her side towards the hidden attacker to reduce her profile. Mistress Zinke emerged from behind a pillar at the end of the main pit area. Zinke was a grey-haired and hooved elder. She wore a black silk robe. She held a slender steel blade in her white-knuckled fist.

"I'm not surrendering," Zinke said matter-of-factly.

Nefra readied the narcabyss whip, making sure Zinke could see it. "This isn't necessary. You're only wanted for questioning. Turn around and place your hands behind your back."

"Over my dead body, Lieutenant."

Yellen loosed the whip, but Zinke was fast. The elder mistress slipped the attack and executed a wide foot sweep. Yellen stumbled and allowed her legs go out from under her, the better to deflect Zinke's darting blade. Shadow chose the moment to lunge with her own sword, forcing Zinke to defend instead of pressing a deadly advantage.

Yellen flanked the skilled elder, who launched a vicious attack at Shadow to free the path to the stairway. Yellen brought the whip to bear and snapped at Zinke's backside, taking the commander by surprise. Zinke hadn't expected her to recover so quickly. Zinke shuddered and launched a hex that slammed Shadow backwards, followed by a gout of magical flame that smoked Shadow's armor. Zinke darted in for a killing sword blow, but Shadow managed to stay on her feet, frantically parrying against the superior opponent.

Yellen summoned the force of her will and executed a desirous kin-hex. The spell caught Zinke off balance. The commander stumbled back. Yellen kicked at the back of the elder's knee and snapped the narcabyss whip across Zinke's bare chest and shoulder, then again, raining blows.

Zinke seized up and dropped her blade as the numbness embraced her. Yellen grabbed a heated wrist and rolled Zinke over. Shadow was quick with the ebon cuffs. Within a minute, the cursing and spitting elder mistress was their prisoner.

The slave girls in their pit cells pressed against the bars, weeping and protesting. There were a half-dozen of them, all youngish with dark hair. They were a shameless bevy of beautiful lesbian slave girls. Gilded collars and matching jewelry were their only attire. A rack of furred headgear featured prominently on the wall. Zinke apparently made her girls dress like kittens. Yellen carefully coiled her whip.

"Why did you fight us, Commander?"

"Why wouldn't I?" Zinke answered. "I only wish I'd known sooner that Lydiah's dogs were coming for me. I have powerful friends. You could both be dead."

"Those are ebon cuffs on you, and Shadow has the ebon wand. Don't try to escape, or you'll feel the pain. We're only doing our duty for the Flames, and you're only wanted for questioning. You might not want to mention your friends to the devils."

"If you try anything," Shadow added, "I'll show you no mercy. Now get up, pathetic lesbian. We're taking you to be interrogated by the devils."

Yellen grabbed Zinke's arm and hefted the Named to her wobbly feet. She and Shadow dragged the Zinke back up the stairs, down the foyer, and out the front door, where they installed the elder in the back seat of the motorcar. Zinke squeezed her eyes closed and shuddered. The grey-haired elder began sobbing openly.

Yellen took a deep breath, grabbed the motorcar wheel, and examined the warrant again. The delivery destination was 115 West Pelagius Street, a downtown address. She fired the engine as soon as Shadow settled into the car alongside her. She trusted Shadow to watch Zinke and have the ebon control wand ready. With one flick of the ebon wand in Zinke's direction, the commander would be incapacitated with pain emanating from her ebon cuffs.

Yellen drove out of the Coliseum District, headed south into the city center, and then turned west. After almost an hour drive through the busy downtown streets with the clumsy motorcar, she found the location. Pelagius was an east-west street that originated behind the old sepulchral grounds on the west side of Lord Hades' palace. The street ran past a lowbrow wedding temple into an inner-city warehouse district. The door on the side of a squat basalt building was old and copper plated, unpainted and stained with oxidation. The copper numerals 115 appeared freshly smithed and screwed into place, however.

Yellen drew the carriage up and stepped down. Shadow was already ahead of her, pulling Mistress Zinke from the back seat. Yellen frowned. She made a mental note to tell Shadow that once they had the lesbian in custody, she herself should be the one to escort the Named while Shadow held the wand at a safe distance.

The investigation was a dangerous game. As Zinke herself had stated, the elder commander could have easily prepared something more deadly than a poorly lying slave girl, a thrown dart, and a sword. Yellen knocked on the grey door. Within a minute the portal opened. A tall, wide-shouldered devil in a yellow robe reached out his mottled grey hand. Another grim devil appeared to assist. Nefra extended the warrant. The devil nodded as he examined it.

"You have the first Named. Excellent."

The devil produced an ebon wand with one hand, gripped Zinke's arm with the other, and dragged her inside the basalt building. Zinke wept and uttered bitter curses at him. The devil threw Zinke forward and swung his ebon wand to contact her ebon cuffs. Zinke screamed and crumpled to her knees in pain. The second devil leveled a kick, sending her forward onto her face. The door swung closed. Locks and bolts clicked and clanged into place.

Shadow wore a little smile. Yellen took a deep breath and avoided Shadow's eyes. She climbed alongside Shadow back into the rumbling motorcar. After another forty minutes of driving through the city, negotiating the slower horse traffic with the car's horn, they completed the tour of the city and arrived back at Befanah's house. Yellen pulled the carriage up and disembarked. She saluted Shadow.

"I'll see you tomorrow morning, then?"

"Yes. For the next Named." The raven-haired tracker slid over into the driver's seat. "We'll get more than one I hope."

"Please come early, no later than the eight. I'd like to meet and discuss our tactics with you a bit further."

"Sounds good, Lieutenant. I'll be here." Shadow threw the motorcar into gear, and the iron beast rumbled off towards the Flames compound. Yellen pushed open Befanah's iron gate. Strangely, the door to the house was locked. She knocked. Befanah's steward let her enter. Befanah was in her study, which smelled sweetly of tobacco smoke. Befanah lowered her pipe and looked up.

"Is it done?"

"Yes. Zinke fought against us with a blade. If I hadn't had the whip—"

Befanah shook her head. "Lydiah and the Council collectively decided they had to notify the Flames in advance of everything that's going to happen. I suspect the lesbian insiders had something to do with that decision."

Yellen raised her hands in supplication. "Is this for real? So the Named will not only be trying to escape, but also trying to kill us when we come for them? We might need a few more Sisters for this. I'm not a coward, but we need a whole team, not just me."

"Lydiah's goal is to keep the operation quiet."

"Maybe Lydiah should do the arrests herself then. The devils at the downtown location aren't exactly treating Zinke with respect, either. They shocked her and kicked her onto her face, and that's just what I could see before they slammed the door on me."

Befanah grimaced. "Yellen, do yourself a favor. Do your job, get paid, and don't ask questions. The situation is bigger than you and me."

"I didn't join the Flames to be at the beck and call of the Hell's Court devils. Is there any way I can get out of this, Befanah? It feels really bad to me."

"You're in this already, Lieutenant. I'll have more names for you and Shadow tomorrow morning. These will be safer, but I agree that if the Named will be fighting, you might need more assistance. How was Shadow as a tracker?"

"Shadow is actually enjoying this."

"She's an ambitious anti-lesbian zealot, and even more so since she was passed over in her last few reviews for a rank promotion. I think Lydiah chose her because she is so motivated. She practically begged Lydiah to let her take the lead in the arrests, but we decided that you'd be better. She begged us again to let her continue despite her injury. By the way, Lydiah is having a few Sisters watching my place at night. If the lesbians try to exact vengeance, I'm in a difficult way to physically defend myself. How is your hunt for a place going?"

"I bought a house. After tomorrow I won't be living here."

"That's wonderful, Yellen! Where is it?"

"The house is just down the way, up Leo from Westmarket. It's a short walk to the west side baths."

Befanah frowned. "Be sure your security is good, Yellen. Your reputation with a blade is fearsome, but you should talk to Lydiah for some magical protection. There is significant possibility of retaliation from the lesbian cliques."

"I'm not worried too much yet, but thanks. Why is this operation running from your personal residence anyway?"

"Lydiah's original idea was to avoid confrontations and possible sabotage at the Flames headquarters. The Council is divided over the issue. There were strong indications of non-cooperation from our security personnel at the monastery, for example. Meeting here was an idea to avoid both publicity and complications."

"How are your feet?"

Befanah struck a match and re-lit her pipe. "They're the same. Dismissed, Lieutenant. Use my slaves to help move to your new place."

Yellen saluted, left the study, and went upstairs to her bedchamber. She didn't have much to move. She had her oil painting, which Henne didn't like, her books, her clothes, and her weapons. Perhaps she could use the grinder's secret room to keep her collection of weapons and armor safe from thievery. She'd have to explore it further and clean it out, along with the rest of the run-down house.

She needed to see Henne. She needed to gauge Henne's interest in an art business before she invested in renovations. Yellen summoned another magical messenger bird. Maybe Henne needed a different tone to motivate her.

Hello, Henne. I want to see you tonight. Stop whatever you're doing and let me know where and when. If I don't hear from you, I'm coming over anyway.

"Do you need anything, Mistress?" Befanah's pretty house-girl stood in the doorway. Her desiring eyes were low, and her stance was inviting. Yellen felt her Hunger surge when she eyed Monica. She knew the solution for her Jinn Hunger, and it wasn't Befanah's bored house-girl.

She'd pack up her coin case, go settle with the Toad, and take the grinder's wife back to her home. She hoped Master Trigo had been telling the truth about the redheaded demoness.

Chapter 13.

Golda slouched in the driver's seat of the Gypsy wagon. She and Gorka had advanced to second in the queue in front of the Grand Auction of Mer. She'd spent all morning helping Gorka load the wagon with knick-knacks. They'd crammed everything into the massive house-sized wagon that belonged to Agron and Pinhas'. In addition to silver, paintings, furniture and books, they'd harnessed up a handful of horses.

They'd found a long queue at the city auction. The sellers and their goods snaked from the hot and sunny auction house side yard all the way into the crowded main market street on the east side of the capital city.

Gorka had refused to sell absolutely everything his parents owned. If Agron and Priebus were released by the Court by some twist of fate, he hadn't wanted them to come home to find their lives erased. Golda adjusted her hat against the sun. She kept her head down and her eyes lowered. Her hair and Pinhas' hat mostly covered her features, but she was nervous at the thought of being spotted by Hell's Court devils.

She just wanted the Gypsy situation to be over with. She cared for Priebus, but her real love was Boudi, and only a true love could overrule the threat of impending doom. Her mind told her to abandon her quest, but her heart refused to leave Haawiyah. She needed to get Boudi. The guards at the

Merian city gate had tripled that day for some reason, which made her quest more difficult that it was already.

Golda scanned the auction yard with impatience. She and Gorka were next. She couldn't wait to out of that place. The Merian auction house was like a monastery of greed with massive old stone buildings organized around a receiving yard that was dominated by a shrine to Lord Hades.

The dark god in bronze held aloft a stack of coins in his hand. The statue was eroded and discolored from the sulfuric rains and the dust storms. Auction-goers had left tributes at the base of the statue—candles, bones and other trinkets left as prayers to Lord Hades for monetary gain. The mess formed a four-foot-tall heap of glinting garbage around the dread god's unseeing feet. The auction owners either didn't employ cleaners, or they were afraid to defile the sacred offerings.

Gorka sat nervously on the running board of the wagon with his youthful arms around his shins, keeping a low profile under the brim of his father's hat. He was watching the half-naked slaves work, most of whom wore whip scars on their tanned backs. The leather-collared humans jumped like dogs at the beck of the hellion auction master. Golda turned away from a muscled human male that kept ogling her, even as her Jinn Hunger stirred.

She hadn't wanted to go into Mer at all. She and Gorka had argued yet again. With Mohilever gone to inquire at Hell's Court, no one else had been left at the camp to help Gorka take his things to sale. All of the rest of the family had taken the road out of Haawiyah, bound for distant destinations with the intent of convening and regrouping at the spring waymeet. While remnants of a few other Gypsy families still lingered in the forest, Gorka, Mohilever, and Trumpeldor were the only Feigns remaining.

The customer in front of them was done. Gorka drove the queue of horses forward into the off-loading area. Golda snapped the reins to pull the wagon up, and then descended to stand behind Gorka. The auction master glowered at them for no apparent reason. He was a hellion—a spawn of some lusty god or goddess with a hapless four-legged animal. Thick horns grew from the auctioneer's temples. His fingers were stunted and hairy. His hands looked hoof-ish.

"Wah orgi wor ooti? Pedidi wo demono?"

Gorka looked taken aback. "What was that? Speak English. Do I look like a hellion? Did horns grow on my head just this morning?"

The hellion sneered at him. "You want to sell everything here?"

"Yes, and take the wagon and the draft horses too, everything except my blue roan and that chestnut there, which belong to me and my friend. This is a fire sale. Everything goes. No minimum."

"Ah, koo cha. Fine then," the hellion said. Golda avoided his eyes when he stared at her. "Your names, young Master and Madame?"

"I'm Gorka Reik," Gorka answered. "I'm a pure-blood covenanted Gypsy. My friend here is a Jinn business consultant for my family here in Mer."

The hellion nodded. "Please wait for your receipt. The standard handling fee is twenty-one percent of the sale price as a base, with a reduced percentage at various tiers depending on the total sale, as described on the back of your ticket."

"Fine."

The hellion signaled to the group of male slaves, who reluctantly broke from their short break and descended like locusts on the carriage, dragging furniture and boxes out of the back. The hellion registered each item as the slaves brought them past, writing with surprising speed in the ledger with his malformed fingers. The horned hellion muttered while he worked.

"You say you're a Gypsy, but I'm thinking about asking you to bend over, Master Gorka."

Gorka blinked. "What? Are you talking to me?"

The hellion eyed the Reik son with a smirk. "An examination of your backside for a brand? It's within anyone's rights here in the capital city of Mer, under the laws of Lord Hades, to stop a suspicious-looking human and ask to see a brand. A citizen's arrest can be made if the story doesn't add up."

"I'm a Gypsy from a covenanted family. You'll do no such thing."

"So your Jinn friend there is just a consultant, helping you in the big city? She isn't your owner?"

"That's what I said."

"This is a highly unusual situation," the hellion said with a hint of nervousness in his voice. "I should call for help and have my superiors ask you some questions. It's strictly business. I've got quite an eye for identifying goods that don't belong to the sellers, you know. We can't deal with illegal clients, and Gypsies are very unliked this week. Whenever the Court devils investigate a client here, it's nothing but a pain in our arse. Do you live here in Mer, Madame?"

Golda opened her mouth with her sketchy planned background—that she was a jewelry trader from Vegasis, but Gorka spoke before her. "Look, we just want to do business. Yes, I'm a free human, and that probably excites your big goat thing down there, but you're wasting your time. I'm a covenanted Gypsy, and I need gold coins, not a brand and a damned slave collar. These things belong to my family. End of story."

The hellion auction master shrugged. "Well, if you're really trying to avoid any more questions, I do accept tips."

"I don't have coin. That's why I'm here, damn you."

The hellion offered a quick smile. "No need to dig in your pockets, good sir. A generous five percent off the top for special handling and excellent service would work. I'll just make a note here and you'll sign for it. Fine?"

The muscles in Gorka's jaw worked. "Fine."

The hellion auctioneer wrote in his ledger. "Excellent, Master Gorka. You have my thanks."

"Just what I always wanted."

The hellion winked. "You know what? I actually like your pretty boy here, my good Mistress. If you're interested in some leisure time activities while you're visiting the capital, I'm a wealthy hellion with pleasure connections, and I've got a big hairy—"

"Get on with it," Golda growled.

"—bill of lading for you that is now ready. If one of you will sign the ledger, I can get to my next important customer. We'll put your things on the block later today. The auction starts at the three. At this point, I'd guess your goods will come up after the seven."

Gorka took the rectangle of parchment from the hellion. Gorka's fingers were visibly trembling. Gorka clenched his hand on the pen and signed. He folded his copy of the bill of lading and pocketed it. Golda wheeled her horse and headed into the street ahead of Gorka. When they reached the street, Gorka drew alongside her.

"Was he seriously threatening me, or did we just get bilked?"

Golda shrugged nonchalantly. "I'd guess it was a semi-bluff, as the werewolves call it when they play at cards. The hellion thought he could get the better of you."

"Wonderful! That's five percent less coin we'll have to help my mother and father, who are probably being tortured to death as we speak. I would expect nothing less from this disgusting city of evil."

"Just calm down, Gorka. We don't want to attract attention. Let's go meet Mohilever at the tavern as he asked. Torch street is two blocks over."

"I'm sorry. I'm trying to be civilized, but my family is in ruins, and this all has happened since you showed up. I've started to wonder if my family would be better off if we'd never met you, Golda. When you walked into the camp from the forest last fall, everything changed. My family has never been the same."

Golda felt a slow burn of anger. She pressed her horse close, grabbed Gorka's reins, and halted them both in the middle of the busy street. "I see how you suffer too in the wickedness of Lord Hades' realm, Gorka. We all suffer. We all do whatever we can to eke out a bit of love and happiness. Love is sacred. Love is the only thing in this existence worth living for. Maybe you've forgotten that."

"Let go of my horse, Golda. How dare you speak of love! You're a Jinn, and your tongue is like a snake. That's probably why my father enjoyed you. You were skilled at licking his bunghole."

Golda felt another growl in her Hunger-stretched belly. "Mohilever is right. You're just an arrogant brat. You don't understand love. Maybe you loved once, but time and Hell have made you forget. It happens to the best of us."

"Mohilever said that? At least I'm not a whore. Don't you dare lecture me about love, Jinn. Lord Tuhan knows love. The Mimos of Heaven know love. My Mimọ Beatrice knows love. She's a far better woman than you've ever been or ever will be. That's why you're here, and she's up there."

"You there, coming through! Move, I say!"

Golda looked over her shoulder and nudged her horse towards the crumbling street curb. She pulled Gorka's roan with her. The driver of a stately carriage waved his thanks and snapped his whip to push a team of plumed steeds into motion, passing in the wrong-direction lane.

A wealthy, bejeweled Jinn sat next to the driver in the carriage seat. The Jinn waved a gilded fan that concealed her powdered, beauty-marked face. Her carriage pulled a gilded wagon behind it—a low-wheeled sled that carried a golden cage studded with gemstones. The opulent cage gleamed in the polluted Haawiyah sunlight.

"Coming through," the driver shouted again, this time to a scurrying hellion. "We're late for a slave auction, thank you!"

The carriage passed with the golden wagon-cage in tow. A pair of handsome human men sat in the cage. Their muscled bodies glistened with oil, and brands were visible on their sacrum's. Slender golden collars gleamed on their necks, and their faces were painted like women. Golden chastity devices winked in the men's' nether crevices. Golda felt disgust in her belly at such a display of obscene wealth. The Merian Jinn likely had enough coin to pay for a Hell's Court bribe two times over. Golda caught Gorka's eye and gave him a hard look.

"So if we don't earn enough coin to save Priebus, are you still planning to ask the other families for help?"

Gorka avoided her eyes. "I suppose. The Akhen are close allies to my family. We have inter-family parties and dances at the waymeets. My mother is close friends with Tahany. I've always been close friends with Tahany's daughter, Lotifia."

"You think they will loan you the money?"

"If Elder Tahany won't help, perhaps I could appeal directly to Lotifia. I haven't seen her in months since I kissed her for the last time at a dance. If I pled my case well, my former love interest could potentially help, although now she is engaged to another man."

"Are the Akhen rich?"

"Lotifia is of royal Gypsy blood, a princess among the Egyptian Luxor. Elder Tahany is her mother. The Akhen are wealthy. Maybe they are still camped in their dells northeast of Mer and haven't left yet. Let's go meet Mohilever and Trumpeldor then."

Golda pushed the pace to lead Gorka west and deeper into the city. Mohilever had requested that they come together at a drinking establishment, supposedly one of the only Gypsy-friendly places in Mer, a place where Gypsies of all persuasions could revel together safely after finishing their business in the Market District.

Within fifteen minutes they drew under the shadow of the stately sign of the Gilded Lion, a tavern that had seen better days. If the tavern's mascot had once been gilded, it had turned brown-grey through exposure to the Haawiyah wind and storms. The interior of the inn was paneled with worn dark-stained oak. Antique flags of several nationalities hung from the high beams that supported the ceiling. Golda examined the place warily. The tavern was a haven but also a potential trap. A kitchen door behind the bar was the only emergency egress.

Mohilever and Trumpeldor welcomed them into a booth by the cloudy front window. Both men were swilling beer from a pitcher. Golda sat next to Trumpeldor. She had the urge to press her thigh against his, such was her simmering Hunger, but she restrained herself from baiting him. She had a second mission while visiting the city, and it didn't involve the sweaty, unappetizing Gypsy men.

"How much, Mohilever?" Gorka said, waving off the portly codger who had arrived to ask for orders. Golda caught the innkeeper's eye, and he smiled knowingly. The proprietor was another hellion judging by his furry cheeks and pointed ears, or perhaps a Kishi, as he lacked a tail. He wasn't a Gypsy. The Gypsies had many freedoms as favored humans in Hell, but residence in the capital city was not one of them.

"Your parents' judge will be Minos," Mohilever said without looking up from his glass of dark amber. "I spoke with a Jinn secretary in Hell's Court. Your father is not for a bribe at any price. He has already been tortured and sentenced to the Bolgia pits in Mer."

Gorka's face shrank in on itself. "Gods. Please tell us we can still help my mother, or all of this is for nothing!"

"We can buy her release, but it will cost three hundred and fifty gold chips. If we don't pay, Priebus is scheduled to work a chain gang down in the Great Blue Hole mines for the rest of eternity, or so the secretary said. I've heard the devils use humans like animals down there, lad. They're given numbers, not names, along with their shovels and picks. They aren't even allowed to speak. If they do, their tongues become devil delicacies."

Golda felt her loins go cold at the truth that she already knew. Gorka ran his hands through his hair, as if the truth was just hitting him. "That price is insane. How much time do I have to put together this bribe, Mohilever?"

"Priebus will be taken to the Great Blue Hole on the next Nanka flight in seven days' time."

"Do you swear, Mohilever, that you have nothing more to give? What of you, Trumpeldor?"

"Nary a denarius, hardly." Trumpeldor shook his head solemnly in the negative. "How did the auction go then?"

"My parents' things will be sold tonight, but I know they won't earn three hundred and fifty. By the gods, that's a lot of aurei. I'm going up the dells to see the Egyptian Luxor—Lotifia, her mother Tahany, and the Akhen family. Maybe they can help save mother."

Mohilever nodded. "I met a Akhen man down at Hell's Court, lad. He said the devils hit a lot of families, not just ours. Everyone is leaving the forest like we are, but Tahany and Lotifia are staying for one more week. Tahany heard about Pinhas'. She sent her own man to the Court to ask about your mother to see if something could be done. I told the man the price of the bribe. He said he'd give Tahany the figure."

Gorka nodded. "That's a bit of good tidings then."

"Have yourself a beer." Trumpeldor hoisted his glass. "To Priebus and Agron, the Fates have mercy on their souls."

"I'll meet you three back at the camp." Golda rose and went to the bar. She felt suddenly hopeless and depressed, and no Gypsy swill could take the edge off of her sour belly. She caught the barkeep's attention. "This is a fine establishment, but I'm looking for my kind of men."

The barkeep looked askance at her. "And here I figured you was with the Feigns. Bad business that. Bad business for my business. I'm off eighty percent this week, and it's not yet the summer season."

"I'd give you a kiss if it would help. I'm just looking for something different and discrete. I wondered if you could recommend anything. I don't know the best spots in Mer so well."

The man grinned. "Well, the Fuchsia Canary might be what you're looking for. It's a dive a few blocks over on the border of the Market and the Ukraine Quarter. It's a slumming hole for the Ukraine nobles. You've got the standard whores—trannies, fatties, four-legged types, and other assorted Jinni and Djinnus. You might find a fix for whatever you're into."

"Thank you." Golda stalked away from the bar. She glimpsed Mohilever's gaze on her backside as she slipped out through the Gilded Lion door. She'd take four legs over Mohilever Reik any day, but she doubted the poor fucked animals at the Canary were her preferred feline variety.

She really wanted a woman, but no ordinary woman would serve. She wanted Priebus, but she wanted Boudi-Ca most of all. Boudi-Ca was sweet in bed, compliant and submissive but also spirited and game for anything. Golda sighed and headed for the Canary. She missed those former days.

If she'd only held tighter to Boudi, and if she'd only been braver to commit fully to Love, perhaps nothing bad would have come to pass. The pursuit of Love could come at a high cost, but never higher than the call of Love ignored and thereby lost forever more.

Chapter 14.

Yellen escorted the demoness into her house, which was refreshingly cool and quiet at the early afternoon hour. Kiree gazed at the shambles of the grinder's shop. The demoness looked uncomfortable, but less terrified than when the Toad's lackeys had dragged her into the slave trader's office to conclude the sale. Yellen sifted her memories for her demonic vocabulary.

"Wor koo cho ba runit. Wee wat rigt penni." Your master went away. I'm very sorry.

"Tee wee tuggi?" the demoness answered sorrowfully. What do I do?

"Wee toggi Mistress Nefra. Wo wee porgi gogh." I am Mistress Nefra. You belong to me now.

The demoness lowered her eyes shyly. "Woggen chai tweri? Wo chai tweri?" Did they kill him? Did you kill him?

Yellen shook her head animatedly. "Nen. Choi pog. Abit choi hetti nen konnig." No. He is safe. But he has no money.

Yellen pursed her lips. Or at least, Master Trigo had no money that he didn't owe. She rubbed Kiree's shoulder. Once she trained Kiree to serve her, the demoness would turn out fine—more relaxed as she became attuned to her new life. A respectable Jinn with a lot of money was a desirable owner for most of Hell's down-and-out denizens, especially a slave-grade hellion like Kiree who wasn't useful for anything except the usual female duties.

"Tee wee tuggi?" Kiree said again.

Yellen put her hands up questioningly. "Podi wee wo maggi pennit abber?" *Can I make you feel better?* She was stretching the limits of her knowledge of demonic, but she hoped it was enough. Kiree looked wistfully at the stairs, then turned and climbed them.

Yellen followed. Kiree's sinuous furred tail would take some getting used to. While the divine blood tended to dominate the beast in every hellion, Kiree almost had the shapely form of a second generation, a quarter beast and three-quarters divine, with less fur, hair, and hooves than normal. Her bruised ass was an inspiring heart shape. She wore five old brands on her lower back from former owners. The brands were the least pretty of Kiree's features, and the demoness would need a sixth brand soon to finish her second row.

Yellen made a mental note to acquire a personal branding iron. She was also required by law to register Kiree with Hell's Court. On the other hand, taking Kiree to the Court could stir up the issues in her provenance that the grinder had alluded to. In truth, she wasn't sure how to proceed. She'd never owned her own slave, much less dealt with a shady slave trader.

Kiree paused in the second-floor hall and glanced at the secret door, which was ajar. Yellen closed the distance, expecting the demoness to enter her old bedroom, where female clothes and worn-out underthings lay in a small pile. Kiree diverted her course instead and entered the nectar-grinding room. The demoness looked forlornly at the stained table.

"Neck-tar?"

Yellen grimaced. Of course that was what Kiree needed—a fix for her longstanding habit. "Wee wo orgi nectar." *I'll get you nectar.*

"Aggrat." *Thank you.* At last Kiree's mood improved a little. Yellen rubbed Kiree's arm. The demoness bit her nectar-purpled lip with her stained, flat, herbivore incisors, but Kiree didn't shrink from the intimacy. Yellen stroked down to Kiree's breast and gently pinched her heavy nipple. Kiree's chest arched subtly with the pleasure.

Yellen brushed Kiree's thick red hair with her fingertips. She leaned in and kissed Kiree's cheek, reaching with the force of her Jinn hunger to feel Kiree's underlying desire-structure. Kiree's reservoir of passion wasn't strong under her skin, but it was solid enough to feed from, possibly even on a daily basis if Kiree could be healed and her soul stoked emotionally. Kiree badly needed a bath.

Yellen stroked her hand down Kiree's soft, flaccid belly and forked her fingertips into the demoness' abundant nether hair, which was thicker and stiffer than a human's thatch, more like a bristly horse's mane. Yellen caressed back up over the swell of Kiree's belly and over her sternum between her breasts.

"Wo rigt kalagi," Yellen breathed in Kiree's ear. You're very beautiful.

"Aggrat," the demoness murmured.

An odd thump came then in the lower level, followed by a scrape and scratch. Yellen turned and dropped her hand to the hilt of her sword, but it was only Henne's brown catbird, which shot from the hall into the grinding room, landed on her shoulder, and spoke in her ear with Henne's voice.

I can see you whenever, Yellen. I'm home now at Nili's, but if you want, I could go out. I'm sorry it took so long for me to reply. It's nice to hear from you.

Henne's voice sounded welcoming but nonchalant. At least Henne had finally answered. Yellen placed another warm kiss on Kiree's cheek. She clasped Kiree's chin in her fingers and turned the mouth of the demoness to meet her own.

She tasted Kiree, claiming Kiree's mouth with her tongue. She clasped the ass of the demoness and pulled her close. Kiree breathed a soft moan into the gentle love-suction. Yellen broke the kiss after several seconds. She hungered, but she was too distracted. She had a far more important priority in that moment.

"Wo porgi higger. Rigt higger," she said softly. "Wo gee poggit. Wo podi pargit?" You stay here. Right here. You'll be safe. Can you clean?

"Rigt gogher," Kiree answered. Very well.

Yellen pointed at the bedroom and the bed. "Wor diggerit. Wo wee gee orgi gabst abber diggerit. Wee wo orgi nectar." Your things. I'll get you more better things. I'll get you nectar.

The demoness smiled and nodded. Yellen summoned a messenger bird for Henne. I'll come over now. I'll be there in an hour.

Yellen descended the stairs out of the house. It took her five minutes to ride fast back to Befanah's, and another hour to bathe and make herself presentable, all while not disturbing Befanah's house-girl, who was dutifully crating things in the bedchamber for transport to the new place.

On her way out of Befanah's house, Yellen picked up the pouches of Blue-Violet Beauty that she'd bought from Master Trigo. She snatched a bouquet of somewhat-fresh flowers from the top of Befanah's piano. It was mid-afternoon when she rode up to Henne's home on Canus Avenue—a modest eighteenth-century stone two-story that Henne had Shared for many years with her mentor, Mistress Nili. Yellen hitched her horse at the same familiar post where she'd been hitching her horse for the last five years.

She'd first met fledgling Henne and Mistress Nili on a mission in Meristyian, where she'd helped Befanah and Lydiah dismantle the hidden lesbian city ruled by the rebel love goddess, Allyssia. Henne and Nili had been living in that distant city as traitors to Lord Hades. Allyssia had escaped with her favorites, leaving many of her lesbian followers behind to be held and punished by Hell's Court.

Mistress Nili still lived in solitary ignominy in Mer, having worn an ebon collar for years as her punishment for her former devotion to Allyssia. As a mere fledgling, however, Henne had been allowed to re-integrate into Merian society and seek a straight and law-abiding life. Henne hadn't been entirely straight or law-abiding during that time.

Yellen knocked on the poorly-maintained oak door. The house-girl named Chen unlocked the door within a minute and allowed her into the foyer. Yellen dismissed the house-girl and found her own way up the stairs. She breezed confidently into the warmth and scents of Henne's intimate bedchamber. Henne lay in deshabille on her old leather sofa. She wore nothing but a maroon under-bust corset lined with satin, with a short peach-colored silk slip that looked attractive against her pale thighs.

Henne was a wiry, pale-skinned artiste with a freckled face. Her burgundy-painted fingernails were trimmed short for her sculpting. Her red-gold hair was longer than during the previous summer and ornamented with gold hairclips above her ears. Henne's perfectly red-painted lips split into a grin.

"You brought fresh flowers. Thank you, Yellen. Welcome back to Mer. It's been how long? I haven't seen you since I received my Mistress Test."

"I assume you passed? I haven't heard from you."

"Yes. Everyone loved my sculptures. I trained my first slave. Nili bought him for me. He's a precious male Mimo, a war prisoner."

"Really? You like him?"

"He was angry and sullen at first, but now he's submissive and sweet. He's very handsome. We'll have to go down into the pit, and you can meet him. Maybe you were involved in his capture in Meristyian, and he's already surrendered to you once." Henne laughed. "That would be uncomfortable."

"I was on special forces. I didn't take many prisoners." Yellen sidled across the room. She dragged the bunch of flowers up Henne's leg, then settled them on Henne's corseted stomach. She leaned, kissed Henne, and handed her a pouch of nectar. Henne was redolent with a head-swimming perfume. "I expect to be in Mer for quite a while this time, not just a temporary leave. I brought this Blue-Violet Beauty as a gift. I hope you like it."

Henne's smile widened. "I like it very much! Thank you, Yellen. Nectar is always appreciated, and purple-violet reminds me of the old days. What a lovely gift."

"How have you been, darling?"

Henne lowered her eyes. "Fine. I'm sorry I didn't answer your birds right away. I was floating in nectar all afternoon yesterday, then I got busy."

"Let me guess. You have a friend?"

"I do."

Yellen winked sweetly. "Well, that's disappointing, but predictable. I hope I can still Share you, as usual? As far as our thing goes, I have some good news."

"What is it?"

Yellen fidgeted. She'd meant to work slowly up to the conversation, but she just couldn't help herself. She felt like a dumb puppy. She wanted to jump on Henne that very second. She'd been thinking about Henne every day for months.

"I bought a house with my back pay. It's in the Westmarket. It's a nice three-story. Now that you're a fully-fledged mistress, maybe you could get out of your current living arrangement. Maybe you could even stay at my place."

"What?" Henne glanced quickly at the bedroom door. "Yellen, this is a little sudden. Are you joking?"

Yellen took a deep breath. "No. To tell you the truth, I want to open an art studio with you as my resident artist. It would be a real, legitimate business in a part of town that doesn't receive much scrutiny. We can fix it up. You'll have all the light and studio space that you need. You complained in your letters about how cramped and dark Nili's basement has always been for your sculpting. I've got the perfect solution for you."

"Yellen, this is shocking. I don't think I could live with you, but I could do gallery showings there, you think?"

"Sure. There's a storefront built in with a small show floor and glass cabinets that could hold your smaller pieces. There are work rooms. I think it's perfect. It's on the west side, which isn't great, but it's still sort of close to downtown."

"Wow." Henne brightened further. "I could actually bring my clients to a space where they can see my work. I could get a real flow of coin going. Will you be living there?"

"Yes. I was thinking about learning to paint. You could sleep there too if you wanted, strictly unofficially and on a professional basis of course. It's an artisanal establishment. Live and work. We could even have room to bring in another artist if the Flames sends me back to Meristyian when my vacation is up. Then you could run the place yourself in my stead. Whatever you want."

"How much would my rent be?"

"None. I own it. Maybe we should pay some insurance, though, especially if you're storing your sculptures."

"If I sold from a shop with no overhead, I'd have coin for nicer clothes, and I could buy my own reinforced carriage for deliveries. I have some debt, Yellen. I spent everything on new clothes last fall for my debutante parties as a newly fledged mistress."

"I'm glad you passed your Mistress Test and finally ascended from fledgling status. Congratulations, Mistress Henneh."

Henne sighed. "Thank you Yellen. It was so much work. So tell me more about this studio. How is the light?"

"The windows in the house are big, but the former owner has them covered over. The place needs a lot of renovation, but in the long term it will be worth it. Maybe you can help me fix it up and pick some furniture and curtains."

"Absolutely. I know a carpenter too. He builds the wood crates I use for transporting my things. This is great."

Yellen smiled widely. For a second time that day, she'd made a beautiful redhead happy. "Can you come over tomorrow afternoon to look?"

"I'll be there. Thank you, Yellen. There's only one thing you should know. I'm engaged to be married in, like, three weeks."

"Well, congratulations again." Yellen tried to maintain her smile, but her heart felt leaden from her throat to the depths of her belly. She'd guessed that her worst nightmare was coming, but she'd dared to pray to Allyssia for something different. "It's an Djinnus, then? You love him?"

Henne giggled. "Of course."

Yellen looked away to hide her pain. She'd never heard Henne giggle. The Djinnus was already changing Henne, making her more feminine. "Would I know this guy?"

"Maybe. His name is Master Andros. You know his father, Archduke Apollyon. Andros is a younger spawn, a wealthy politico from Hell's Court. This doesn't mean we can't still be friends and do this gallery together, Yellen. I just won't be able to spend the night or hang out with you most evenings. I'll be keeping my husband's household and managing our slaves.

I'll be hosting parties. I'll be helping my husband with his Hell's Court career. We're getting married on Ostara Day at the end of the Spring Festival."

Yellen drifted towards Henne. She couldn't help herself. It was her inner tiger coming out, wanting to fight for the kill. She pulled Henne's hair back and bent to plant a kiss on Henne's shoulder. She moved her lips up to the sensitive skin of Henne's neck. She could feel Henne's inner tension relaxing into the kisses.

"Is there any way I could persuade you to put off this wedding just for a couple months until I leave again?" Yellen planted more kisses.

"I admit that I missed you," Henne answered quietly.

Yellen pressed Henne. Henne's mouth was wet, sweet, and tingly with sweet nectar. Yellen kissed for long minutes, re-acquainting herself with Henne's nimble, smaller tongue and slender, pampered body. Finally she felt Henne's fingers at her waist, tugging at her sash, and she drew back to undress.

"Turn and I'll take off your corset," Yellen whispered. "I'll put it back on for you after."

"Fine." Henne turned, yielding her backside and her corset lacings. "Could you put some music on the phonograph and crank it? Just pick anything."

Yellen eyed the copper box with the metal armature that sat on Henne's side table. She tugged at Henne's corset laces, taking her time. "I'd like to hear it, but I've never used one of those things. I don't know how a machine could sound good, anyway."

"Technology keeps accelerating, doesn't it? The humans are inventing everything now. They're way ahead. Our businessmen here are trying to keep up, and they're making a ton of coin at it, along with the Gypsy merchants who manage the transport. Pretty soon the business people might be the wealthiest people in Hell, and many of them are just lowly hellions or humans. It's a scandal, and the Court establishment isn't accepting this. Lord Hades is raising taxes on the factory owners and the Gypsies, and it's causing major outrage."

"Technology is an advantage for Hell. The Mimos haven't kept up either. They still have their holy books, but they haven't upgraded their armies with heavy cannons."

"I'm glad because I worry about you, Yellen."

Yellen swallowed. It was nice that Henne worried, but sometimes that wasn't enough. "You could teach me how to use the phonograph."

"Of course. You know, it may sound strange, but it's nice to talk with someone without feeling like I'm being judged. The old aristocracy and the people at the Court can be such snobs, and not just with technology. It's so different in the upper-class circles downtown, Yellen. You can't imagine what happens."

"I learned to drive a motorcar today. It was a loud, bumbling beast. I ended up wishing for a nice carriage."

"Let's not listen to the phonograph. We'll just do some purple. I know you don't like to, but it will be better if we're more relaxed."

"I'll do some purple with you. I'm off duty."

Henne reached for the pouch of Blue-Violet Beauty and opened it. Yellen kept pulling the laces, taking her time and savoring every inch of Henne's freckled, powdered skin as it emerged. She tried not to think of Henne's Djinnus fiancée in the same position. Was he an expert on using phonographs? Was he an expert nectar-user, like Henne?

Likely the phonograph had been a gift. Henne spent all of her money on clothes, jewels, and nectar, not technological mechanisms. By the time the corset came off, the lines of purple were ready on the side table, and Henne bent to snuffle one of them up with a thin silver cylinder. The cylinder was elegant, with turned-back florette petals on one end.

"Take it. Snort it," Henne said with her voice faint from pleasure. "Swallowing nectar is so cheap and passé these days."

Yellen took the cylinder, pressed it to her nose, bent and sniffed. She was clumsy. Henne giggled and tried to hold the end of the implement for her, which didn't work. Yellen blinked and swayed as the intense pleasure burned through her nasal passage and down her throat, lighting fire to the insides of her head. Her body lightened, and she felt an amazing floating sensation. It had been ages since she'd done any nectar.

She pivoted into Henne, and they pressed fully nude against one another, flesh against flesh, stumbling towards the unmade bed. Yellen softly crashed Henne down onto the sheets. She bit and licked like an animal. Under the influence of the nectar, she let her Jinn Hunger get the best of her. She needed to claim Henne. She needed to take every advantage of the minutes Henne was giving her if she wanted to win Henne's attention. She had to cling to a vain hope that her deepest desires weren't hopeless pipe dreams.

Yellen lingered long on Henne's breasts and nipples, finding the sensitive places under Henne's arms with her tongue, every place that Henne's Djinnus likely didn't. Henne sighed with silent thanks. Yellen went lower and pressed her lips into Henne's flat stomach, and still lower over Henne's infinitely attended mons, which was freshly smooth, waxed, and scented. Yellen tongued the crevices inside Henne's thighs, and then met the crease of wetness in the center.

"No, Yellen," Henne murmured, tugging her head. "I don't want you to venerate me down there. I don't want to influence your mind any more than I already have. It isn't good for you. Leave the cunni for my slave."

Yellen slid up, licking Henne's taste from her lips, those Jinn fluids that had a long-term seductive effect on those who imbibed, just like Djinnus seed but to a lesser degree. She needed to ask Kiree for such attention, the better to sway the demoness to faithfulness. Henne sat up to turn the tables then. Yellen allowed it, recognizing a need in Henne to be with a woman, a need that resonated with her own. Henne only pressed against her, however, locked her arms, and pressed breast against breast.

Yellen caressed Henne's shoulder. "What is it?"

"I don't know if I can do this," Henne whispered.

"Why? Are you crying?"

"Yellen, I've been working up to this wedding for months, convincing myself that I really want to marry Master Andros. I'm not sure that's what I want."

"You're like me," Yellen whispered. "You need a woman who truly understands you, not a husband."

Henne sighed. "I know, but it would be good for me too. If I marry Andros, the doors of the inner Court circles will open for me. It's an absolute dream for any young beauty mistress. If I don't marry Andros, I'll be unwelcome forever in polite society. Nili would disown me. It would be unthinkable to call off my wedding. I know how this is supposed to go, Yellen."

"Listen to me—"

Henne shook her head. "It's our Lord's law for all Jinni. It's time for me to take responsibility and become a fully-fledged married mistress. I need to do this for myself and for Nili. I want him very much. It's a yearning inside me that I can't deny."

"It's his seed. He's been taking you?"

"Yes, but only once a week. When we go away on our honey moon, the floodgates will open. He'll fill me to bursting, and I'll adore him forever with all of my soul like everyone else adores their husbands. Everything will be fine, and I'll be a happy and devoted Jinn wife. It's a rite of passage for a Jinn. I just need to do it."

Yellen bent and kissed Henne's lips. "It isn't you. You're independent by nature, like me. You're an artist, not a wife."

"I have to." Henne sniffed. "I have to, Yellen. Please understand. You can't just walk back into Mer and expect me to reverse my life. I just passed my Mistress Test."

"A lot of Jinni delay marriage for various reasons even if they aren't in the Smokeless Flames. At least come look at this gallery with me. You need to keep up your art, and I can help you. Your art is more important than a husband."

Henne's tight lips softened into a smile. Her eyes went dreamy. "I'd like that. I'd like to have my own gallery for my sculpture. Is there enough space for a party, and to have openings and classy shows? Is it nice?"

"It's big enough. It's intimate. It needs work, but I have the coins. The shop is already there with the display space, but it needs improvement. I need to talk with you."

"The classiest art galleries have trained slaves working in them. A skilled assistant would be the most expensive and important thing I can think of. A strong male slave could help us fix things up, and then he could help with all of the lifting. My bronze and marble pieces are very heavy."

"Can your Mimọ work? You said he was a soldier for Heaven."

"No. My handsome Mimọ needs to live with me. I wouldn't want him trooping back and forth from my house downtown to your gallery. Andros likes him too."

"Right. I need a strong male slave, then. Fine."

"He should be handsome, so he can tend the shop. It would be nice if he had some musical abilities too. The best galleries all have music."

"Would you like to pick him for me? We could go to an auction together."

Henne's smile widened. "Yes. Let's do this. I'd be honored sell my art at your gallery, Yellen. Fuck me now, and then we can do more nectar. We can think later."

Yellen took the invitation to top Henne again. She just wanted to be against Henne, entwined and enveloped in their mutual nectar-heightened pleasure. She trailed more kisses. She suckled at Henne's small, pale nipples. She reached low between Henne's thighs and staked her claim on Henne's high-society prize.

Henne's prize felt used and owned by someone else in that moment, both literally and figuratively. Yellen felt her belly quiver with both fear and hopelessness. Perhaps she was only torturing herself. The law was the law, and she'd already gone too far. She was rude to keep pushing Henne to go against Lord Hades and everything Henne believed was right for herself.

Yellen eased her pressure and slowed her efforts. Perhaps she needed to find another steady, trustworthy lover, but she couldn't go near the private clubs in Mer with the purgation underway. Worse yet, she would meet plenty of lesbians in the coming weeks, but her job was to arrest them all and send them to the devils.

Chapter 15.

Boudi-Ca climbed a slanted path through the cactus garden in front of Moshe's ramshackle north side home. She'd snuck out of Fennel's house as soon as Lydiah had left on her Flames duties. It was the early morning of dies Saturni, and she was trying to summon the courage to visit Breanarachelle as the she-devil had requested.

She hadn't dared say anything to Lydiah for fear of the consequences. She'd said far too much to Breanarachelle, and she needed to fix things. She had an idea, but she'd hardly slept all week. She'd buried herself for endless hours in her bed, wracking her brain for solutions. She'd had a good excuse to stay in bed. The persistent headache from her nectar withdrawal was killing her. She'd even cancelled her piano and sword lessons each morning without telling Lydiah.

She'd decided that she'd have to face Breanarachelle and argue for a delay, but she needed to smooth over the pain and craving. She couldn't deal with her problem if she couldn't think straight. She needed Moshe's nectar and some sex, and then everything would be better. She'd gain the strength to face Breanarachelle.

Boudi-Ca walked through the entry hallways to the inner courtyard. Compared to Fennel's well-maintained estate, Master Faisil's fix-up investment was a heap of medieval rubble surrounded by collapsing stone walls. Moshe and Master Faisil had relocated north to acquire more space while escaping from the high rents in the near east side Quartier Francais.

The courtyard of the home was bright in late morning. The morning sunlight accented the ridges of the spiral Moorish columns. Moshe's easel loomed in the shadow of the roof overhang. He sat on a low stool with a long brush in his hand.

"Boudi-Ca, ma petite poupee," he said over his shoulder at the sound of her heels on the stone tiles. "I was hoping to give you a lesson while I work. You've always said we might paint sometime together."

"Who is she?" Boudi-Ca drew up to Moshe and gazed at his figure painting. The painting depicted a corpulent Jinn with an overflowing saffron-colored robe, a belly like a wheelbarrow, and breasts like flour sacks. The figure leaned back with seeming pleasure, yet imperiously at a high perspective. A sepia photo of the same Jinn sat propped nearby on the table with Moshe's paints.

"She is the great Empress Wu," Moshe answered with an overaffected tone of stentorian importance. "She's an elder Chinese Jinn from the Tang dynasty. She's a patapouf and stinking rich. Apparently she spends most of her coins on pastries."

"You're painting her from a photograph?"

"Oui. I did a session at her place in the Asian Quarter yesterday, and I'll finish from the photograph. It's better this way. The light in her throne room was horrible, and there was no way I'd ask her to make the trip up here. You can see why, right?"

"Did you fuck the empress then, or does she only want a picture?"

Moshe chuckled. "When you're working for royalty, you don't kiss and tell. I sold Wu pink nectar. I'll say that. It's all the rage with the patapoufs these days. It's red nectar mixed with refined sugar crystal. They use pink nectar to glaze their pastries and sprinkle their sweetcakes for that extra special pleasure."

"I want some cheap purple, and then I'll paint with you."

"I can't do that." Moshe cleared his throat. "Lydiah had a conversation with me, and she visited your usual places in the Denmark quarter too. She told everyone and their uncle to give you no more nectar. Lydiah's second fledgling is pledging to the Smokeless Flames."

"I can't believe this. Lydiah says she's so busy, but she has plenty of time to go all over Mer and threaten people to not give me nectar." Boudi-Ca felt heat steal over her cheeks. She felt suddenly faint, and she grabbed Moshe's strong shoulder to steady herself.

"You're too talented to live for nectar, ma petite poupee. I've got some skill with paints and brushes, but you're going real places in your life. You don't want to be like me, a workman for rich peoples' vanity. 'Anything you wish, Empress Wu. I'm honored, Empress Wu. Yes, the painting doesn't do your breasts proper homage, Empress Wu. I'll fix it immediately.'"

Moshe rose and pressed her with a warm Djinnus hug. His open white shirt smelled pleasantly of linseed oil and chemicals. Boudi-Ca edged away. She didn't want to get paint smudges on her expensive skirt and jacket, which would give Lydiah further conniptions.

"My head hurts so much. I just want to feel better."

Moshe grinned. "You will eventually. Until then, stay here and paint. I want you to try to paint me. I'll set you up my second easel. Wait." Moshe vanished into the hallway towards his workshop.

Boudi-Ca paced. She didn't have time for a painting lesson. Her embarrassment turned into a slow burn of fury. She'd made a rational decision to take just a little nectar, but Lydiah had embarrassed her and treated her like a child in front of Moshe and the Denmark Djinnus. Moshe returned within a minute, carrying a second easel under his arm. She brushed up to him and kissed him on the cheek.

"I'm leaving."

"Aw, Boudi-Ca baby. Stay."

Boudi-Ca turned on her heel and tried to keep her courage on her way out of Moshe's house. She directed the driver to take the carriage downtown. Her ass still felt uncomfortable from the small punctures that Breanarachelle had left in her skin a few nights previously. She summoned her messenger bird.

Mistress Breanarachelle, I would like to request an audience this morning as planned. May I present myself?

Boudi-Ca fidgeted. Perhaps Breanarachelle would be too busy, and she could use the excuse of no response to turn the carriage back to Tanjie. The carriage was approaching Pee-Hill when Breanarachelle's return bird came winging up the street. The huge black bird startled her, like a sudden ominous omen. The bird flew straight at her face before darting to the side. It disappeared in a swirl of Breanarachelle's sibilant syllables.

Present yourself. Yes.

The wide gravel driveway of Rhadamanthus was eerily devoid of visiting carriages that afternoon. A gardener watched her disembark while pruning the rose bushes by the steps. Boudi-Ca steadied on her heels. She wore a coquettish knee-length pleated black skirt and a black day-jacket with ruffled sleeves over her favorite burgundy corset, which sported a little pink bow between her breasts.

She shouldered her leather purse and directed herself towards the gardener. She walked up, pried his clippers from his fingers, and cut a red rose from his bush. The gardener silently accepted the return of the clippers with his eyes fixed humbly on her feet. Boudi-Ca examined the red rose, even as butterflies bounced in her belly. The roses at the estate were the thorniest species she'd ever seen, with quarter-inch orange-tipped barbs.

She climbed the front steps and entered the cavern of Rhadamanthus' foyer. A slave boy was waiting. He beckoned to her. She followed him down the quartz-floored hallways to a darkened parlour, where Breanarachelle was waiting in a sunken leather chair.

The elder she-devil was in deshabille, wearing only a loosely-buttoned white silk blouse over a grey brassiere, a charcoal slip that rode high on her thin yellow-grey thighs, and strappy stiletto heels that appeared fashioned from yellowed bones.

Another slave boy sat on the floor next to Breanarachelle with a stack of printed fashion plates in his lap. Boudi-Ca curtseyed as she entered the room.

"Leave us," the she-devil said.

Boudi-Ca blinked, but then she realized Breanarachelle had meant the slave boy, who climbed to his feet, bowed to his mistress, and hurried from the parlour. The shaved and groomed boy was nude except for a bejeweled locking sheath around his flaccid cock. His skin was a remarkable map of raised scars from his nape all the way down his legs.

"Good morning, Mistress Breanarachelle. It's nice to see you again." Boudi-Ca stepped to place the red rose next to Breanarachelle on the chair arm, but Breanarachelle grabbed her hand and squeezed. Boudi-Ca suppressed a gasp. The thorns from the rose stem penetrated her flesh, digging deep until Breanarachelle finally released the pressure and allowed her to drop the gift. The she-devil lifted the rose to the thin froggish slits of her nose. She sniffed the length of the bloody stem, not the petals.

"Don't let your beautiful blood drip on my carpet, child." Breanarachelle murmured. She extended a laced doily from the fine wood side table. "Use this. Then sit."

The she-devil's sensual amber eyes were piercing and bright. Small wrinkles were visible around Breanarachelle's eyes in the cool low light that came through the shuttered parlour window. Boudi-Ca wrapped her bleeding, painful fingers in the fine white lace. She blinked tears from her eyes and took a seat in the leather chair opposite Breanarachelle.

"That really, really hurt. Is your husband at the Court?"

"No. My husband is upstairs dressing for the downtown service," Breanarachelle answered. "Does Lydiah not take you to week-end cathedral services?"

"Sometimes. We mostly pray to the Lord and Lady at home."

Breanarachelle examined her nails. "Well, put your cards on the table, then. What's it going to be? You have fifteen minutes before I get dressed and leave."

Boudi-Ca took a deep breath and tried to collect everything in her head. She mentally reminded herself that whatever happened, she couldn't lie to the elder she-devil with any success. "Remember when you said that you could feel my suffering, and that Lydiah was mostly responsible for it?

Well, I agree. I would like to see her suffer as much as me."

Breanarachelle's thin freckled lips turned into a small grin. "Interesting. You're on board with my plan, then. You're going to give me Lydiah, and in return I'll give you leniency. I'll call my secretary, and we'll start with a sworn statement that your Mistress molested you against your will on multiple occasions. You can work on it while I'm gone to services."

"No."

"No? Shall I call my husband and have him arrest you now instead? He can have the devils here in ten minutes, and they'll torture you this afternoon. We went over this. We either do this my way, or you get the knives, pincers, and split canes."

Boudi-Ca felt her heart pounding hard in her chest. "I mean I agree with your plan, but it isn't as good as it could be."

Breanarachelle's eyes darkened dangerously. "Pray tell how so, child?"

"That works fine for your vengeance or whatever, but your hatred of Lydiah means nothing to me. Your plan doesn't make my Mistress suffer enough. You just want to ruin her quickly and get it over with. There's no fun or subtlety."

"The time is ripe," Breanarachelle retorted. "I haven't seen Lydiah so active since the aftermath of her Meristyian debacle. Hell's Court has given her a chance to get back in good graces by leading the purgation. If I wait, and she succeeds, she could regain her credibility. When the purgation comes to an end, and Merian society is dead tired of hearing anything about lesbians, my bid to discredit her might come with a whimper instead of a bang. It could even rebound on me. This is a timing issue. Still, how are you suggesting we could make her suffer more? You're intriguing me."

"Lydiah loves me. She cares for me more than her own reputation, although she won't show it. I can feel it when she's close to me."

Breanarachelle sank in her chair and stroked her knee thoughtfully. "Yes. Her protectiveness of you seems completely irrational. She's battling tooth and nail to keep you instead of letting you go to the Flames. She really has it bad for you, doesn't she? It's pathetic, but it makes sense."

"Yes, and when someone is in love, they are very vulnerable to exploitation. They make mistakes. Lydiah herself taught me that."

"Go on."

Boudi-Ca stretched her legs sensuously and crossed them one over the other, flashing her inner thighs to Breanarachelle as she shifted. Her most difficult stretch was ahead, but she felt more and more confident. Her next words were as close to a lie as she dared get. "The other night when you put your claws on me, I felt something between us. I wanted you very much, and I still do."

"You want to play and make Lydiah jealous? Is that your proposal?"

"Yes."

"Seriously?" Breanarachelle laugh-snorted. "I'm not a lesbian, you overconfident and prickish little bitch. I thought you could do better, but clearly I've been swayed by Lydiah's deluded high opinion of your assets. Let's restate the issues. Lydiah is an Mimọ-obsessed hypocrite who fucks her own freak of an Mimọ fledgling and then orders the arrests of other Jinni in Mer who dare to have similar interests. The proof of that history of illegal lesbianism is sitting right here with me in this room. I don't need more than you to get Lydiah."

"Maybe you're overrated too, and you're just proving that Lydiah is cleverer than you. I can't believe that you're not interested in ripping Lydiah's guts out before you ruin her and send her to prison. What devil worth her salt wouldn't jump at that chance?"

"I agree with the merits of your idea. I only object to your juvenile meth-ods." Breanarachelle's froggish nostrils flared, and the room descended into silence except for the clip-clip of the gardener along the drive outside. "If I've made one mistake, it's assuming that you're just a dumb little Mimọ with ill-begotten Jinn gifts. You're in fact an inverted sadist. You enjoy seeing others suffer, but you feel guilty over it, so you settle for enjoying things done to yourself. It's the only way you could have been wet for me on Egyptian New Year's eve."

Boudi-Ca bit her lip. She had never seen herself that way, and her throb-bing headache prevented her from delving too deeply into Breanarachelle's words. "So teach me."

Breanarachelle laughed. "I am nearly four thousand years old. I don't enjoy babysitting, but maybe we can make an agreement. My question is why are you stalling?"

"It's asking a lot of me to betray Lydiah. I want a lot of things in return. I need to be sure that I'm going to get protected. I need to go to the Flames. I need—"

"You need nectar. There is some in that drawer. Get it."

"Thank you." Boudi-Ca opened the drawer of the polished oak table next to her chair. A thin red box with flower designs squatted inside. She carefully pulled it out and lifted the lid to reveal a beautiful little sea of precious red with a sniffer perched on a cradle. She lifted the sniffer to her nostril. The intense nectar pleasure hit the insides of her skull like a blast of super-heated wind off the Mare.

"Yes, I agree you'll need protection," Breanarachelle said casually. "You're my proof, so I can't have you dead or your memories gone again. Lydiah would do anything to get rid of your testimony if necessary. She already tried to cover her abuse of you by keeping you nectared for so long and destroying your diaries. This is the complication. She could make you disappear, and I could be left with nothing. So how do we prolong her suffering without the risk of my leverage slipping from my fingers?"

Boudi-Ca returned the sniffer and settled back into the chair, which seemed suddenly much deeper and more comfortable. The pleasure bloomed through her blood, and her headache and discomfort both lifted like a fog from her mind and body. She felt happy, and a deep relaxation stole over her being.

"Well, she wouldn't even know what we're doing until you're ready. I wouldn't say anything."

"How can I trust you?" Breanarachelle countered. "If we go slow as you request, then I want insurance that I'll get something one way or another. Two birds in the bush are only better if one bird is sitting in a trap."

Boudi-Ca swallowed and rubbed her nostril. She didn't like the sound of that. "I don't know why this is a problem. I want her to suffer as much as you. We just aren't agreed how to do it. Maybe we should just wait until the purgation is over."

"Lydiah loves you," Breanarachelle persisted. "What do you love, Boudi-Ca? I think you love your beauty. When people speak of you, it's always your beauty. I've heard people at shows ask why Masia-Ca is modeling instead of you. Doesn't Lydiah know she has a prettier fledgling? I think so. I think she loves you so much that she doesn't want you gang-fucked by the fashion public. She wants your lovely assets all for her secret lesbian self."

"You flatter me." Boudi-Ca felt a blush stealing over her cheeks, along with a warm rush of pride that rose in her throat. She felt a dizzy sensation and a queer sadness that Breanarachelle's words were true—deep down Lydiah loved her that much. Boudi-Ca winced and blinked. Her eyes were suddenly watering, but she wasn't crying. Her throat was beginning to burn, and the burning climbed to pulse in her nectared nostril, intensifying with every second. She lifted her pricked finger to rub her nose, but the rubbing only made the pain worse. She moaned as the pain pushed heat and tingling pain through her eye sockets and throat.

"It's Nefertiti Pepper from Tisiphone's gardens in Vegasis." Breanarachelle winked with a wicked little smile. "It's one of the most powerful peppers in Hell, and it's excellent when mixed with red nectar. Tizzy gave us a few boxes of it last year when she visited. You're lucky it's lost a lot of its potency. You want to play? Then take the other nostril for me now."

"No, thank you." Boudi-Ca sniffed and swallowed, resisting the urge to take another bump to make the pain go away. Her eyes were starting to itch and water, and her breasts and buttocks felt hot and sweaty. She forced herself to stay focused and think, even while half of her face was starting to burn with fire. "So what do you want if my promise isn't good enough?"

"Your beauty might suffice."

"What do you mean?"

Breanarachelle leaned forward intently in her leather chair. "A few centuries ago, after Fennel married Lydiah, Rhada asked him what he would do to blunt Lydiah's pride. She was the most arrogant Jinn imaginable, and everyone loved her and praised her. Rhada asked how Fennel planned to claim his wife in the devil way. What mark would he make on his new wife besides a piece of signed paper? Fennel told Rhada that he planned to turn Lydiah into a patapouf. He planned to turn her perfect body into an enormous mound of Jinn flesh. Her beauty would end forever with her marriage to him, and Fennel would write epics of pain and pleasure on Lydiah's grand canvas. Fennel said he would feed Lydiah sweets until she was the size of a Nokian Oliphant, and she would no longer be able to do her ambassador duties. She would only stay home and mind the slaves. I was looking forward to seeing that, of course."

"Nothing happened?"

"No." Breanarachelle sighed. "Of course not. Lydiah still has the figure of a wine glass with volume only where it counts. She always gets everything, but this is the end. If Lydiah isn't convicted because you fail to deliver a signed statement of her lesbian uses of you, then your penalty is to become a huge patapouf. That's my price if we agree to delay the proceedings."

Boudi-Ca blinked. She couldn't believe what she was hearing. Meanwhile the burning from the pepper felt like a hundred ants biting her nasal passageway and throat. Sweat was trickling between her breasts. She wanted to get up and leave, but at the same time her legs and limbs were filled with a nectared torpor. "I've heard that devils love patapoufs," she managed. "Is that true?"

Breanarachelle smiled and re-crossed her slender greyish legs. "Yes, but it depends on the taste. I don't enjoy spending my playtime lifting whales, but most devils swear that more flesh is always better, and who cares if a slave can never leave her cage. Rhada and I have two enormous humans that we play with, one of each sex, but a Jinn patapouf is the most lovely. A Jinn patapouf always feels empty and hungers intensely and endlessly for sweets and sex both. She's the most pathetically needy creature in all of Hell."

"If I agree to this deal, what would I need to do?"

"You'll need to eat. If Lydiah squeaks free yet again despite her magnificent failures, then forever more she'll look at her dearest love and see how I ruined you. There is no return from having your stomach stretched by Hell's foodstuffs. There is no going back from your skin swelling three or five times its size, except by painful and scarring surgeries, yet few patapoufs ever quit once they've begun eating. That's the penalty for failing to deliver Lydiah to me."

"That's extreme. I need time to think."

"No. You have three choices. You can be arrested now. You can write a three-page Court statement that Lydiah is a lesbian and submit it to the Court as evidence. Or we will wait, and you will sign a contract that you will eat three pastries from a gourmet bakery each day until you deliver said statement that I require. You'll visit me to eat each morning while Lydiah is working the lesbian purgation. If you skip a day, I don't care, but you'll have to eat the balance on your next visit to make up for the miss."

"How long will I have before I get fat?"

Breanarachelle smirked. "I would imagine with your thin figure only a week will pass before the pastries start showing on your perfect little tits, tummy, and ass. Jinni can't process Hell's delicacies like humans' process food on Earth. You'll feel a little improved energy, but the pastries can't really go anywhere. They melt straight into your flesh."

"Pastries sound disgusting."

"They are pomegranate sugar baked with flour, honey, and many other special ingredients. In antiquity, our Lord wanted his bride Persephone to stay with him forever in the Underworld, so He made her eat pomegranates. Pomegranates became all the rage in the capital. Everyone wanted to pay homage to our royal couple. Orchards were planted by the score in Erebus where the weather is favorable. Chefs began to make pomegranate bread and candies, and Jinni began to swell up. Jinni in particular have a weakness for sweets, especially the Ukraine, and the patapoufs have been a respectable part of Hell's society ever since."

"I think I have another choice. I could leave Mer. I could run away and go to Erebus or something. You have nothing without me."

"Very well. I'll sweeten the deal. Every time you visit me to eat your ration of pastries, I'll tell you more about your past. I can also give you nectar to make your headache go away, if you like. I can get you some nectar without pepper."

"I can't get fat. I'm supposed to join the Flames."

"Once you learn the truth, you might not like Lydiah, and you might not want to join the Flames. Your entire life is a lie, Boudi-Ca. Are you ready to sign the contract?"

"You have to promise to tell me everything about my past."

"It will go into the contract, so I will be bound to tell you everything I know."

Boudi-Ca felt her legs queerly trembling. To her humiliation, she turned, bent over the open side-table drawer, and lifted the sniffer again. She drained another pile with a trembling hand. Pleasure exploded into her other nostril, washing away her pain. Her head went light, and she was floating above the chair and the floor. "Fine. I'll sign, but when I eat the first pastries you have to prove that Lydiah has been lying to me all this time."

"Proof will be difficult, but I promise to do my best. If you'll allow me, I already invited a Hell's Court notary to be present this morning. She's my part-time secretary, and she'll help us. Lacharrah, come in now please!"

Breanarachelle snapped her fingers at the open parlour door, and within seconds heels clicked in the foyer. Lacharrah was a younger-looking she-devil than Breanarachelle, with a pinched waist and a form-fitting mid-thigh skirt that make her look like a walking yellow-grey ant. A wave of ashen devil perfume filled the room. Lacharrah hefted a small stack of official-looking documents in her long-nailed fingers.

"Here we are," Lacharrah purred. "Boudi-Ca, the fledgling of Mistress Lydiah, who is the wife of Archduke Fennel, will write and sign a statement of at least three thousand words condemning Lydiah as a lesbian predator with examples of specific instances of lesbian molestation, or Boudi-Ca will eat at least three sweet pastries each day until she does so. In return, Mistress Breanarachelle, wife of Rhadamanthus, will verbally inform Boudi-Ca all that she knows about Boudi-Ca's past. Are there any last-minute additions?"

"Wait." Boudi-Ca felt her face heating again both with embarrassment and with the bump of painful pepper. "How are the papers already written?

We just now talked about this."

Breanarachelle's lips split into another wicked grin. "My dear child, you can't think Lydiah is cleverer than I am. I already knew how this conversation would go before you even got here, and I'm just getting started. The deal is that Lydiah won't know any of this."

"She won't. If she does, then you have to protect me from her."

"Agreed. Meanwhile, you'll keep eating your pastries until you write a satisfactory statement of lesbian condemnation and submit it to the public record."

"I will when the purgation is over."

"That might be a while. If you choose to never betray Lydiah and eat your pastries every day as your new lifestyle, protecting her from a new life in the Merian prison, that's fine. That will satisfy my desires. For now, I'll buy the pastries for you every day, and you'll eat them in my presence. If any pesky details come up, we can have Lacharrah add an amendment. Everything will be fine. Devil contracts are more common in Mer than most people realize."

Boudi-Ca felt fear flooding her limbs even while her head was swimming into the ceiling. "What happens when Lydiah sees me getting fat? She'll be angry. She might forbid me to leave the house. She might try to lock me away."

"Precisely. She will try to counterattack. This could get exciting." Breanarachelle stroked her knee as if lost in thought. "Provide Boudi-Ca with a pen so she can sign, Lacharrah. After she picks the pastries she wants, I'll have them delivered up here regularly. Lydiah is busy each morning with her Flames operations, correct Boudi-Ca? You can come down the hill and visit me?"

"I think so."

"Good. Pastries are so delicious. You're going to love them. The Ukraine pastries are the best, but Lydiah has far too many friends in the Ukraine Quarter. We'll go with Italian instead. Mistress Giacondah is one of my oldest allies. She's discrete and has excellent puffs, cupcakes, and coffee crêpes. You can pick your own poison, child. I'll see you here dies Lunae at the same time and place, and we'll go get started."

Breanarachelle chortled as she rose and smoothed her silk slip. She strode from the parlour without a backward glance. Lacharrah drew up a chair, seated herself with a polite smile, and arranged the legal papers on the side table.

Chapter 16.

Yellen drove her horse at a canter up Leo Street towards Befanah's home. She was late for a sixth day of ridding Mer of lesbian corruption. The week had gone more smoothly after the first day, when Lydiah had decided to personally attend the daily arrests. The Councilor's presence had proved to be an intimidating asset. The arrests amounted to eight more Named delivered to the mysterious grey door, including two corporals, a fledgling, and a retired Flames trainer with a brazen collection of kitten girls similar to Zinke's.

Yellen turned her horse into Befanah's neighborhood, letting her legs relax in the stirrups. She was sleeping better in her new house. The demoness had proved to be pleasant enough in bed—willing, responsive, and sensitive, although a bit noisy.

She still needed a boy slave, both for appearances and for the art gallery, assuming she decided to push through the complications with the business plan. Kiree was flighty, nectar-addicted, and only spoke demonic. The demoness had potential as a sculpture model, but she wasn't a workable shopgirl or heavy lifter. Kiree had been set to the task of polishing and oiling the slave cages that morning in the pit under the old house.

Yellen guided her horse over the final stretch up Befanah's quiet tree-lined street. She'd been going over the situation with Henne in her head. She really couldn't have hoped for a better reaction to her business proposal, except for the wedding. She'd met again with Henne on dies Martis, and they'd agreed to meet again that afternoon with the carpenter to make more plans for renovation.

Unfortunately, she needed to comply with her Flames obligations before she could meet with Henne. She wanted to get the day's mission over quickly. She hoped the arrests would be short, straightforward, and preferably not negotiated with swords.

When she arrived at Befanah's gate, there were two motorcars at the curb in a line with Lydiah's familiar sleek two-seater. Councilor Lydiah and Mistress Shadow-Under-Moon were waiting on the walk. Lydiah's eye sockets were bruised, and her face wore a gaunt shadow of tired irritation. Her usual perfect black lips looked smudged, and her thin smile was as icy as her diamonds. She held three small black boxes in her black-gloved hands.

"Mistress Befanah informs me that you aren't normally late, lieutenant."

"No—my sincere apologies." Yellen dismounted, led her horse through Befanah's gate, and hitched the loyal animal to the post in front of the house. She avoided Lydiah's eyes and sent a messenger bird to Befanah's steward to come stable her horse.

"So as for our status." Lydiah took a deep breath. "Posters and handbills went up all over the city in the last few days to protest the Smokeless Flames purgation. The handbills were tracked to the east market district. The printer cooperated with Court officials in order to save his own skin, and after an internal investigation, we now have three more Named. We're going for maximum impact today, sending a message that this protest is a disgrace and cannot be tolerated, especially during the sacred Spring Festival." Lydiah patted the coiled whip at her belt. "I'm going to assist again. Today for the first time we're heading into sacred Flames precincts. We're raiding the training building at the monastery during scheduled drills."

Yellen frowned. "Who are the protestors?"

"A small group of blade fledglings apparently made the handbills. Their names are Anna-Ca, Trun-Ca, and Griselda-Ca. Hell's Court has dispensed to us three sets of ebon cuffs and three ebon wands. Each of us will have one set."

Yellen accepted her cuff box. The small black box was heavier than it looked. She could feel the dark devil magic between her fingertips. She shook her head. "With due respect, Councilor, I hope we're not making a mistake arresting these fledglings. I thought we were going after the older lesbian establishment like Zinke—the inner clique."

"Lieutenant Nefra, do you think you won't be able to do your duty to Lord Hades in rooting out the lesbian corruption today? If not, perhaps you'd like to come before the Council and explain why. This isn't a debate, and I'm not in the mood for hesitance. The young lesbians will be arrested, and their interrogation will reveal their older mentors. That's how the devils are working the purgation."

"I meant to just discuss, not question the orders. It's part of making decisions in the field." Yellen turned away. She needed to just shut up and do her duty, but it was difficult.

The motorcars reached the Smokeless Flames monastery on the north side of Mer within thirty minutes. The red flags over the quadrangle buildings had been replaced by purple ribbons for Allyssia's Day, which commemorated the graduation of the First Fledglings, Astaarteh and Ereshkigeh, from Allyssia's tutelage into full mistresshood. Allyssia's Day would begin the Spring Festival—a week of celebrations and contests of combat among the Flames fledglings in training.

Yellen drew the motorcar up to the front of the training building. A Hell's Court cage-carriage already sat at the curb. A team of Hell horses were harnessed to a sturdy wagon that sported a massive silver cage mounted behind the drivers' seat. The cage was large enough to accommodate at least half a dozen prisoners. Yellen shut down the motorcar and dismounted with Shadow. Lydiah joined them to stride up the walkway to the Flames training gymnasium, where a pair of hooded figures in black waited outside the entrance. Their mottled grey faces revealed their identities as devils—inquisitors of Hell's Court. The devils held gaffs and nets that bristled with cruel hooks.

Lydiah bowed shortly in greeting. "Nefra, this is Master Nargchuk and Master Glumstak. They'll be helping and observing this morning. They'll watch the building exits with their nets, and they'll be ready to snag the fledglings if they try to flee."

Master Glumstak saluted with a grim smile, and Yellen returned the salute. She followed Lydiah and Shadow through the door into the monastery gymnasium. Nearly thirty fledglings worked at swordplay and gymnastics inside the high hall. She recognized only two of the fledglings. The fledgling Minnie-Ca, an old friend of Henne's, was practicing hateful kin-hexes with the perky blonde who worked the log books at the Flames Nanka landing. Minnie directed a hateful kin-hex at the blonde, who rocked backwards, then recovered to throw one of her own. Lydiah signaled at the robed training instructor and drew her fingers across her throat. The instructor nodded.

"Stop sparring and line up," the mistress called, raising her hand for attention. "Form ranks at the north end of the main training mat, fledglings. One-two, on the double."

The fledglings around the hall dropped their practice blades, rose from their floor exercises, and hopped off of balance beams. Minnie and the blonde aspirant hurried across the room with the others to rank up in a double line. Three fledglings, however, were not lining up with the others.

"There they are, Yellen," Lydiah barked. "Get them." Yellen surged into a reluctant sprint across the gymnasium. Shadow loped gamely right behind her. The three renegade fledglings darted through the inner doors.

"I'll try to hold their tracks in the tapestry," Shadow said. "The weave is chaotic in this place, though. Threads are everywhere. I think they're splitting up."

"Just do your best," Yellen said. Tension gripped her core. It was absolutely horrible to arrest fledglings in the training compound. In fact, she secretly hoped the fledglings could hide from Shadow or otherwise escape. Shadow moved like a cat into the inner hall, however, and then turned left towards the dormitory complexes. The hallways were empty except for the distant patters of feet and a slamming door.

Yellen eyed the printed notices on the hall bulletin board. She scanned the old archway into the armory. The layout of the place was still familiar to her. She hadn't been in the training complex for many years, not since Befanah had identified her potential and fast-tracked her into a rising star in the Smokeless Flames. The place brought back a lot of old, emotional memories.

Shadow took the lead through an archway into the warm humid air of the dormitory baths. The tracker swept her braid over her shoulder and stalked along the marble edge of the largest bathing pool. Shadow veered and quickened her pace into the dressing rooms. Yellen matched Shadow's urgency. At the end of the first marble-tiled dressing room, one of the Named—a young, muscular fledgling with short bobbed hair—had pried open an old round window to the building roof. Her legs wriggled as she climbed through.

Shadow threw a strong desirous kin-hex that made the fledgling grunt with her upward motion arrested. The tracker bounded across the room and grasped an ankle. Shadow leaned back. The fledgling kicked ferociously, but she couldn't wrench free from Shadow's grip. Yellen reluctantly grabbed the fledgling's other ankle and helped Shadow disengage the fledgling from the window opening. Shadow slipped her grip upwards and locked the fledgling's arm.

"No!" The fledgling shouted, even as her voice broke into a sob. "Please no! Please don't take me! Just pretend I got away! In the name of Lady Allyssia, have mercy! Please no!"

Yellen sighed. "We're just taking you in for questioning."

"That's a lie!" the fledgling whimpered. "Everyone knows the Named aren't coming back! I'm going to die! They're going to execute me!"

"No one knows that. If you'd been discrete and hadn't participated in the handbill protest, you wouldn't have been a Named in the first place. These are ebon cuffs we're putting on you, so I wouldn't recommend protesting anymore."

"No! Please!"

Yellen helped Shadow wrestle the fledgling down. The fledgling fought like a wild cat. Yellen pinned the fledgling on the dirty marble floor so Shadow could cuff first one wrist, then the other. The fledgling finally fell limp and defeated. She was crying openly with tears streaming down her cheeks.

"By the balls of Cerberus," Yellen muttered.

"I still have the track of the next one," Shadow said. "I think she's in the dormitories. Let's go. Bring that one, Nefra."

Yellen lifted the Named up and escorted her back out of the dressing room and the baths, following Shadow. The baths gave onto a curved rising hall that led to the fledgling dormitories that crowned the training complex. Yellen followed Shadow up a set of wide stone stairs that had been worn down by the feet of countless monastery residents over the centuries. A few magical messenger birds winged back and forth, channeled by the wide bird slit over the closed doors at the top of the stairway.

Shadow led the way through the doors into the dorm common area, which was a high room with a domed ceiling and cracked old oil paintings. The paintings rendered homages to Lord Hades and Allyssia. Old rugs and divans were arranged around a great hearth. The near-extinguished coals of a morning fire shed extra warmth. The room smelled of tobacco smoke, perhaps laced with a bit of nectar, both of which were forbidden substances in the monastery.

Shadow led the way onward through a connecting hall into the sprawl of the slave-taking areas—those darker, low-ceilinged feeding rooms with wide columns and high-backed divans to offer privacy for the young Jinni. A nude rosy-cocked male slave scurried barefoot out through a nearby archway.

Shadow raised her hand as if to wait. Yellen took the Named to the side and pressed her down onto a sex-stained divan. Yellen patted the Ebon Wand in her pocket and gave the fledgling a warning look. The expansive L-shaped feeding room was gloomy and spawned countless dark niches in which to fuck a slave boy in private. It was a perfect place for hiding. Yellen felt her skin prick. Her senses were on edge. Something wasn't right.

She advanced after Shadow, who had almost moved from her sight. Shadow was a sitting duck in the middle of the room. Shadow, as if sensing the same thing, eased her blade from its sheath. The tracker turned in place.

"Yellen! Behind you!"

Yellen drew her blade and whirled to see silhouettes in the low wash of light coming from the doorway. A surprise desirous kin-hex caught her knees and threw her off-balance. She rolled to the shelter of a column and kipped to her feet in time to raise her sword to parry a vicious blow. Two Smokeless-Flame Sisters in hooded assassin garb assailed her. Out of the corner of her eye, she saw Shadow engage the Named fledgling they'd been chasing, who had emerged from the shadows to attack with a blade. The fledgling's angry face was a mask of hate.

Yellen slipped aside, avoiding the dart the first assassin threw, and then countered the hateful kin-hex of the second one with a counter-kin-hex of her own. The first assassin flourished a blade. Yellen countered the flurry and spun to avoid being trapped against the wall. The assassin attacked again, coming in low in an Exquisite Form style. The assassin was a highly skilled blade mistress—no mere fledgling student.

"Stop," Yellen said. "It doesn't have to be like this." The mistress didn't answer. Her thin mouth was grim and determined under her cowl. She attacked again with a higher tactical line. Yellen countered by the book, matching thrust for thrust. The room suddenly brightened and a wave of heat blasted through the feeding room.

"Help!" Shadow screamed. Yellen glimpsed fire out of the corner of her eye. Shadow's robe was on fire. The smell of burning skin and hair filled the air. The second assassin had flanked Shadow and launched a sorcerous attack. Yellen felt sweat bead on her forehead from the sudden magical heat. She launched a fierce counterattack against the first assassin, and then sprinted to assist Shadow, who was back-pedaling. The cowled sorceress sent another bolt of fire that scorched into the tracker, and then drew a narcabyss whip.

Yellen squinted her eyes against the flames and defended, even as she glimpsed Shadow reeling, trying to extinguish the flames that were consuming her. The first assassin was pursuing with fast harassing blows. Yellen blocked them all and launched a dervish stance, a wild, reckless attack that was entirely inadvisable for the close quarters, but she was a master. She took both assassins by surprise. She scored a deep cut on the arm of the whip-wielding magic mistress. The assassin dropped the whip and cried out.

Yellen followed with a kick and a hateful kin-hex that sent the mistress reeling. She spun away from a kin-hex launched by the Named fledging in time to see Shadow speared by the first assassin's sword. Yellen felt her stomach lurch. She'd made a small mistake. She had switched targets, but so had the first assassin. Shadow slumped rigidly to the floor with her mouth open. The flames were out, but her brown hand was covered in blood.

Yellen countered another weak attack from the Named and entered the dervish stance again. She was alone against three. The second assassin had recovered. The first assassin side-stepped quickly to block the door. The assassin's mouth arched a grin of victory. Yellen countered the Named fledgling again and counter-spelled another hateful kin-hex. She issued block after block, scoring hits on repartees but never a finishing blow.

The magic mistress hurled a gout of flame. Yellen edged to the side. The incendiary ball seared the skin of her arm and set fire to one of the divans. Smoke billowed through the room. Yellen jerked away from sudden movement in the corner of her eye, but it was only a messenger bird that flitted to land on her shoulder and speak in Lydiah's voice.

Master Nargchuk caught Trun-Ca trying to leave by the back exit. How are you and Shadow progressing, Yellen?

Yellen counter-attacked hard against the Named fledgling, who was the weakest point of the ring of attackers that had formed around her. She followed with a swift lunge that pierced the fledgling's shoulder and sent her reeling back in agony. The sorceress had retrieved her narcabyss whip and summoned a spell. A cloud of concealing, choking smoke rose.

Yellen held her breath against the noxious vapor. In the second of distraction, the whip flew through space. She felt intense numbness bloom in her hip and down her leg. At the same time, however, the smoke had slowed the first assassin, buying time. She quickly summoned a bird and sent it to Lydiah.

Under attack. Need assistance in the dormitory.

The assassins glimpsed the bird winging out and redoubled their efforts. The whip flew once more, sending eddies through the smoke. Yellen growled. This time she was ready. She knocked the whip to the side and swept around her block to take a finishing attack to the blade mistress.

The numbness from the whip was spreading in her leg, however, impairing her movement, even as the magic mistress launched another bolt of fire. Yellen twisted and took it off her shoulder. She smelled her hair burning. She countered the blade mistress again with desperation, and this time scored a direct hit. The assassin cried out in agony, reeled back, and tossed a handful of caltrops. The little spiked balls skittered across the floor. Yellen danced away from them gamely, and almost fell to her knees.

Shadows crossed the opening of the great room. Had Lydiah come so quickly? No. The interlopers were Minnie-Ca and the blonde fledgling from the Nanka platform. Yellen saw the whip coming again and twirled her sword, slicing it in half in midair. Her assailant looked shocked at the incredible, desperate backhanded flick. Fledgling Minnie-Ca charged into the room from the doorway and sneak-kicked the blade mistress, sending her flying forward.

Yellen pommeled the assassin in the forehead—a blinding blow with the blunt end of her sword. The red-robed mistress went down in a heap. Minnie turned to face the whip-wielding mistress.

"Be careful, Minnie-Ca!" Yellen warned.

The sorceress threw more smoke. Minnie jumped to the side along with the blonde fledgling, and the sorceress sprinted away into the great room. Yellen grimaced. She couldn't give chase with her half-numbed leg, and she wasn't about to order Minnie-Ca and her friend into danger. The blonde fledgling from the landing platform scurried forward to the fallen Named, who moaned on the floor with her hand grabbing her bloody shoulder.

The assassin blade mistress also lay on the floor, clutching her face and moaning. Blood ran from between her fingers. Shadow lay on her back on the floor along with the two other fallen, as quiet in her suffering as she was in her tracking. Shadow lay deathly still and breathed in soft wheezes. The blonde fledgling looked up angrily from where she crouched.

"Anna-Ca needs to be healed, not arrested!"

Yellen pursed her lips. "She'll live. It wasn't smart of her to attack us, or to participate in this little cabal, was it? What's your name?"

The blonde fledgling frowned. "Why do you want to know?"

"Well, whoever you are, you should leave immediately. You should go too, Minnie-Ca. Scratch that. Too late."

Running footsteps sounded in the common room. Councilor Lydiah and the Court devil named Glumstak appeared in the low lamplight. Lydiah gazed down at the three wounded Jinni on the floor. Her powdered face was pinched with fury and concern. She worried her diamond earring between her fingertips.

"Yellen, what happened here?"

"We were attacked by assassins. I don't know how they knew we were coming, but it looked like a trap. One of the assassins is right here. The other escaped while my leg was numbed. The Named that Shadow was tracking is on the floor over there. She aided the assassins with the ambush. Shadow took a sword. She needs medical attention."

Lydiah glanced at Shadow and the blonde fledgling, who had moved to examine Shadow's wound. "And who are these other two fledglings, Yellen?"

"They happened to be in the dorms and assisted with the capture. They defended me from the assassins and should both be commended. This is fledgling Minnie-Ca and—"

The blonde fledgling crossed her arms warily. "Yilka-Ca."

Lydiah shook her head and looked down at the fallen assassin, whose hood had come free from her blood-smeared face. "The lesbian corruption runs deep. I'm disappointed in you, Mistress Na'armeh. You're Anna-Ca's mistress, yes? You're willing to go to prison for her? You're willing to murder these deputies of the Court? What a waste. So they tried to kill you Yellen? They weren't just helping the Named escape?"

"They had ample opportunity to finish off Shadow once she was helpless, if that had been their purpose, but they didn't. I think they wanted to send a message, and we were better than they were expecting, with a little help."

"This message cannot be tolerated any more than the lesbian propaganda," grated Master Glumstak. "Clearly the Smokeless Flames has serious internal issues, Councilor Lydiah. I'm beginning to wonder if you're capable of carrying out this inquiry internally. The involvement of these other fledglings is suspicious. They will come with the rest for questioning."

"No!" Yilka-Ca blurted; her face contorted with horror. "We just heard the noise and we were curious—"

"Allyssia's Flames has always policed its own, Master Glumstak," Lydiah said tersely. "These fledglings are not Named, so they are not be going anywhere. Mistress Na'armeh has clearly committed a grave breach of conduct by attacking Nefra, so I agree that you should take her, but we need her for internal questioning first. Leave her to me."

"Hell's Court will give the orders here, Councilor Lydiah," countered Glumstak. "I will take Na'armeh personally along with the fledglings. I'll send you the next names when we have the results of the torture."

The devil knelt and snapped an ebon cuff onto the wrist of Na'armeh, who struggled, but Glumstak was quick to wave his ebon wand in his other hand. Na'armeh writhed and groaned with pain. The devil rolled the mistress over and clipped the other ebon cuff to her twitching wrist.

"Nefra," Lydiah said. "Cuff Anna-Ca and get her up."

Yellen brushed past the blonde fledgling named Yilka-Ca, who gave her a look of simultaneous hate and gratitude. She cuffed the Named. Yellen beckoned to the other Named, who still sat motionless on the divan, shaking and afraid. The fledgling rose to her feet with her head bowed.

"Excellent," Lydiah said. "This is Griselda-Ca, and Trun-Ca was caught outside, so we have all three Named. Lieutenant Nefra, take these suspected young lesbians in your motorcar to their destination. I'll send a bird to Mistress Yehudit at the Flames infirmary. We'll take care of Shadow."

"I can't take these two on my own. Without Shadow, I have no way of watching over them while I drive. I'd need a cage-carriage like Hell's Court."

Lydiah sighed. "Master Glumstak, Lieutenant Nefra seems rattled by her combat. Could you and Master Nargchuk deliver the fledgling Named for us? You have the cage-carriage. You can fit all four of your ladies into it."

"Very well." Glumstak said. "That's what it's there for."

Yellen nodded. "Thank you, Master Glumstak. Councilor Lydiah, if you don't need me further, may I leave?"

"No," Lydiah answered. "Stay here, Yellen. I want you to come back with me to the Flames council chambers. The Council will want a full first-hand report of this incident. We need to investigate Na'armeh's associates to see whether she was directed by higher-level lesbians. Obviously they are a step ahead of us. Master Glumstak will interrogate Na'armeh while we work everything on our end."

"How long will this take? I had personal plans this afternoon."

"Cancel your plans. Help the devils load the Named into their cage. When the healers get here for Shadow, we can leave for the council building."

Yellen guided Anna-Ca and Griselda-Ca out of the dormitories. She nodded silent thanks to Minnie-Ca, who bit her lip, saluted, and lowered her eyes shyly. Yellen suppressed a smile. She hoped Lydiah hadn't seen that exchange of glances between her and an admiring young blade fledgling. As a former resident of Allyssia's city, Minnie-Ca perhaps knew certain secrets just like Lydiah, or perhaps Minnie-Ca was merely respectful of a Flames blade legend.

She realized that Lydiah was right. She was rattled. She was a huntress and a killer, but it hurt her to hunt her own kind. Still, she couldn't see a reasonable way out of it, unless she was taken down like Shadow. In that moment, she almost wished the assassins had broken a few of her bones. Her emotional pain was almost worse than a physical wound.

Yellen descended the stairs and walked out of the gymnasium complex behind Glumstak, who unceremoniously dragged Na'armeh with him like a doll. Outside, Master Nargchuk stood alongside the cage-carriage. Trun-Ca curled on the cage floor. Yellen helped the devils load Na'armeh and the two other Named fledglings into the silver cage as well, which was large enough to accommodate all four cuffed Jinn prisoners.

A group of fledglings and trainers had gathered outside the gymnasium to watch the proceedings. Most of the Sisters seemed pleased about the arrests, but some faces betrayed thinly-veiled outrage.

Yellen straightened and addressed the nearest instructor. "Get these aspirants back inside, sergeant. There's nothing to see here."

"I agree, lieutenant," the red-robed mistress said. Yellen turned away from the dispersing crowd and summoned a silent messenger bird in brazen plain view of the devils.

I'm not going to be able to make it to the gallery this afternoon, Henne. I'm delayed, but I'd like to see you later. Would you join me at my place for some three-way love-taking? I have a lovely red-headed demoness. She reminds me of you, which is why I got her.

Yellen sent the bird and stalked back into the gymnasium. The fledglings were back to their practice, but all of them watched her as she walked through. She left the gymnasium and paused in the inner hallway, lingering to let the memories from her fledglinghood sink in. She herself had passed wild rebellious nights in the confines of the training facilities.

She diverted her course back into the humidity of the baths. Three bathing pools occupied a space almost the size of the gymnasium. Two fledglings had gone to bathe.

Yellen lurked in the doorway, watching them. One fledgling was swimming nude in the larger pool, butterflying with long strokes. Her bare ass surfaced with each strong, sensual, undulating movement. The other fledgling soaked near the wall of one of the smaller heated pools. Her dark hair was undone and lying over the worn azure edging tiles.

Yellen gazed on those beautiful youths. She'd had her first lesbian experiences with an older instructor right there in those baths. She remembered Mistress Simhonit's foot caressing her thigh under the water. Simhonit's sultry brown eyes had seduced her with promises of forbidden pleasure.

Yellen turned away from the pool. She hadn't seen Sim in years. Was

Sim still an instructor for the Flames and potentially in danger from the investigation? Surely Sim knew what was happening and didn't need to be warned. Yellen flinched. Henne's catbird landed on her shoulder, surprising her.

I'm already at your place, darling! I let myself in. We need to get this door fixed. Your furry new friend is friendly, although I don't know what she's saying. I can't see you tonight. I'm going to a few parties.

Yellen felt a rush of jealousy—a thick syrup of envy and rejection poured over the layers of disappointment. She knew Henne, and she knew that Henne could be as sensitive and chary as a fallen leaf, blowing from one course to the next on the tide of her artist sensibilities. She needed to get a grip. Henne went to lots of parties and had lots of relations with lots of people. She summoned another bird.

Let's go slave-shopping together. I have the name and address of a dealer named Hillel Yaffe. I'm going to stop by and meet him this afternoon to see what he can do. I love you, Henne. I really want this to work. I want you to have the best.

Yellen climbed the stairs back to the training-complex dormitories, turning over in her head what Henne had said. Shadow still lay on the floor in the slave-taking room. Mistress Yehudit had arrived with a bag of herbs, an assistant, and a stretcher from the infirmary. Lydiah signaled.

"Yellen! Let's go."

"How is Shadow?"

"She'll be fine, but she'll need to recuperate. Thank Allyssia it takes more than a stabbing to send a solid Jinn to the void. I've decided that with Shadow out of commission, you're going to need to step up and become my new assistant. You'll come to the Flames council chambers each morning instead of Shadow to get the motorcar. I'll find you another tracker. Do you think you can handle that?"

Yellen nodded. She could handle it, but she didn't want to. "Of course, Councilor. I'm honored."

"Good. We have a lot of work to do. The lesbians are tipping their hand with their actions. I have a feeling that with the Hell's Court interrogations of the sympathizers we arrested today, the number of Named will rise exponentially."

"I'm not good with math."

Lydiah led the way back down the stairs and through the gymnasium. The cage-carriage holding the Named had already left for downtown. Yellen climbed into her motorcar and fired the engine. She threw it into gear and loosed the clutch to keep pace with Lydiah, who was already driving off with the other motorcar.

The Smokeless Flames council building was only a few blocks away on the north side. It was a squat building constructed of the same black basalt as many buildings in Mer. Yellen pulled the car up behind Lydiah and climbed down. Lydiah barked orders to the lazy slave boys who loitered at the curb. The boys jumped into motion and climbed into the cars. They directed them towards the nearby stables, which had apparently been converted in recent years to accommodate cars as well as carriages.

Yellen joined Lydiah, who wore a small smile on her black-painted lips. Lydiah reached with a leather thong and gathered her windswept platinum blonde hair into a ponytail. "Have you been into the Council building before, Yellen?"

"Only on the occasions of my rank promotions, Councilor, and when Befanah adopted me as her fledgling so she could train me personally."

"Ah yes. You were quite the prodigy back in the day. Are you still a prodigy, Lieutenant? Do you still have the fire to succeed for the Flames and Lady Allyssia like I do?"

"I'd like to think so, Councilor. My nickname used to be The Tiger. I'm always ready for a fight."

Lydiah's silver-grey eyes turned to cold, hard steel. "As you know, I was officially demoted a few years ago from ambassador status. This is my first high-profile undertaking since my former failures. I cannot fail again. I will succeed in purging the lesbians from the Flames. Are you with me, Nefra? Can I count on you?"

"I will do my duty."

"Good. I'd like to get to know you better, Lieutenant. I'd also like you to start giving my fledgling blade lessons. Dimona says she can't teach Boudi-Ca anything else, which is ridiculous. Perhaps you can do better. Afterwards, perhaps we can relax and talk together. Tomorrow afternoon?"

Yellen met Lydiah's eyes. The Councilor was staring at her intently—glaring at her like one deadly predator facing down another. Lydiah turned her diamond ring slowly on her finger. Yellen felt her skin prick just as it had in Befanah's parlour.

"I'm busy tomorrow. I was planning to purchase a new slave."

"Oh, yes. For your new home. We can meet the day after that, perhaps? Come. Let's go inside. We can arrange a time. Do you know my home in Tanjie on the south side? I'll make sure Fennel is away." Lydiah winked over her shoulder as she turned and headed down the sidewalk. "My husband makes my guests nervous sometimes."

Yellen followed Lydiah down the walk into the council building. The social visit sounded more like an order than a thing between friends. She wasn't Lydiah's friend. A social visit with Lydiah would likely involve a lot questions, and answers would potentially involve lies. How did Lydiah already know that she had a new home?

Yellen felt nervousness creep through her bones as Lydiah continued through the council reception room and into the close office hallways. Lydiah was a legendary beauty mistress and a genius negotiator. Any frank social discussion with Lydiah about life, lesbianism, and sexual desires would be as pitfall-ridden as a vampire nest in the dead of night.

Things were getting serious quickly, even as the arrests were beginning to revolt her even more. Her raise in position to Lydiah's assistant was unwelcome, but perhaps she could turn it into something good. Were the lesbians really organized? Were they trying to assassinate her? If so, then they would keep trying and possibly succeed.

She was beginning to feel isolated, stuck between a rock and a hard place—between the lesbians and Lydiah. Did she dare play both sides? With Lydiah breathing down her neck, her choice of allegiances was a matter of survival. Perhaps she needed to see her old lover Sim. Perhaps Sim could help her negotiate with the lesbian cliques.

It would be bold to seek out Sim, but she instinctively felt the need to hedge her bets. Playing the game too passively could be a fatal mistake. She followed on Lydiah's heels into a cozy wood-paneled office with two chairs. She sat quickly and spoke first.

"Councilor Lydiah, this week won't work for a social visit. I'm very busy with my new home. I need furnishings. I need to repair the door. It's hardly habitable. So much is going on. Can we postpone a social visit until next week or even next month?"

Lydiah sat at the desk, which was laden with papers and file folders. When she spoke, her tone was low and pensive. "I need you to tutor my fledgling. She's lonely, and she needs counseling. We're trying to wean her of nectar so she can start with the autumn novitiate class as Allyssia and Astaarteh wish. I'll cancel Boudi's lesson with Mistress Dimona for dies Martis, and I'll see you at the nine. Plan on an hour or so, or however long Boudi-Ca lasts. I'd like to make the training a weekly thing."

"What about the morning purgation mission?"

"Let's mix it up a bit and keep the lesbians on their toes, Lieutenant. We'll go in the afternoon on dies Martis, and you'll come to my home in the morning. I'll tell Befanah and Hell's Court that we're meeting for a procedural review. Thank you, Lieutenant."

"It will be my pleasure."

"To repay you, I can help with your new home." Lydiah leaned back in her chair with her eyes hooded. "Fennel and I have some old furniture that I wouldn't mind getting rid of. Perhaps you can see when you visit."

"I'm sure it's elegant."

"And after the attack today, I'd be remiss if I didn't assign you some real protection at your new residence. I don't want to lose you like Shadow."

"That won't be necessary. I don't want to draw attention to myself in my new neighborhood. I'm trying to start a gallery business. I can't have my clients and artists being stopped by armed guards. I can handle my own security." Yellen forced a confident smile. She'd hardly spoken with Lydiah for thirty seconds, and she'd already resorted to a half-lie. She didn't like the security of her old house at all, but she couldn't allow herself to be placed under any surveillance. She'd chosen the run-down home to avoid scrutiny in the first place.

"I'm going to insist on this one," Lydiah said. "Now that you're my personal assistant, you're a key asset to the investigation. You've heard of a sacra vipera, right? I'll have Mistress Karmallah perform the ritual to place a vipera in your house later today. You'll have your protection. The serpent won't bite your customers unless those people wish you ill."

"I've heard those things are deadly poisonous."

"You took the Smokeless Flames venom trainings didn't you? You survived the serpent trials? You faced the serpent king and earned your poison immunities as a Sister?"

"Of course, but what about my customers, visitors, and slaves?"

"As long as they don't assault you, steal from you, or spy on you without your knowledge, the vipera will not send them to the void. We can remove the spell once this is over if you wish. Let's focus on the report."

Lydiah rolled up her sleeves and prepared a blank parchment and a pen. Yellen took a deep breath and settled deeper in the chair. She didn't know whether to feel honored or threatened. The sacra vipera was a powerful protective spell bestowed upon the highest officers of the Smokeless Flames.

She would feel safer with the summoned serpentine servant guarding her house, but the invisible protective anacondas were loyal to Allyssia and the Flames as much as their homeowner. Worse yet, they had two magical eyes like any snake, eyes that could see things. Lydiah gazed at her darkly from across the desk.

"Go ahead, Lieutenant. Please describe in detail what happened after you left the gymnasium. I'll write things down and go from there. Don't worry about the vipera. I have one in my summer house. It won't look twice at your private activities. In fact, it will eat any mice. Now, recount the events of the arrests when you're ready."

Yellen stared into Lydiah's cold silvery orbs. What had Lydiah meant by private activities? Were the words a threat, or were they something else? Yellen felt her heart congeal in her chest, even as the close air in Lydiah's office thickened around her. She'd already suspected that Lydiah knew that she was a lesbian, and in that moment warning bells were going off. Meanwhile, the lesbian powers in Mer were apparently trying to assassinate her.

She needed to see Simhonit. She needed to communicate with the inner cliques of the Flames lesbians. She needed to choose sides, and the further she went under Lydiah's zealous thumb, the more in trouble she was. If she did nothing but serve as Lydiah's bitch, things couldn't possibly end well.

Chapter 17.

Golda stripped her clothes and changed to cat form. She stalked from her tent and into the forest. She headed in the direction of Gorka's tent. The common auction on that afternoon of dies Saturni had gone smoothly despite the turbulent weather over Mer. Most of the Reik goods had sold for handsome sums, but the proceeds only amounted to two hundred and five aurei. The sum was a small fortune, but it wasn't close to what Hell's Court demanded for Pinhas' soul.

The Reik son had returned empty-handed from his first meeting with the Akhen family, but Lotifia Akhen had been waiting in the camp when they had returned from Mer, an event that had re-animated Gorka with a modicum of hope. Golda bristled her cat whiskers as she closed the distance to eavesdrop on Gorka's tent. She padded close to the tent wall and pricked her furred ears to overhear the conversation inside.

"Your father made mistakes, Gorka," Lotifia said. "He was too overt in his dealings with the vampire clans and the rebel Jinni who follow Lady Allyssia. He flaunted too much the hard-bought freedoms of our people. Lord Hades is punishing him."

"I can only guess why my father was taken," Gorka said. "But mother can be saved from the Great Blue Hole if I can get three hundred and fifty aurei.

I need a hundred and fifty more."

"It pains me, Gorka," Lotifia said in a barely audible voice. "Truly it does. We just can't. All Gypsy families must abide by the code. If a family borrows and fails in their business, they must pay their own debts. My mother and I can't ignore this. The Avvoca Ordine has helped our people for ages, especially through hard times like these."

"Lord Hades is changing the laws on us and ignoring our old covenants. It isn't right. It isn't fair. We didn't fail in business. Hell's Court and the insurance companies conspired to ruin us."

"The gods have rights to their interpretations. Any organized Gypsy resistance against the will of Lord Hades would be viewed poorly by the Hell's Court. Lord Hades needed to punish our people to make an example of what happens to those who trade with the rebels in His kingdom. We would do well to accept this."

"My father is nothing but a sacrificial bull then, and my mother a lamb. They are elders of a venerable family. This cannot stand."

"I'm sorry, Gorka." Lotifia hesitated. "You're a good man. Your father is a great man, and your mamma is a dear friend of mine, but—"

"If you won't help, there is no more reason for you to be here. I imagine you have better things to do, Lotifia, so just be on your way."

"Do you really want me to leave?"

Golda settled her belly on the ground, the better to silence her heart. The tent was silent inside. She listened for telltale sounds of kissing or fucking, but she heard nothing for a long minute, then two. She willed Gorka to seduce the Akhen princess, but Gorka didn't sound out of breath when he spoke again.

"So how is your promised, Lotifia? Does he know you're here?"

"I suppose my younger brother Treno might have told him where I was going. Treno and Rodrigo have become something of friends. I think they're about the same age soul-wise."

"Well, I hope Rodrigo isn't too upset that you're with me."

Lotifia spoke after a pause. "Should he be?"

"I don't know. We have a history, don't we?"

"I still like you, Gorka, if that's what you're asking, but I didn't come tonight to discuss what happened between us. I'm here because I care. You were very distraught earlier when you came to visit us."

"You care about me, but not my family then."

"You're handsome. Interesting. Intelligent." Lotifia hesitated. "You're usually self-confident. Sometimes you're just unfathomable, almost in the way of a woman more than a man. What do you want? Should I write another poem for you? I will if it will make you any happier."

"It would make me happy to get my mother free from an eternity of toiling on a chain in the Great Blue Hole. I'm sorry, Lotifia. My entire life is turned upside down, and there is nothing I can do about it."

"I wish I could help."

"You could marry me instead of marrying Rodrigo. Then we could be the same family, and the Avvoca Ordine wouldn't keep your mother Tahany from helping my parents."

"I had a feeling—"

Golda focused her ears, but a wind sprang up through the forest then, and the susurrus of the dead leaves washed away the lowered voices inside the tent. For long minutes she listened until Lotifia's voice came louder and clearer.

"No. I can't do this. You're playing me. That's what this is about. There is nothing to explain, Gorka. You're seducing me for my family's money. You disappoint me."

"No, Lotifia—"

"You almost had me fooled."

Lotifia emerged from the tent with her gun in hand, mounted her horse, and rode off into the forest night. Gorka emerged after her. Golda crept after Gorka, who wended his way alone through the dark and windy forest to Mohilever's grove. A small fire burned near Mohilever's wagon, shedding flickering light wide across the gnarled trunks of the blackened trees.

A haphazard pile of wood sat near the fire. Mohilever had gleaned the firewood left over from the hasty departures of the others. The old man sat on a wooden chair near the fire's light, carving on a block. He dropped the block and grabbed his long gun from where it sat next to him.

"Gorka?" Mohilever squinted. "You shouldn't be sneakin' up on an old man. Thought you might be a devil."

"No Mohilever, I'm no devil. I wish I could be an Mimo."

Golda melted into the darkness outside the firelight, close enough to overhear. She mourned for the fate of Priebus, but she felt relieved that the effort to save the Feigns was almost over. The men would leave the forest, and she would have decisions to make. Her living situation was far less safe without the Gypsies, and she was no closer to saving Boudi.

"Come to pay me a visit then, lad?" Mohilever continued. "Making any progress in your quest to free your parents?"

"Yes."

"Let me guess. You serviced the lusty Lotifia Akhen, and she gave you a big pile of aurei for your brilliant man-whoring."

Gorka leaned close, and when he spoke again his voice was low, barely audible. "No. This has to do with Golda, but you must swear not to breathe a word of it. Agreed?"

"Of course," Mohilever answered. "You have my solemn oath—"

Golda crept still closer and pricked her ears. Her senses were suddenly on high alert. She poured her energy into hiding herself in the tapestry, making herself invisible on the edge of the firelight. She could barely hear the men.

"—mother confided some time ago that Golda is actually wanted by Hell's Court," Gorka whispered. "She's a rebel Jinn, of course, but she has an old slave brand on her lower back. She's a former slave."

Mohilever shrugged. "Aye. I know the whore's secrets."

"You know? Well, she might have a bounty or two on her head, placed by Hell's Court. Golda could be worth some aurei—aurei that could help with the rest of my mother's bribe."

Golda clenched her claws into the dirt. She couldn't believe what she was hearing, after all she'd done to help Gorka. Mohilever looked in the direction of her tent, where a glow of dim lamp light was visible through the trees.

"Easy, boy. You're talkin' dangerous things. Aye, your father told me about Golda some time ago when he was floatin' on nectar. When I went to the Court, I checked into it." The old man winked and grinned. "Great minds think alike, eh lad?"

"What did the Court say? How much is her bounty?"

"Golda is wanted for a long list of crimes, or so the Court clerk said, but there's no bounty any more. She had an official bounty of a hundred aurei put on her head just a week ago by Hell's Court, but then it was removed a day later."

Gorka's brow furrowed. "That's curious."

"Aye. That's what the clerk said too. She told me there's a base finder's fee always paid on top of what's posted for an escaped slave, but it's only ten aurei coins, lad."

"Something then, but not enough."

"Discourages people from bilking the Court, methinks. They could let their own slaves escape, just to let a friend catch them. It's a nice heap of coins for a Gypsy, but not much for the rich Disians."

"Could Golda be re-sold?"

Mohilever tilted his head. "That'd be illegal in the eyes of the Hell's Court, but rest assured that re-sales are done. Papers are forged. Brands are altered or burned off with acid. Collars are switched and such. I'm sure there be people out there who deal with such things, but I don't know them, lad."

"Nor do I."

"You dislike Golda that much? You'd see that lass snatched up by the devils after everything she's done to help you?"

Gorka sighed. "I'm not sure she's more of a help than a curse. I saw some male slaves in the Merian street, and I was thinking if I had a few slaves, I could sell them. A few good souls might be worth more than my parents' old horses."

"They'd be worth a heap more, yes." Mohilever's wattles jiggled as he nodded his head. "The wealthier Djinnus and Jinni take their slaves very seriously. Collect them, they do."

"How so?"

"Some of 'em collect fallen Mimos from Heaven. Some collect a-certain human ethnicity, like Asians or younger, prettier types." Mohilever lingered on the last words. "I'd reckon a fine lad like you would go for a nice penny to some lusty Jinn."

"Me? I don't know whether to be insulted or flattered, Mohilever."

Mohilever gave a grin that looked ogrish in the low firelight. "Aye, maybe you should sell yourself. You could cover the difference of coin and save your mother."

"That's the most repulsive idea I've ever heard."

"Well, I don't really know how much you'd fetch, but you're a pretty lad. Just a fancy I've had. It's the red nectar, you know. It goes to yer head."

"I'm done with you. Good night, uncle."

Mohilever cleared his throat. "I'll likely be harnessing up the horses to ride out in the morning, Gorka. I know I said you could ride with me, but Golda and I talked earlier, and it looks like I'll be taking her instead. You're welcome to ride along behind, but I've no room fer your belongings. You're on your own unless Trumpeldor will help."

"I'm going to go see Golda."

Gorka turned, and Golda backed away quickly, hiding the sounds of her paws in the whisper of the wind. She scampered through the forest, re-entered her tent, and retook her female form. She brushed the forest loam from her fingers and threw herself on her bed. She heard Gorka's footsteps. She pretended to be asleep. Through squinted eyes, she watched Gorka poke his head through the tent flap. He stopped short and ogled her body in the low lamplight, surprised by her state of undress.

"Come in, Gorka." Golda rubbed her eyes.

"Were you asleep?"

"Just a bit. Let me rinse." Golda crawled to her water basin, conscious of Gorka's eyes on her as he entered. She wetted her face with the stale water in her pot while she tried to control the simmering anger in her bones. She wasn't sure yet of Gorka's intentions in her tent. Why had he come to her? Was he off-kilter enough to think her ten-aurei bounty would help him?

She composed herself and went back to her bed, where Gorka had seated himself on the edge.

"You're a beautiful woman, Golda," Gorka said slowly. "Your Jinn nature makes you more beautiful, really. There is a glowing intensity to you, and not just the silver in your eyes."

Golda cautiously picked up her shirt from the dirty rug and slipped into it, but she left it unbuttoned and made no effort to cover herself. She'd fed well enough from an anonymous Djinnus in the Fuchsia Canary back alley, but her Hunger was once again hollow in Gorka's presence.

"How did things go with your beautiful friend Lotifia then? Did she give you anything for Priebus?"

"No." Gorka shook his head as if defeated. "Lotifia was compassionate, but she wouldn't give me any coin. She cited the Gypsy code. It's hard to explain. My family is cursed it seems. We can't seem to escape this coil of misfortune afflicting us."

"I weep for your mother's fate, Gorka. She must be in so much pain, but we have no way of getting such coin. I've thought of trying to rescue her when the devils transport her to the Great Blue Hole mines, but I think they take slaves to the mines on Nanka back. They don't bring them through the forest."

"Tell me about your own slave brand, Golda."

Golda sat down on the bed next to Gorka and reached surreptitiously with her hand to verify that the pearl handled shiv was still in position under her pillow. Gorka was often direct, but it was a question that she hadn't been expecting. "Can you be more specific?"

"I don't mean to pry. I'm just shocked. Who owned you?"

Golda clenched her jaw. She was willing to divulge, but only to a point. "My mistress was a cat goddess named Basteh. I was a collared cat-girl slave a long time ago. Basteh was a cruel four-breasted bitch. She exploited me for coin. She sold me to the men of Vegasis. If I misbehaved, I was whipped. I was abused mentally and physically for many years. I was very lucky that Allyssia's rebel Jinni recruited me for my skills. Eventually the love goddess converted me into a Jinn as my reward."

Gorka nodded. "I'm sorry for asking, Golda."

"I don't mind."

"How did you become a slave in the first place?"

"I don't remember all of the details. I've had too much nectar since then. I only know what I've been told. I was Egyptian royalty. I was Golda of Egypt, the wife of a ruler of Egypt, a man named Natat. He ruled in the tenth century, or maybe the eleventh, and I stood by his side. I died on Earth, and I was judged by the Mimos. The Mimos rejected me for my many sins, and I was cast from Heaven."

"How did you sin on Earth?"

"I don't remember." Golda looked away. She wasn't sure of Gorka's motives. Was he fishing for more information to use against her, or was he truly sympathetic? Her senses told her the latter, and if she could strike a chord of empathy with the young human male, so much the better to inspire him to get out of Haawiyah and end his efforts.

"How were you enslaved, then?"

"I must have been sold. The cat goddess purchased me. I think she liked my red fur, if you get my meaning. She gave me a lot of nectar to make me behave and make me forget. I was humiliated, but I finally learned to accept my slave life. It wasn't so bad except for some of the men who treated me like an animal. Eventually I rose to some fame in Vegasis, however, and I attracted the attention of some important people, including some agents of Lady Allyssia. They helped me escape."

"You're still an agent of Allyssia?"

"I still consider her to be my goddess, but she has abandoned me. No one has seen her in three years. I've been studying the arts of tracking with Masad, the rebel son of Lord Hades. He is my mentor."

"This is really your fault, isn't it? Hell's Court was here for you, not my family. You're the rebel they were looking for. Why won't you admit it?"

"You might be right. I may have made some mistakes. Masad said I wasn't ready. I hadn't completed my training, but I left anyway. He wouldn't come and help me save my friend. Fighting Hell's Court seems hopeless, but I can't bring myself to just give up and let the devils win."

"I know exactly how you feel, Golda."

"Maybe so." Golda stared at the floor. She could feel Gorka's conflicted moil of sympathy. A tangible connection had formed between them.

"I can only imagine how you must feel for your losses," Gorka continued. "While I was riding this afternoon to see Lotifia, I decided you were right when you said I'd forgotten about love. I never pursued Lotifia because I still love my wife who went to Heaven, and now Lotifia is betrothed to another. Sometimes I think that love doesn't exist in Hell—only lust. Love is an illusion created by our desire, nothing more."

"No. True love exists."

Gorka's downcast eyes lifted. "You really believe that?"

"Yes. As a Jinn, I have felt love in ways that a human cannot. Allyssia is proof in herself. If you've never been in the presence of the goddess of Love, then you can't know what I'm talking about."

Gorka nodded. "I think true love cannot be selfish. It is only found in giving—in charity and evenhanded compassion. If you abandon someone to focus on yourself, you never loved them. My Beatrice taught me this, but I was a horrible student. Any selfishness is a taint that cannot come from Heaven or the Mimos. Sometimes I feel it when I play my guitar, or last summer when I was close to Lotifia at the waymeet. I know that I have no way left to help my parents except one, and it's a terrible one. Yet in a way it's charity. It's love."

"What is it, Gorka?"

"First let me ask you this. You helped me yesterday without complaint, despite the fact that you don't like me, and I don't like you. We were united by a common cause—saving my parents from their fates. Are you still committed to saving my mother?"

"Yes. I suppose, although—"

"Does the Reik family, what's left of it, have your support? Are you willing to sacrifice more to see my mother freed? I know you've given all the money you have, except your personal effects and your horse. I'm only asking if you're willing to further help me."

"I said I would help, and I meant it." Golda took a deep breath, even as she slid her hand again under her pillow and grasped the hilt of the shiv. "I can't blame you for refusing to give up on love. I've felt that too."

"It's strange, but I'm glad to hear you say that, Golda. I could feel the same way if I were in love. I'm sorry about the cruel things that I've said to you. You can only imagine how I must feel."

"Apology accepted."

"Thank you." Gorka closed his eyes and rubbed his forehead. "My plan would be to sell myself at the slave market in Mer, assuming my humble soul is worth enough coin to the wealthy Djinnus and Jinni. You and Mohilever could then take the coin and pay the judge at Hell's Court for my mother."

Golda tried to remain calm, even though her heart was suddenly stirred with mingled hope and much darker emotions. "I'm shocked, Gorka. I didn't realize you had such conviction. People say they will sacrifice for love, but few really mean it."

"I wouldn't stay a slave, of course. I would escape as soon as you and Mohilever get my mother and take her away from Mer."

"How would you do that?"

"That's why I came to you. You escaped, didn't you? So you know how to do it. I simply refuse to let Hell's Court and Lord Hades get away with this injustice. I could somehow sell myself and save my mother, and then you could help me get free with your Jinn skills. That would satisfy me. Hell has stolen from my family, so it is time to steal back from them. We just have to figure out how."

Golda blinked. Her mind boggled with the possibilities as well as the problems. She released her grip from the shiv. "I'll think on it."

"How much might I be worth in a Merian auction?"

"You're a handsome young man. Possibly a lot. I've only ever sold a human once, and it wasn't by auction. I have little idea of the current market prices in Mer."

"How much does—" Gorka looked away. "How much does the size of a male slave matter? The Fates cursed me with the manhood of a youth. I've been afraid enough of what Gypsy women will think, much less a Jinn who sleeps with a dozen different men every week. I'm worried about what

Lotifia was really thinking a bit ago, honestly. She saw me once when I was drunk."

"I wouldn't worry. We Jinni want to drain lust. We aren't so interested in having our own pleasure, at least from male slaves. We lose precious energy that way. You're capable of orgasms though, I hope?"

"Yes, although I've tried to lead a chaste afterlife, in honor of my heavenly wife."

Golda bit her lip. She felt a little guilty for visiting Gorka in his dreams, where she'd been far from chaste with him. She could only hope Gorka's noble Beatrice hadn't been watching from on high. "Your physical youth is an asset for this, actually. I'll help you if you truly wish. I might even pose as your Jinn seller."

Gorka nodded nervously. "Yes. When I escape, I can ride hard out of Haawiyah. My mother could be saved. I could go far away to Meristyian. I could see the family at the waymeets. I could never return to Haawiyah. My owner will never see me again. Are you sure it's possible for us to bilk the slave market?"

"It depends on what your owner does with you. If you're always locked in a cage like I was at first, then you can't escape. You may need to earn your owner's trust first like I did, and that could take years. Maybe I can't let you do this. If your mother were here, would she agree?"

"It's my decision."

"I could make up a story that I'm visiting from Vegasis. It will be hard to explain why you don't have a brand or papers already. All human slaves must have papers."

"I didn't think about that."

"Often a Jinn will seduce a human through the dream world, and I've heard of a few werewolves being captured by collectors who like slaves who are exotic and dangerous to tame. They wouldn't have papers. I also know bounty hunters hunt fallen Mimos in Meristyian and bring them back to Mer, so the legalities must handle a lot of odd situations. Maybe I could claim that I own you through a trade with a Kishi. The Kishi don't register slave papers with Hell's Court."

Golda stilled her tongue. She had a sudden inspiration in a completely different direction. If Boudi-Ca were cuffed, gagged, and drugged, any devil or Hell's army soldier might assume that she was a beautiful young slave, not a kidnapped Jinn of the most exotic and unique origins. The plan would require high quality gear and a powerful poison.

Gorka rubbed his head pensively. "Fine. I'm willing to try if you're willing to help me. I'll tell Mohilever and Trumpeldor the new plan in the morning."

Golda hesitated, and then put her arms around Gorka. She hugged him with her warmth. She felt genuine compassion for the young male in that moment, despite his persistent insults. Gorka broke the embrace, but only to lift his feet up and curl next to her on her bed. Golda felt her Hunger stir in her belly. She leaned and kissed Gorka gently on the shoulder. She rubbed his hip, then snaked her hand slowly over his hip and felt for his cock.

"Perhaps I should show you what you can expect from a Jinn," she murmured. "I'm sure you'll be less nervous."

Gorka disentangled himself and bolted from her bed. "What in the hells?"

"I'm sorry."

"You should be, whore. This is all your fault. Why don't you go see Mohilever again? He'll be happy to have you." Gorka pushed out of the tent and disappeared into the night. Golda sighed, reached for her perfume, and touched her breasts with scent. She exited the tent and stalked barefoot and half-nude through the dark to where Mohilever sat alone, whittling his wood.

"Gods," Mohilever said. He gave a low whistle. "I thought you were a lost nimfa for a minute, come to bless an old Gypsy. It happened once to me in Meristyian. The girl came buck naked from the forest while I was carving and slept with me. The next day I helped her find her way back to her rake master."

Golda closed the distance, giving her best sashay. "I do need something from you, Mohilever."

"What, lass? Let me guess."

"Not that. I understand you know a bit about chemistry. I need a poison that will knock out a Jinn. Do have any idea where I could acquire such a thing in Mer?"

"What for, lass?"

"Gorka has decided to sell himself as a slave in Mer so he can save his mother. Afterwards, I'll need to take care of his new Jinn Mistress, because she'll have the keys to his slave cage. I don't want to kill her. I'll just poison her, and use some strong cuffs and a gag to make sure she stays under control until Gorka can escape."

"Bollocks and bosh. The lad doesn't have the balls for that."

"You suggested it to him, didn't you?"

Mohilever laughed. "Har. I didn't mean for him to do such a thing. You talked him into it, didn't you? You love Priebus, and you don't give a goat's ass for Gorka."

"Maybe he'll change his mind, or maybe it's just his fate. I said I'd rescue him, but some things are easier said than done. It isn't a sure thing." Golda avoided Mohilever's eyes. She loathed lying, but she had no choice. Her plan was to use the Reik coin to buy a quality paralyzing poison, a gag, and some cuffs, and then try to get Boudi-Ca with an old fashioned Mimo-napping. She could use the poison and bondage gear on Boudi-Ca while abandoning Gorka.

Golda straddled Mohilever's legs. She pushed her perfumed breasts into his bristly face. The old man breathed deeply. She caressed her fingers through Mohilever's grey hair. "Where is Trumpeldor tonight?"

"He went back to the Golden Lion," Mohilever answered. "Said he was lonely without the ladies around. So I can have you for myself, lass. I was prejudiced against you when you were with Agron, but you're the best damned sex this old man has ever had."

"Once Gorka is sold, you'll need to take the coin to get his mother from Hell's Court. I'll need whatever coin we have left. I can buy the poison and gear to rescue Gorka after his mistress takes him home. You'll need to get Priebus and take her to Erebus. I'll meet you there with Gorka. In a few days, hopefully all of this will be over."

"It will all be over except for my brother Agron." The old bugbear laved her nipple with his rough tongue. "He's sentenced to the Bolgia pits forever."

Golda snaked low and grabbed Mohilever's hard cock. Her mind wasn't on Agron. She was imagining how to knock Boudi-Ca unconscious and export her from the city as a bound slave. The east gate was swarming with soldiers for some reason, though. She was capable of slipping through alone with her skills, but not with Boudi. She might find another gate less guarded, but scouting the perimeter of Mer for a safer route might take another day.

Chapter 18.

Yellen made her way through the cool, blue-shadowed vomitorium into the afternoon warmth and sunlight of the Merian Coliseum. It was scarcely midday. The day's Named had been two Sisters living together in secret. The lesbians gone easily, cuffed separately while doing their daily duties for the Smokeless Flames. Neither had resisted, but both had cursed and spat with rage. The two arrests had been a respite from the previous day's life-or-death confrontation at the Flames monastery, but still very unpleasant.

Lydiah had produced a new tracker to replace Shadow. The new tracker was Mistress Canthah, an Asian Jinn of less skill than Shadow but more submissive and ready to take orders in her support role. Most Asian Jinni paid more attention to the order of the Flames ranks, and Canthah was no exception. Canthah waited for directions and obeyed, which made her easier to coordinate.

They were still waiting to hear from Master Glumstak and the devils about the results of Mistress Na'armeh's interrogation. Lydiah had warned that the arrests would quickly escalate, and they might need to bring Shadow back to form a second arrest unit when she recuperated.

Yellen climbed the worn steps towards the primum seating in the Coliseum. Like Simhonit, she was afforded a primum seat as an officer in the Smokeless Flames. She'd arranged to meet Simhonit via exchanges of messenger birds the previous evening. She'd needed to be persuasive. Simhonit had suspected a trap, but had agreed to a public meeting.

The Coliseum had almost no regular Flames clientele. The sands of combat were more popular with Gypsies, lowbrow Djinnus gamblers, Hell's army grunts, and horny she-devils who flocked to the Coliseum to masturbate in the seats while they watched the fighters screaming, dying, spilling blood, and dripping their intestines. It wasn't unusual in the Coliseum to see a she-devil sitting on her husband's lap, engaged in pleasurable coitus while enjoying the spectacle of pain and death.

Yellen searched the sparse midday crowd in the Coliseum. She didn't spot Sim until she was almost on top of her. Sim was sheltered in the shadow of a wide umbrella, warding herself against the droppings of the vultures, which circled in the orange-tinged Haawiyah sky.

Yellen made her way along the seats and settled silently next to Sim. The seat was relatively cool, made from a travertine that didn't soak up the heat. Sim kept looking straight ahead. Simhonit was as beautiful as ever, as if she'd hardly aged a day in decades, wearing her dark hair short as always in a pageboy style. Simhonit's lips were painted with a dark Venetian red that complimented her almond complexion, a lighter half-tone of Shadow's tanned skin.

Below on the Coliseum floor, a tiger squared off against an ogre. The tiger was lean and hungry. Its thick ribs were visible on its tawny flanks. The ogre was muscled and clumsy, possibly a deserter from Hell's army, or just a hopeless oaf who had stolen something. A Hell's Court conviction meant the loss of a hand for thievery, but the condemned was always offered a cruel alternative—to fight in the arena. To a capable fighter, the limb was worth more than the risk of going to the void.

Yellen watched the fight, working her sensibilities around the complexities of the moment. She wanted to savor the slow-boiling memories of Sim that were surfacing in her mind—those hot encounters in the Flames dormitories and the nights in bed at Sim's home. Their relationship had ended when she'd started traveling for many months at a time, and Sim had stayed at her job in the capital city as a Flames hex trainer.

As a Flames veteran, Sim had never married. Instead, she'd taken many lovers over the years. She was an accomplished dream-traveler in her spare time. She frequented the fluid medium that allowed Jinni to take love from humans living on Earth. It was on Earth that Sim cleverly found her female companionship, far from the judging eyes of Lord Hades, the Djinnus, and the devils of Hell's Court.

The hungry tiger evaded the ogre's slow spiked club and scored a ripping wound in the ogre's arm. The massive bald ogre howled and dropped its weapon, leaving itself fatally exposed to further attack. The tiger went for the knee, then the throat. The spectators cheered. A group of rowdy Hell's army soldiers went to their feet to fist pump for the bloody kill. As the ogre breathed its last, its entrails began to litter the sands, and wager winnings changed hands.

"So how have you been?" Yellen ventured without turning her head.

"I've been fine," Sim murmured. "What of you? You're hungering. I can feel your need from here, and it's distracting me."

"Councilor Lydiah had a sacra vipera installed in my house yesterday. I have only one slave—a demoness—and I didn't feed from her last night. I'm afraid the serpent will watch me. I'm also afraid I'll go home and find my demoness poisoned to death. I don't keep her caged."

"The vipera can't pass through solid doors. Close them. I'm impressed they gave you a vipera for protection, Yellen. Maybe that's a good thing."

"Maybe. Seeing each other is also a good thing, isn't it?"

"I can't believe I agreed," Sim replied tensely. "You're a betrayer. You're arresting lesbians. I'm still terrified this meeting is a trap. Is it? Am I surrounded right now?"

"That's absurd. You know me. You can trust me."

"I don't know you any more, Yellen. How can I know you're not spinning lies? You're in Councilor Lydiah's pocket. Admit it." Sim turned to her questioningly. The Jinn moon-silver in Sim's eyes was a hard grey shimmer over her sparkling blue irises. "How can you do this even if ordered?"

Yellen slid her hand to the hilt of her blade. "It's my duty. They were persuasive. Befanah is going through her elder change. She can't walk well. She asked me for this favor."

"You're doing this as a favor?"

"I owe my former teacher everything. I didn't come here to fight or be criticized, Sim. I just wanted to ask if you have connections to the higher-ups who are trying to assassinate me. I'd prefer to live without my life in jeopardy. They need to know—"

"Know what?" Sim' voice was heated. "You're kidding me. Where do you stand, Yellen? It sure looks to everyone like you're against us."

Yellen hesitated. She knew that she needed to face the moment of truth, but she hadn't expected it to come so soon. "I am loyal to the Flames and to Lady Allyssia, but I am also loyal to my own people. I swear this to Lady Allyssia. Are there high-level lesbians in the Flames that I could consider friends if I allied with them?"

"If there were, how would they know you're trustworthy? Can you prove that you're loyal to the lesbians? Because otherwise—"

"I have a girlfriend. We made love yesterday."

Simhonit's lip twitched. "What's her name?"

"Mistress Henneh. She's a recently-fledged beauty mistress. We're planning to open an art gallery together. I'm going to run it and sell her sculpture. Unfortunately, she's engaged to be married in a few weeks, which complicates things. I hope we'll see each other secretly after her wedding."

Sim' lips finally curved into a bitter smile. "Yes, I was in love once with a fledgling on the cusp of her mistresshood. She passed her Mistress Test. An Djinnus got a hold on her, and his seed set its hooks into her belly. She married him, and she never answered my messenger birds again. That's how we lose young lesbians. Good luck."

"I'll always love Henne even if she leaves me."

"If you're not lying, Yellen, then I admit you're impressing me."

"I serve Lady Allyssia and the Flames first, and then Lord Hades and Hell's army. I didn't sign up with the Flames to persecute my own people."

Sim' eyes turned sultry. "I can feel your passion, Yellen. You're brave to indulge your desires despite the position you're in. You're braver than I would be, which is why it's so hard to believe."

"I'm telling the truth. This meeting isn't a trick planned by Councilor Lydiah or Hell's Court. I don't have any ebon cuffs. I'm meeting someone I loved once—someone I need something from."

"Vague assurances and confided fantasies are appreciated, Yellen, but we need real proof of your commitment."

Yellen felt the tension creep over her shoulders even as the arena workers dragged off the dead ogre and surrounded the tiger on the arena sands, catching its neck with a collaring staff. The workers leashed the tiger and led it off towards its cage, where it would rest from its win and slowly starve again, awaiting its next chance to meet the end of its doomed and bloody existence.

"So you're admitting that you're one of them, Sim? You're in direct contact with the lesbian cliques?"

"I can't say that. I can say that they'd sooner kill me than allow the devils to get me for questioning. Either that, or I would need to kill myself. I'm just warning you."

"Are they watching us now?" Yellen looked over her shoulder to scan the stands. She knew that she hadn't been followed in, but any of the several dozen Jinni in the awning-shadowed rows of seats above her were potential allies of Sim—allies that could fire a gun or unleash a destructive spell.

"More importantly, are you being watched yourself?" Sim countered. "Even if you're sincere in your overture, how do you know you weren't followed here?"

"I've worked in the field out in eastern Meristyian for many years. I wouldn't have survived the werewolves and vampires if I were stupid. What sort of proof do you need? I'm not saying I can comply. I just want to know."

"I have everything to lose by coming into contact with you, Yellen. If the matchsticks start falling, the lesbians in the Flames could be wiped out. Future young lesbian fledglings will live lives of private hell without friends or guidance. They'll be persecuted and eventually lost to unfulfilled false lives addicted to Djinnus seed for centuries."

"I understand that."

"Yet you could be our strongest ally in this fight. You are Lydiah's right hand. You could communicate to us. You could serve as a spy."

"Yes. I suppose that's right."

Sim took a deep breath. "We just want to be sure that you have everything at stake like we do before any arrangement is made."

"You're already trying to assassinate me. That isn't enough?"

"Not even close. We'll want to know your lover, Henne. We'll want to know where she lives. We'll want to know your slave girl. We'll want to know everything closest to your heart, because if you screw up, you should plan to lose everything too."

"Fine. We can make a deal?"

Sim pursed her lips. "If it wasn't for your old relationship with me, you would have no chance to strike an alliance with the inner cliques. I'm taking a huge risk vouching for you. Still, I think it's early in the game."

"It isn't early for those arrested in the next couple days. It's very late."

Sim nodded. "Touché. So what will it be, then? Let's say for the sake of argument that you've convinced me of your sincerity. When can I meet your special friend who will die if you fail us?"

Yellen rubbed her fingers on her sword hilt. She'd never seen Sim so tense and distrusting, and the conversation was depressing. "I don't see why Henne is important. She's marrying in a few weeks. She won't be thinking of me much after that, nor I of her. It's pointless to drag her into this."

"You're lying now, Yellen. You love her deeply, and it pains you to lose her. I told you the terms. If we lose everything, so do you. If you want to help us, you need to commit."

"My address is 773 South Leo Street. Perhaps you'd like to stop by sometime. I just moved in. I still have that fighting tiger painting you gave me. It's hanging above my bed."

"Yes, I remember your old nickname at the Flames academy. My tiger cub." Sim smiled. "I miss those days with you, Yellen. We were reckless and uncaring, and lesbianism was everywhere. It was like a forbidden game that all of the fledglings played. We assumed we'd get married someday, so it didn't matter. For some of us, the wedding never happened."

"Things change. Those old days can come back."

"Not if all of our beloved old guard is carted off to rot in the Merian prison for eternity, or worse yet executed. Not if our very identity is a forgotten thing, an anathema. No one will be left to show young Jinni there is an alternative to glorious cock."

"Some things can't be erased. We all love who we love."

"Like you say, Yellen, things change. The veneration of the old gods is dead on Earth. The Mimoic Hierarchy has taken over everything with their holy nonsense and biblical gibberish. The solution to lesbianism on Earth is reformation, guilt, and belief in Lord Tuhan and his son. Today I whisper the name of Allyssia in the dreaming ears of Earth women and nothing registers in their heads."

Yellen nodded. "Yet the tide is turning back against the Mimoic Hierarchy. Thanks in part to technology, we're obliterating the Mimos and sending them scurrying behind the shelter of Heaven's gates. If the rumors of Lord Hades' ambitions are true, we'll be pressing the war into the churches and cities of Earth soon, and this time we will win."

"That's bad for me, then—more risk that my activities could be discovered if a devil happens across me while I'm having my way with someone."

"It's also good. You'll be in less danger when you travel the dream world. You'll be safer on Earth from Mimo guardians."

"Danger? You're telling me about danger? The danger isn't in the dream world. Do you know what they're doing with Commander Zinke and the other Sisters you've arrested up to this point?"

Yellen took a deep breath. She didn't know as much as she wished. "The devils are interrogating them to get more names. There is a grey door at 115 West Pelagius downtown. I deliver the Named there, and the devils take them."

"We know that much. You're being watched, of course."

Yellen looked at Sim Sharply. "I hope you know Shadow is a skilled tracker. She might have picked up on someone following us."

"It was a concern, but precautions were taken. What is Shadow's status after what happened to her? How long will she be out?"

"I spoke with her this morning at the headquarters when I met with Lydiah. Shadow is in bad shape, but she insists that she can continue tracking in a few days. She's committed to getting the lesbians, and she believes in the purgation. She hates lesbians now more than ever."

Sim cleared her throat. "I'm very sorry to hear that information, for her sake. Shadow should have quit while she had the chance."

"Is that a threat, Sim?"

"Yes. Shadow needs to go to the void."

"You know, I've decided that I don't want you to meet Henne. I refuse to drag her into this. On the other hand, I also refuse to stand by and not do something. This arrangement will be on my terms. You may receive a bird from me in the mornings to come. The bird may tell you the Named of the day. Perhaps you and your friends will be interested in doing something with it. In any case, you can't stop me from sending a message."

"Always the tiger, aren't you Yellen? Fine, if you want to play that way, then I think I can extend a gesture of good faith. Discretely send those birds as early as you can, and I promise no more assassination attempts will be made against you. I won't make the same promise for Shadow."

"Are we good then? I swear I want to help."

"The powers will still want that leverage over you, and will insist on getting it regardless of your wishes. You'll make your move, and they will make theirs. I'll try to see you safe, but if something happens and they decide you're a traitor, then you will pay."

"I'm not, and I'll prove it to you. Maybe when this is all over, we can even see each other again some time."

Sim smiled faintly. "Maybe. I'm busy these days. I have hex classes seven days a week. I assist in blades and Nanka flight training. I have a blacksmith shop, although I don't do the work. I own the facility. I go to parties. I write a bit of poetry. I have three slaves. I'm training one of them. I took advantage of the war with Heaven to buy a male Mimọ. They're going for much cheaper than normal."

"I need to find a male slave too, as soon as possible. Councilor Lydiah knows a little too much about my living situation."

"Well, we're doing a little counter-investigation of our own on that bitch. There are a few rumors floating around Mer that she indulges with her fledgling, Boudi-Ca. Since Lydiah is spearheading the lesbian arrests, if we can find something on her, it might disrupt and delay the purgation."

"If I learn anything along those lines, I'll tell you. I'm going to Lydiah's home on dies Martis to have blades practice with her fledgling. I only know Lydiah has a centuries-old record as an outspoken anti-lesbian. She's also married, of course."

Sim slouched deeper under her umbrella and extended her ringless fingers as if examining them. "She's married to a devil, not an Djinnus. Archduke Fennel is often away from the capital, and Lydiah winters in the north country without her husband. Lydiah dotes on her fledgling, and she had Boudi-Ca in the north country with her. Boudi-Ca's history is well-known to those of us who pay attention. Even if Lydiah isn't a closet lesbian, she can still be framed. Please don't breathe a word of this, of course. Now please go. Allyssia willing, I hope I don't see you again until this is over."

"Sure, but you might get a bird from me soon, or three or four." Yellen rose and made her way back down through the seats. She resisted the urge to look over her shoulder. She sifted the possibilities as she walked through the vomitorium and out into the fresher air of the city street. Was she truly willing to risk her own life to save the Named, or was she only trying to impress Sim? Was she willing to risk demotion, arrest, and torture by the devils? Was she willing to face execution as a traitor? What was truly at stake? What was happening to the arrested lesbians?

Was it possible that Lydiah could have relations with Boudi-Ca, given her high public profile and proximity to the Hell's Court devils? Yellen scanned the street outside the Coliseum for a rickshaw. She'd never considered that Lydiah herself could have lesbian inclinations, although Boudi-Ca had a conspicuous history. Meanwhile, Lydiah was pressing her to tutor the talented fledgling.

Yellen ran her fingers yet again over the hilt of her blade. Perhaps she could take advantage of the situation. If she could get into Boudi-Ca's head, she'd have more than one way to help Sim, a way that she could also help herself. If she held something over Boudi-Ca, she'd have something to hold over Lydiah.

She wasn't tutoring Boudi-Ca until dies Martis. Meanwhile, she had personal affairs to deal with. After the slave auction, she planned to ask Henne to go to bed with her again. She'd plead once more with Henne to delay the wedding with Master Andros. She couldn't seem to let Henne go.

Yellen grimaced when she raised her arm to hail an approaching rickshaw. Her chest wound was suddenly hurting her out of the purple, in sympathy with her emotional weakness. Perhaps she'd imbibed a little too much of Henne's pampered and perfumed sex over the years, as Henne had suggested, or perhaps she was just in love.

She had no problems with making the correct decisions with a blade or with business, but love had always proved a more difficult two-edged weapon to handle. If she kept pursuing Henne, she was probably more naïve than Boudi-Ca. Meanwhile, despite Kiree's presence, she was feeling more alone than ever.

Chapter 19.

The slave trader's house was located at the end of a cul-de-sac in the outskirts of the market district, within view of the high, decrepit stone ramparts of the eastern walls of Mer. Golda sat next to Gorka in the cramped reception room that smelled faintly of cinnamon. Gorka had decided to go forward with his grand charitable sacrifice. She hadn't argued with him. She wanted to save Priebus as much as he did.

She and Gorka had entered Mer yet again, while she had used her skills to bypass the heavy gate guard. They'd spoken with the auction master from the Merian auction house. Apparently the auction master still appreciated the tip, and had informed them of the basics of public slave auctions in Mer. Unlike a hard goods auction, a licensed agent was required to handle the formal Court papers. The hellion auctioneer had recommended Master Hillel Yaffe, a small-time but ambitious agent who wouldn't ask too many questions.

Golda stared straight ahead at the classical figure painting on the wall. She knew Gorka's fear instincts were triggering. She needed to keep his mind on the task of saving his mother. She'd trained him intensively that morning in the basics of slave behavior. The rules had bounced around in Gorka's head, some sticking in his human skull, and some not.

She'd assured Gorka that they could scam the slave market and then effect an escape. She wasn't so sure, but that didn't matter as long as the coin was procured for Pinhas'. Golda licked her hungering lips. Priebus would be forlorn at the loss of her family and would need a shoulder to cry on. Their relationship would bloom anew, and Mohilever could go screw himself.

She'd already spoken briefly with Yaffe. The slave trader had asked them to wait while he researched the selling of Kishi slaves. Golda fidgeted. Every minute of sitting in the slave trader's office increased her tension beyond bearable levels.

"Mistress Darlah?" Vanessah, the trader's Jinn secretary, appeared in the inner hallway and motioned with a silver pen. "Please follow me with Stefan."

Golda rose and motioned to Gorka to follow her down the hall and through the doorway into the trader's cozy back office. She carried Gorka's guitar in its case. After careful consideration, she'd guessed that Gorka's musical abilities were his best asset for Merian collectors. She sat down next to Gorka in front of Hillel Yaffe's expensive-looking oak desk.

Yaffe was a smallish Djinnus with a round, easy face, big ears, and greying hair. He wore an unbuttoned mustard yellow waistcoat and a narrow yellow cravat that rested like a lizard on the paunch of his round belly, which was barely contained by a peach-colored shirt.

"I think we can do this, Mistress Darlah," Yaffe said with a professional smile. "I've consulted with a colleague about the legalities. We've got no problem selling a slave boy who once belonged to the Kishi. I'll simply need a small additional fee associated with a first-time registration for him. It's trivial, really. How much did you pay for him in the Seelie Court?"

"I traded horses to the Kishi, not coins."

"I've heard the Seelie Court is a beautiful place. It's on an island, isn't it?"

"Yes. It's an island in the Sea of Desire, not far from the coasts of Western Meristyian. The Kishi patrol everywhere, from the Alpacians to the Asphodel Meadows, so they need good horses as well as boats. They don't trade so much with the hard coins of the King's realm though, at least not the Seelie. So first I need an estimate of what my Stefan is worth in real aurei. I need a certain amount for an investment here in the capital city, and I can't accept anything less."

Yaffe leaned back and clasped his fingers together. "Of course, yes. It's actually standard practice. We can't have nasty surprises when we put him up on the block. Please take off your clothes, Stefan, and stand over there on the dais by the wall."

"Everything?"

"Yes, Stefan." Golda answered quickly. "Strip and be quick about it. What have I told you about asking too many questions?"

Golda cleared her throat. She'd warned Gorka to not say anything, to keep his eyes lowered, and do everything that he was told. Hopefully her story that Gorka was mostly untrained would explain his inevitable failures. She watched Gorka go to where Yaffe indicated, a low dais in the corner of the office about a meter wide and a few hands tall. Gilt-framed mirrors graced the walls in the corner to provide multiple views of a slave's nude form.

Gorka removed his shoes, trousers, and shirt. He stepped onto the dais. Golda eyed Yaffe, who was rubbing the short bristles on his chin as he watched. Gorka resulted to be modestly endowed as he'd admitted, and Yaffe's eyes lingered low and skeptical for a long time. Finally Yaffe spoke.

"You need shaving and waxing, my dear Stefan. You need a good work-over from head to toe. Don't get me wrong. You're as pretty as a peach. We just need to remove your fuzz. My assistant will take care of prepping you. Can you turn and bend over, please? Excellent."

"Stefan is fully functional both in the front and back. I've had him long enough to assure you of that." Golda tried to keep her voice as smooth and relaxed as silk. "Is he to your satisfaction, Master Yaffe?"

"Yes," Yaffe answered. "Stefan can sit down."

"Don't bother getting dressed again, Stefan. Get your clothes and sit. So how much do you think my little darling will earn at auction, Master Yaffe? I hope a lot. I'm sure there will be Jinni in Mer who will appreciate him."

Hillel Yaffe tilted his head and tapped his knuckle with his pen. "Well, let's just go on to the next part. What enticing abilities can I put on the card for this boy?"

"He's a talented musician."

"I am, sir," Gorka added. "I know modern music as well as the classics."

"Excellent," Yaffe said. "Skilled song-slaves are in high demand. Can I assume since you brought the instrument, Mistress Darlah, that the boy is prepared to demonstrate?"

"Absolutely." Golda handed the guitar to Gorka. He pushed his chair back, and he began to play a Chopin nocturne. By the end, Yaffe was beaming.

"Fantastique, Stefan. Fantastique. Is it fine with you, Mistress Darlah, if he plays when he's up on the block?"

"Of course. I'll be selling his guitar along with him as a bonus." Golda ignored Gorka's veiled angry look. "So how much, Master Yaffe? And when? We need to do this as soon as possible."

Yaffe leaned back in his chair. "A talented and virginal artist like Stefan shouldn't go in the common daily auction with all the rest. It would be a waste. We need to wait for the high dollar Night Auction. It takes place once a week."

"And when is that?"

"We just had one last night, so in six days—on the eve of the next dies Saturni. If Stefan can play a wide repertoire of music like that, I'll bet he could fetch you upwards of two hundred aurei. I'll just need to find and inform the right clients."

Golda frowned. "Six days is too long. I don't have that much time. I need the coins immediately. How much would he go for in the common daily today?"

Yaffe gestured with his open hands. "Hypothetically if I could still get you on a card this afternoon? I don't know. It's a dies Solis. The buyers with the real coin are attending our Lord's temple services like gentle folk, and they don't venture out with the common swill anyway. They leave the heat and crowds for the less distinguished people. I deal with only the best, Mistress Golda, or at least I aim to."

"Give me your best guess for today."

"He could sell for less than a hundred, even with me representing him. No, that's not advisable for a handsome, talented boy of his age. I'd get less commission, and you'd get less than he's worth. He deserves better."

Golda shook her head. "I need the coin immediately."

"Unless," Yaffe ejaculated. "I could set up a private show with my best clients. Yes, yes. It will take some work, but I could get that together within three days."

Golda shook her head again. "Still not good enough. A private auction tonight sounds like the best option, tomorrow night at the latest. Can you do it, Master Yaffe? And promise at least a hundred and sixty aurei? Otherwise we're walking out of here."

Yaffe winced. "Stefan is very handsome. You have me at a disadvantage. Fine. For you, I will try for tomorrow night."

"Just understand that I must get at least—"

"Understood. I'll bill it as a unique opportunity to acquire an exquisite and spirited song slave. I could find more buyers if I had another couple days to advertise, but he'll sell, and I'll bet you I can get at least a hundred forty chips. Will that plan work for you, Mistress?"

"It's moving in the right direction."

"Good. He's special even with his shortcomings. He's young enough to attract the lovers of the young, and skilled enough to attract the lovers of the skilled. Stefan can look forward to playing many a love song and lullaby for his owner. Why are you selling him, again?"

"I need some coin for a lucrative business investment here in Mer," Golda answered. "I can't sell him for anything less than one hundred sixty after your commission. That's what I have to have, or nothing."

Yaffe grimaced. "I suppose we'll agree that's the base price then, but I warn you it will be difficult. The commission on the private show will be higher than my usual rate, but I expect his price will absorb that along with the first-time Court registration fee. So. We can go ahead and sign the consignment papers. Right there, and there, on the lines where the owner would normally sign."

"Fine." Golda clenched her throat. She felt a weight on her shoulders, like the Fates themselves had entered the room to witness that cruel moment. She picked up the ink pen and signed her alias with a clumsy, unpracticed script. In all of her hundreds of years in the Underworld, she had never in her memory signed anything. She was adding a fake signature on Court documents to her long list of crimes. Yaffe rubbed his hands together when she was done. He collected the papers and stood up brusquely.

"Excellent. I'll see you tomorrow night then, no later than eight o'clock. You may come to my back door. You'll find a gate just out there down the alleyway. I have a display room where we'll do the show and sale. Stefan, you may now come with me. I have a cage in my basement where you'll stay."

"Wait." Golda said quickly. "I need Stefan until his sale. I can't let you have him yet."

Yaffe slowly stacked his papers. "No. Gorka has to stay here. It's part of the procedure for my shows. That's why we call it a 'consignment', right? These papers are consignment papers. I'm insured. I have steel cages. I've never had a slave escape. What if I get my best clients and you don't show? It would be bad for my reputation."

"This isn't the way things are done in Vegasis."

"Well, I'm sorry." Yaffe looked annoyed. "That's the way it's done here. My clients might also want a preview. You don't understand how things work here in Mer—"

"Oh, I know how this works," Golda said Sharply. She felt her inner heat rising, a strange animal rage that came from a deep, forgotten place. "What happens at these little 'previews' exactly, Master Yaffe? Will the clients pay to abuse him for free? Will they whip him, prod him, and poke him? Will they slip him a cock to see how he responds? You have my promise that I will bring him tomorrow night. We can do this the Vegasis way."

"Well, I never—" Yaffe sputtered. "I admit the legalities are obscure in this situation, but fine. Have it your way. I'll assemble my clients with no previews. They'll come on my word. If you don't show, or if there are problems that keep me from making a sale, we may have a problem. People tend to get hurt when they hurt my reputation."

"Thank you, Master Yaffe. I appreciate your honesty."

Yaffe turned away to look out the window. "Just be damned sure you bring your slave at least two hours early so we get him properly bathed and shaved. I'm a high-class trader. I don't do anything half-assed, and your Kishi slave is a bit scruffy, to be honest."

"Of course, sir," Gorka interjected tersely. "We certainly respect and appreciate your expertise, and I apologize for my 'scruffiness.'"

Golda dragged Gorka by his arm from the office. She resisted the urge to slap him for his stupidity. She walked him quickly down the hall past the tall Jinn secretary named Vanessah. They passed back out into the bright sunlight and stink of the Merian street.

"You made a horrible mistake talking to him like that, Gorka. You were glaring at him while he was examining you, too. I'm sure the slave trader thinks I'm either an idiot or a swindler."

"Oh, I'm so sorry I reflected badly on you, Golda," Gorka retorted. "You're not the one who is going to be abused by some wicked Jinn. I'm doing my best, but this is sick. Why did he ask me to bend over?"

Golda sighed. "Why do you think? You could be attractive to men, and you can take a cock anywhere if you have to, Gorka. Who knows—you'd probably like it."

"If my Beatrice can see me from Heaven, I hope she understands this is for charity and self-sacrifice. I'm trying to make things right. Why did that Djinnus call me virginal? I was married on Earth. I've had sex here in the afterlife, although not recently."

"I have a feeling Master Yaffe knows his boys. You've never been with a Jinn or Djinnus, have you? No, I didn't think so. Think of all that coin. It's enough to free your mother from her torture. Now let's go. Mind you behave until you're back in the forest. We're close to freeing Pinhas'. We can't afford any more mistakes."

Golda climbed onto her horse. She breathed deeply to release her tension. Her dangerous visit to the slave trader had terrified her. She didn't feel safe in the city, where she was at the mercy of too many stone walls and prying eyes. She wended her way through the crowded city streets back to the east gate. She slowed when she confronted the unusual number of devils and Hell's army guards at the exit lane. Gorka drew alongside her. She stalled her steed off the line of travelers and caravan wagons.

"They're watching the exit. It's never been like this until last week."

"Are we doing the same thing?" Gorka's voice sounded strangely submissive and boyish in that moment.

"Yes. You'll go back through alone as a Gypsy with the horses, and I'll wait and sneak out later tonight. I'll use my skills of stealth to hide myself."

Gorka nodded. "Do you think I'm making a mistake, Golda?"

Golda met Gorka's steady gaze, staying calm and confident even as she lied to him. "No. We're going to get your mother free. Then we're going to get you free too. Trust me."

"Everyone else has failed my parents except you, Golda. Thank you for helping my family. I mean that." Gorka's brown eyes were haunted. His composure was starting to unravel.

"Don't worry. Human slaves in Hell don't escape because they have nowhere to go. They don't have friends. They don't have a horse. They don't have a family waiting for them at a waymeet."

Golda dismounted and handed Gorka her reins. She planned to head for the Fuchsia Canary again, where she would find someone to feed her. Then she'd stalk the Merian near west side at sunset and again at morning, hoping to find Boudi's thread in the tapestry. She wouldn't approach the fledgling yet, but if she wanted to plan an abduction, she needed to know more about Boudi's comings and goings.

Chapter 20.

Boudi-Ca fidgeted with her purse, a beautiful black silk affair with gold thread and yellow pearls arranged into a bumblebee around a golden latch. Lydiah refused to give her the physical love she needed, but the Mistress gave her things in other ways. "I'm afraid my Mistress is going to find out."

"Of course she'll find out soon. That's part of the fun." Breanarachelle glanced over her shoulder, where two Hell's Court escorts sat in the rear carriage seat with their grim hoods and whips. "The question is what your Mistress will do next. She could kill you. She could try to kill me. She could erase your memories again with black nectar, but that won't negate our agreement. You'll still need to keep eating, or you'll go to prison for breach of contract."

"Well, I already have a problem. My Mistress told me last night that she scheduled a special blades training for me tomorrow morning with Lieutenant Nefra. She said it will be a few hours at least, and I don't have any excuse to skip it. So I won't be able to have pastries tomorrow morning. There is no way."

Breanarachelle shrugged. "The contract says you must eat three pastries per day. It doesn't say you need to eat every single day, child. You'll just need to make them up later."

Boudi-Ca slumped in the carriage seat. She felt grey inside, as grey as the hollows of Breanarachelle's wicked salamandery eye sockets. She'd risen early that morning, gotten dressed, and then watched from her window until Lydiah's carriage had rattled out of the estate. She'd saddled a horse and ridden out through the grounds, downtown to Pee-hill, where Breanarachelle had been waiting as planned.

A sense of doom hung over the arrangement, a feeling that mistakes had been made. She'd confessed her lesbian tendencies, and then she'd gone back and crawled into Breanarachelle's trap. It was inexplicable, but she felt horribly pulled to Breanarachelle's presence. The she-devil casually looked right and left, and then over her shoulder again.

The carriage rolled into the Italian quarter, one of the oldest neighborhoods on the Merian near north side. The Italian quarter was a dense conglomeration of classical columns, archways and sidewalks of cracked black marble that had been worn down by millions of feet over the centuries. The narrow streets were connected by even narrower alleyways.

The driver brought the carriage to a slow stop in front of a shop. Bakery smells drifted from the open door and the nearby alley to mingle with salt smells from the public baths across the street. A warm yellow glow came from a small shop window under a hammered lead awning.

A small fat human wearing a waistcoat sat on the rounded front step. The man grinned and lifted a flute to his lips. Staccato notes of music rose on the air for short seconds until the Court devils hopped from the carriage and advanced on the man.

"Begone, piper," one of the devils said, threatening with his whip. The man skittered, and the devils formed a twin guard at the shop door. Only then did Breanarachelle descend from on high, clutching her haute couture purse made from the shining silvered scales of some serpentine hellion or other hell-beast.

"Come along, child. Let's see Giacondah's pasticceria." Breanarachelle sauntered up the steps. The she-devil turned and beckoned. Boudi-Ca finally descended from the carriage, cautious with her stiletto heels on the ancient stones. She sniffed more of the sweet smells of the pasticceria when she rounded the carriage horses. The shop smelled warm, inviting, and cinnamony.

She climbed the steps and entered with Breanarachelle. The wonderful bakery smells filled the interior of the store, multiplied into an infinite complexity of olfactory pleasures. A magnificent crystal oil-lamp chandelier hung over the main room, which was ringed with elegant glass display cases. The cases were piled with manifold incarnations of foodstuffs in all shapes, textures, and colors of the rainbow.

Square pink breads made love with each other in a gilded basket where orange crescents also wrestled. Gleaming purple ovals formed a wild orgy on a filigree silver platter. Black bars with white stripes squatted more solemnly on a rectangular basalt board. Beside them sat yellow cones draped with orange lace. A Jinn pushed through a curtain at the rear of the room. The Jinn was rotund, with an enormous swollen belly and puffy arms around a porcine neck. She waddled on flat slippers instead of heels. Her low-cut ruffled dress revealed breasts of such girth that they would have served as buttocks for a sturdy pony.

"May I help you?"

"Yes," Breanarachelle said. "We're here for pastries. I haven't visited in a few years, and I've forgotten the selection. Which are the house specialties, again?"

"The sugar-clove sweetbreads are the seasonal special," the Jinn answered. "They are only five denarii per each. We also have the cinnamon witch-sickle tartufi and the lemon crush torta. The nectar coffee biscotti is popular, as are the lemon pepper horns. We also have pomegranate cioccolatto biscotti, pomegranate pepper cocks, sweet candy-coated mushrooms, and charcoaled cioccolatto fairy rings. We use the best imported ingredients from Erebus."

"What are these?" Boudi-Ca pointed to a group of small brown mounds in a case near the door, which were sprinkled with white dust. Amidst the many bold colors of the other pastries, the simple brown mounds looked small and non-intimidating.

"Those are sugar honey strudels," the Jinn answered, shifting her girth behind the case to grab the plate with her pudgy fingers. She slid the plate on top of the counter, then produced a small knife and cut a sample off a strudel. Boudi-Ca took the proffered morsel. It seemed innocuous, although it was sticky on her fingers.

"Go ahead and taste it," Breanarachelle murmured.

Boudi-Ca pushed the pastry between her teeth. A rush of what could only be described as sweetness filled her tongue. She chewed and savored the complex honey and sugar taste. She swallowed, just like she swallowed Moshe's seed on occasions, and amazingly she felt a pleasant, happy sensation in her throat. "It's like nectar, but it's more subtle and heavy. It's nice, Mistress Giacondah."

"Oh, I'm not the Mistress." The Jinn beamed. Her smile puffed her cheeks. "I'm her fledgling. My name is Golosina-Ca, or Scaramucci if you wish. I work the shop."

Breanarachelle bent and sniffed the strudels. "These will do. We'll take three."

The fledgling nodded. "An extra for your husband, Mistress?"

"Do you even know who I am, fool girl? I'm Ambassador Breanarachelle, and my husband, Judge Rhadamanthus, does not eat pastries. Pretty young Jinni eat the pastries, and then my husband eats their sweet flesh. Prepare three strudels please for Boudi-Ca on a plate, with one charcoaled fairy ring for me, and then let us see Giacondah. I sent her a bird and told her we were coming this morning."

"Of course, Ambassador," Scaramucci said quickly. "My apologies. One moment. That will be eighty-five denarii, please."

The fledgling bent low and retrieved a hidden plate of perfect white porcelain. She tonged three of the brown sugar honey strudels alongside a small crispy blackened ring of candied mushrooms. The fledgling kept her eyes lowered, and she was breathing heavily by the time she was done. She waddled across the room back through the curtain.

"Well then," Breanarachelle said. She opened her purse and counted coins onto the glass counter with her fingernails. "Your poison is chosen, child. The strudels are rather bland-looking I must say. I expected you to choose lemon. The girl did a good job of selling the devil-flavored delicacies. I was tempted for myself."

"So what about my past? You have to tell me. We agreed."

"Very well. You were never a spy for Heaven as Lydiah tells you. You were one of Allyssia's rebel Jinni. Allyssia made you into a Jinn, not Allyssia. The black nectar was part of your reformation. It wasn't voluntary. It was ordered by the Court."

"How did I meet Allyssia?"

"You joined her when you fell from Heaven. I don't know the details."

"What else? Why did I need to be reformed?"

"I'll tell you more next time." Breanarachelle's lips turned a small grin. "Now you need to focus on eating."

Boudi-Ca gazed down at her strudels lined up neatly next to Breanarachelle's fairy ring. Strangely, her mouth had gotten wet, just as when Moshe enjoyed her orally. From everything she'd heard of the politics of the purgation, Allyssia's rebels were lesbians, which confirmed why her reformation had been considered necessary. Lydiah had claimed that her black nectar protected her from her past, but the nectar seemed more like a punishment instead, a punishment ordered by the devils. Scaramucci's head popped back through the curtain. She beckoned.

"Please come in. The mistress will see you."

Boudi-Ca started towards the curtain, but a hand grabbed her shoulder. She gasped when she felt Breanarachelle's nails dig into her skin. Breanarachelle spun her around. "Carry the plate, fool child. I hope don't expect me to do it for you."

Boudi-Ca carefully lifted the plate and followed Breanarachelle. The rear room of the sweet shop was even thicker with bakery smells than the front. The enormous bulk of a woman filled the rear end of the room. Giacondah was so large that she appeared like a tent with her head, arms, and legs sticking out from under a large purple-paisley drapery.

"Breanarachelle," Giacondah's mouth was barely visible amidst the puffs of fat that were her face. "I'm so sorry I didn't warn my fledgling. It's not her fault. I'm doing pink nectar. I just had my seasonal surgery."

Breanarachelle drifted forward. "May I see?"

"You can see my legs. He removed a hundred kilograms." Giacondah gestured at the edge of the sheet, but her arm was too short to reach over her bulk. Breanarachelle lifted up the sheet and exposed the giant leg underneath, which looked like a human torso wrapped in bandages stained with blood. Breanarachelle ran her fingertips over the dressings almost lovingly, like an artist examining a masterpiece. The she-devil's nostrils flared as she leaned close and breathed deep.

"You use Master Dremelle, then? I've heard he's one of the best surgeons in Mer. My husband could take some scalpel lessons from him."

"Oh yes," Giacondah sighed with a smile. "Dremy loves working with me. He gives me just enough nectar so I don't fall unconscious. He's so sweet, and of course he gives me his happy ending when he's finished. If I could cope with the pain, I'd have him six or eight times a year instead of only four. So who is this pretty thing with the strudel plate?"

"This is Boudi-Ca," Breanarachelle answered. "She's a little friend of mine who attends my parties. I've recently convinced her of the merits of patapoufery. She's very ambitious, and I believe she can be special as a patapouf. She has the most delicate, porcelain skin. If she does well, I might consider adopting her as a personal plaything someday."

"If we could all be so lucky." Giacondah winked. "I've heard her name, Breanarachelle. Isn't she Lydiah's girl?"

"She is. Lydiah doesn't need to know about this."

Giacondah's enormous foot twitched. "Oh! I love an intrigue. These pastries are her first, Breanarachelle?"

"Indeed, and one for me. So let's get to eating, shall we?"

Giacondah's chest heaved, and she gestured with her arm. "Have a seat. Boudi-Ca should have consecrated goat milk. It will help everything go down easier. Get the girl a cup of warm milk, Scaramucci, and bring my afternoon snack early."

"Yes, Mistress." The fledgling Jinn disappeared through another door, from which wafted intense smells of the bakery, along with the clinks and clatters of trays and pans. Boudi-Ca allowed Breanarachelle to escort her to the small round table next to Giacondah's bed. The table was surrounded on two sides by padded benches. Scaramucci returned with a silver pitcher and poured a teacup full of thin yellow-white liquid, then bustled off again.

Breanarachelle picked up her charcoaled fairy ring and nibbled. She licked her yellow-grey fingers. "Delicious. It has just enough sweet to go with the charcoal, with undertones of smoke in the mushrooms. Go ahead with your strudels, child. Take sips of milk in between swallows. Is that right, Giacondah?"

"Just pretend you're swallowing a cock, and you'll be fine," Giacondah breathed, reaching for the cioccolatto that Scaramucci was extending over the bed. Giacondah levered her arm with difficulty, dragging her enormous portions of flesh over the amorphous mound of her left breast. She wedged the pastry between her lips with a sigh of distracted satisfaction.

Boudi-Ca felt a strong pull in that moment, but not to the pastries. A nectar box sat as the little table's centerpiece. She grabbed one of the strudels, bit and chewed. The sugar and honey were a little trickle of pleasure, almost like nectar but coarse, textured, and thick. She took a second and third bite. The little lumps sank into her belly and formed a pleasant warm weight. She drank the warm milk, which was less pleasant, but another bite sweetened the milk, and then she tested the milk and strudel together. Breanarachelle nibbled and watched her closely.

Boudi-Ca finished her first strudel. She could feel the pastry like a sweet satisfaction in her belly. Her belly was happy, and so was her mouth and throat. She bit into the second strudel, suddenly aware that the room had grown silent, and the three other women were all watching her.

She worked quickly to chew and swallow the second strudel. The pastry was a definite weight in her stomach, a fullness that was almost sexual, as if she'd been penetrated orally, and then impregnated through her throat. She felt a small quiver of fear as Scaramucci stepped forward at the behest of Giacondah to refill the mug with more goat milk.

"I'm feeling full," Boudi-Ca said. She really didn't want to eat the last pastry. "Can I just have two this first time?"

"That wouldn't be satisfying," Breanarachelle said quickly. "Eat it."

"She can have a bit of nectar to calm her stomach and throat," Giacondah murmured. "It will help soothe her nerves, certainly."

"No," Breanarachelle answered. "There are times for nectar, and there are times to feel something going down your throat. I want her to feel her throat."

"She might vomit," Giacondah countered. "The girl has eaten enough for her first. Until her stomach stretches, she won't eat much. On the other hand, if she ate a sugar oat cake for her third pastry, it would thicken in her stomach, and she won't be able to vomit. I always recommend a topper of oatcake for aggressive stomach training."

"Then bring one."

Boudi-Ca tried to catch Breanarachelle's eyes to express her anger, but Breanarachelle didn't look at her. Breanarachelle's eyes were lingering again on Giacondah's surgical bandages, which were visible under the hem of her enormous dress. Scaramucci returned with the oat cake. The oat cake was rich red and smelled of cinnamon. Boudi-Ca tried the cake. It was dry, and her throat clutched. She took more milk to soften the lump, and then she swallowed. She pressed the cake to her lips again.

"Eat it quickly, fledgling," Giacondah said. "Tarrying will only make it worse. Swallow the cake down as fast as you can, and it will go better."

Boudi-Ca did as she was bid, swallowing the cake fervidly. When she finished, the big lump in her belly felt like lead, and she felt a small pain in the center of her chest. She felt feverish, and her throat quivered and throbbed. Her stomach heaved suddenly, and heaved again. She opened her mouth, but nothing was coming out. She tried to sit perfectly still, in hopes that her belly would settle.

"This is such a beautiful moment." Giacondah sighed. "I agree with you, Breanarachelle. Boudi-Ca has beautiful skin. Her breasts are underdeveloped, though. I'd recommend a few surgeries to inflate her assets. A young patapouf needs to top up, or else she grows horribly out of proportion."

"I'll want a delivery of two strudels and one oat cake each morning at my estate for her," Breanarachelle said airily. "Perhaps around the eight?"

"Of course."

"Except for tomorrow, when she won't be available. Start the deliveries on dies Mercurii."

Boudi-Ca felt her stomach heave yet again, a heaving that swelled to embrace her whole body. She opened her mouth again and shuddered, trying to expel the pastries back onto her plate, but again nothing would come out except for a gagging sound.

"You see, Breanarachelle?" Giacondah said pleasantly. "The oats absorbed the milk and thickened. Everything is stuck well in her belly, and it's starting to stretch already."

"Lovely," Breanarachelle said. Her voice was throaty and sensual. "Lick up the rest of the crumbs, child. Finish your plate, pastry slut."

Breanarachelle's clawed hand gripped the edge of the table. She was bracing her slender yellow-grey body backwards on the low bench. The she-devil's skirt was hitched high up her thighs, and her other hand was low and levered. Breanarachelle appeared to be masturbating openly.

Boudi-Ca felt her stomach heave yet again, and again she leaned open-mouthed over the table, clenching. She only had to lean a little further to lick as Breanarachelle had bid. She actually wanted those crumbs. She wanted those little happy morsels. The morsels wanted to be in her stomach with their brethren, their sugary purpose fulfilled.

The cinnamon, honey, and sugar were delicious and melted together to renew the sweet gentle rainbow of flavors on her tongue. On impulse, she stuck her tongue out as far as she could manage. She the plate slowly to give Breanarachelle a good view of her licking efforts. Breanarachelle's eyes fluttered closed, and the she-devil moaned with transported pleasure.

Chapter 21.

"Ah, Stefan," Master Hillel Yaffe said, rubbing his hands together. "You're almost ready, and so are the clients."

"Your advertisement for him was poetry, Hillel," Mistress Vanessah added. "'Young Stefan has the ass of Adonis. His nipples are the sweetest pomegranate flesh, and his cock and balls are the fruits of the Earth, beckoning with the rustic, seductive charms of his old Kishi home. And those are the least of Stefan's virtues. His skilled musician's fingers would charm the cruel loins of Cerberus and arrest the momentum of Charybdis."

Hillel smiled. "Old money likes references to Greek myth."

Vanessa drummed her chin with her perfectly manicured and painted fingernails. "What does the ass of Adonis look like exactly?"

"Like that statue over on Rue De La Chartreuse," Hillel answered.

"You're talking about the hanging statue in the arch over the fountain, right?"

"Yes, but he isn't hanging. He's sitting on a swing, on the edge of leaping into a pool. It's Le Petit Adonis by Master Fragonard."

"Oh yes, I know Fragonard." Vanessah minced. "I love it when you talk Ukraine, Hillel. You've outdone yourself. This pretty boy must have inspired you."

"Be a good girl and finish him up quickly." Hillel slapped Vanessah's ass.

Golda lurked in the corner and watched the portly, well-dressed Djinnus stride down the dark hall towards the show room. She prayed that Gorka could hold himself together until the coin changed hands. So far, the boy had been strong. He'd accepted the leather collar around his neck. Mistress Vanessah stepped back and surveyed her work.

"There we are," Vanessah purred. "Perfect."

Golda cleared her throat. "Mistress Vanessah, would you mind if I spoke to my slave alone for a moment? I'm sure you understand. I'd like to say goodbye to him."

"Oh! I'd almost forgotten you were over there, Mistress Darlah. Of course. I'll just peek and see if Hillel and the bidders are ready yet." Mistress Vanessah sashayed out of the prep room and closed the door behind her. Golda sidled forward. She had one last moment to bolster Gorka's resolve. The boy needed to perform to earn the coin they needed.

"You can do this, Gorka," she whispered. "Stay true to yourself and never stop believing in Love, something divine beyond the endless pleasures and sufferings that the Jinni and Djinnus will make you feel."

Gorka's eyes were wild. "What do they actually do to you, Golda? I've heard stories, but I've never really spoken about these things with a human slave."

"The Jinni, Djinnus, and devils all want different things. Of the three, only a Jinn physically needs you to survive. She'll make you release sexually, and that's how she feeds her eternal emptiness, her Hunger. She'll drain your lust, which sustains her and gives her strength. Without it, a Jinn hungers for lust like a vampire hungers for blood. An Djinnus is something different. An Djinnus is a son of Lord Hades, and is constantly driven to spread his addictive seed into all female creatures, and males I suppose, if they prefer."

"Utter perversions."

"Yes, but the Djinnus and Jinni are experts at giving pleasure, beyond anything you're likely to imagine. Sex with Gypsy women won't satisfy you after you've been with the children of Hades and Allyssia."

Gorka lowered his voice still further. "Yes, but you and Mohilever will come to rescue me from my owner as soon as possible once my mother is safely away from Mer. I don't expect to suffer such pleasures for long."

"Of course."

A soft knock sounded on the door. Vanessah walked back in. "Are we ready, Mistress Darlah? Hillel says we can bring him."

"Yes," Golda said. "I hope my handsome slave boy will sell at a high price. Don't forget to sit perfectly straight and smile, Stefan."

Vanessah held a long leather leash in her hand. The Jinn lifted the end of it meaningfully. The silver clip on the strap snapped into the sturdy metal hoop on the collar. The Jinn tugged Gorka forward like a horse.

"Keep your back arched and your chin as high as it will go," Vanessah said airily. "You'll look like a trained song slave that way when you play. Be sure to spread your legs on the bench like I told you. And when I say wide, I mean wide. Your outer thighs should be pressing against the uprights of the armrests."

"I'll try."

"Don't just try. Every inch is another aureus, Hillel likes to say, and you need every extra inch that you can get. Arouse your phallus a little if you can still play."

Golda followed Vanessah down the hall. Vanessah guided Gorka by the leash through a doorway into the slave trader's show room, which was lit softly by candles in bronzed ivy wall sconces. The buyers held elegant masks to their faces, as if for a courtly masquerade ball, preserving their anonymity. Some of the buyers were Djinnus, well-dressed in long evening coats, waistcoats, and cravats. Gold and silver glittered on their fingers and ears. Most of the buyers were Jinni. Golda held up her own mask, hoping it would hide the pounding of her heart as well as her criminal visage.

To her relief, she didn't see Mohilever. She'd persuaded the uncle to wait outside the rear door, where two burly goat-horned hellions stood guard with armor and swords. Hillel Yaffe hovered at the foot of a low dais with a pleasant smile on his round face. He tucked a gold pocket watch into his mustard yellow waistcoat and nodded politely at her.

Gorka stepped towards the dais in the center of the room. The round wooden dais was a low platform for a low sturdy chair. A burgundy tapestry draped the chair, a backdrop to show off Gorka's body like a living sculpture. The tapestry appeared Kishi-woven with gold embroidered stars. Gorka climbed onto the dais, guided by Vanessah on one side and Yaffe on the other, and then he was sitting on the tapestried chair. He didn't spread her legs as Vanessah had ordered. He pressed his legs together coyly instead, kept his eyes lowered, and set his guitar on the dais such that it rested against his thigh.

"Here he is for your pleasure, ladies and gents," Yaffe said with a flourish of his arm. "Stefan is a very special slave for discriminating collectors. Remember to keep your mask on and refrain from naming names. I take every effort to ensure you are all law-abiding citizens, but the mask is for your own additional protection and anonymity during the bidding process. Spread your legs please, Stefan."

"Quite wide," Vanessah added.

Gorka opened his legs, putting has modest little cock on display. The buyers drifted closer to get a better vantage point. The rotating show-dais jolted into motion, propelled by Yaffe's firm hand on its wooden lip. Gears whirred. The platform rotated slowly. Yaffe stepped back and gesticulated at Gorka with a polished cane.

"This young, boyish beauty is looking for his very first Djinnus master or Jinn mistress. He is a virgin to the world of our fine capital city, soft as kitten, subservient as a lamb, but eager and energetic as a colt—"

"So he's never been trained?" interrupted a male buyer.

"Young Stefan is a former slave of the Kishi," answered Yaffe in a breathless tone, filled with magic and mystery. "This is a once in a lifetime opportunity, ladies and gents, to own a slave imported from the distant Seelie Court."

A Jinn buyer chuckled. "The boy looks smart, and the Kishi are notoriously lazy. I'd wager he'll be a donkey to re-train by civilized standards."

"Ah, but look at those firm little nipples and the room is barely cool," continued Yaffe. "Such sensitivity will make your plans for him difficult to resist, even while his taming and stoking will be uniquely satisfying. Now I present the pièce de résistance. Please listen to him play. Stefan will melt your heart with his music."

Gorka raised his guitar on cue and put fingers on the strings. For a moment he froze there, and then he closed his eyes and strummed. He played an old Gypsy song, the opposite feel of the classical piece that he'd played in Hillel Yaffe's office. He didn't miss a chord for several minutes, even while Yaffe was calling for bids and forgot to keep the dais spinning. Vanessah stepped in and jolted it forward again. Yaffe's secretary climbed onto the dais then. She reached under Gorka's guitar, and by the time the dais made a full revolution, Gorka was stiff. The bidding pushed higher with murmurs of approval.

When Gorka finished the Gypsy song, he went on to a Debussy. The buyers drifted away from the dais, some for the exit and others to give more persistent bids to Hillel Yaffe. When Gorka finished the mini-concert and lapsed into silence, there were only a handful of Jinn buyers left in the room, whispering amongst each other. Some had dropped the formality of masks, including the highest bidder, a wiry, strong-looking Jinn with a sword and a petite, better-dressed redheaded companion by her side. Golda blinked. She vaguely recognized the redhead as Henne-Ca, and with a girlfriend, no less.

"One-hundred sixty-five is the going price," Hillel Yaffe said with a smile. "Do we have another bid?"

"Yes." A Jinn in a voluminous pink dress raised her hand and waved a folded fan. Perfume wafted through the air from her enormous body. "One hundred eighty."

"Mon dieu," exclaimed Yaffe. "The bid is back to you, fine Madame with the sword. No? Sold then to the lovely mistress in pink. He'll make an excellent song slave in your famous establishment in the English quarter, Mistress. Will you be taking him in your carriage?"

"I'd like a delivery for that price," the Jinn said. She spoke wheezily as if breathless. She waved her fan to cool her face. With her other hand, she leaned her massive weight on a stout cane. "Bring him to The Absinthe

Cask."

Yaffe nodded quickly. "Yes, of course. Anything you need, Mistress. I'm here to serve."

"Tomorrow, I think. Late afternoon. I must arrange accommodations."

"Excellent." Yaffe bowed deeply. "Just send me a messenger bird to let me know when you're ready. I'll bring him right over then."

The Jinn gestured to her assistant, a collared slave boy who pulled handfuls of coins from a leather pouch and counted them. Yaffe readied a clipboard. He dipped his pen into an inkwell offered by Vanessah. He made entries in the paperwork before handing the clipboard to the Jinn buyer in exchange for the stacks of gold coins.

Golda pressed close. She could hardly suppress a jovial feeling. Gorka's buyer was three times the young man's size. The barrel-like thighs and the pillows of her ass would swallow Gorka and spit out a subservient young man who for the first time would know a purpose in his life. She hoped Yaffe didn't notice her hands trembling when she reached out to take her cut of the aurei.

When Yaffe handed her the heavy bag of coins, her heart was buoyed still further. It was almost over, and she'd be safe with the coin once she made the forest. She upended the little bag in her palm to count the shining aurei with her eyes. She'd never in her life held so much coin in her hands.

"So that's it ladies," Yaffe said with a white-toothed smile, adjusting his waistcoat over his paunch. "Mistress, will you brand your new slave tonight before you leave? My advice is always to brand when the money changes hands."

"Yes," the Jinn wheezed. "My slave will fetch my tong. It's in my carriage. You can heat it for me, Yaffe?"

"I have a furnace ready downstairs. It's part of my service."

"Downstairs?" the voice of the enormous mistress dripped with displeasure.

Yaffe put a pixie-smile on his businessman face. "Vanessa will heat your tong down there and bring it up here. Would you like more tea? Please slap me for not serving pastries and sweetcakes."

The mistress licked her lips. "You're a clever rake, Hillel. You should flirt more with me. I could bring you a lot of business."

Golda felt a twisted urge to stay and watch Gorka get branded by his new mistress, but she didn't dare stay longer than necessary, nor stop Henne-Ca to say an awkward hello. She didn't even stop to thank the slave trader or have any words with frog-jowled buyer, who had rotated to face her as if desiring a conversation about her new slave and his idiosyncrasies. Golda turned and hurried out the rear entrance into the alleyway where Mohilever was waiting with the horses. The old uncle stared at the coin bag with a curl on his lip.

"So you've done the dirty deed and got the coins? This will kill the lad's good mother if the devils haven't. You know that, Jinn."

"Yes, but this will also save Pinhas' soul from an eternity of torment. I'd say that's better. Did you buy the steel cuffs and the poison?"

"I surely did, lass. I have some wee skill as an apothecary. I picked something that can knock a Jinn right off her feet and keep her in a bad way for a while. I told the shopkeeper it was for a horse. The handcuffs were easier. Every corner cart in this damned city sells 'em in all shapes and colors."

"Wonderful." Golda leapt onto her horse and pressed hard with Mohilever through the stinking city streets. She was ready to nab Boudi. She just needed a time and a place. She was so sick of Mer and the fear that gripped her whenever she re-entered that ocean of stink and sin. She could see Henne-Ca's thread weaving away through the tapestry, but she ignored it. In a few days, Allyssia willing, she would never return to the capital city. She led the way back to the Merian east gate. Once again, she handed her horse off to Mohilever and used her stealth to evade the eyes of the wary guards.

It was eerie traveling at night through the corrupted forest of Haawiyah. Mohilever led the way with a torch outstretched in his hand. Golda urged her horse behind Mohilever along the last league into the camp. For the umpteenth time, she patted her small purse, assuring that Gorka's coins rode safely. She refused to feel guilty for helping the boy into slavery. She'd seen the humiliation in Gorka's eyes, but he deserved it.

Golda reined in alongside Mohilever in front of his tent. The Reik camp was eerie and dead silent at midnight, bathed faintly in the light of a moon tinted yellow by the spring sulfur blooms over the Great Blue Hole. Mohilever had been uncharacteristically quiet. His cheeks sagged more than usual, and he walked with a stoop. The Damp Delirious binge had taken a toll on the pathetic old codger. Mohilever shook his head grimly.

"So when are you going to try to spring him, lass?"

"We need to take the bribe in the morning to get Priebus before she's sent to the Great Blue Hole. We can't help Gorka immediately, because it will be too obvious that it was a trick. We need to let Gorka settle into his slave life while we bide our time."

"Aye. We'll Gorka suffer a little bit. How do you plan to help him then?"

"I have a few spells, and of course I'll use the poison and cuffs if needed to take out Gorka's new owner while we steal him from her. Can I have them now?"

Mohilever yawned. "I'll hold onto those, lass."

"I need the cuffs."

"Nary a Gypsy should trust a Jinn, and I'm no different. Just hand me the coins, and I'll make sure everything is locked up safe in my wagon."

"Fine. If you want to play that way, I'll keep the coins from Gorka's sale for tonight. I have a good place to hide them."

Golda ignored Mohilever's furious look and gave her horse a swift kick to send it skittering towards her tent. She was sick of looking at Mohilever's extrusions of unplucked nose hair. She tethered her horse and went to the hoary old oak behind her tent. She slid the coin bag into a dark hidey hole under the dead exposed roots, a little hidden hollow she'd discovered while watching two Gypsy camp children at games. She finally slipped into her tent and shucked her boots and clothes. She lit the stub of a taper candle and collapsed onto her bed.

She allowed her mind to drift back to Gorka sitting nude and playing in Hillel Yaffe's auction room. Gorka's hair had been handsome after

Vanessah had tended to it. Golda rolled onto her stomach, ignoring her pang of Hunger. The risk had been worth everything. In the morning, the Fates willing, she would see Priebus free. She just needed to wrangle the poison and cuffs from Mohilever, and then she could give the old man the slip. She'd hunt for Boudi-Ca and abandon Gorka. Perhaps she would return for the boy later, or perhaps not. She could only save one at a time, and Boudi-Ca was the priority. Golda closed her eyes. She allowed the weariness in her bones to convey her into the world of dreams.

She awoke to a noise in the night. The leaves outside her tent were crackling under soft footsteps. She shook her head to rouse her senses and felt for her shiv under her pillow. A rustle alerted her to an intruder entering. The footfalls suggested more than one. She could feel the heat and desire in front of her. She lunged and stabbed, and she was rewarded with a flood of warm blood over her fingers. A hand seized her arm. A cloth pressed suddenly over her nose.

She jerked and grappled with the next assailant, even as her nasal passages writhed from a sickly-sweet odor that made her brain explode. She beat the man away, but not before her limbs went rubbery. She hit at her attackers with her fists, but her arms wouldn't obey her. When the men leapt on top of her again, she couldn't resist. Stars burst in the darkness of her eyes. A hum sounded loud in her ears as the toxin took control of her body.

Chapter 22.

"Lieutenant Nefra is here," Lydiah's voice was low and conspiratorial. "I want you to make friends with her, fledgling. I won't always be there for you. You'll want friends and mentors in the Smokeless Flames. Nefra knows about your hidden past, but you can't speak of any of that. Understand?"

"I guess, Mistress." Boudi-Ca examined herself yet again in the mirror. She didn't look fat yet from her first pastries, just tired and depressed. "I can't talk with her though if I don't know what she knows. It's like fighting blindfolded."

"She's in no position to expose your weaknesses. She knows it would be mutual suicide, so the point is moot. I'll be speaking with Nefra about some furniture for a few minutes. Come down whenever you're collected and ready."

Lydiah left the bedchamber. Boudi-Ca drew a final stroke of lip paint over her upper lip. Vladimir resumed his efforts to tighten her cured leather corset, which would provide protection while also lifting her breasts to reveal her assets. Her nectar headache was back already, but at least the feel of the pastries had dissipated in her belly. She no longer felt the dread-inducing weight or urge to expel them. The memories from the previous day were engraved in her brain, however, especially

Breanarachelle's obscene pleasure.

That morning she'd considered turning Lydiah over to the devils, and thereby satisfying Breanarachelle. Her fear was in implicating herself. She had no faith that Breanarachelle would help her. Boudi-Ca felt her belly tremble. She hated the devils, and she secretly loathed Lord Hades. It was stupid to make lesbian love illegal in the first place.

Meanwhile, she was going to meet Lieutenant Nefra, who was in charge of arresting the lesbians. She would do well kiss ass with the lieutenant as Lydiah suggested, although once again Lydiah was telling her nothing of importance. How did she know Nefra? What did Nefra know about her?

Boudi-Ca stepped into her sparring flats and collected her fencing gloves. On impulse, she gathered her sheathed Oya-blade from behind the door. She never practiced with the elegant gemmed sword, but perhaps it would impress the lieutenant. The citrines in the pommel glittered mystically. Boudi-Ca descended the east wing stairs to the first floor, where she found Nefra speaking with Lydiah on the rear patio.

Lieutenant Nefra was a weathered-looking, attractive Jinn with shoulder-length brown hair pulled back into a pony tail. Her body was corded and strong, neither old nor young. She wore a fine-looking metal-plated fencing vest. The vest wrapped her white linen chemise, which was lacy with flouncing around the sleeves. A plain black mid-thigh leather skirt completed her ensemble. The skirt was ribbed with front and rear reinforcements.

"Here is Boudi-Ca." Lydiah gestured. "She's had regular lessons with Mistress Dimona for the last two years. I want you to run Boudi-Ca through a real Flames-style training regimen, Nefra. She needs to know what to expect if she becomes an aspirant in a few months."

"I'll do my best."

"Boudi!" Lydiah barked. "Form ranks!"

Boudi-Ca looked sullenly at Lydiah. She really wasn't in the mood for the Mistress that morning. She sifted through excuses in her brain for going back to bed, but as usual her headache impeded her thinking. "I have a bad headache. I don't think I can practice today."

"And there you are, Lieutenant. That's what we need to work with." Lydiah turned on her heel and stalked off the stone patio towards the garden pool.

"When they say form up, you're supposed to stand at attention facing the instructor." Nefra smiled calmly. Her silvery brown eyes appeared tired with inner strain. Nefra wore no powder or paint on her face. Boudi-Ca sighed and slung her heavy Oya-blade over her shoulder.

"My Mistress said I knew you before. Where did we meet?"

Nefra glanced warily at Lydiah, who had settled on the wide brick edge of the garden pool just out of hearing distance. Vladimir had emerged from the nearby château doorway to stand behind her. Curiously, the slave boy was unlacing Lydiah's corset. "I don't think this conversation is appropriate at this moment," Yellen finally answered. "You should ask your mistress."

"Just tell me. I won't tell her."

"You seem tense. Let's go ahead and spar."

"I won't spar until you tell me how I know you. Lydiah won't tell me, and that's ridiculous. It's almost as ridiculous as her getting undressed right over there by the pool. She never even goes near that pool, so what is she doing?"

Yellen's eyebrow arched. "Perhaps she's getting some sun, but it's a strange time and place. I assume she's doing it for a reason, and I'm not going to look over that way."

"Well, I'm tired of her not telling me the truth. I used to be a lesbian, right? Were you the one that arrested me, like you're arresting all of the lesbians now?"

"No. I fought you, but I didn't arrest you."

"Why not?"

"You were better than I was, and I didn't want to hurt you. I still remember your beautiful eyes in the sunlight, shining silver-blue and bright. You wanted so much to beat me, and at the time I thought you were cute. I was smiling at you, even though I was a nervous for a lot of different reasons. You soon taught me that you were no one to be trifled with."

"I'm not. That's why you should never try to arrest me."

"I'm not really interested in arresting lesbians. It's just my job, and I'm doing my duty for the Smokeless Flames. I secretly believe in loving freely."

"Oh." Boudi-Ca could feel her cheeks heating. She had no idea what to say, and she could hardly believe her supposedly beautiful eyes in that moment. Lieutenant Nefra's brown, worn eyes flickered down. Nefra was giving every impression of drinking in a desirable figure.

"In fact, I don't think such a thing can even be reformed," Yellen persisted, raising her eyes again. "What do you think?"

"I don't know. I just feel."

"I know what you mean."

Boudi-Ca gazed into Nefra's brown eyes. She couldn't believe what she was hearing and seeing, and she could feel something in Nefra, an emotional openness, a vulnerability beneath her tough exterior. "So what are you going to teach me?"

"Whatever you want. That's a nice blade."

"It's a Oya-blade. Mistress Lydiah gave it to me, or at least that's what she says. I don't remember." Boudi-Ca half-drew the sleek mid-length blade and showed the polished, oiled steel. "I'm not really in the mood to train. Dimona's lessons are usually so boring, and I have too many other things I'm thinking about."

"Like what?"

"Like how you fight a devil. What are the best tactics?" Boudi-Ca blinked her eyes and tried to look innocent.

It was Nefra's turn for minor shock. The Lieutenant looked uncertain and glanced again over at Lydiah. Vladimir had removed her corset laces, and Lydiah emerged bare-chested with her impressive assets in sunlit glory. She was nude from the waist up, wearing only a short black skirt. She posed her body over the worn retaining bricks beside the placid, yellow-brown pool. Vladimir returned to the château with the corset, and then the lush thorny gardens stilled again except for the trickle of water from the urns of the Rake statues.

"No one would fight a devil, and I have never fought one," Nefra said in a low tone. "Did your Mistress tell you to ask that, Boudi-Ca? Is this another tactic to get into my head?"

"No." Boudi-Ca shrugged. "I was curious, that's all."

"Why? Are you worried?" Yellen's eyes were suddenly feline and huntress-like. "Maybe you're not as reformed as your Mistress says you are?"

"I want to learn hand-to-hand techniques today." Boudi-Ca knelt and abandoned her Oya-blade to the patio stones.

"You mean for when you're disarmed?"

"No, like an Djinnus is trying to rape me, and I don't have a weapon. So what am I going to do to him? Dimona only wanted to teach me with a blade. I know more about blades than she does, and I know there is much more than blades. So you can be the Djinnus and try to grab me from behind, and I'll try to fight."

"Like this?" Nefra dropped her blade and approached her. Boudi-Ca turned her backside into the Lieutenant, and for a moment Nefra gently embraced her from behind. Boudi-Ca dared to grab Nefra's muscled thigh, as if to balance herself.

"You love someone, don't you, Lieutenant? I can feel it."

Yellen flinched and released her grasp, as if slapped. "You're telepathic?"

"Just with love."

Nefra took an audible breath, as if to ease her tension. "Your feelings are like your blade, Boudi-Ca. They have a double edge that cuts to the truth."

Boudi-Ca pivoted to face the Lieutenant, who stood just inches away from her. She could almost feel the heat of Nefra's broiling emotions. "What do you mean? You mean the truth of who we love?"

"No. The path of the sword is a spiritual path, and the sword is a symbol for a Sharp mind. Our swords cut through our enemies from within as well from without. Ignorance is a great enemy. If you want to know the truth, you must cut through the enemy of ignorance, and that includes illusion and delusion."

"So illusion and delusion come from ignorance?"

"No. Illusion and delusion are ignorance. They come from passion."

"Why passion? Passion is our strength. Passion makes us strong. It's ridiculous to say passion is our enemy. I don't know who I'd be without my passion. I'd be really bored, for one thing."

"Maybe that says something. Passion blinds us to the truth. I learned this recently in fact. Passion fools us, so it leads us back to ignorance. Passion blinds us. If we can't see our real enemy, then we can't fight it. That's why it's important to let go of endless passion and just step back. If you start to think of your blade as a symbol of cutting through to truth, that will be enough for today. A blade cannot lie."

"What about a feint attack? That's a trick. That's a lie."

Boudi-Ca gasped. Nefra seized her bicep and yanked her close. Nefra's lips were an inch away from hers, and for a moment they braced against each other in frozen balance, poised at the brink of a kiss. Boudi-Ca sought Nefra's eyes inches away from her own, and then Nefra released her again. The lieutenant drifted back to arm's length. "Was that a trick, Boudi-Ca?"

"No. I don't think so."

"Exactly. Even in a feint, there is truth. A feint has to be a real potential threat, or else it's a failed feint. I could have followed through if I'd wanted to. A feint opens the eyes of your opponent to the possibility of death, and that is the essence of the blade. It cuts through all of the nonsense and bares your soul to the essentials. If you just came an inch away from death, then what really matters in life? The things that don't really matter melted away in that moment, and they no longer seem so important."

"A kiss seems really important," Boudi-Ca countered. She felt flushed, and for some reason she was thinking clearly for the first time in days, as if she were suddenly wide awake. "So apparently it really matters in life."

"If you think so. That is your truth."

"What's going on here?" Lydiah was approaching across the lawn onto the patio, striding in half nudity. "Why aren't you two practicing at blades?"

"I wanted to learn hand-to-hand combat," Boudi-Ca answered. "Mistress Dimona refused to teach it to me, but it's really important. Lieutenant Nefra is teaching me all sorts of things already."

"Right. That's what I hope and expect. Carry on then." Lydiah quickly turned on her heel and sashayed back across the patio, striding like a pale goddess with perfect posture. Boudi-Ca grabbed Nefra's hand and pulled her towards the gardens.

"She doesn't know fighting. I want to take you someplace more private."

For a moment, the lieutenant resisted, but finally gave in. "Where are we going?"

"You'll see." Boudi-Ca pulled Nefra forward to where two plump rose beds came together like rosy buttocks at the beginning of a narrow path. The path led away from the lawn and the patio, and soon they were out of sight of Lydiah. Beyond the hyacinths and thorn-leaf ivy, the gardener's shack loomed in the shade of a stand of cobra-leaf trees. Boudi-Ca pushed the door open into the dark wood-floored cabin, where a few old wheelbarrows cozied up with rakes, shovels, and hoes. She pushed the door closed behind Nefra.

"What are you doing?" Nefra asked in a warning tone.

"This." Boudi-Ca threw herself against Nefra, pressing with her lips to cross that forbidden extra inch, that one desperate inch to death. She pressed the lieutenant against the closed door, refusing to be denied. Nefra dipped forward finally and took the kiss in earnest, fencing tongue tips, as if they were first-time sparring opponents circling for control. Nefra's lips were soft and vulnerable, just like the softness under her armored shell. Boudi-Ca moaned when she felt Nefra's hands grab her buttocks. Yellen half-lifted her from her feet, pivoted her, and turned the tables, throwing her hard against the shed wall.

"What in the hells are you doing?" Nefra pulled back. Her brown eyes recoiled in the half-dark like a rabbit in a hole. "Why did you do that? Is this some sort of trap?"

"No."

"Did Lydiah order you do to this? Are the devils watching us?"

"No!" Boudi-Ca fought sudden tears. "I just suddenly wanted to kiss you. Maybe I was trying to make my Mistress jealous."

"Maybe you're insane." Nefra yanked open the door, and then she was gone into the sunlight. Boudi-Ca hugged herself in the dark interior of the shed, fighting tears that wanted to stream down her cheeks. She slumped and sat alone on the hard floorboards. She hoped she wouldn't be in horrible trouble for what she'd done on impulse, but she was already in horrible trouble. Everything was overwhelming and out of control—the Flames, Breanarachelle, her nectar headache, Lydiah, and now Lieutenant Nefra.

Chapter 23.

Yellen drove slowly. She held the red-painted wheel with her left hand and draped her right arm over the back of the motorcar seat. She tried to do it casually, not like she was putting her arm around Shadow. Yellen mentally formed the messenger spell, and the bird flitted away across the street, over the tops of the cobra-leaf trees.

Shadow hadn't noticed the forewarning to Commander Changeh, who was the Named of the day. Shadow was supposedly medicated with a bit of nectar for her pain. Yellen looked straight ahead. She was feeling the pain as well. Her chest was aching again from her stress. The ache had started the previous day when she and Boudi-Ca had gone toe-to-toe, fencing faces instead of blades.

She'd decided that Boudi-Ca's kiss had been genuine and not a game. She'd felt a magical connection, a magic that had come from deep within the troubled fledgling. The spark had thawed her in places that hadn't felt warm in forever, not even during her recent, tense meetings with Henne. Phar gripped the motorcar wheel more tightly in her fingers. She hated herself already for scolding Boudi-Ca, and she was punishing her own cowardice by growing bolder with her rebellion against the purgation.

Thanks to her daily forewarnings, the lesbian purgation over the previous three days had been shocking in its futility. Each morning when they'd arrived to make an arrest, the Named had vanished in the nick of time. Canthah had been able to track the Named in the tapestry, but the threads of the hunted kept disappearing into the pits and warrens under the capital city, or at the precarious cliffs of Erebus outside the city where the quarry had somehow fled, despite the devils guarding the gates. All ten Named in the previous three days had escaped.

According to Lydiah and Befanah, questions had already been raised in Hell's Court. All of the focus had been on Canthah and her abilities as a tracker compared to Shadow, which had turned into a perfect distraction from the real fact that the lesbians were in fact being forewarned by a mole in the chain of command. As a consequence, Shadow had been re-instated.

Yellen turned into a quiet northside neighborhood, keeping a slow pace. She was nearing the home of the quarry, and she hadn't allowed much time for the Named to escape. Commander Changeh was close by on the north side, so she'd sent the warning to Changeh directly. She'd warned two other Named directly in the previous days under similar circumstances. In her heart, she'd wanted to defray the weight of culpability from Simhonit and take more upon herself.

She knew that she shouldn't send warnings either directly or to Sim every damned morning. It was too suspicious, yet she couldn't help herself. It was only a matter of time before eyes would turn in her direction, and she was surprised that Lydiah hadn't questioned her already. Once committed to sabotage, however, she hadn't been able to decide which suspected lesbians to condemn to torture and which to save. It was a dilemma that she needed to solve before she landed herself an interrogation.

Yellen wrenched the heavy metal wheel and tooled the motorcar left onto Cherry Blossom Street, the address of Commander Changeh. It was a quiet, well-to-do and well-landscaped neighborhood. It was peaceful except for the shrieks splitting the morning air.

Carriages lined the crumbling street curb. Figures struggled in a front yard. Yellen pulled the motorcar up behind a sturdy Hell's Court cage-carriage. Lydiah was already there, standing by her personal sleek black two-seater. Lydiah looked on as the devils incapacitated the Named and dragged her towards the waiting cage.

Yellen quickly disembarked along with Shadow. In the front lawn of the residence, four devils wrestled with Commander Changeh, who was flailing, shrieking, and hurling powerful hexes, even though she was ebon cuffed and writhing in pain as the Hell's Court devils swung their ebon wands at her. Changeh finally slumped and stilled in submission in the middle of the gang of devils. Yellen tore her eyes away from the terrible scene.

"Councilor Lydiah? What's happening?"

Lydiah gave her an icy glare. "I could have sent you a bird, Nefra, but I thought you should see for yourself. The devils pre-empted us this morning. I got a warning from them twenty minutes ago and came straight here. I don't know where we stand now, but given our string of failures, I can't say that I blame Hell's Court for invoking the clause in the Purgation mandate that allows them to take over."

Yellen watched the devils thrust Changeh into the cage. She took care to keep her face impassive, although she couldn't manage Shadow's level of coldness. She'd taken lessons a few times with Changeh, who was a well-known instructor at the northside Smokeless Flames monastery. Changeh was an Asian mistress wearing a beautiful handmade batik kimono that had been ripped apart mercilessly. The kimono hung in shreds over her whipped and bloody body. Yellen stepped closer to Lydiah.

"Any word yet on what's happening with the lesbians who have been taken, Councilor? It's been weeks now. Will there be Court trials?"

"I don't know," Lydiah answered. "I've asked Master Glumstak for a one-month report on the status of the incarcerated Sisters, and he said he would refer my request to his superiors. Well, his superiors include my husband, among others. I begged Fennel to tell me something. He told me to wait, but he appreciated my service to Lord Hades."

"I'm not surprised."

Lydiah glowered. "I used to be a lackey like you, Lieutenant, following orders, but I happened to be a little more ambitious. I married an

Archduke—a true son of Lord Hades. Shadow's husband is a respectable man too. Perhaps you should have a husband before you pass judgment on others."

Yellen kept her eyes even, but she noticed Shadow's little smirk. Meanwhile, one of the devils had approached. The morning light dappled his mottled grey skin with colors of ochre and sickly gold.

"Good morning, Councilor," the devil said. "We'd like to inform you that we saw a bird fly into the residence before we made the arrest, and when we broke in, the Named was in the process of hastily packing a bag. We're certain now that the Named are being forewarned."

"That's unfortunate, Master Nargchuk," Lydiah said. "Perhaps we need to re-examine the process of how things are happening. What sort of bird was it? What color?"

"It was a small and green. Is that a bird you recognize, Councilor?"

"Not particularly."

"The Flames internal investigation will be on hold until a decision on this is made. This weekend is the sacred day of Ostara and the end of the Spring Festival. I expect no more arrests will be made until the following Dies Lunae."

Lydiah's face was pinched. "And then?"

The devil smiled. "The clause that allows Hell's Court to take over the investigation will probably be invoked. The formalities will require a few days. We'll see if we have better success, and if so, then perhaps we'll open another investigation into your failed effort, Councilor."

Lydiah bowed curtly. "I doubt if you have the authority to assure me of that, and your brazen speculation isn't appreciated, Master Nargchuk."

"Thank you, Master," Shadow interjected, with a feminine tone of deference in her voice that could only be reserved for males. Yellen didn't meet Nargchuk's beady probing eyes. She managed a polite nod. Nargchuk saluted and stalked off towards the cage-carriage.

Yellen avoided Lydiah's eyes, which she could feel boring into the side of her face. She felt unhinged, like the paving stones under her boots had turned to sand, yet she still stood on them. She tried to remember whether she had ever sent a messenger bird to Shadow. She'd sent several green finches to Lydiah over the previous weeks. Lydiah wasn't an idiot.

"I guess that's it then." Lydiah's voice was as cold as ice. "I was worried about this. Hell's Court is taking over. The Council will be disappointed, and I'll likely be required to describe what might have happened. Meanwhile, we've been threatened with an investigation, which will surely involve questioning."

"I'm so sorry," murmured Shadow. "If I've failed the Flames, then please give me a demotion."

Lydiah's jaw worked. "If anyone has failed, it's the leadership of the Flames for allowing lesbianism to increase to such levels during this last century."

"It's a disease," Shadow agreed. "It will spread if left unchecked."

Yellen wanted to open her mouth to argue, but she held her tongue. Lady Allyssia was the leader of the Smokeless Flames, and the goddess had condoned lesbianism in Her ranks since the Flame's inception. The first two Jinni, Ereshkigeh and Astaarteh, were said to have experimented with each other. After the institution of Lord Hades' laws, the consorting between the firstborn had been stricken from Hell's written history.

"So, Yellen," Lydiah said with an acerbic tone. "Since we don't need to file a report at the Council building, why don't we go back to my home and have another social visit. I'd like to speak with you a little bit more. Let's call it a debriefing."

Yellen tilted her head as if pretending to consider. Lydiah's tone had implied an order, but she had zero intention of going. It was a rule of swordplay—treacherous footing demanded movement, not getting pinned down and nailed by Lydiah. She needed to consider her options and whether she needed to flee Mer. It would kill her to miss Henne's wedding, but it could literally kill her to stay and face Lydiah's vengeance.

"I need to go elsewhere, actually," she said. "I have a gift to buy and some clothes to get pressed. I need some supplies for the slave that I'm training, and then there's a bridal party this afternoon. A friend of mine is getting married on dies Solis."

"Ah, yes." Lydiah turned to watch the Hell's Court cage-carriage recede up the street with Mistress Changeh moaning and weeping in tow. "The biggest weddings are on Ostara day. I'll be attending one myself. Very well, Lieutenant. I suppose you get your vacation now. I hope you enjoy it, at least while it lasts. I won't need you to instruct my Boudi-Ca again, of course, since clearly you failed at that too."

"I think I made some progress. She's had a lot of black nectar, correct?"

"She's had less than you might imagine, and much less than Hell's Court might imagine." Lydiah turned on her elegant heels and stalked off in a cloud of anger to her sleek black carriage. The Councilor didn't look back. A flicker of movement came from the residence of the Named. The form of a forlorn slave girl haunted the wide-open front door. The girl rubbed a tear from her cheek. She was nude except for a gold chain around her hips and a wide gilded collar with side-mounted D-rings. The girl was an Asian with long dark hair that hung over her shoulders and breasts.

"I wonder who is warning the named." Shadow said. "I haven't noticed anyone following us. I've been watching. Now it's too late. It's not you, is it?"

Yellen shook her head in the negative, avoiding Shadow's eyes. "Of course not. I need to do some shopping here on the north side. I'll hire a rickshaw."

Shadow offered a slow salute and paced back to the motorcar. The tracker climbed in, fired the engine and shifted it into gear. Yellen watched with relief as the car drove away. She crossed the yard of the Named toward the girl. As she went, she summoned her messenger bird.

Henne, I don't think I can come to your party today. As far as a wedding gift, the art gallery is my gift to you. I'm sorry we didn't get that male slave, but we'll find another one. I hope to have the gallery renovations under way when you get back from your honey moon.

"Where are they taking my mistress?" The slave girl exited the house and crossed the front patio. Her eyes were bold and upset, abandoning any pretense of deference.

"To Hell's Court," Yellen answered. She stopped at arm's length from the girl. "I'm not sure when you'll ever see her again. You're the house-girl?"

"Yes," she answered.

"You'll need to take care of the others. If your Mistress doesn't come back soon, I'm sure someone else will come and tell you what to do. Hell's Court never leaves loose ends."

The girl wiped her tears. "Thank you, Mistress."

Yellen squeezed the girl's bare shoulder and caressed her soft neck. The girl shied away, but lowered her eyes submissively. Yellen turned and headed back towards the street. She hadn't considered the fate of the slaves of the arrested lesbians. The answer could well provide a clue as to what the Court was planning for the Named. If the slaves were left alone, that would be a good sign. If the slaves were taken and put up for public auction, that would be bad.

Yellen pushed away her soggy feelings. She needed to be strong, and she needed to avoid being cornered by Lydiah. She was no match for the Councilor. Even her sword was an underdog against Lydiah's sorcery. In reality, Lydiah could simply turn her over to the devils, who would demand to see her messenger bird, and she would have no recourse.

She dared to hope that wouldn't happen. Perhaps her brief lusty encounter with Boudi-Ca had been a blessing in disguise, pushing her into the realm of knowing too much. If Lydiah gave her to the devils for torture, Boudi-Ca was also in jeopardy.

Yellen walked two city blocks to the edge of the Asian district before she found an available city rickshaw. She climbed into the seat just as Henne's brown catbird swooped over a stone wall and alit on her shoulder.

That's fine, Yellen. I'm really busy today. I'm floating on nectar before I get dressed for my prenuptial party. I know it's a long way, but could you please come and give me just one last kiss?

Yellen winced at the horrible tone of finality. She hoped Henne meant a last kiss before the wedding, not one last kiss forever. If she could never kiss or touch Henne again, then running the art gallery and showing Henne's sculptures would be torture more than a labor of love.

"Driver, please turn around," she called out to the barebacked male city-slave. "I'd like the Coliseum district please—Canus Avenue and

Reichstrasse."

The driver took twenty minutes to angle down across the near north side towards the neighborhoods between the Denmark district and the Coliseum. Henne met her at the rear door of her house. They climbed the stairs and locked themselves in the bedroom. Yellen pressed and met Henne's infinitely soft lips. They fenced tongues. Henne slipped from her robe and pulled her towards the bed. Yellen fell on top of her.

"This is crazy," Yellen breathed. "My coming here today."

Henne winked seductively. "Someone gave me Charleton Red as an early wedding gift. I was supposed to wait until my honey moon, but I wanted to sample a little bit."

"So you invited me over just to do red nectar with you?"

Henne giggled. "Silly. No, I wanted to see you. I've secretly been sleeping with women for so many years, and after my wedding everything will change. I'll have my husband's seed in me permanently, and a lust for his cock will be one hundred percent in my soul. I just wanted—"

"What?"

"I wanted to taste your love for me. It's so much different and special than his." Henne pressed upwards. Yellen straddled her, tonguing and licking. She slid down, peppering Henne's breasts and nipples with more kisses. Henne smelled and felt so good—soft, feminine, and exquisite. Yellen kissed over Henne's belly, but Henne was pulling her up, reaching low, tugging at her sword and sash.

Yellen slipped from the bed to disrobe, glancing at the door to be sure the bolt was thrown. One last kiss. The words of Henne's messenger bird still echoed in her head. No matter what happened, she could only make the most of it, yet she desired for so much more. Henne slid from the bed and went to the phonograph. She manipulated the arm of the device and vigorously turned a crank. The machine began to play music—tinny but nonetheless a marvel, a mechanical symphony to drown out the sounds of the impending physical concerto.

"It's nice, Henne," Yellen said. "The music. You're so cosmopolitan. I feel like rube. I've been out on the war fronts for so long that I'm behind the times with these inventions. I know we're making a lot of guns. Musket balls never used to hurt much, but they keep making bigger and better ones. I'm sure the vampires, werewolves, and everyone will soon get their hands on them."

"But there are wonderful things coming out too, like the vibrating song-slave stools. Oh Yellen, you should get one for our gallery boy for when he plays at my shows. They're expensive, but it would be lovely to have him sit in the corner of the showroom on a phallus-mounted song stool. You're going to look for cheaper boy, right? One less skilled but with bigger biceps and a bigger cock?"

"Yes." Yellen met Henne again at the bedside, and they crashed together into the sheets. She showered kisses on Henne's freckled cheek and neck, the softest and most compelling surfaces in all of Hell. "By the Lady, I wish you'd change your mind. Please?"

"I can't." Henne's eyes were wistful as she returned the kisses. "Have you heard about those arrests? Hell's Court is cracking down on lesbians everywhere. I hope you're safe from that? I've heard a lot of rumors this week. I'm worried about you."

Yellen nipped. "I'll be fine. I'm more worried about you."

"Don't be worried. My husband is going to take good care of me." Henne smiled. "He's filthy rich. It's ridiculous. I'm lucky, Yellen. Please find it in your heart to be happy for me. I don't blame you for not showing up at my prenuptial party, but you're going to my wedding this week's end, right?"

"Of course. And when you come back from your honey moon, you'll come see me, and we'll open the gallery together. We'll think of a story for your husband about how we met, and why I'm your art dealer."

Henne sighed. "Right. After my honey moon."

"Where are you two going?"

"Andros wants a hunting trip. We're going to the Carthago promontory. Andros has a stone tower there that belongs to his father. It's supposed to be a quiet place with wide views of Haawiyah over the Great Blue Hole mines. I was worried the mines might raise a stench, but Andros says no—the wind mostly blows from Erebus along the cliffs. Of course, the tower has a big and luxurious bed, and that's all we really need. The slaves went up last week to clean, fill the flower vases, and get everything ready. I'm going to be a very wealthy wife, Yellen. It's a whole different world of high society."

Yellen felt her kisses clutch in her throat. The thought of Andros emptying everything into Henne during her honey moon, addicting her body and soul to him and his seed, filled her with queasiness. The way Henne spoke of it with pleasure made the feeling even worse.

"I can't do this." Yellen forced herself away from Henne and off of the bed. She grabbed her robe from the wooden floor.

"Come back, Yellen."

"I love you more than he ever will. You should know that." Yellen climbed back into her uniform as fast as her shaking fingers manage.

"Oh, Yellen. Please don't torture yourself. I have to do this. Hell's Court left me off with a warning years ago. They gave me this chance, just like they gave a chance to Boudi-Ca with Councilor Lydiah. I'm proving that a fledgling lesbian can be reformed. I'm setting an example. It doesn't have to be a bad thing. It's all in the way you look at it."

"You should know that I might be in trouble. I'll try to make your wedding, but it's possible I might not see you again." Yellen hurried out the bedroom door. She was a fool, and she was finally convincing herself that the gallery was a big mistake. She needed to let Henne go, hide herself away, and hope for everything to blow over. Mistress Nili was waiting in the front foyer. Henne's former Mistress and mentor stood in a tired patched robe with her arms crossed. The heavy ebon collar was unflattering around her neck.

"Don't come to my home again," Nili said in a low, menacing tone. "Henne doesn't need your presence in her life anymore. Just leave her alone."

"She asked me to be here," Nefra countered lamely. "I'm done." She yanked open the door and passed back out into the street. She suppressed a slow, burning energy that heated her breast, mingling with the low ache of her pain. She had half a mind to visit the Smokeless Flames monastery and find a sparring partner at the gymnasium. She needed to act. She needed to beat on someone for a few hours with a practice blade. She summoned a messenger bird to her fingertips. She thought of Boudi-Ca.

I'm sorry I was rude to you. You took me by surprise. Maybe we could have a chat again sometime, if you like. I enjoyed your company very much.

The bird flitted off. Yellen admonished herself for her clumsy, laughable words, wishing immediately that she could recall the spell. She'd been far too long in the field away from Mer. She was blundering like a dumb, desperately horny ogre through the battlefields of love, and with the purgation still in play, at best she was going nowhere.

Chapter 24.

Boudi-Ca gathered her skirt and stepped from the carriage. She'd just received a messenger bird from Lieutenant Nefra, and she was struggling to keep Nefra's surprising message all collected in her head. She stopped while Breanarachelle's two devil bodyguards shooed the piper from the bakery steps again. This time the short human didn't move. He fondled his flute, and his eyes rolled back in lyrical rapture.

Where the lilacs bloom
   Frogs croak a honeyed tune
   Sweet cakes, sweet cakes—
   Mounds of liquid delight
   To please any child, and
   Jinn with hungry eyes—

"Move, piper," one of the devils said. The human didn't move. The devils pulled their whips and looked at Breanarachelle for the signal.

"Move, idiot," the she-devil hissed. "Do you know who I am? I'll clean the steps with your tongue so my shoes won't be sullied by your buttocks. First your tongue needs to be cut and mounted to a handle."

Boudi-Ca looked away, even as the idiot put his pipe to his lips and played in Breanarachelle's face. She rubbed her belly as the piper's shriek of pain echoed down the street. Her belly seemed infinitesimally fuller than normal under her fingertips. Her skin was turning a bit resilient instead of flat and firm. She couldn't imagine that Lieutenant Nefra would be attracted to a pastry slut, much less a huge patapouf. Nonetheless, she was looking forward to her morning pastries. She could think about Nefra's provocative message later.

It was dies Veneris, her fourth day of eating with Breanarachelle, not including dies Martis when she'd skipped to train with Lieutenant Nefra. Over the previous two days, she'd gone to Breanarachelle's estate just like on dies Lunae. She'd waited until Lydiah had left for the purgation, and then she'd ridden her horse alone down to Pee Hill, where the pastries had been delivered by Giacondah's slave boy. The pastries had been better than the first ones, if anything. She'd felt filled to capacity, and she hadn't heaved again.

On dies Jovis she'd even gone to visit Moshe to spike her feeling of fullness, breaking the two-week rule. He'd seemed pleased that she was willing to addict herself to him. In truth, between Moshe and the pastries, her nectar headache had finally gone away, and she felt more relaxed. She felt like she could continue eating the pastries for a few more weeks until the purgation was over.

She didn't want to betray Lydiah, but perhaps Lydiah would only be disgraced and avoid prison. She'd casually questioned Moshe in vague terms about Court evidence and the lesbian purgation, saying that she'd seen two Jinni together at a party like everyone else in Mer at one point or another.

According to Moshe, the Court needed more than a testimony and an unreliable witness with a sketchy memory. The Court would need a devil witness, hard evidence, or a legal confession. A wealthy, important Jinn like Lydiah would likely get a slap on the wrist. The plan seemed to be coming together. She was simply delaying Breanarachelle until the purgation was over, the importance of which Lydiah had underscored for her career and status.

On that morning, however, Breanarachelle had loaded her into the carriage instead of hosting her in Rhadamanthus' parlour, and thence they had ridden through downtown again to the Italian Quarter. They were visiting Giacondah, and the bloody-mouthed piper was lying in the nearby gutter. Breanarachelle beckoned with a long black-nailed finger.

Boudi-Ca stepped into the sweet shop and breathed the wonderful scents of sweetness and honey. A queer smile came unbidden to her lips. She felt her neck tingle when Breanarachelle gripped her shoulder with a gloved hand, urging her forward. She ran her eyes over the many delicacies, an abundance of sweetness that made her mouth water and her belly warm with a feeling that felt more and more sexual as each day of eating passed. Her desire for delicious pastries merged with her Jinn Hunger, creating a compelling whole-bodied feeling of need.

Scaramucci was waiting in the entry room, serving a bag of pastries to a demoness. The demoness was a pudgy horse-like creature with a shaggy tail and a grotesque horse head. "Go ahead into the back," Scaramucci said brightly, taking the coins from the demoness' fat fingers.

Boudi-Ca stepped up to the case and examined the fresh pastries. "I'd like to try lemon wedges today instead of the strudels."

Scaramucci smiled. "I'll bring those, then. They're the same price."

Boudi-Ca felt Breanarachelle's hand again on her shoulder, as if patting with approval. She continued through the curtains into the rear room. Giacondah was in her usual position, sprawled in her gilt-framed bed, her horizontal throne. A silver tray was perched on her stomach with a pile of pastries that surely numbered a dozen. Giacondah shoved a pastry into her mouth and beckoned to the table and chairs in the corner next to her. She drained a cup of milk while they seated themselves.

"So how are you, Gia?" Breanarachelle said cordially. "How are your legs feeling? Thanks for entertaining me and Boudi-Ca again."

"The pleasure is all mine," Giacondah managed, wiping her chin with a white cloth. "I love training a new patapouf. It's one of my favorite things."

"Mine too," Breanarachelle said. "Boudi-Ca has been lovely. She's eaten three pastries a day all week quite comfortably with no more problems in her little tummy."

"It's a long road." Giacondah picked up another pastry, and then seemed to think better of it. "I'm still in quite a bit of pain from my surgery. I don't suppose I could trouble you to have a look?"

Breanarachelle rose and pulled back the covers from Giacondah's enormous legs. The bandages were stained with dark dried blood, and the exposed skin was mottled with purple splotches. Breanarachelle slid her hand over the bandages, as if savoring an object d'art. "Master Dremelle hasn't taken the stitches out?"

"I know Dremy is a busy man," Giacondah said quickly. "He'll come pull them when he's ready. You don't see an infection?"

Breanarachelle squeezed and worked the thigh with both hands. "I'm not seeing anything. How many pastries do you eat per day? I'm not sure I've asked."

"Twenty or thirty, depending on the type." Giacondah sighed. "I wish I could afford to eat more, but such is the life of a patapouf. I'm a lucky one."

"Indeed you are," Breanarachelle said. "And so is Boudi-Ca."

"Are we stretching her today?"

"Oh yes," Breanarachelle said. "She owes me an extra three."

"Wait," Boudi-Ca said. "The contract says three a day. I'm not eating more than that."

Breanarachelle re-seated herself. "You skipped dies Martis. It's time to pay the piper."

Boudi-Ca frowned. "You said I could skip. You said I didn't have to eat every day."

"I said the contract didn't stipulate that you have to eat every single day, but for each day that passes, you need to eat three. I thought you understood that. How many does your Scaramucci eat per day, Gia?"

"She takes twelve," Giacondah answered. "Six in the morning and six in the evening, on average, and no more. She likes the honey pastries like Boudi."

"I want to see your fledgling stretched this morning too." Breanarachelle lips curled into a smirk.

"Oh, no." Giacondah shook her head. "I keep her on a strict regimen. I need Scaramucci to run the shop, and I can't afford the surgeries for her."

"Boudi-Ca feels alone. The child needs some morale support. I'll make you a deal, Gia. Let me see Scaramucci stretched this morning, and I'll pay for the pastries. I'll also pay for her next surgery if I'm allowed to attend. I'd like to watch your Dremy at work. I'd be very appreciative, Gia. I'm bringing you business."

Giacondah paused and looked at Scaramucci, who had poked her head through the curtain to listen to the conversation. Giacondah gestured at her. "Get yourself fourteen strudels and two oat cakes along with Boudi-Ca's order, our box of Hot Pink, and a fresh amphora of goat milk."

"Yes, Mistress." Scaramucci's voice quivered.

"Hot Pink is a nectar mix, yes?" Breanarachelle said.

Giacondah's jowls bulged when she nodded. "Yes. It's the usual sugar and red, which helps relax the stomach and let sugar absorb more quickly. Breanarachelle, I don't mean to criticize, but your girl needs to be off with her corset. Should I send for a boy?"

"Yes. Please, Gia."

Giacondah sent a messenger bird, and a boy quickly appeared from the kitchen. The boy wore an apron and a fair amount of flour on his forearms. Boudi-Ca reluctantly stood up, allowing the slave boy to take her dress. He worked at her corset lacings. She felt like she was melting and paralyzed. Above all, she felt embarrassed. After five minutes of sartorial efforts, she sat back down on the padded bench. She was clad only in her stockings and panties.

Scaramucci returned with a tray laden with pastries and a jug of milk, which she placed on the table ceremoniously. The patapouf fledgling left again and returned with the small wooden box that had graced the table on the previous visit. Scaramucci settled her bulk at the edge of the table, took the lid from the box, and reached for the little silver spoon inside. Breanarachelle's thin, avian fingers wrapped Scaramucci's.

"May I, Gia?"

"Certainly. One spoonful for each fledgling."

Boudi-Ca felt an even intense desire burn into her belly then, spiking her Hunger up further, and when Breanarachelle lifted the spoon to her lips, she gulped the sparkly lump of pink powder. A wave of intense pleasure burned down her throat. The pleasure lit her belly on fire, and then her sex, followed by her feet. Even her toes tingled with pink warmth. Breanarachelle fed a spoonful to Scaramucci. A sheepish, eager smile spread over the fledgling's pudgy face.

"Oh, it looks like they're enjoying this," Breanarachelle murmured. "Let's begin. Go ahead and dig in, little piggies."

Boudi-Ca reached for a pastry in unison with Scaramucci. Her first big bite of the lemon wedge soothed her fears. The wedge was an exciting, intense rich flavor of tart and sweet. She could already imagine the exciting new heights of pleasure that four wedges and two oat cakes would deliver to her belly.

She swallowed bite after bite, and the nectar pleasure drifted higher and higher into her head. She reached for her second wedge, only vaguely aware that Breanarachelle was tipping back and hitching her leather skirt. The she-devil's hand levered low. Boudi-Ca bit, chewed, and swallowed. She nibbled, chewed, and swallowed in a rhythm until she finished the second wedge.

"An oat cake for you next, Boudi-Ca," Giacondah said.

Boudi-Ca reached for an oat cake. Her mouth watered even more when she bit into the drier cake that would stopper the first two pastries in her stomach. She grabbed some milk and gulped a few mouthfuls to wash the oat cake down. She filled her mouth with more cake, and a sudden inspiration came to her head. She wanted still more pleasure. She hitched up her skirt and grabbed Breanarachelle's left wrist. She pulled Breanarachelle's hand over to her stockinged thigh. Breanarachelle's clawed fingernails seized her tender skin.

"You tempt me, child." Breanarachelle's eyes were hooded and dangerous. "I know you've wanted this since the first time I touched you."

Boudi-Ca gasped with secret happiness when Breanarachelle's fingers slid over between her thighs, deeper until those cruel digits pinched her nether lips. Pain splintered, and wetness washed into her crevice. She picked up the oat cake again and nibbled up another mouthful. Scaramucci was silently eating with her eyes tactfully lowered, and Giacondah still looked on.

Boudi-Ca stuffed the oat cake in her mouth, squirming, begging with her hips to get Breanarachelle's fingertips onto her clitoris. The she-devil denied her, pinching and probing in her crevices instead. The ensuing little splinters of pain each seemed to be perfectly placed to send waves of both pleasure and pain up into her abdomen or down into her legs.

Boudi-Ca groaned. She quivered, already close to an orgasm, and Breanarachelle eased immediately, denying her. She reached for her fourth lemon wedge.

"That's a good little piggy," Breanarachelle hissed. "Good piggy. Eat it, piggy."

Boudi-Ca bucked slowly while she chewed and swallowed, dancing shamelessly with Breanarachelle's fingertips, which kept coaxing and goading her nethers without allowing her any relief or any respite. Breanarachelle's fingers seemed to know her every nerve center intimately. Boudi-Ca took a deep breath. The fourth pastry was heavy in her stomach, and she felt an uncomfortable fullness. She couldn't eat any more.

"That's all," she said. "Please let me—"

"Oh no," Breanarachelle said. "Maybe you need more of this." Breanarachelle abandoned her personal ministrations to take up the nectar spoon and fill it. Boudi-Ca hesitated when the she-devil pressed it to her lips, but opened and took it in. The wave of red-pink pleasure spiked higher, transporting her. Her thoughts disappeared, and her head felt like it was floating up towards the ceiling.

"You can do it, Boudi-Ca," Giacondah's voice encouraged from a distance.

Boudi-Ca took the fifth wedge and bit into it. Breanarachelle's finger hit her clitoris. She nibbled again, and again Breanarachelle rewarded her with a rub on her clitoris. She nibbled again and again, and soon the fifth pastry was down, and her stomach felt like it was bursting.

Pain surged. Breanarachelle pinched, slowly increasing the pressure on her nether lips. Boudi-Ca winced. She felt her inner thigh trembling as the pain increased. She reached for the sixth and last pastry, another oat cake. She nibbled. The pain lessened and went away. She drank some milk and nibbled more. Breanarachelle's fingers nibbled in symphony with her clitoris. Whenever she ate, Breanarachelle gave her pleasure. Whenever she hesitated, Breanarachelle gave her pain.

When she shoved the last piece of cake into her mouth, she was so close to her orgasm. Breanarachelle's fingers pushed inside her and rubbed quickly. Boudi-Ca groaned and heaved. The pleasure waved up and hit like thunder against the big lump of pastries in her belly. She moaned and shuddered, shaking loose the little crumbs that were clinging to her milk-damp chin. Her heavy, pastry-filled stomach jiggled. It was the most intense orgasm that she'd ever felt.

She leaned over the table, wide-eyed and open-mouthed. Her belly suddenly heaved of its own accord, attempting to expel the pastries and cakes, but they were thoroughly stuck. Breanarachelle's wet fingers seized her sex again and pinched. Boudi-Ca reached low to dislodge the she-devil's fingernails, but she was no match for Breanarachelle's strength. She squealed. The pain became agony.

"Please stop! Please! Oh, please!"

Breanarachelle's own body went rigid as she split into her orgasm. When the she-devil's long moan drifted into silence, a contented smile played on her froggish lips. Boudi-Ca took a deep breath when Breanarachelle finally let her go. She realized her forehead was dripping with sweat. Her stomach hurt. Her sex hurt. She eyed the pastry plate feverishly.

She wished in that moment that she could eat even more pastries, and she envied Scaramucci, who was still working on the rest of them. She wanted more, but she was beyond full. She was beyond full, and she was beyond empty. A queer horror arose as her senses returned, and her intense pull towards Breanarachelle tipped back towards revulsion. She slowly licked the remaining crumbs from her lips. She wiped her damp chin with the back of her hand.

Breanarachelle stood and composed her skirt. The she-devil edged behind Scaramucci. Breanarachelle leaned and whispered close in Scaramucci's ear.

"Good piggy. So delicious. Oh, yes. So delicious, isn't it piggy."

Scaramucci didn't look up, but she nodded her head and grunted a gustatory acknowledgement. The patapouf fledgling laved her lips and shoved another big bite. Scaramucci's plate was disappearing quickly. She was down to her final set of stomach-stretching pastries. Breanarachelle slowly massaged Scaramucci's shoulders, offering sensual encouragement.

Boudi-Ca caught Breanarachelle's wicked eyes over Scaramucci's shoulder. If Breanarachelle intended to make her envious of the attention, it was working. A queer sadness descended on her soul, pressing on the lump of the pastries in her belly. She felt alone sitting by herself on the other side of the table with the empty pastry plate. She'd cleaned her plate. She was left with nothing—not even a crumb. She felt both good and bad, so wonderfully filled but so horribly empty.

Chapter 25.

Golda lay quietly on the narrow sleeping pallet. Her skin was chafed. Her body was cramped. Her mouth was gagged. Mohilever's smelly wagon was her prison. The strong steel cuffs still bound her wrists. The cuffs in turn were tied to a steel eye-bolt fixed to the head of the bed.

Mohilever had made her suffer for Trumpeldor's painful death by her blade. He'd slapped her. He'd beaten her. He'd called her a wicked Jinn whore. He'd tried to intimidate her into telling him where she'd hidden the coin from Gorka's sale. She hadn't given in. She'd only spat at him. She hadn't told Mohilever the location of the hidden cache even after two days had passed, and even after the old man had assured her that it was too late to save Pinhas'.

She wasn't sure where Mohilever had abducted her. The wagon had rolled for many hours through the forest before stopping again. They hadn't gone as far as Erebus, but they weren't close to Mer anymore. Mer was distant in the tapestry. Golda tried to stretch her tied and cramped legs. Mohilever had denied her his seed, so she hadn't fed. She was desperately weak. She couldn't know exactly how long he had kept her prisoner, but it seemed like forever.

She'd begged him to let her go, but he only seemed amused by her mingled fury and pathetic begging. Golda frowned and focused. She hadn't been attuned to the tapestry, but she and Mohilever were no longer alone. She saw the threads converging on the Mohilever's wagon, and soon she heard hoof steps. Horses and riders were approaching in the forest. The riders stopped outside the wagon. Mohilever was asleep on his bunk just three feet away. The old man's eyes jerked open when the loud knock sounded on the wagon door.

"Who is it?" Mohilever reached under his bed and withdrew his pistol.

"This is Tahany of the Akhen family," answered a commanding female voice. "I'm here with my daughter Lotifia. Open up, please."

Golda watched the fear register on Mohilever's face. He leaned close and made sure the bit of the leather gag was tight in her mouth, and then he bent and squeezed through the center of the wagon to unlatch and push open the wooden door. Golda craned her neck. It seemed to be sunrise outside, or sunset. She could see a faint light through the trees beyond the narrow silhouettes of the visitors.

"Mohilever Reik. It's nice to see you," Tahany said. "What are you doing in this camp?"

"I could ask you the same question, lass. On yer way into Erebus with your family, I take it? A little late, aren't ye?"

"Yes," Tahany said. "We stayed to help Priebus, but Lotifia suspected something was amiss with Gorka. I understand she spoke to you at the Reik camp some days ago?"

"Aye, yes. I spoke with yer daughter," Mohilever answered. "I told her about that foul plan Gorka had, and how the Jinn whore stole all of the coins and ran off. Ye can't ever trust a Jinn. That was Gorka's mistake. I weep for poor Agron and Pinhas'. I've been camped up here drowning my sorrows, you know."

"Well, don't mourn for Priebus, because she's free. I had second thoughts about denying your family aid, and we got the coin to Hell's Court for the bribe at the last minute on the last morning. Priebus is safe. She is here, actually, riding south with us to Erebus."

"Is she now? Well praise the Fates."

Golda shoved her knees desperately against the hard wall of Mohilever's wagon. She wriggled violently against the ropes, working herself inch by inch to tip off of her narrow bed. Her knees hit the floorboards with a loud thump. Mohilever stirred and shifted his body to hide her from sight, but she tipped forward towards the wagon door with all of her strength and kicked Mohilever's backside. The man grunted.

"Who's in there with you?" Tahany said.

"It's me!" Golda yelled as loud as she could through her damp gag. She could see Tahany pushing Mohilever aside. Golda blinked up at the swimming silhouette of the elder Akhen family leader. Tahany was tall and wore a brown leather vest and matching pants, tooled and studded elegantly in Gypsy fashion. Her hair was done in a bun. A thin rapier glinted at her hip.

"It's the Jinn," Tahany said. "She was here all along. Men, get her out of there and get her gag off."

"I caught up with the whore yesterday," Mohilever quickly muttered. "I was going to explain that. She refused to tell me where she hid the family coins that she stole, so I had to get a bit rough with the lass."

Golda felt strong hands on her shoulders. The Gypsy men cut her cuffs from the bolt and dragged her unceremoniously from the wagon floorboards to stand upright in the cool morning air next to Mohilever. She tottered. She couldn't hold her weight on her aching, cramped legs. Her belly was hollow and desperate with her Hunger. Her eyes went low of their own accord, wanting any of the human cocks in front of her. A man pulled the gag from her mouth.

"Please," she said. "This horrible hobgoblin took me prisoner and tortured me. I didn't steal from the Reik family. I love Pinhas'. Why would I have tried to take the coins instead of seeing her free?"

Tahany arched her eyebrow. "I think both of you are lying. I'll speak to each of you separately and see what you have to say, starting with you, Mohilever. Men, keep your weapons pointed at the Jinn. Untie her legs, but keep those cuffs on her. We'll set up camp here. Go ahead and pitch the tents. Mohilever, you have the cuff key? Give it to me."

Golda stood still as the Gypsy men cut the remaining ropes from her body. She avoided meeting Mohilever's beady, sagging eyes. The old human was turning schemes and stories in his head, trying to come up with a combination that would condemn her. Tahany and Lotifia Akhen would surely trust Mohilever's words over hers. She needed Priebus to vouchsafe her character. The men escorted her to the Akhen caravan that sat parked in the nearby forest heather. A few Gypsy women emerged from the wagons with disapproving looks at her nudity.

Golda stretched and thrust out her breasts. She knew she could affect the men by her mere presence, and a few eyes were drinking in her form. Any advantage was an advantage. She watched and waited while the Gypsies pitched tents through the forest, hung oil lamps, and lit fires against the blackness of the coming night. After what seemed like forever, Tahany strode through the gloom.

"Explain yourself," she said. "I've heard Mohilever's story."

Golda tried to collect her thoughts. She was distraught, and her mind was foggy and unclear from her Hunger. "I was kidnapped by Mohilever Reik. He wanted to steal both me and the coin from Gorka's sale, but I hid it where it was safe. He tortured me to try to reveal the coin's location, but I wouldn't tell him. He must still have his coins from the auction of the horses and wagon—the half that Gorka gave him."

"He says you took all the coins," Tahany replied.

"Search through Mohilever's things. You'll find a couple hundred aurei that isn't his. It's coin that belongs to Agron and Pinhas'. That will be your proof that Mohilever is lying. I didn't steal it like he claims."

"He also says you killed Trumpeldor Reik."

"Both of those men came into my tent in the middle of the night and tried to rape me. I killed him in self-defense."

Tahany stared at her with hawk-like eyes. "I'm willing to consider believing you. Mohilever Reik hasn't impressed me with his honesty. Tell me something else. Why would Gorka sell himself into slavery? It's absurd. I'm wondering what insanity drove him to this. I wonder if you coerced him, as Mohilever says. That's the best explanation."

"Mohilever gave Gorka the idea, and the boy himself came to me for advice about it. He wanted to sacrifice himself for his mother. He was speaking of love, charity, and Mimos."

"Did anyone try to talk him out of it?"

Golda glared at Tahany. "I may have expressed reservations."

"Really? Yet Gorka went ahead with such a hare-brained plan anyway. Curious. You're sure you didn't trick him so you could steal the value of his freedom?"

"No. I wanted to free Priebus with the money, and Gorka wanted that too. Why do you stare at me like that, Elder Tahany? Why are you assuming that I'm a traitor?"

"I'm staring at you because I can't read the truth or non-truth of your words, Golda. I do believe that Mohilever is lying, but I can't read you. I have a gift. I can read anyone, even Jinni, but I can't read you. This is very, very strange. It's like your truth doesn't exist. It's like your truth is a blanked slate. There has been only one other person who I wasn't able to read the truth of, and he was a divine. He was a son of Lord Hades."

"You mean Masad?"

Tahany blinked. "You know him?"

"He was my mentor until recently. If you know where he is, then he will vouch for my honesty and tell you to let me go. Maybe you can't read me because I'm a tracker. I'm connected to the tapestry."

Tahany looked skeptical. "This whole business is bad, Golda. Are there any other things you can tell me?"

"I didn't steal the coin, because it's still hidden back at the Reik camp. Take me there, and I'll show you. You can actually have it to compensate for the bribe you paid for Pinhas'. It was supposed to be for her release anyway, but it was several days delayed thanks to Mohilever's pathetic betrayal. He raped me. If you can find Mohilever's coins, then you'll have your fortune back, because I'll tell you where to find mine."

Tahany eyed her thoughtfully. "I admit you look roughed up."

"Can I please just see Priebus? She can vouch for me."

"Fine. Come with me."

Golda almost groaned with relief. She was finally getting somewhere. Tahany escorted her down the line of wagons, closely watched by the guards. Golda turned her face to the sky. It was growing late. Night had fallen over the Haawiyah forest, yet Tahany was in no hurry. Tahany pushed into a low tent and gestured.

The Gypsy tent interior smelled strongly of herbs and tanned leather. An oil lamp glowed where it hung on a hook. Priebus was stretched on a narrow bed in a plain linen nightgown. Priebus looked haggard. Her eye sockets appeared shadowed and bruised, even in the low and flattering light of the lamp. A livid scar ran across her cheek from her ear to the corner of her lip, which appeared horribly disfigured.

"Pinhas." Golda bent and kissed Priebus softly on her forehead. Pinhas' eyelids flickered wide open.

"Golda?" Pinhas' lips formed a smile as her face brightened with recognition. "Golda, my love."

"Yes." Golda felt her tears flow, but in that moment she couldn't decide if they were tears of horror or joy. "You know that I've been working day and night to try to save you from the devils."

"Yes," Priebus sighed. "I was thinking of you the entire time I was locked in the prison, and the entire time they tortured me. I was thinking of you, and how you're the only thing that means anything to me in this world aside from Agron—you and my son. They told me what Mohilever says. I don't believe Mohilever. I don't believe you would sell my son into slavery."

"It was his idea. He loves you, and I love you too." Golda leaned forward for another kiss, and she could feel Priebus respond. Golda felt Tahany's hand on her shoulder then, pulling her away. Tahany's voice sounded distant and acerbic.

"Priebus isn't herself, as you can see. The devils hurt her severely. We can only hope she'll recover some of her sanity during the months of the spring tour. Meanwhile, you must do three things, Golda, to regain your favor with the Gypsies."

Golda felt the urge to growl, but she allowed Tahany to pull her back. She turned and faced the human elder in the low light of the oil lamp. "What are these three things? Tell me."

"The first is to hand over Gorka's coins. The second is to remain in my custody until your story can be further investigated. I want to find this slave trader you spoke of. I want to speak with Gorka's owner to see if we can get him back. I owe Priebus that. I'll hold my caravan here in the rim country until this business is settled."

"You still don't believe me after everything I've told you, Tahany? You think I'm lying just because I'm a Jinn? You can see that Priebus trusts me."

"I don't understand why Gorka went willingly into slavery to save his mamma, only to have a heap of aurei mysteriously disappear and turn up weeks later along with a complicated story involving kidnapping and rape. The fact that you're a Jinn raises my suspicions, and Priebus told me you're formerly Natasa of Egypt. I know the history of my home country. I know your history in Egypt and the stories of the corruption and greed around you and the Coptic popes. You used people for your own reasons, with no respect for Lord Tuhan and the Mimos."

Golda shook her head. "I know what I've been told, but I have no memories of those old days. My slave life took that away from me, and I imagine I'm a better soul for it. Suppose I agree to help you get the coins and put myself at your mercy until you can track down Gorka. What's the third thing I must do to appease you?"

"Prove to me that you're not also an illegal escaped slave as Priebus has told me. Show me your backside, please. If you're on the run from the devils and a fugitive from Hell's Court, that greatly changes the ways I can negotiate."

Golda felt the growl in her throat again. "I'm surprised that you would treat me like this, like a dog. I've been poisoned, kidnapped, and raped by one of your people, and you speak to me like I'm the criminal."

"So let me propose something," Tahany said. "A fugitive from Hell's Court—an escaped slave—used Patriarch Reik and Lady Priebus as convenient shelter. I don't know how a Jinn can even be a slave, but I know you used your charms to seduce the Feigns—"

"No. I was their welcome guest."

"I won't traffic an escaped slave to Erebus." Tahany drew her sword and held it extended. "As an officer of justice for the Gypsy people, and as the leader of the Egyptian Luxor, I'm arresting you, Golda of Egypt. You're going back to Mer. Perhaps your bounty at Hell's Court will help free Gorka. I'm not making the same mistake as the Feigns."

Golda edged forward, allowing the tip of the sword to graze her breast. She twisted suddenly and threw a desirous kin-hex, pulling the Gypsy leader towards her and the sword under her armpit. She kneed Tahany in the stomach and brought her cuffed fists down on woman's head. Priebus cried out.

"No!"

The deed was done, and Tahany slumped. Golda bent over her and fished for the key in Tahany's pocket. She ignored the soft whimpering of Priebus behind her. Her relationship with Priebus was over, and it would be a long time before she could entertain relations with the Gypsies. She found the cuff key and offered a silent prayer to Allyssia. Within seconds she had the cuffs unlocked.

Golda snatched Tahany's sword and cut a silent slit through the rear of the tent. She poked her head through. There were no guards in back. She slipped out the crack and padded into the forest, placing her feet with infinite care. The forest floor was littered with ancient stones from the escarpment. She crept among them, back to the dark clearing where Mohilever had parked his wagon. The wagon was unguarded. She climbed inside, closed the door, and made a tenebris lux. If the Gypsies wanted her to be a thief, she would oblige them.

The hood and gag were hanging above the bed. She collected the bottle of poison from a drawer, but she found none of Mohilever's aurei coins. She shoved the things into a small pack, along with a knife, some rope, and Mohilever's nectar stash. She slipped back out and found her horse tethered with Mohilever's sturdy draft specimens.

She carefully untied the steed, and then she was away into the trees. After several minutes, she heard the alarm barks of Gypsy dogs, but they were nowhere near her. After an hour of riding relentlessly through the dark, she recognized the terrain. She was heading down through the forest into the heart of the Gypsy dells. She almost didn't notice the turnoff into the Reik camp with no one in the forest, but she could see the thick knots of recent presences in the tapestry. There was no Reik camp anymore—just the worn patches of dirt, forlorn corral fences, and beaten down tracks.

Golda wandered through the trees in the deep of the night. She found the clearing where her tent had sat next to Gorka's. She dismounted and paced back and forth under the moon until she found the old oak. She pawed under the roots and found the hidden coins. Relief washed over her.

She dragged herself back onto her horse. She wanted to sleep, but she needed desperately to feed. With the coins, she could hire a lover and a bed. Her days of being Mohilever's slave had reminded her of the important things in life. She would throw caution to the wind. She would trust in the Fates and Allyssia. She would rent a room at the Fuchsia Canary and do whatever it took to get Boudi-Ca out of Mer immediately.

Chapter 26.

Master Andros was an impressive wall of manly muscle. He was a formidable Djinnus—almost the size of an ogre in his shoulder-padded, tailored suit. He lifted the black veil from Henne's upturned face and pressed down for a kiss as the devil attendants looked on with their usual monastic dispassion. Henne looked perfect in her black silk dress. She arched her hips up to submit to her husband. Her hand gripped his ass as if clinging to life itself.

Priest Phanes smiled and lifted high the smoky long sleeves of his divine robes. "And so let Mistress Henneh and Master Andros be wedded forever with the blessings of our great Lord and Lady."

Yellen averted her eyes as applause thundered through the cavernous central hall of the most magnificent and prestigious temple in all of Hell—the Templum Mortum. Henne turned and strode arm-in-arm with Andros down the center aisle towards the exit. The hundreds of guests turned out of the seats, forming a flowing procession of well-to-do Court devils and other Merian residents who had come to see the wedding. Per tradition on that sacred day of Allyssia, many of the guests were decked out in colorful Ostara fineries instead of the customary blacks.

Henne's parade went past, and the crowd swarmed out of the Templum doors into the evening. Yellen slipped into the shadow of the side aisle behind the enormous Doric pillars. She examined the two-meter-tall bronze statue of Tisiphone, the half-avian Fury and ruler of the city of Vegasis, which graced a lamplit niche.

She didn't want to watch Henne climb into her new husband's stately gilded carriage. She didn't want to see Henne ride away for her lavish wedding night. She didn't want to see Henne head off for her honey moon, where Henne would spread her legs and receive buckets of Andros' sticky addictive seed. Yes, the honey moon with her Djinnus would be a permanent Hell's Court seal on Henne's bisexual love-envelope.

Once most of the guests had exited, Yellen gritted her teeth and followed them. In truth, she didn't feel as much pain as she'd expected. She'd always known that the day would come when she'd lose Henne, even though she'd foolishly held onto hope for a different outcome. She was so lost in memories that she almost collided with the other stragglers at the massive golden Templum doors. She stood face to face with Councilor Lydiah.

"Lieutenant Nefra," Lydiah exclaimed. "Fancy bumping into you. I noticed you sat on the side of the bride, but surely you didn't know that ragamuffin redhead? Oh yes. I remember now. You two met ten years ago in the rebel lesbian city of Lady Allyssia."

Yellen hesitated. She'd been taken by complete surprise. She looked around swiftly, but none of the surrounding wedding attendees seemed to be paying attention. She milled with everyone else down the steps alongside Lydiah.

"I know Master Andros."

"Do you?" Lydiah matched her strides across the Templum plaza, grasping her arm and leaning close to whisper. "You lie. You were here for your little lesbian, Lieutenant. You were afraid to meet with me yesterday because you were afraid of making a mistake. Well, you went and made a mistake anyway, on top of betraying the purgation effort."

Yellen wrenched her arm away from Lydiah and kept her eyes straight ahead. So the confrontation was finally going to happen. Yellen glanced over her shoulder and kept her fingers on the hilt of your blade. Boudi-Ca walked right behind, alongside Lydiah's other fledgling, a dark-haired Asian beauty. Boudi's silver-umber eyes were worn, tired, worried, and wide.

"What do you want, Councilor?" Yellen muttered. "You have me outnumbered."

"Let's go for a ride. I'm going to insist on having a cup of tea at my home."

"Fine." Yellen walked cautiously to Lydiah's four-seater and settled herself in front. Masia-Ca and Boudi-Ca squeezed into the rear. Lydiah expelled her driver boy and ordered him to walk, and then hauled her long extravagant dress into the front seat and cracked the whip.

The carriage rolled away from the Templum towards the public downtown gardens and amphitheaters, which were lit by rows of gas lamps that glowed in the polluted evening haze like will-o-wisps. The spired black bulk of Hell's Court loomed adjacent to Lord Hades' Palace, which was silhouetted against the dirty pink-puce wall of the dying Haawiyah afternoon.

Yellen squared herself in her seat, resisting the urge to look back for one last glimpse of Henne and her wedding procession. She needed to think, not disassociate into self-pity. She watched Lydiah instead out of the corner of her eye.

"I just want you to know that you aren't immune, Nefra," Lydiah said over the rumble of the wagon wheels, as if reading her mind. "You're well aware of the curious number of lesbians that have been escaping their arrests—in fact most of them."

"Yes. It's unfortunate." Yellen kept her face a mask as she looked straight ahead. Her starting strategy was to say as few words as possible.

"Of course, Hell's Court knows that someone is tipping them off," Lydiah continued. "I don't know if they've identified the owner of that little green messenger bird, but I have. Yes? Are you willing to admit it?"

"Admit what?"

Lydiah snapped the whip again, urging the carriage horses to strain harder in their leather harnesses. The carriage picked up speed down the old cobblestones of the lightly trafficked Merian street. "I spoke with Master Glumstak at the Court just this morning. He confirms the

Purgation has been an abject failure for its first three weeks, so last night the Court officially declared that the Flames is too corrupt to conduct the investigation. The devils may open an investigation of our investigation next. This reflects extremely poorly on me, of course. How do you feel about that, Lieutenant?"

Yellen tried to stay calm. The confrontation couldn't have come at a worse time. She was already in an emotional turmoil over Henne's wedding. She flinched when the brown catbird landed on her shoulder. The bird spoke with Henne's voice.

Thank you for everything, Yellen, and thanks for coming to my wedding. I've known you longer than anyone else in Mer, and you've been the most loyal of all of my friends.

Yellen drummed her fingers on her sword hilt. She was short on both patience and tactical acumen, and her frustration was again converting into a desire for violence. She entertained a vision of taking a little trip up to the Carthago promontory and accidentally murdering Master Andros. She suppressed her tension and shrugged.

"I'm getting the names of the Named, and I'm going to the places, Councilor. I can't help if the lesbians leave before I get there."

"Right. Well, you're going to have one more chance. According to Glumstak, tomorrow we'll see the largest list of Named yet seen. The interrogations of the arrested lesbians have yielded dozens of names during this little break for Ostara's day. The devils want to get these Jinni all in a major one-day sweep. They are allowing us to help them as a test. If the devils get their Named, but we fail at ours, it will be proof that you and I are guilty. The lesbians cannot be warned tomorrow, or there will be direct consequences. I'm talking directly to you, Lieutenant, and I hope you're listening."

"Is that supposed to be a threat? If you know that I'm betraying the purgation, why aren't you having me arrested immediately?"

"If any lesbians escape our raids tomorrow, you can count on spending tomorrow night answering to the devils. This is a fact, not a threat."

Yellen stretched. Her tension was spiraling. She never like being threatened. She also didn't like that there were witnesses to the dangerous conversation. Both of Lydiah's fledglings sat quietly in the back of the carriage, overhearing everything that was said. She wondered what Boudi-Ca was thinking.

She had a potential dagger left to play. She was still waiting for the results of Sim's investigation into Lydiah's own private lesbianism, yet after three weeks, she'd heard nothing. She'd seen a feint attack win countless swordfights, however, and in moments of desperation, it was best to go on instinct. She looked over her shoulder at Boudi-Ca.

"You're a hypocrite, Councilor," she said over the rumbling carriage wheels. "You're committing lesbianism yourself, and yet you accuse me? If the devils arrest me and interrogate me tomorrow, then you'll go down next with what I know about you."

Lydiah slowly turned to look at her. For a fraction of a second, the gleam in Councilor Lydiah's moon-silvered eyes revealed a tortured soul that bordered on pure insanity. Yellen looked away resolutely. She couldn't believe it. She'd actually scored a dagger to Lydiah's heart. Yellen slid her hand again to the hilt of her sword, and this time she drew it. The inches of carriage seat between her and Lydiah were charged with energy that could explode at any moment, and if Lydiah exploded, she'd do it at sword point.

"You're bluffing," Lydiah said, folding her whip in her hand.

"I'm not." Yellen weighed her words carefully. "You know about me and Henne, Councilor Lydiah, but by the same token I know about you and your lesbian fledgling. I also know about Boudi-Ca's former relationship with Henne. If I go down, you both do too."

"My fledgling is reformed from her old lesbian ways," Lydiah said. "You have no proof."

"I have enough. I suggest that you protect me from arrest, or you'll put yourself and your fledgling in more jeopardy than you might guess. I know you spent months alone with your fledgling in the north country without your husband. I know you weren't in the garden shed a few days ago with me and Boudi-Ca. Are you jealous of the way your fledgling looks at me? Are you jealous that she kissed me?"

Lydiah remained silent. Yellen dared to look again at the Councilor. From the blanched look on Lydiah's arrogant face, the counter-threat had again landed solidly. Lydiah leaned close, and when she spoke, her voice was low and ice cold.

"Why do you think I called you all the way down here from Meristyian in the first place, you fool? I thought I could trust you, but now you've gone and done something stupid. We'll leave each other alone for the moment. We need to focus. Glumstak suggested that this last sweep of arrests will finish things. In forty-eight hours, this lesbian Purgation may be over, Allyssia willing."

"Let's hope so."

Lydiah tightened her leather glove around her whip. "Is the sacra vipera that we put in your home working for you? Is it catching your mice, Lieutenant?"

"I imagine it is. The invisible serpent stays out of my way, but I hear it slithering around sometimes. Now if you don't mind, could you stop the carriage? I need to get away from you."

Yellen poised and leapt from the carriage as soon as the horses slowed. She didn't look back at Lydiah or Boudi-Ca, but she kept her hand on the hilt of her sword. She was almost afraid to go home. Why had Lydiah suddenly asked about the vipera? The Councilor had surely leveled yet another veiled threat. She nearly turned and raised her blade when she felt the touch on her shoulder. The messenger bird spoke with Boudi-Ca's voice.

I'd love to see you again, but right now I have a lot of problems. Maybe soon. I think you're beautiful too.

Chapter 27.

The carriage was rolling up the driveway when the black rook flew across the house grounds, clipping the top of Lydiah's head. Boudi-Ca felt a wave of fear when the bird landed her shoulder and spoke with Breanarachelle's voice.

I want your piggy ass at my villa right away. You skipped another day yesterday, and you skipped this morning, so you get six. I already have your pastries delivered, and I'm arranging more piggy pleasure for you, since you enjoyed it so. I'm waiting.

"Was that Breanarachelle's bird?" Lydiah drew the carriage to a stop in front of the carriage house doors.

"She invited me to a party. I'm sure Masia must have gotten a bird too."

"No," Masia said shortly. "I didn't get any invitation, but we don't need one so—"

"Everyone is staying home tonight. I'll bring up some boys." Lydiah coiled her whip. "Boudi-Ca, you're doing nectar again, which is unacceptable. You don't think I've noticed how your headaches magically disappeared? You're not complaining any more about how horrible you feel, either. I know how this is goes. I hold Masia to blame as much as you. She's supposed to be looking after you."

"Mistress, I can't keep track of her every move," Masia protested. "I shouldn't have to follow Boudi-Ca everywhere just because she's out of control. I think she's also addicted to her Djinnus boyfriend."

"I'm going to my room." Boudi-Ca hopped from the carriage. She felt a quiver of need in her being, and her mouth was already watering at the thought of sweet, delicious pastries. She wanted so many pastries, a whole big belly full. She wanted her stomach stuffed with a big weight of comforting sugar-nectar pleasure. She'd skipped a day out of disgust with Breanarachelle, but the desire for more nectar and pastries had returned with a vengeance.

She stalked across the driveway and through the side door into Fennel's house, hoping with every step that Lydiah would just let her go. As she climbed the steps into her east wing bedchamber, however, she heard the heels of the Mistress following her, and when she closed her bedchamber door, it popped open just as quickly.

"I'm sorry, fledgling." Lydiah's face showed a questionable, breezy contrition in a way that only she could manage. "I've been ignoring you, and I apologize. I wanted so much to get back into the good graces of Hell's Court. I wanted to be relevant again. They gave me a chance, and I failed."

"I still love you."

"I know." Lydiah's chin trembled, and she brushed her white-blonde hair over her shoulder. Her diamond piercings glittered in the half-dark. She went to the writing desk and lit the oil lamp, prolonging the pregnant moment. "I want to be closer to you. That's why, after the big purgation sweep tomorrow, we're going back to the north country. I'm having Vladimir and Kveta pack our bags tomorrow morning. We can take Tajee from his cage and free him together from his chastity. He's so sensitive, don't you think? I'm sure he's already desperate for that, and I'm tired of the intrigue in the capital city."

"What about the summer storms?"

"We can weather them in the north. I've done it before. When the northern Nanka routes are closed for the summer, so much the better to dissuade Hell's Court and any Flames officials from coming up. They'll have to come on horses through the storms off the Mare if they want to question us. We can relax and enjoy life with the boys. We'll keep the house storm-shuttered and dark, like no one is home. I can write my books with no politics for a while."

"That sounds nice." Boudi-Ca dared to press herself against the Mistress. Lydiah bent and kissed her head. She almost felt a burden lift off of her shoulders for a moment, but then a heavy fear weighed her even more. She couldn't leave the city without violating Breanarachelle's devil contract. She either needed to give Lydiah to the devils, or she needed to keep eating pastries. In neither case could she leave the city.

"When times are most horrible, we realize what matters most to us in this life," Lydiah murmured. "You are my most precious gift. I'm responsible for you, and I don't want the Smokeless Flames to have you. I made a promise to Hell's Court, but I only signed a devil contract to give you black nectar, which is all that matters. You have no legal requirement to join the Flames, and I have no legal requirement to deliver you."

"What happens if someone breaks a devil contract?"

"Well, the devils come for you. When a Jinn breaks a contract with the devils, her suffering and punishment become a first priority in Hell's Court. No one breaks a devil contract. That's the whole point. The devils are the sacred judiciaries of our Lord, and they can't be lenient. There is Hell to pay, and the power of a contract comes from everyone knowing it. We don't have to worry, because we don't have a contract for you to join the Flames."

"I don't know if we can leave yet, though." Boudi-Ca kept her eyes low, afraid that Lydiah would see right through her and realize that she'd ruined everything.

"Why not?" Lydiah drew her away at arm's length.

"Someone knows about us."

"Yes." Lydiah's black-painted lips curled into a tight smile. "Lieutenant Nefra and Golda both need to die. I'm planning to kill Nefra tomorrow morning during our raid. I'm going to claim that I coerced her into admitting her betrayal, and she attacked me. I'll simply direct the devils to

Befanah for confirmation of the green messenger bird, and Nefra will be history."

"I like Lieutenant Nefra. She's my only real friend."

"I'm sorry, fledgling. She was a good soldier, but her disrespect is unacceptable. If the Council knew the truth, they'd agree with me, and perhaps even with my methods as well. I haven't won, but I haven't lost so much. I'll claim fatigue and a need for a vacation. I've hired a trustworthy bounty hunter with a gun to hunt Golda, since you're not quite ready."

"I don't want Golda to die either."

"Well, sometimes we don't get everything we want in life, fledgling. I'm proof of that. I've used Billy at times for private hire. He's a hellion tracker, and he never fails. If Golda is still hiding out in the forest, she won't even see him coming. She's as good as dead."

"Yes. That's perfect, Mistress." Boudi-Ca shivered. A queer horror gripped her spine. Lydiah caressed her shoulder gently, sensing her inner distress.

"I want you to stay away from Breanarachelle. Stay away from her villa. I want you ready to leave Mer by tomorrow afternoon. With a bit of luck from Allyssia, the devils will officially close the purgation soon, and the more cautious and sensible lesbians can keep fucking each other in private, except for Lieutenant Nefra, of course. Everything will be fine."

"Yes, Mistress. I love you." Boudi-Ca watched Lydiah turn on her heel and leave without another word. She'd never felt more hopeless. She curled up alone on her bed. A tear wetted the corner of her cheek, and she wiped it. She summoned her messenger bird.

Kveta, come help me dress.

The scarred, half-nude dressing girl appeared in less than a minute. Boudi-Ca rose from her bed, and Kveta stripped her full-length formal gown. She ordered Kveta to remove her corset, and she replaced it with a laced brassiere that covered only her ribcage, while leaving her stomach unrestrained. She added a slip of a summer skirt that barely reached her thighs. Finally she ordered Kveta to bind her hair in a bun while she freshened her face powder and perfume. She applied only a lining of lip paint.

When she slipped out of the house, she felt an agony of mingled fear and anticipation. She was disobeying Lydiah, and she was more scantily dressed than she'd ever been in public in Mer. Her panted crotch was surely visible when her skirt shifted. Her desire drove her recklessly to the stable and onto a horse. She pushed the horse down into Pee-hill, and soon she was striding on her petite stiletto heels up the steps into Rhadamanthus' villa and across the smoky quartz vestibule, where a devil guard accosted her.

"You're here for the party?" The devil's ugly porcine eyes scanned her assets.

"Yes," she answered. "I'm looking for Breanarachelle."

"This way."

Boudi-Ca followed the devil guard. The smell of his sulfuric skin seemed to queerly increase her anticipation. He led her down a marble side hallway in the direction of the guest quarters, past magnificent gilded Italian oil paintings into the stony west wing of the villa, where classical music lilted from somewhere in the still, dead air.

A row of niches down the hallway boasted a collection of bronze statues—humans frozen in molten metal, their flesh carved away artistically to reveal the shafts of bones and the curvatures of intestines. The devil guard turned at an intersection, where he indicated a doorway. Voices came from the crack in the door.

Boudi-Ca pushed through the door. The room was high-ceilinged and vaulted with ornate carved columns that arched over towering bookcases, which in turn were interspersed with gilt-framed geographical maps. Glass display cases contained a variety of long guns, whips, and hunting knives. A low fire burned in a blackened hearth. A glass case on one wall displayed a row of preserved bones, and above the case was mounted a great boar's head with a hairy snout.

The room sported two leather armchairs. Breanarachelle sat in one of them, and a devil master sat in the other. Between the two devils, two patapoufs lounged on the wooden floor amidst plates of pastries. The fat patapoufs were stuffing their mouths with sweetcakes. Both patapoufs were fully nude except for headbands sporting porcine ears. The wonderful smells of sugar and spices wafted on the warm, smoky air.

"Welcome to the piggy party, Boudi-Ca." Breanarachelle's grey lips split into her usual wicked smile. "The other piggies aren't too far ahead of you. I imagine you've never seen my husband's private hunting room. Go to the veranda and have a look at the view."

Boudi-Ca walked past the two patapoufs to the open double doors on the far side of the room. The doors gave onto a small balcony with a view of a magnificent night garden with fountains and antique statues. Little magical wisps danced and sparkled in the garden, providing pools of light through the darkness. Boudi-Ca shivered when she felt clawed fingers stroke the skin of her back. The devil master had followed her.

"You are beautiful, but you should be nude," he intoned in her ear. "I am Master Tarnak. Breanarachelle has told me a lot about you, and it's a pleasure to finally meet you."

"The pleasure is mine," Boudi-Ca said politely. She allowed Tarnak to press her to the warm stone railing, unfasten her brassiere, and unbutton her skirt. He slid his fingers into the band of her panties and slowly removed them. The devil's fingernails caressed down the skin of her naked legs, as if exploring her pressure points and contours.

"Your wing scars are artistically jagged." Tarnak rose again to examine her shoulder blades. "Fennel is a true master."

Boudi-Ca shivered. For some reason, she'd never wondered who had cut her wings. The scars were ugly and disturbed her, so she rarely looked at her backside in her mirror. She edged away from the devil, but Tarnak grasped her arm. He escorted her back into the warm, sweet-smelling hunting room.

Tarnak's yellow fingernails were filed into little points that pricked her skin. Dog-like pink and white splotches ran up his yellow-grey fingers and forearms. His sallow face was angular and shiny, like half-melted candle wax. His nose was prominent and arched, and a pair of gold beads glinted in his dark goatee, which was slick with oil like his tight ponytail. He wore a sleeveless black leather vest and matching trousers.

"Little piggies don't walk," Breanarachelle said. "Get on the floor, Boudi. This headband is magical and will affect you, and so will this nectar. I want you to just enjoy and surrender. You won't need to speak much, and you'll be a little numb. I promise you'll love it."

Boudi-Ca knelt warily on all fours in front of Breanarachelle, who rewarded her with her very own pig-ear headband, even while she felt Tarnak working on her feet. He removed her shoes, leaving her completely nude. Boudi-Ca felt her throat tickle. The pig-ear headband made her head buzz. Her eyes blurred and refocused. She was much more aware of the smells in the room, and her vision seemed shortened.

Breanarachelle smelled of sensuous, smoky devil perfume as usual. The she-devil wore a short skirt and matching brown stockings. Under her skirt, she wore no panties. A gold-handled knife glinted where it was tucked into a thigh sheath. Breanarachelle crossed her legs and shifted. A little spoon crouched next to a round box on the cylindrical side table. The she-devil grasped the sniffer handle in her metal finger-claws.

Boudi-Ca felt the spoon press to her left nostril, and she sniffed. Pleasure exploded through her face, followed by a prickling numbness that raced under her headband and around her scalp. She moaned her appreciation. The much-wanted pleasure spread quickly through her tongue, her face, and slowly into her body, diffusing into a deep peacefulness and contentment. The nectar was a high-quality blue-purple. Her body seemed to melt, and she settled on all fours with the stability of the floor underneath her. She snorted and rubbed her nose when her nostril started to burn.

"She'll be a very pretty piggy." Tarnak settled back into his armchair. "She needs a lot of fattening first."

"You can start eating, child," Breanarachelle added. "Giacondah sent us a bit of everything. These are your new friends, Schiller-Ca and Leeanna-Ca. Leeanna is a boy, just so you know."

"Heroink," Schiller-Ca murmured with a wan smile. "Soink you're newoink?" The fledgling's fat cheeks were rouged pink, and her lips were lined in black. A heavy silver ring pierced her nasal septum. Her nipples were also pierced with dozens of studs. Schiller was completely nude, but her sex was invisible under the sea swells of her heavy belly and thighs.

"I don't understoink," Boudi-Ca managed. "Which roinks should I hoink?"

Breanarachelle chortled. Boudi-Ca felt heat run through her cheeks. When she tried to speak, the sides of her head felt strange where her pig ears were pressing. Breanarachelle's heeled shoe planted on her buttock, shoving her forwards towards the pastry plates.

"Piggies don't need to understand. They just want to eat so much."

Schiller nodded and pushed another big bite into her mouth, erasing her smile. The young patapouf wiped honey from her puffy chin and turned her attention to licking her fingers. On the far side of the pastry plates, Leeanna-Ca rocked backwards, upending a pastry over his face. His generous curves glistened with oil in the firelight. The head of his cock popped like a little mouse from under his grand bulges, and his thighs were striped with long ragged scars.

Boudi-Ca crawled over Schiller's thick calf to inspect the pastry plates. She didn't see her usual honey strudels, so she selected a lemon wedge. She lifted it to her mouth and moaned softly when she bit into the sweetness, tartness, and textured pleasure. A small wave of happiness and contentment soothed her soul.

She settled comfortably against Schiller's warm leg, not far from Breanarachelle's feet. She bit and chewed. She swallowed and bit. She finished her first pastry, and a huge relief came over her. She wanted more, much more, and a plate full of more was right in front of her. She was happy, and all of her cares seemed unimportant.

She reached and selected a cinnamon chocolate roll next, aware of Breanarachelle watching her closely. She chewed and swallowed. The feeling in her body seemed to change with the cinnamon into something spicier, something even more delightful.

Boudi-Ca sighed. She'd had no idea pastries could be so complex and fascinating to the taste, an entire universe of new wonders. She couldn't possibly go to the north country with Lydiah, not unless there were pastries.

She watched when Master Tarnak approached her with a flask in his yellow-grey hand.

"What are you doink?"

"Oiling your skin," Tarnak replied. "Get up on your knees, please."

Boudi-Ca tongued her mouth to swallow the pastry, the better to attempt a full sentence. "Why are you oinking my skoink?"

"We always butter up the piggies. It makes them more tender." Tarnak smiled.

Boudi-Ca took another bite and climbed to her knees. Her mouth, belly, and throat felt so warm, happy, and sugary. Her whole body was filled with a happy contentment from getting filled. Tarnak's hands were pleasant when they slicked her. He ran his pointy-nailed fingers around her legs. He dumped oil onto the small of her back. He spread the oil up, lingering over her wing scars, and then he pushed the oil down over her buttocks and other warm furrows. Finally he half-embraced her from behind to smooth the oil over her breasts, chest, and stomach.

Breanarachelle had lit a pipe, and the warm room filled with an even richer scent of comfort, like a blanket of intoxicating happiness. Boudi-Ca gasped when a little splinter of pain shot through her left breast. She looked down to see a heavy metal implement attached to her nipple. She reached to remove it, but Master Tarnak's hand grabbed her wrist.

"Bad piggy," he admonished. "Piggy needs to keep eating."

Boudi-Ca frowned and desisted, accepting the discomfort. She took a big bite to push away the pain with pleasure. She felt Tarnak's hand drift to her hip. He tugged, twisting her down and onto her back. Schiller flopped onto her back in turn like a domino to complete a three-sided circle of beached patapoufs around the pastry plates in the center. Tarnak reached again. Boudi-Ca winced when the second clip was affixed to her other nipple. The clips were heavy and beetle-like in shape, with silver pincers that held her little nipples painfully imprisoned. Thankfully, the numbness and pleasure in her body made the discomfort acceptable. Tarnak rounded the room, adding clips to Schiller and finally Leeanna-Ca. Boudi-Ca gazed up at Breanarachelle. The she-devil was watching her from on high with a smile.

"Lydiah pierced you with a diamond down there too." Breanarachelle drew on her pipe and breathed a circle of smoke. "Very nice. Lydiah likes the devil ways, and it's nice to see her starting you."

"Yoink." Boudi-Ca licked her lips. "I like my noink piercing moink." Boudi-Ca felt warmth come to her cheeks again. She twisted her buttocks away from Breanarachelle while she finished her second pastry. She looked for an oat cake, but she didn't see one on a plate. She fished for a second lemon wedge.

Schiller squealed when Tarnak pushed his hand between her thighs. Boudi-Ca stalled the lemon pastry at her lips, distracted by Tarnak, who knelt at her buttocks next. She felt his fingers briefly, and then pain splintered through her nethers from a third metal clip. A squeal came unbidden to her lips, and tears wetted her eyelashes. She almost sat up, but Tarnak pushed back her down.

"You're a sensitive little thing," Tarnak murmured lovingly. "Just keep eating."

A knock sounded on the door then. Breanarachelle rose to greet the interloper. Whispered words came across the threshold. Boudi-Ca bit into her third pastry. She just wanted the pleasure. She wanted more pleasure to fight back the persistent pain that was continuously bleeding from the metal clips into her breasts and sex. She didn't need to worry about anything. She had lots of pastries and nectar.

"Well, tonight's the night." Breanarachelle returned to her chair, even as Schiller squealed again. Schiller's long squeal broke into a breathless animal bleating. "Lydiah is asking for her fledgling at my front door. I had her thrown out of the house, but when we're finished with you tonight, Lydiah will finally know the truth. I'm sending you home with a copy of your contract, as well as my marks on your pretty skin, Boudi-Ca. You're mine, child." Breanarachelle laughed with a laugh of triumph.

Boudi-Ca wiped the tears forming on her eyelids. She sniffed and glared at Breanarachelle, even as she took another big bite. "You're horrinkable. You're the moink horrinkable, ugloink—"

She winced when pain exploded across the side of her face. She fell sidelong across the floor, such was the force of Breanarachelle's slap. Her pastry flew and crumbled up against the stones of the hearth. Just as she pushed herself up, the she-devil's fingers pushed her head down again.

"Lick it up, little bitch. Piggies don't make messes on my husband's floor. You've sealed your fate little piggy, and now I'm going to enjoy watching you wallow in it."

Boudi-Ca obediently sucked and licked, denuding the dirty floor of the sweet crumbs. She wanted all of them. Breanarachelle drew away with a chuckle, satisfied with the submission. Schiller was squealing in the background, and then Leeanna-Ca joined in. Leeanna-Ca had a low voice like a boy. Boudi-Ca turned her head to watch Breanarachelle working her claws between Leeanna's thighs, where his mouse-cock had emerged a little more boldly from its hole.

Meanwhile, Tarnak was kneeling behind Schiller, jamming her big puffy posterior. Schiller oinked and grunted with the devil's rhythmic thrusts. Her nipple clips swayed and glinted in the firelight, and she was still nibbling at her pastry, pressing it to her mouth with her fat fingers. Boudi-Ca rose slowly to her feet. She was drifting in such pleasure and happiness, yet the suffering in her most sensitive places was sickening her, and she was afraid her pastries might heave up.

She braced herself on a glass display case. The firelight in the hunting room was just bright enough to reveal the hunting weapons inside. Boudi-Ca gazed down at the knives in wonder. Somehow she knew those knives in the case. The knives were all shapes and sizes. Some were straight, some curved, and others serrated. Some had hilts and others none. Some were for slashing, and others were for skinning. Some were made for dissecting, and others were made for a deadly low-bleed puncture in a public place.

Boudi-Ca licked the last crumbs from her lips. Somehow in that moment she knew every possible use for every possible shape of knife. An intense compulsion came over her then—an intense urge to grip one of those knives and see a river of blood flow from her fingertips. Twisted thoughts of rebellion entered her skull, thoughts so much more powerful than her own. Lieutenant Nefra wasn't her only friend. Somewhere deep inside her mind, she had another friend, a very powerful friend.

"Get down, piggy."

Boudi-Ca ignored Breanarachelle's command. She opened the display case and reached inside. When she grasped the serrated hunting knife and turned, time seemed to go still. Breanarachelle's brows were frozen in a furrow. Her cruel mouth was pursing, and her hand was reaching for the knife on her thigh. Tarnak was oblivious with his eyes half-closed, close to his devil orgasm. His hips arched, thrusting joyously with abandon into Schiller, whose little painted mouth was agape with unbearable sensation.

The door of the hunting room was wide open, revealing the silhouettes of Fennel and Judge Rhadamanthus. The room suddenly unfroze, and the two men strode forward. Fennel cradled a heavy-looking black object in his blotchy yellow hands, an oblong pyramid with the face of a clock. Rhadamanthus held a long gun. Boudi-Ca tried to focus her eyes. Rhada's face was contorted with fury, and he was pointing his gun directly at her.

"Rhada?" Breanarachelle relinquished Leeanna-Ca. "I hope you've come to join us. My stupid new piggy isn't following orders. She needs a punishment."

"She certainly does," Rhadamanthus growled. "Five minutes from now, Breanarachelle, you and Master Tarnak were found bleeding out. You were on your way to the void, and this little viper had sawed your head clean from your neck. These two pigs were found shrieking and stumbling down the hallway, smoking and burning with the acids of your sprayed blood."

"I'm not quite following." Breanarachelle gazed at the dark black object in Fennel's hands. "I see you have the Ebon Timepiece, my darling Fennel. I assume that has something to do with this interruption?"

"Yes," Fennel answered. "Rhada arrived at my place a while ago, and he proposed a way to save your life. The Ebon Timepiece is not to be used lightly, but I agreed in this unique case. We interrogated the guard who let Boudi-Ca into the villa. We interrogated the house maid who was the first to arrive on the murder scene. The house maid was able to tell us the approximate time on the wall clock, the time when Boudi-Ca stabbed you in six different places with surgical precision."

"You saved me then," Breanarachelle breathed. Her froggish nostrils flared, and her grey face contorted into hideous rage. "You had to save me from this pathetic little lesbian snake. Thank you, my husband, but I feel ashamed."

Rhada smiled grimly. "You should thank Fennel for using the Timepiece. He reminded me that Lydiah is far too easy on her dumb little Mimọ freak. Boudi-Ca needs a lesbian interrogation to be sure, and then something unique, perhaps something public after we break her, a good old-fashioned puppet show."

Fennel flicked his cane, and the tip retracted to reveal a shining needle-like blade. Fennel's thin lips contorted into his characteristic look of amusement, which wasn't quite a grin. "Let's arrest this bitch."

Boudi-Ca felt her heavy stomach turn to jelly under the withering gazes of the devils in the room with her. A wave of fear spiked into her yielding sweet pleasure, making her dizzy. "I didn't doink anythoink."

Breanarachelle edged forward with her metal claws outstretched. "Oh, you'll be doing something very soon, girl. You'll be screaming. You'll be weeping. You'll beg for me to give your flesh back, but I won't. I'll stretch it and cure it, and soon I'll have a new leather handbag. I'll wear it to every party that Lydiah attends."

Fennel advanced, kicking Schiller in passing. Schiller squealed. Boudi-Ca gripped the hunting knife more tightly in her fingers. Tarnak had come to his senses and disengaged from Schiller. The younger devil master rose to cut off the breezeway to the balcony. Breanarachelle muttered words of magical power, and the flame from the fireplace arced to burn on her metal fingertips.

Rhada reached and grabbed the she-devil's bicep. "Easy now. We don't need to set fire to my library. Let Fennel handle this. The girl is a viper."

"She's clipped and stuffed," Breanarachelle snarled. "I gave her a sniffer of Professor Visek's Purple #13. I don't know why she's standing on two feet, or why she'd even want to be."

Boudi-Ca flashed. The room froze. She tiptoed down a black ribbon over Leeanna-Ca's shoulder and past Breanarachelle. She twirled behind the she-devil. The room unfroze again, and she backhanded, angling the knife deep under Breanarachelle's ribcage, and again. She stepped left away from the fireplace, interposing Breanarachelle's body between her and the three devil men.

"Oh yes, child," Breanarachelle moaned. The moan was a guttural expression of pleasure, not pain. "Dance with me."

Boudi-Ca gasped when the metal fingernails seized her naked shoulder. Fire from Breanarachelle's spell burned up the side of her neck before the spell fizzled. She turned the knife and sliced a third time, opening a deeper wound that gushed blood. She stabbed again into Breanarachelle's stomach. The she-devil moaned louder, as if in ecstasy.

Fennel's cane snaked forward. Boudi-Ca attempted to evade, but her body was too torpid and numb to get out of the way. She flashed at the last fraction of a second to arrive behind Rhadamanthus. She backhanded her knife deep under the Judge's ribcage, in the same spot where she'd speared Breanarachelle. She struck a second time on the other side. Somehow she knew the exact angle of attack to sever a devil's most vulnerable organs. More devil blood spurted over her fingers. Rhadamanthus grunted and dropped his gun.

She attacked again. The intense burning pain of devil blood shocked her skin further, and she almost dropped the knife. Tarnak was next, and she managed to ravage him, interposing his body between herself and Fennel. Fennel raised his cane and muttered foul syllables.

Anakh nothra. Ipsakh nothra.

Mystical smoky snakes darted from his fingers and twisted forward. Boudi-Ca cried out when the snakes slipped around Tarnak and hit her. The room blurred and dimmed. The snakes piled onto her, battering her backwards. She left her feet and fell through the open double doors onto the hard stones of the garden balcony. She tried to rise, but the summoned snakes relentlessly pummeled her neck and head. Pain jolted her spine like lightning, and a loud hum ushered her into unconsciousness.

Chapter 28.

Golda skulked in the twisted trees outside the fence. She could see the arched windows of Fennel's house through ornate iron bars. She'd worked up her nerve to try for Boudi-Ca that day, but she couldn't find Boudi's track in the tapestry. Thankfully, the private wealthy neighborhood was like a little patch of Great Blue Hole rim forest near the Merian downtown, offering opportunities to hide in the black-boiled oaks, witch sickles, and brittle brushes.

Perhaps Boudi-Ca had slept elsewhere. Perhaps Boudi-Ca had slept on the north side with her Djinnus boyfriend. Boudi's absence in the morning wasn't normal, and Archduke Fennel had visitors. The estate had extra presences aside from the usual vicious Hell hounds, housemaids, and stable boys—the twisty black threads of Hell's Court devils.

Golda roused at the glimpse of movement in the tapestry. She melted into an oak and made herself invisible. A sturdy slave girl was approaching at a run through the oaks inside the estate. She was nude, collared, and running as fast as her small feet could fly. She ran with a whip in one hand and a leather satchel slung over her shoulder.

The girl leapt at the iron fence. She threw her whip over the top crossbars and used it to help pull herself up. She eased her body over the iron fence spikes. The girl landed heavily on her feet and skittered through the thorny underbrush, as if running for the road.

Golda loped and closed the distance. She was no stranger to interrogating a slave, and the girl smelled of desperation. The girl slowed. Her brown doe eyes held a look of surprise. The girl's collared neck was laced with old scars, and a coin piercing swayed on her cheek. Golda drew close and patted the hilt of her sword.

"Going somewhere? I don't think so."

The girl coiled her whip slowly and pushed her satchel behind her hip. "You. I've been looking for you."

"Me? I want to ask a few questions. Where is Boudi-Ca? Tell me." Golda glanced over her shoulder. Something wasn't right. The howls of Hell hounds rose over the sigh of the wind through the oaks. Black threads detached from the tapestry inside Fennel's estate. If the slave girl was trying to escape from Master Fennel, a chase was already underway. The girl smelled faintly of a familiar, expensive nectar perfume.

"If you help me, I will help you," the girl answered.

"You want me to help you run from the hounds and devils? That isn't going to happen. Just tell me where I can find Boudi-Ca." Golda glanced over her shoulder again. The howls were growing louder, and the devils were accelerating, possibly mounted on horses. She drew her sword. She needed to disappear quickly.

"You look like a tracker," the girl persisted. "If you help me, I'll tell you where Boudi-Ca went. You'll never see her again without me."

Golda grabbed the girl's arm. She'd prowled the neighborhood many times in both cat and human form. She knew every tree, fence, and twisty pathway. She dragged the slave across the road. A small crumbling gap in the stone wall of the neighboring home allowed narrow entry, and soon she was running with the girl through a luxurious thorn garden. The girl took long strides through the thorny paths with her bare feet, as if she hardly noticed.

The far side of the garden offered a more difficult obstacle in the form of a stone wall, but soon they were over and descending the hill on the far side. They followed a gully between two other fences. The gully turned into a trail, and the trail led into a maze of a downtown neighborhood. The baying of the Hell hounds faded. The black threads went aimless in the tapestry and doubled back, a hopeful sign that the devils had no tracker of their own.

Golda adjusted her pack over her shoulder. She was carrying her horse poison, a fresh pair of purchased cuffs, and a small fortune in gold coins. She wore Elder Tahany's sword on her hip. Her horse was tethered in a copes along the lower hill road. She was ready to make a bold play for Boudi, but once again she'd been turned away.

"Are we safe?" the slave girl asked.

Golda shrugged. "Yes, for the moment. The devils are still looking for you, but they're running in circles. This isn't my lucky day, so it must be yours."

"There's no luck, only the cursed spinning of the Fates." The girl's visage wavered and seemed to melt. She grew four inches in height, and her sturdy figure converted into more generous, womanly Jinn curves. The girl's appearance and nudity had both been an illusion. Her brown hair changed to stark white, and her eyes turned cold, grey, and gloomy. Instead of a slave collar, she wore a bloody, ripped silk nightgown. Golda stepped warily away from Lydiah. She'd known Boudi's captor had great magical powers, but she hadn't known what form they might take. "Why in the hells were you running from your own home?"

"I was escaping," Lydiah answered. "Obviously."

"You're some sort of shifter or doppelganger?"

"I'm an illusionist. My spells aren't common knowledge, and I like to keep it that way. I don't expect you'll be telling anyone soon."

"Are you playing a game with me? Is this some sort of trap?" Golda leveled her sword. Lydiah raised her whip defensively.

"How quickly the claws come out with you, cat. This is no game. I'd almost forgotten about you, honestly. Boudi-Ca was arrested last night. The devils came to arrest me this morning. I took the form of my dressing girl, Kveta, and left my home. I've sealed my guilt, but still I'm free to do what I will."

"Where is Boudi-Ca?"

"I'm not certain, but I think Boudi-Ca is in the Bolgia pits. The devils have a blank grey door downtown at 115 West Pelagius Street. It's the place where they are taking the suspected lesbians for the purgation."

"What purgation?"

"You don't even know? The devils haven't questioned you coming in and out of the city, or have you been living in the city all of this time, Golda?"

"I'm sneaky. The devils are hard pressed to find me."

Lydiah rolled her eyes. "The devils can't find their own buttocks sometimes, but once they sink a few steel hooks into your flesh, you've got problems. The purgation is a city-wide hunt going on for lesbians. The devils intended to arrest at least a dozen lesbians this very day."

"What are the devils doing with the lesbians, then?"

"No one knows," Lydiah answered. "It's very strange. No one has heard a peep from any of them, and my own husband won't tell me. Boudi-Ca is arrested for murder, however. She assassinated Judge Rhadamanthus and his wife Breanarachelle last night, along with one of Breanarachelle's young man-friends. According to my husband, she stabbed them dead with a hunting knife. Her cuts were perfectly placed, the work of a master butcher."

Golda gritted her teeth. She couldn't believe what she was hearing, and all of her brazen hope to save Boudi-Ca was in serious jeopardy. "That sounds bad, Lydiah."

"Well, it's wonderful but very bad, yes. The devils don't suffer any attack on their own, and Breanarachelle and Rhadamanthus were devil royalty. Boudi-Ca is still alive and in bondage, counting each second of her unthinkable suffering. She can only pray to the Fates for the devils to make a mistake and let her die too quickly. They've probably started to flay her skin. They'll do that first to expose all of her nerves." Lydiah's cheek twitched. "I don't know what charges they are bringing against me, personally. Perhaps it's for conspiracy, or perhaps it's for fucking my own fledgling. I didn't wait around to find out."

"Well, I can't be waiting around while there is any chance to save Boudi-Ca. Where is this door you're speaking of?"

Lydiah snorted. "So you're going to just ride in and rescue her, is that it? Let me ask you a question, Golda. Do you truly love Boudi-Ca?"

Golda lowered her eyes. Lydiah was asking the same question that she'd asked herself a thousand times, with no definite answer. "I think so, yes. I'm still here, and that's the best proof I have for it."

"There is likely no saving Boudi-Ca, but will you try to save her anyway?"

"I don't know."

"Well, if you hesitate, then maybe you don't love her after all."

"Some say true love is sacrifice." Golda ran her gaze down Lydiah's barely-protected body. She gauged her chances of thrusting her sword between Lydiah's breasts. She feared the elder sorceress, and she was afraid to put her sword away in that moment. "I think we Jinni have difficulty with sacrifice. We are creatures of need. We take from others endlessly. We have trouble giving."

Lydiah's eyebrow arched. "Truly, or is that just an excuse? You've never known a Jinn to sacrifice herself? I know many Jinni who give their very lives and souls to their husbands. They practice—"

"I'm well aware of the sad, sick devotion of Old Order Jinni to their husbands. Addiction to Djinnus seed doesn't mean undying love."

"—vodun dollification to become their husband's living doll, or they pierce themselves with rings and play as his puppet on strings. Or perhaps they practice self-mummification, never again to move or speak, serving as only a lifeless vessel for their husband's seed. Most Jinni want to be owned totally by their husband. In uniting with him, they are united with our Lord. I know at least five Jinni who ritually killed themselves after Boudi-Ca killed their husbands in that Isandlwana massacre. I personally received many death threats, but I threatened them in turn and assured them they couldn't have my Boudi's head. Some of those Jinni refused to continue living."

Golda felt a queer emotion well from deep in her chest. "Maybe I do know someone who sacrificed herself. Maybe I'm a fool for following in her footsteps. Maybe I'm sacrificing myself right now. I've been hunting Boudi-Ca in Haawiyah for months, but I've heard the Bolgia pits under Mer are an unspeakable, impregnable place. No one ever leaves until the devils are done making them suffer."

Lydiah's glittering cold eyes brightened. "You're correct. No one escapes from the Bolgia pits. Once the devils bring you in, they own your body, soul, and mind. I've visited prisoners there on a few occasions. Normally I'm unaffected by devil presences, but if Mer is the heart of the garden, the Bolgia pits are its soulless roots. After only ten minutes down there, I began to feel drained and empty, like the will to live was sucked out of me. My bones and brain began to ache. After twenty minutes, my brain throbbed with despair, and I was desperate to see Dawn's chariot again. After thirty minutes, I couldn't bear to stay any longer."

"Yes. There is no hope." Golda lowered her sword and planted her rear on the ground not far from Lydiah's feet. In that moment, she queerly lacked the will to face Lydiah, or anything. She didn't care anymore. Everything was hopeless. She allowed her sword to slip from her fingers into the thorny dirt of Haawiyah. Warmth flowed up from her depths however. A sudden animal warning broke the overwhelming wave of despair.

She snapped awake when the coil of Lydiah's whip slipped over her head and around her neck. She grabbed the coil and yanked forward with all of her strength. Lydiah tipped off of her feet and landed hard in the thorny ravine underbrush.

Golda flexed her fingers and picked up her blade. She was surprised that her neck and hands weren't numb. The whip was only an ordinary slave-driving implement, not a wicked narcabyss whip from the Smokeless Flames. Lydiah climbed to her feet, brushed herself off, and slung her leather satchel back onto her shoulder. Lydiah sighed with exasperation.

"You're very strong, Golda. You shouldn't have resisted my domination spell. I expected to see you strangled, but instead I'm impressed by your tenacity. Maybe you're not such a loose end. Maybe you can be trusted. Maybe your death can wait a while longer, if I deign to—"

"Just shut up. I felt we had an issue, and now I see how it is." Golda glanced over the stone wall at the nearest Merian abode. The commotion in the ravine had roused the attention of at least one of the neighbors in the adjacent homes.

"You want me to shut up?" Lydiah snarled. "I'm a former ambassador for Hell. I was the mistress of two kings of France. I'm married to a son of our Lord. If anything, you need to stop interrupting me when I speak."

"I'm a former senator and first lady of Egypt. I was the mistress of two Popes. I'm the student of a son of our Lord. Let's call it close to even."

Lydiah's eyebrow arched. "I'll assume you're lying, like all of your rebel ilk. Why should I believe a renegade shifter? I'm better off trusting an Choshek hobgoblin."

"That's amusing coming from you."

A messenger bird winged through the forest. The bird alit on Lydiah's shoulder and disappeared. Lydiah's face went pale. "That was a bird from my first fledgling. Masia-Ca says my husband has her in a cage. He is holding a knife to her face, and he's going to cut her once every five minutes until I return to him. Fennel has always wanted to play with my fledglings, and now he has a chance to get both, I suppose. Meanwhile, even the devils know the trick of following the birds straight to me. So I don't have time to stand here and exchange petty insults all day with your cat brain."

Golda hefted her blade meaningfully. "Well, maybe we can parlay, like the werewolves. If you help me find a way to rescue Boudi-Ca, I'll use my tracking skills to help you avoid the devils. Just to be clear, this doesn't mean we're friends. You took Boudi's life away when you took her memories. You changed her fantasy into a nightmare. For that, there's no forgiveness, not to mention the fact that you just tried to kill me."

Lydiah glared at her for long seconds that stretched into a minute. "I didn't ask for your forgiveness, Golda, but you can help me get my fledgling back. I might have a plan. You can live to help, but the Fates have a way of catching up with everyone eventually."

Chapter 29.

Yellen rode up Leo Street towards Befanah's house. She pulled her hat over her eyes against Dawn's brightness. Dawn was flying low and lazy that morning, and the day after Ostara was breaking hot over the heart of Haawiyah. She was nervous for the big day of arrests, but she was looking forward to getting it over. She needed to take her mind off of Henne's honey moon. She had to let Henne go. Their relationship was over.

After two weeks into the Flames Purgation, she faced one more sweep and then, as Lydiah had intimated during their exchange of words after Henne's wedding, the first phase of the Purgation might arrive at a stopping point. She felt horrible for the arrested Sisters, but she seemed close to surviving the ordeal. She'd struck a détente with both Lydiah and Simhonit, although the uncertainty still weighed on her.

Strangely, there were no iron carriages waiting at Befanah's curb—no Shadow or Lydiah in motorcars. Yellen advanced through the door, which stood ajar and unlocked. Befanah sat behind her desk in the study, looking up at the ceiling and chewing on the stem of her reading glasses. Befanah tilted her head.

"Hell's Court arrested Lydiah's fledgling."

Yellen froze. "Which one?"

"The one."

"That's horrible. What about Lydiah?"

"I'm not sure if Councilor Lydiah is under arrest yet, but if her fledgling was arrested, it's a bad omen. I think Lydiah was worried all along about the Court turning on her. She told me a few weeks ago she had sacra viperae installed in both of her homes. Those are fine against mice, but not against lesbian assassins from the Flames."

"Why not?"

"We're immune to the poison, of course. From the rumors I've heard, I wouldn't be surprised at all if Lydiah were secretly a hypocrite, and she was hiding illicit activities."

"I don't understand. Lydiah said something about the viperae eating mice. I always thought Allyssia's invisible vipers were given to Flames officers for better reasons than catching local vermin. I assumed she was joking."

"The viperae catch magical mice, Nefra." Befanah dropped her reading glasses and reached for her desk drawer. She extracted her smoking pipe. "It's a little-known fact that the devil sorcerers of Hell's Court use magical eye-spy mice to catch people in unlawful acts. Those spy spells allow for remote viewing through an obsidian ball or some such. Yes, the viperae will bite intruders who have bad intent and inflict a paralyzing venom, but they'll also eat magical mice. The Flames leadership never speaks of this openly, but the sacra viperae mean protection from Hell's Court if they pry too deeply into our business. Bless our mother Allyssia."

Yellen averted her eyes from Befanah. She felt like a fool. If the viperae protected Sisters from devil spies, that would mean Lydiah had given her the vipera to protect her from Hell's Court, not vengeance from the lesbian cliques.

"This is bad. This is very bad."

Befanah snapped her fingers, and a flame sparked in her pipe bowl. "I wouldn't be surprised if they arrest Lydiah next. I wonder if the Councilor was responsible for warning the Named. I assume you wouldn't do such a thing."

"What's happening with the arrests today then? Lydiah said we'd have a final list to help the devils."

"That's not going to happen now. I expect Hell's Court will take full control. Our involvement in the arrests is over. I haven't heard anything about the purgation ending either. I expect the devils to continue arresting Jinni in Mer for as long as it pleases them, or unless we have divine intervention."

"Why isn't the Flames more outraged?"

"I've caught enough messenger bird updates in the last hour to see some outrage, yes, but key Council members plan to send a formal apology to the Court. We'll cooperate, of course. The Council will toss Lydiah to the devils in an eye blink if there is any implication that the Councilor protected the lesbians. My concern now is the fallout from any interrogations. How much did she know about you, Nefra?"

"She knows a lot more than I'd prefer."

Befanah nodded gravely. "So I suspected. You're dismissed, Lieutenant. I'd advise to get far away, and quickly. I'll complete the paperwork approving your health leave immediately. I can try to schedule a Nanka flight for you to Erebus, but that might take a little more time. You're clearly fatigued, and you need to heal from your war wound in a better climate. The purgation was too much effort for you. I'll keep you apprised."

"Yes. Thank you, Mistress." Yellen met Befanah's pained eyes. She felt a chill run down her spine. She turned and strode from the study, out of the house and into the harsh Haawiyah sun slanting over the tiled rooftops. The cobra-leaf trees hissed at her, as if they knew all of her secrets. She climbed onto her horse and directed it back towards her home. She summoned a messenger bird for Simhonit.

Councilor Lydiah's fledgling was arrested, and Lydiah might be next. The devils are taking over the investigation. I'm going to try to leave the city. Watch yourself and your friends. There is a big raid today.

Yellen directed her horse back down Leo Street towards home. She needed a plan. She had to admit a high probability that the arrest of Lydiah's fledgling could lead in any number of ways to her also getting arrested. Boudi-Ca's memories were sketchy, but if Lydiah were arrested and broken, dire secrets would surely be revealed. If she herself were arrested and broken to the point of confession, that meant Henne and Simhonit would be next.

Yellen felt her guts turn wretchedly. She urged her horse to a full gallop down Leo Street past the baths. She'd made mistake after mistake, incautiously compelled to sate her deep Jinn needs. She refused to allow the devils to make her feel guilty, however. She was a Jinn. She loved who she loved. Allyssia had made no mistake in creating her. She only wished that her desires could cause less pain.

The best thing she could do for Henne was to not get arrested, which meant that she needed to leave the city immediately as Befanah had suggested. Her preference was to take Kiree to Erebus, but how could she even escape the city with the gates locked down? She couldn't steal a Nanka from the Flames without implicating herself further as a criminal. She could only wait for Befanah and the paperwork to make her trip official.

Perhaps she could fabricate a fictitious husband or a military fiancée stationed in Erebus, wear her uniform, and try to talk the guards at the east gate into letting her leave. Hundreds of military personnel passed through the east gate of Mer daily from the Hell's army camps outside the city along the Mare. Surely they weren't barring all military Jinni outright. She could buy herself a cheap secondhand wedding ring at a Westmarket trinket cart. She arrived at her house within minutes. She was tethering her horse in the run-down stable when the return bird from Simhonit landed on her shoulder.

In that case, we may raid today too. We have twelve sisters committed. We're planning to attack 115 West Pelagius while the devils are out arresting more victims. We've mapped a secret route through the Bolgia pits. Will you help us, Yellen? You owe it to our friends and Sisters whose lives you helped ruin. Are you still a tiger, or are you a coward?

Yellen clenched her jaw. The harsh words from Sim stung as intended. She had to respect such a daring plan for vengeance, but an attack on 115 West Pelagius seemed inadvisable at best. Sim and company were skilled blade mistresses, but likely none of them were elders. They could scarcely defeat Master Glumstak and the legion of algolagnite torturers who held the lesbians imprisoned.

Simhonit was risking even more exposure, more arrests, more torture, and the entire lesbian establishment potentially wiped out. On the other hand, the timing was excellent. If the devils were out in the city arresting more victims, they couldn't defend the Bolgia pits. Yellen pressed through her rear door and made her way to the front shop room.

The house was quiet. Kiree had closed down the bird slits for some reason, although the morning was calm, with no sign of a storm. Yellen gazed at the glass display cases that Kiree had carefully cleaned. The plaster patches on the walls were waiting for a final coat of paint. Thanks to Hell's Court and the laws against lesbians, it would all go to waste.

"Kiree!"

Normally the demoness scurried to greet her at the door, but Kiree was apparently sleeping. Yellen strode up the stairs at pace, sifting through her head where she could get a second horse for her slave. Perhaps it would be wiser to return Kiree to the Toad on her way from the city, but she hated that idea. Kiree was her first real slave. She had no desire to discard her First like a piece of rubbish.

Yellen topped the stairs and glanced into the empty second-floor studio room. Kiree was supposed to be refinishing the floor of the studio-to-be, but the demoness was nowhere to be seen. Yellen climbed the narrow stairs to the third floor and rounded the corner into her cozy loft bedroom. Kiree was stretched out on the bed in the nude. The demoness lay in an inviting half-asleep stance. Her slender legs were awry, and her ruddy-tufted, well-worn slit was angled in invitation.

"Kalagi cha cha," Kiree said in a sultry tone. Pretty girl.

"Yes, you're very pretty, but we don't have time for that." Yellen reached under her bed for her travel bags. She hunted for her favorite rucksack, but it appeared to be missing. "We need to leave the city."

"Poggi wee? Wo kala wee?" Will I be safe? Do you love me?

"Of course I love you." Yellen tossed a worn saddle bag towards her armoire and pressed low with a quick kiss. Kiree's thick lips were unusually cool. Kiree's face suddenly blurred, and her hair changed tone, bleaching from red to pale white. Yellen jerked back. Kiree was gone, and Lydiah lay on the bed instead, licking her unpainted lips slowly.

"Good morning Lieutenant. I appreciate the kiss." Lydiah stirred and sat. The Councilor was in deshabille, wearing only a bloody, tattered silk nightgown, as if she'd been dragged from bed that morning and assaulted with Sharp instruments. "Your taste in slaves is terrible, however."

"What do you want, Councilor? Where is my slave?"

"I gave her a few gold coins and told her to go away, permanently. Kiree stole your nectar supply and one of your knives."

"She's one less thing to worry about, but I don't feel any better. What do you want with me? I'm packing up to leave before the devils arrest you along with your fledgling." Yellen went to the wardrobe. She fished for her favorite army coat, but selected her best dress instead. She folded the dress and pushed it into her saddle bag, followed by her best corset. She could feel Lydiah's hard eyes on her back. She hoped Lydiah hadn't come to kill her. She tried to work with her left hand only, keeping her right hand free to draw if needed.

"I'm sorry," Lydiah murmured. "My husband betrayed me, and the devils tried to arrest me. I'm a bit put out of my home."

"Your own husband tried to arrest you?"

"He's been bored of me for the last century, really. Lesbian love is as good an excuse as any, and he loves to see me helpless in handcuffs. It's an instant arousal for him."

"So you aren't really a lesbian."

"I'm cursed by Love," Lydiah answered. "I've fucked my own fledgling on several occasions. I admit to loving her more than I've loved anyone in the last millennium."

Yellen abandoned her attempts to pack. She turned and faced Lydiah. Lydiah's confession upped the ante yet again. "Why are you confiding in me? It's nice that you're a complete hypocrite, but I can't believe you need a shoulder to cry on. Are you just toying with me before killing me? What do you want?"

"I want to apologize."

"Apologize?"

"I know you loathe me, Nefra. I try to be fair with everyone I work with. I apologize for dragging you into this. I was selfish. I just thought you could be a friend for Boudi-Ca. I thought you could help her and mentor her—"

"Excuse me? You risked my life and put me in a difficult, dangerous situation just so I could be your fledgling's friend?"

Lydiah raised her hands in mock surrender. "I love my fledgling. She was lonely, and I couldn't give her the things she desperately needed."

Nefra swallowed. She could hardly believe what she was hearing, yet she'd never heard such an honest, heartfelt tone from Lydiah's cold and calculating mouth. "Well, that's very charitable. Sometimes love can make people better, and maybe that happened to you. Congratulations."

"Has love made you better, Lieutenant?"

"I've had a strong urge to kill the Djinnus who is taking Henne away on her honey moon, so no. I'm not better today. I'm angry. I'm also angry at Hell's Court. I'm afraid I'm going to lose more friends soon." Yellen sighed and let the tension drain from her face. "On the other hand, I'm more compassionate. I warned the Named. I ruined your purgation on purpose."

Lydiah snorted. "I knew it was you."

"Why in the name of Allyssia did you want me to do this job? I never believed your story that I was less likely to be bribed or influenced by the cliques in Mer."

"You want to know the real truth? Fine. You were my insurance. The Flames Council knows you, so by choosing you, I effectively informed them how I truly feel on this issue. Meanwhile, Hell's Court is clueless. I never imagined you'd have the balls to disobey orders and go rebellious like that, but you did it. I'm impressed. I'm sorry you lost your lover to an Djinnus, but you had that coming anyway."

"Yes. I'll find someone else."

"I won't," Lydiah muttered. "I'm doomed, or at least I'm cursed to flee from Hell's Court until I go to the void. I try not to flatter myself, but I know things. I'm just glad our Lord is still in His conjugal bed with Allyssia, or else He himself might take an interest in seeing me brought to heel. I could give Prince Masad some competition for selling Hell's secrets to the enemy."

"The shoe is on the other foot then, isn't it? Boudi-Ca leads the devils to you. You lead the devils to me. I lead the devils to everyone I ever cared about. This is an issue." Yellen drummed her fingers on her sword belt. She had a strong intuition to pull, like a pricking on the back of her neck. She was less worried that Lydiah was going to kill her, and more worried that killing Lydiah was her own best course of action.

"Yes, now we get to the heart of the matter, which is your involvement." Lydiah's voice went from warm to cold again. "Oh, I'm so sorry for your pain, Lieutenant Nefra. Never mind the dozens of lesbians who are already in the Bolgia pits at this moment, probably undergoing weeks of torture, including my beloved Boudi-Ca."

"I hope you don't really love that girl, for her sake."

"Of course I do. I told you."

Yellen cleared her throat. "You're a scheming, lying, conniving, two-faced devil-lover. Hell's Court never would have appointed you ambassador if you weren't. Boudi-Ca deserves a lot better, or at least someone closer to her own age."

"Precisely. That's why I have to insist on your help in saving her before her flesh splits open and all of her secrets spill out with her intestines."

Yellen drew her sword. She tried to gauge the ramifications of killing Lydiah in her own bedchamber. "You gave Boudi-Ca the black, which means her memories are gone. She doesn't remember me stealing her girlfriend in Meristyian. Except for a little kiss in a certain garden shed, where I cut Boudi-Ca off and left her, she hardly knows me. I just need to sever the link between her and me, and I might be free."

"I gave her less than half the black that Hell's Court required of me." Lydiah's eyes were lidded. "I couldn't bring myself to completely ruin her. I put a blanket over her memories, but they are still in her head."

"I'll take my chances."

"No." A voice came from the hallway then, accompanied by the sound of a drawn sword. Yellen caught the movement out of the corner of her eye and stepped away from Lydiah, raising her sword in defense. The interloper was a tall redhead with wild hair almost down to her full breasts, which strained her shirt lacings. She wore a white linen buccaneer's shirt with brown leather pants. The redhead's gloomy eyes were a baleful silver-blue under the shadows of her mane. She was a Jinn, and she held an antique Gypsy-style sword extended.

Lydiah nonchalantly examined her nails. "I have a tracker. Her name is Golda."

"No." Golda said again. "We have a Lydiah. I don't think we've met, Lieutenant Nefra. I serve Allyssia, and I'm trying to get Boudi-Ca out of the city. We're wasting time, and we need your help. Boudi-Ca could be dying this minute. Please give Lydiah some clothes, and let's go do this."

Yellen lowered her blade. "Well, I suppose you have me outnumbered."

"No." Lydiah said. "It's still two against two, Lieutenant. Your sacra vipera is waiting nearby, ready to strike. Move slowly like I told you, Golda. Stay calm and lower your sword."

"Calmness is not one of my strong points."

Yellen eased back from her two powerful, uninvited guests. The presence of the vipera on her side was hardly comforting. "I remember you, Golda. You're a well-known lesbian criminal, correct? You have a Hell's Court bounty on your head?"

"At your service. Any other questions?"

"How are you planning to get into the Bolgia pits?"

"I'll pose as my husband," Lydiah interjected. "I'll walk right up to the door. When the devils open it, I'll talk my way into seeing Boudi-Ca. I'd like to pretend that Golda is my prisoner, but Golda isn't excited by handcuffs. It's the best I've been able to think of. I may need more muscle in case of any problems, and that's where I'd like you with me, Lieutenant. I can't imagine I'll fool the devils for very long. They're wary against all sorts of escape efforts and magical trickery. They've seen everything over the centuries, and I believe many sections of the pits are dampened against some forms of magic."

"What's the exit strategy? If you find Boudi-Ca, what happens next?"

Lydiah stood at full height on her hooves and brushed her white hair over her shoulder. She sifted under the bedcovers and withdrew a hidden whip, along with a leather satchel. "I have a lot of friends in Hell, of course. I plan to take my Boudi-Ca to a secret location, far away from Mer. She and I will need to be hidden in a private patch in the tapestry, a place that can't be tracked. I know someone who offers such a temporary refuge for a few stacks of gold coins."

"She isn't your Boudi-Ca." Golda lowered her blade and stepped further into the room. "I'm taking Boudi-Ca back to Eastern Meristyian with me. I know a werewolf enclave where she'll be safe."

"I would not be safe there, however," Lydiah countered tersely. "And I have no intention of sending my fledgling to live like a wild thing amidst a pack of dirty animals, even if they're willing to protect her. She likes nice clothes. She likes nice things. I know her."

Golda made an animal sound low in her throat. "She's lived with the werewolves before, and she enjoyed it. Mostly."

"Well, where is Lady Allyssia these days?" Lydiah's eyebrow arched. "Maybe I'd like to apply for an ambassador position, assuming the pay is up to my abilities."

A veil of pain darkened Golda's face. "I don't know. Masad believes she's on an island somewhere in the Sea of Desire, having renewed an alliance with Poseidon. He isn't willing to help me hunt high and low for her, and I don't have a boat. I decided to come to Haawiyah alone and find Boudi-Ca. My plan is still to take her with me when I leave."

Yellen frowned. "Well, if you're leaving the city completely, how are you getting out? Hell's army and the devils are guarding the gates and walls of Mer for the purgation. They're watching for Jinni like us, especially. We'd need a major diversion, a Nanka, or spells of invisibility. Just how good of a tracker are you, Golda?"

"I'm one of the best in the realm. I was mentored by Prince Masad."

"You're still just a shifter, not a goddess." Lydiah waved dismissively. "And if we stole a Nanka or stormed a gate, Hell's army and the Flames would chase us like hounds after a hare. Our best choice is to go in stealth through the under-Bolgia. We'll head through the eastern tunnels of the lowest levels of the Bolgia pits and into the depths of the Great Blue Hole mines. From there, we climb back up to emerge under the Erebus rim country, just like Allyssia's followers left the city originally in the old days of the Jinn schism."

Yellen slowly sheathed her sword. She hadn't considered leaving Mer through the tunnels underneath it, mainly because such a thing seemed impossible. "I thought all but one of those passages were destroyed, and to guard the last passage through those old ways, the devils unleashed the great Beast."

Lydiah shrugged. "That was centuries ago. Perhaps the ancient Beast is sleeping in the deep, and perhaps it won't stir if we find a way to go quietly. If it confronts us with an intent to devour us whole, then we'll just have to say hello."

Yellen felt her chest wound began to ache again, as if in sympathy with her emotional turmoil. "I remember stories of the Beast from when I was a fledgling in the Flames. It rules over the dead passages in the pits, and no one goes through those places. The Beast is worse than the devils. No one faces it and lives to see daylight."

"So are we agreed?" Inanna continued. Her silver-grey eyes were shimmering brightly in that moment. "We'll use my illusion magic to go right through the front door, and then we'll fight to the death against the Hell's Court devils to save my fledgling from an even worse fate, if necessary?"

Golda stirred restlessly. "You said we were using trickery and stealth, but now the plan is to start killing everything? I agree we need to go right away, but fighting the devils seems insane."

"Well, the plan is trickery, but like I said, the devils aren't idiots. If you truly love your Boudi-Ca, I just assumed you're willing to sacrifice your life, like I am."

Golda's moody blue eyes turned even more dangerous, and the tracker glared at Lydiah from under her wild mane. Yellen winced and rubbed her sternum, willing the ache to abate. At least she'd found an escape route from Mer, but she agreed in principle with Golda. Lydiah's mental state was in question if the Councilor thought a frontal attack on the devils to rescue her fledgling was sensible.

The route through the Bolgia to the Great Blue Hole was equally treacherous, threatened with ancient, nasty things that had lurked for ages in the dark holes and tunnels deep under the bowels of Haawiyah. The Beast was only one of the potential dangers. Yellen glanced at her saddle bag. If she was going through the Bolgia, she'd leave her nice clothes behind. She'd take a hefty stash of gold coins in a belt pouch along with her blade, but no Flames uniforms or decorations. Her old life was over. She met Lydiah's intense eyes.

"I have a better plan. There's another rescue party heading into the dungeon this morning while the devils are out arresting the suspected lesbians. They're friends of mine, and they've apparently used old maps to find a backdoor into the Bolgia pits through private connecting pits downtown. I'll send a bird to Simhonit. She said she has twelve sisters. I'll tell her we also have a tracker, and I'll tell her we have a Lydiah."

"Excellent. I'm so glad you're willing to help us, Lieutenant." A messenger bird flitted into the room and landed on Lydiah's shoulder. Her small smile disappeared, and she took a step back in surprise. Her knuckles went white where she squeezed her leather satchel more tightly. "Have you opened one of your bird slits? We closed them."

"I may have left the back door open a crack. Is there a problem?"

Lydiah shook her head. "Not yet. That was another bird from my fledgling, Masia-Ca. She says she's hanging upside down, and Fennel is torturing my slaves. Vladimir and Kveta have both confessed to seeing me fuck my Boudi-Ca. Masia-Ca is weeping and begging me to come home. Nefra, if you have this force of renegade sisters, perhaps we should pit them against my husband first. He has a few Hell's Court devils to record the testimonies, but he may be mostly alone."

"I can't command them. Simhonit's objective is to save the arrested Serpent Sisters from the hell of the Bolgia pits."

"We're going to save Boudi-Ca. That's our first priority," Golda added. "We're not here to solve all of your personal problems."

"Fine. Nefra, I'd like to borrow a nice black skirt and blouse. I'd also like to trade my ordinary driving whip with one of your lovely narcabyss variety."

"Anything you need, Councilor. My wardrobe is yours."

Lydiah shucked her torn nightgown and strode to the wardrobe. She dropped her leather whip and withdrew a pulpy magical replacement. She coiled it almost lovingly. "I didn't expect your cat brain to understand, Golda, but Lieutenant Nefra knows that some battles have to be fought sooner or later. We could be making a strategic mistake if we wait until later to face Fennel. Even if we rescue Boudi-Ca and get past the devils and the Beast, he'll still be coming for us. Breanarachelle was his lover, and Rhada was his best friend. Boudi-Ca killed both of them."

Chapter 30.

Golda led the way down the dark tomb-like passageway. She held a sheaf of ancient architecture plans folded in her left hand, but she preferred not to use them. She explored the under-texture of Mer with her inner sight instead. She was descending into the Bolgia pits under the Merian downtown. She could feel the oppression already. The fear felt like weights in her legs, urging her animal self to leave that place immediately.

Perhaps the dread was foul devil magic. Perhaps the dread was a psychic remnant of the many thousands of souls who had been imprisoned over the centuries in the black cells and tombs under Hell's capital city. The Bolgia pits dated from ancient Sumerian days, even before Lord Hades had assumed kingship over the lower realms. The Bolgia were over two millennia old.

Over those centuries, Merian homeowners had tunneled innumerable private pits and holes of their own, and then dug still deeper via mine shafts and secret passageways. Simhonit and the Smokeless Flames had mapped a wind-about route through such passages under Mer, and so they had entered through the private home of a Hell's Court official, after binding and gagging his devil wife and their abused transgender houseboy.

Golda tried to ignore the clinks, thumps, and scuffles that followed her down the tunnel. The well-armed and armored band of Serpent Sisters weren't much for subtlety, but she was glad to have their help in her quest to save Boudi. She'd forever hated and feared the narcabyss whips, but now she had several whips at her back, ready to defend her.

She almost trusted the Smokeless Flames assassins in that moment, despite not knowing their names. No personal introductions had been made—only exchanges of fierce nods and handshakes. Aside from Simhonit and Lydiah, who were clearly known by all, some of the grim lesbian Sisters had offered only code names in lieu of their real identities.

The Weasel was a wiry, boyish Sister with short-cropped hair and a quick, nervous smile. The Tower was an older woman who wore a robe with a belt pouch stuffed with healing herbs and unguents. The Mountain was a tall, hulkish fighter with a spiked mace in her hands and a sword on her back. The Sparrow and Hawk were a roguish couple in matching black leather armor. They'd kissed each other several times in defiance of their potential deaths, and to defy Lydiah, who was an unpopular and controversial presence. Lieutenant Nefra had only introduced herself as the Tiger.

Golda ducked a big cobweb, wary of the creatures that lived in the nearby crevice—clots of evil in the weave. Twenty or more beady black eyes glistened in the darkness, accompanied by a cacophony of demonic chittering.

"Watch the crack on the left." Golda raised her blade. The first beast sprang. Simhonit was ready to defend. The sword fell, and the giant spider screeched before the sword fell again. The remaining spiders retreated. Golda nodded her thanks, but inwardly she admonished herself. She'd boldly introduced herself by the code name of Lion. She felt as brave as any of those well-trained military assassins, but the dread of the pits made her as skittish as a kitten. Even after a few years of training with Masad, she still found it difficult to stay aware of the tapestry while staying alert to every movement in the physical environment at the same time.

A myriad of fears kept nagging at her. While she felt safer with the Sisters at her back, she couldn't say the same about Lydiah. Lydiah had tried to kill her, and probably would try again when their shaky agreement no longer had any mutual benefit. Lydiah had more or less said to her face that her death was only delayed.

Golda descended another set of crumbling, dusty stone steps, ever deeper under the volcanic rock under the capital city. She needed to deal with Lydiah sooner or later. Even as she seemed close to saving Boudi, she could easily lose Boudi-Ca forever, and not just with her death at the hands of the devils. Lydiah had no intention of giving up ownership of her beloved fledgling.

The dust was thicker at the bottom of the stairs, a layer of grit disturbed by the trails left by the spiders. The tunnel bent and ended at a massive bound door, just as the map had indicated. The door supposedly led into the pits under the Court building. She reached for the handle.

"Hold, friend Lion," Simhonit muttered from behind. "It could be cursed, or worse. Let's let the Weasel see this."

Golda backed away from the door while Simhonit ushered one of the Serpent Sisters forward. The Weasel removed her gloves and tucked them into her belt above the coils of her whip. She pressed a small gold monocle to her eye. "Aye. There's a death magic trap as well as a conventional lock. I have a few cantrips."

The Weasel uttered words of power. Golda blinked. Unless her eyes deceived her, the dungeon door seemed to relax in its hinges, appearing less foreboding and threatening. The Weasel nodded and motioned at Simhonit, who stepped forward with an array of lockpicks. Simhonit bent to the task, working the lock in silence with only her brilliant red-painted lips visible under dark pageboy hair. Two or three uncomfortable minutes passed until the Sisters began to mutter and bicker in the low light of a tenebris lux. Golda eased back against the stone wall, comforted that she wasn't the only one feeling the pressure. Lieutenant Nefra sidled close to her.

"I wish I had your skills," Nefra whispered.

Golda shrugged. "I wish I had your bravery, Tiger. I feel like a cowardly Lion right now. You're the only one of us who seems unafraid."

Nefra nodded. "I used to be afraid of the void, but not anymore. I think most of our fear of death comes from losing everything, even ourselves. In the field of battle, I had nothing except my sword, and my sword was only an extension of my mind. So everything I have, I know I will take into death with me. Everything else is an illusion, including the self. If you become one with the energy inside you, you can let go and just be. The flow goes in, and the flow goes out. You watch it go, round and round. The most important thing in life, like with fighting, is to stay calm and open your mind."

Golda nodded, aware that the other Sisters had quieted, as if to listen to Nefra's monolog. A loud clunk sounded then in the passageway. Simhonit edged back. "It's done. Are the guards coming, Lion?"

"I don't feel anything ahead, only more empty passageways." Golda forced her mind open to the tapestry again. She realized that was closing herself instinctively. Deep down, she didn't want to go into that multi-level tapestry where the darkness crept over the edges and horrors lurked under the surface. She pushed through the door, and the scene in the tapestry shifted completely. Simhonit advanced alongside her into a storage room filled with barrels of chemicals, canisters, and bundles of dried herbs.

"Still nothing?" Simhonit whispered.

"Wait. We've entered a proprietary weave, and everything just changed." Golda scanned the tapestry, even as her skin pricked. "There are six devil presences nearby. I see two devils in a room down the left passage and three to the right, while one is farther away. The far one is a big one, with a presence more like an ogre. I see a few prisoners to the right, but far more are in the levels underneath us. I see a sign of Boudi-Ca's thread, but it's very faint, like she is close to death. And the devils to the left are now coming this way."

"They smell our fear." Nefra advanced to the fore and motioned to the Sisters behind her. "Mountain and Tiger are going defensive sinister. Sparrow and Hawk go defensive dexter. Take care of our tracker and mages."

"Thank you Lieutenant," Lydiah said. "It's nice to know you care. If they attack us, we need to kill everything that moves, and quickly. Watch for the blood sprays, and let none escape. It's time for me to play as my husband, and of course no one should mention my name. When the underlings are dealt with, I'll handle with the Pit Master as well."

The Serpent Sisters pushed forward even as Lydiah's figure shifted. She gained three inches in height, and her black-skirted feminine figure turned into a handsome, muscled, dark-haired devil with a widow's peak and glittering, hard yellow eyes. Golda felt a chill at the mere sight of Archduke Fennel.

Fennel smoothed his tweed trousers, examined his nails, and unbuttoned his waistcoat to show his mottled, ashen-yellow male chest. He attempted to brandish his cane and dropped it on the floor, where it sounded an odd slap instead of a clatter.

Whips snapped, and blades rang in the left corridor. The Mountain swung her mace. She was a burly woman, but she roared with pain when a devil barreled under her mace and straight into her stomach. She fell backwards. The devil ripped his heavy steel hooks across her buttocks before sinking them triumphantly into her chest, piercing through her leather armor towards her heart.

The Mountain screamed like a horse, even as Nefra patiently slashed the devil's neck. Blood sprayed and smoked. The Mountain made choking sounds and shielded her face with no breath left to scream again. Sulfuric acid bubbled over the stones. Horrible odors of burning flesh and leather filled the room.

A barbed net flew. Nefra ducked, half-escaping another devil, and grimaced when a net hook raked her forearm, deflected by her leather armor. She met the devil's vicious polearm attack with a sword parry until Simhonit and two other Sisters came to assist. Golda tried to keep her mind open to the tapestry. The battle in the left tunnel was turning in favor of the Sisters thanks to sheer numbers, but more devils were coming from the right. She gestured with her hand. "Dexter."

"What goes there?" the feminine voice of a she-devil called. "Who are you, and what are you doing in the pits?"

"They are under my supervision." Lydiah strode forward in her illusory form.

"Archduke? What means this?" The she-devil's face went confused, even as she was joined by two male comrades. All three devils wore the decorated black and silver uniforms of Hell's Court.

"This little skirmish is a misunderstanding," Lydiah answered. "We were just following a lead on fledgling Boudi-Ca. The Smokeless Flames has discovered that the assassination of Judge Rhadamanthus and Breanarachelle was a high-level plot to avenge the arrested lesbians. Councilor Lydiah mind-controlled her own fledgling to compel her to do the deed."

"So it was really mind control then." The she-devil nodded sagely. "Interesting. Given the fledgling's murders and the trial we all remember so well—"

"Yes," Lydiah interrupted. "So we need to see Lydiah's fledgling and interrogate her with this new information. Where is she, please?"

"She's in the primum seat of course, being flayed. She's just down the corridor, my Lord. You put her there yourself. Wait. Is this a trick?" The she-devil's baleful eyes narrowed, and she reached for her blade. "I smell magic. You aren't really—"

"Correct." Lydiah swung her cane, and the cane transformed into Lydiah's narcabyss whip, and then the whip turned into a spray of smoky tentacles, which grabbed and twisted around the feet of the three devils, holding them in place. Lydiah motioned at Sparrow and Hawk. "Kill them."

Hawk surged forward and speared the surprised she-devil before she could even protest. The other devils brandished their curved blades and swung at the Sisters, but toppled off balance from the magical cords that held their feet in place. Golda stepped forward to assist, but the other Serpent Sisters darted ahead of her with faces full of hatred, joining Sparrow and Hawk to hack grimly at the devils.

The devils defended their lost position ferociously with flurries of hooks and blades, but they fell one by one, all moaning and sighing in an orgy of pleasure as the Jinni opened cut after cut, causing blood to run. In the final seconds, the Hawk cried out and fell. Her body crumbled amidst the fallen devils.

"No, please Allyssia!" the Sparrow shouted. When all three devils had stilled and gone silent, the younger Sister bent and tried to rouse the Hawk. The Hawk's face was pale, and her eyes were closed. Her right leg was shattered, and the pieces of her leg formed a pile like black charcoaled wood. The Sparrow moaned and tried to shake her lover back awake. "No, oh no!"

"Clear," Nefra said from the left. "We need medical here as well."

Lydiah knelt and examined the Hawk. "Your friend's desire structure is completely broken. She is going to the void, and let that be a note to the rest of you. If a makumbacer casts a spell, and a part of your body starts to weaken and burn horribly, you need to do something about that. You can't just keep hacking blindly as if nothing is happening. Aren't they training Sisters properly these days?"

"I'll look at Jan—I mean the Mountain," the Tower said in a low, pained tone.

Golda re-scanned the tapestry. The Pit Master wasn't coming, at least not yet. Five devils were down, along with one Mountain and one Hawk. The Mountain moaned and held her hands to her face. The Tower knelt over the fallen Sister with her leather healing satchel at the ready. The Tower applied a salve from a flask, and then prepared herbs.

"Onward," Lydiah said. She advanced into the right-hand passage. "My fledgling is in pain."

Golda followed in Lydiah's footsteps with the other Sisters, who closed ranks. The Sparrow rose from her dead lover. Her face went from mourning to ice cold, as if already bent on vengeance. The passage led to a well-appointed, marble-floored office room with a desk and several chairs. A short hallway led opposite the office into a high-ceilinged chamber full of cages. A nude, bleeding Djinnus lay in one cage, and a pig-headed demoness lay curled in another. Both wore ebon collars and cuffs. They barely stirred.

"This looks like a holding facility until sentenced prisoners can be assigned to torture or a cell." Simhonit shook her head. "I can smell the fear."

Lydiah pushed onwards past a devil prayer room with hooks, bundles of thorns, anatomical diagrams, and various ritual tomes. She turned a corner and passed through an archway into a larger room that looked like a laboratory for the infliction of torture. Racks of Sharp and pointy instruments festooned the old walls, and a Sharp, acidic odor hung in the air. A familiar blonde figure sat in a chair in the center. A huge figure hulked over her.

The elder devil was half again as large as any of the others. He was clad only in a sash and skirt around his waist in ancient Sumerian fashion. His nipples were pierced with thick golden hoops, and his black beard was polished, oiled, and glinting with golden beads. He held a curved, bloody knife in his equally bloody hands.

"Is that Master Fennel? Where is your wife's pretty flesh?" The Pit Master flashed a yellow grin through his thick beard. "I thought you were bringing your pathetic bisexual whore-slut down for some fun."

"Oh, yes. I'm here for fun," Lydiah answered. She shifted back into her feminine form and hefted her whip. "And soon you will not be, Pit Master Gonthrass. You're the boss in this upper level of the pits, correct? So let's get the fun started then."

"Ho, there!" Gonthrass raised his bloody hands in supplication. "No fun intended, Councilor. I surrender."

Lydiah blinked. "You surrender? You surrender after calling me pathetic?"

"Yes!" Gonthrass grinned. "I'll just put down my knife."

"I don't think so. We're raiding this dungeon to save my fledgling. I tried to negotiate, but you opened with an inexcusable insult to my character. Now there's supposed to be a big fight, but maybe you're right. Maybe you can prove more useful if you're not a corpse on the floor."

Gonthrass held up his hands again. "I agree completely. So go ahead and rescue your fledgling, take whatever loot you can find, and be on your way. Deal?"

Lydiah sighed. "I suppose—"

"Where are the other Sisters?" Simhonit interrupted. "Where are the other lesbians being held?"

"They're in next level, of course," Gonthrass answered. "So it's a big rescue, then. Well, the stairs are right over there. You might not want to find your friends, though. You might be disappointed. You're a little late, don't you think?"

"What do you mean—"

Golda felt a low growl again in her throat. She could barely concentrate on the conversation. Her emotions were almost out of control. She slipped past Pit Master Gonthrass, rounded the massive leather-bound torture chair, and gazed down at Boudi.

Boudi's tear-washed, puffy face was barely recognizable. Her neck was tightly wrapped with steel wire, which held her neck to the chair. More wires restrained her wrists, which were red-striped like candy from her attempts to struggle.

Boudi's legs were completely stripped of skin up her to hips. Her underflesh was red and dull, showing every vein, a few of which had broken to bleed, leaving trails of crusty scars like maps around the cylinders of her flayed thighs. More wires held Boudi's ankles tightly, bloating her feet, which appeared to be missing toenails.

The tips of thick spines protruded from Boudi's chest, dark things inserted between her ribs. Golda blinked back sudden tears. She couldn't believe the unbelievable horror of what she was seeing. For years she'd lived only with her best memories of Boudi—of a beautiful, mostly happy girl of innocence, desire, and perfect beauty, an Mimọ who loved and smiled, mostly free from Hell's horrors, but no more.

"—well you can't go on finger-fucking each other forever, you little vixens," Pit Master Gonthrass was orating, gesticulating with his bloody hands. "Our great Lord has laws, righteous laws, just and good laws, laws that enforce the proper conduct in service of all that is properly unholy—"

Golda felt her belly heave, and then her dread was over. She only felt calm. She stepped forward and plunged her sword into the back of Gonthrass, who roared and swatted at her. Nefra surged forward then with a serpent strike, and then the other Sisters attacked en masse, eager to kill. The raging battle was over within a minute, and Pit Master Gonthrass twitched in a pool of his hissing, smoking blood. The blood ran in rivulets through an ancient iron grate in the worn, stained floor tiles.

Golda lowered her sword and searched quickly for the mechanisms to remove the bondage wires from Boudi's limbs. Boudi-Ca didn't stir. The fledgling was still as death. Nefra joined the effort, bending to attack the wires around Boudi's ankles. Lydiah approached to assist from the other side. Golda searched the faces of her allies for the same emotions that she was feeling. Lydiah's face was a pale mask, while Nefra nodded with grim sympathy.

"You have real claws on you after all, friend Lion."

Chapter 31.

Boudi-Ca lay on her back and looked up at the plain, slate grey sky. Her soul was the stone she lay on—a ravaged, pock-marked landscape. Her soul was her world, stretched under the flat grey sky like a dead, desiccated insect under glass. There was a handle to the lid of that trap somewhere, but it was out of reach, made hopeless by those who had pinned her.

A light exploded in the sky then, and a rushing wind pulled her back under the stone. She was vaguely aware of the torture room again. She could feel the chair underneath her. She could feel the long spines that were locked in her chest, penetrating her wet and bloody lungs. She quivered and heaved into a blood-bubbly coughing fit, longing for that grey landscape, but she would need more pain to go back to that happier place.

Her ankles were still anchored in the landscape. She jerked her leg, a rattling appendage in a world far away. She could lift the anchor, but only for an inch until the unbearable pain bit back. She twitched her other leg, and she felt a coolness in the spaces between the pain, a lovely numbness, and a pressure that set the wind to rushing in her ears.

Could she leave from that place and go to the solace of the void? No, not while her ankles held her fast. She tried to reach down and unfasten herself. She imagined her hand grabbing her ankle, but her hand passed straight through. There was no hand there, and she kept trying to grab her ankle to free herself. She wasn't moving. She wasn't bending over.

Pain ripped through her right ankle, echoing her left. The pain shocked her sex, like a bolt of lightning attracted to a paradisiacal island. The pain returned in a flood up her legs. She was sitting in the sea of pain, and her legs were submerged up to her hips. Boudi-Ca opened her swollen eyes. She could see the three women. The women loomed over the red messes of her knees. Pain rose, a slow pain through her core, reminding her of how much she hungered. She was empty, so empty that she'd lost the sensation of how empty she'd become. She closed her eyes again, the better to search for a sunken chest of pleasure in the sea underneath the stone, a shell holding a pearl of oblivion.

She didn't want to wake up. She felt tears tickling over her cheeks, as if the pain had metamorphosed in her body and transposed to her brain. Her tears were not enough, just oozing of the clots of pain in her skull. The pain was too big to escape.

A hand slapped her, and again on her other cheek. Boudi-Ca stiffened. She opened her eyes again. Pain laced through her chest, a horripilating echo from so long ago, an age when the barbs went inside. She could feel the pain everywhere in her bone cage, her prison.

"No," Boudi-Ca sobbed. "Please."

"By the gods," a voice answered, a voice unlike the devils. The voice was Lydiah's voice, the voice of a goddess, a protector. "Nefra, grab those pincers and see if any of those vials contain alcohol or nectar of some sort."

Boudi-Ca braced against the persistent agony. The room wanted to resolve around her, but she wanted to go back to the numb grey space. She didn't want any more pain. She looked down to see a spine emerge, held tightly in Lydiah's fingers. It was a red tapering spine from some hellish plant with blood on two inches of its needle-like tip.

She clenched the arm chairs and focused on Lydiah's face—the steel-silver eyes, the pale white eyebrows, and the mane of platinum hair. Lydiah's lips looked less sensuous without her customary black paint, but still kissable. Boudi-Ca felt her belly heave. Her Hunger was a hollow beast through her innards, and she welcomed the distraction from her suffering.

She groaned with pain when Lydiah used a pair of metal pincers to withdraw the remaining devil barbs from her chest. She rolled her eyes and let her head loll. She tongued the taste of blood from her lips. She glimpsed the Pit Master on the floor. A flush of dread went through her as the memories came back into her head. Lydiah wasn't alone. Lieutenant Nefra was there with Golda, along with several other Jinni.

"I'm so sorry, Mistress," Boudi-Ca managed. Her chest ached, and her voice almost wasn't her own. "I thought I could kill Breanarachelle for you. I wanted to make myself useful."

"You've made things worse." Lydiah's words seized up, and she composed herself. "Still, I'm very proud of you, fledgling. Breanarachelle is in the void, and I suppose she had it coming to her."

Boudi-Ca clenched her throat. Dark and scattered memories surged into her head again—memories of the binding with wires, of the interrogation, of the spines sliding into her, of the incessant accusations and questions, the only features on the sea of pain that never ended. "I'll do it again if I have a chance. I'll kill all of the devils. I won't stop until—"

"We need to leave," Nefra interrupted. "Are we ready, Simhonit?"

"Yes," the Jinn named Simhonit answered. "This is just one prisoner. We're looking at least for twenty more. Can the fledgling walk?"

"I'll try." Boudi-Ca lifted herself bodily from the chair. Pain shocked her feet and ankles. She stifled a cry and flopped back onto the chair seat. She wiped her tears fiercely. A wave of hopelessness washed over her dread. "My feet. I can't stand on my feet."

"She has no skin on her feet," Golda muttered.

"We don't have time for this," Simhonit said. "The rest of us are taking the stairs, staying ahead of any counterattack."

"We need to stay together in case my husband comes with reinforcements," Lydiah countered.

"No," Nefra said. "Sim is right. Boudi-Ca isn't the primary objective. Go, Sim. We'll be right behind. Lydiah, can you look at Boudi-Ca? The Tower is still working on the Mountain, apparently. Should I run and get her?"

"No," Lydiah answered. "Hold and be ready to defend against devils if necessary."

The band of armored Smokeless-Flame Sisters filed quickly from the room. Boudi-Ca sighed and settled back into the chair while Lydiah knelt and examined her feet. She looked around to distract herself from the suffering. The room was more of a laboratory than a prison, with vials of caustic chemicals, pots of poisonous herbs, and other ingredients for the practice of pain and foul devil magic. The torture chair sat in a clear space in the center of the room, with doorways leading off into dark black hallways.

She tried not to look at her bloody, stripped legs. She coughed suddenly, and Lydiah raised her arm to shield her face from the blood spray. Lydiah collected herself, poured olive oil from an old flask, and rubbed gently for a long minute, then two.

Lydiah shook her head. "The oil might protect your flesh and keep it from drying and cracking, fledgling, but I think you're beyond the abilities of the Flames healer. This is a real problem. We can wrap your feet with bandages, but walking will be even more—"

"I'll carry her," Golda said. "Grab onto my neck and shoulders, Boudi. We need to move. I'll use my shirt."

Golda removed her shirt, draped it over one arm, and knelt low. Boudi-Ca shifted forward onto her feet again, suffering the intense pain long enough to fall into the strong arms of the mysterious, redheaded cat-shifter. Golda was very strong. Boudi-Ca went limp, even as her head went light and dizzy. Golda's warm breasts pressed against her, reminding her belly of its intense emptiness. "I need to feed."

"She needs a cock, but that won't heal her missing skin," Lydiah said. "Perhaps she could use shoes. Where is her clothing? If you hadn't stupidly attacked Pit Master Gonthrass, Golda, he could have—"

"He was a monster who needed to die," Golda interrupted.

Nefra looked over her shoulder at the dark hallway. "We're never going to get through the Bolgia pits like this. Even if we find a way, it's several leagues of walking. We also needed Boudi-Ca to help fight the devils. The devils will find these bodies soon, and when they do, there will be Hell to pay."

"Boudi-Ca needs a real healer and a real cock," Lydiah said. "I know where we can find both. I'm thinking of an Djinnus physician, Nefra."

"As soon as the devils finish their raid this morning and turn their attention to handling this counterattack, we're going to take enough heat to melt us. You really want to go back up into the city and look for a physician?"

"No." Lydiah rubbed her forehead, as if pained. "The plan is to go down, not up. There are many prisoners here in the Bolgia pits, and I happen to know one who might help Boudi-Ca. You three go down the stairs after the others. I'll run back to the front room and look at the Pit Master's register. I believe it lists the long-term prisoners in the Bolgia pits with their cell numbers. They use it as a reference for important visitors."

"Let's go." Golda surged into motion. Boudi-Ca winced at the wave of abrasive pain. The linen shirt under her thighs was a rough bandage for her stripped skin. Nefra followed with her sword drawn. The dark passage from the torture chamber dropped onto a steep stairway. After an interminable descent, they entered a long, low room with an array of heavy wooden tables in a grid.

Candles burned in the eye sockets of old skulls. The deeper room was filled with a still stronger fetid odor of chemicals and death. A rack of butcher knives and steel saws hung on the wall. A candlelit devotional shrine to Lord Hades rose a corner. Dead bodies sat arranged on two long tables, or rather parts of bodies—women without legs and one with a detached head. Nefra ran her fingers along a table edge and shook her head.

"That's Trun-Ca. Or rather, what's left of her. She's one fledgling that we won't rescue. Let's keep going. Lydiah will catch up with us. How are you feeling, Boudi-Ca?"

"I hunger," Boudi-Ca answered. In fact, her belly had never felt so empty. When she looked down at the chunks of preserved flesh on the work tables, they looked like pastries. The pieces of dead body were the color of oat cakes. Golda hefted her, and she pressed her head against the tracker's shoulder for support. She caught Nefra's eyes in that moment, and she suddenly remembered the brief kiss and the flirtation through messenger birds. She managed a smile of thanks, and Nefra nodded solemnly back at her.

Golda surged forward into the opposing passageway, an arched affair of ancient stone etched with rows of devilish inscriptions and sigils. Antique brass lamps threw intermittent pools of light in the darkness. The air grew ever more stale, lifeless, and suffocating. Halfway down the passage, voices and clinks of swords heralded the band of Smokeless-Flame Sisters, who swept up the tunnel at a fast march. Simhonit approached Nefra.

"We only found five alive. The rest are dead or dismembered. They didn't even get a fair trial. The devils just brought the lesbians down here and started cutting them up. We found a few magical grimoires. The devils are doing some sort of horrible ritual with the prisoners. I don't even want to know."

"I'm sorry. I'm sorry I was ever a part of this." Nefra fiercely embraced Simhonit for long moments while the other Smokeless-Flame Sisters looked on. Boudi-Ca felt her belly burn with envy. She desperately needed a kiss too, preferably one with an orgasm attached. Like Lydiah, Lieutenant Nefra was more emotional and passionate then she showed. Quick footsteps heralded the return of Lydiah down the passage from the first level, and then the full group was rejoined.

"Enough lip-locking, Lieutenant," Lydiah said. "Are the prisoners found?"

"Yes," Simhonit answered, breaking her embrace with Nefra.

"Is the Smokeless Flames heading back to Mer?"

Simhonit wiped tears from her cheeks. "Yes. If you intend to go deeper into the Bolgia pits, Councilor, then this is where we part ways. Two of the five living prisoners have chosen to go your way instead of coming back with us and risking Mer. Mistress Na'armeh and Mistress Changeh are waiting for you ahead at a door to the lower levels."

"That's wonderful news." Lydiah's lips registered a faint smile. "Na'armeh has spirit, and I'm glad she's still alive."

"We found them a few weapons," Simhonit added. "With your help, they might have a chance to escape through the Bolgia underpasses. You might want to know that our hexes and the Sparrow's spells failed in the chambers ahead. The devils have dampened this level against magic, and Allyssia only knows where the anti-magic areas end. Good luck in your quest, Councilor. May Allyssia smile on your love for your fledgling."

Lydiah lowered her eyes. "Thank you for your assistance, Sergeant. I appreciate it, and I apologize for this entire fiasco. May Allyssia smile upon you and your friends as well."

Simhonit pressed once more against Nefra and planted a kiss on her lips, and then she signaled the other women and pressed ahead of them. The group of grim Smokeless-Flame Sisters filed past with tramps of boots and rattles of bared blades.

Boudi-Ca gripped Golda with the remnants of her strength. She so desperately needed to feed that she had the urge to ask Nefra to feed her. She wanted Nefra's lips against hers. She wanted to taste the heat that Simhonit had tasted. She knew well the urgency of her Hunger when left unchecked. She would feed from anything.

Golda's warmth and bare skin were much closer however. Golda's wild red-brown hair smelled earthy like leaves in a forest, and her strong arms seemed tireless. Boudi-Ca bent her head again towards Golda's shoulder. She tried to stay focused on her Hunger-heightened sensual perceptions. Her desires distracted her from the pain in her thighs.

She winced when Golda hefted her again, and again the pain burned. She met Golda's stormy eyes, and she felt a silent wave of love. Golda wanted to kiss her. The moment passed, and Golda's face went resolute. It was time again to move.

Yellen watched the rescued prisoners filing past. She nodded with silent apology at the one who looked at her. She'd personally arrested all three of them. She saw no hatred or desire for vengeance in their eyes—only a haunted look of trauma. Their heads were shaved bald, and their bodies were marked with boils and fresh scars of devil inflictions. At least they still had their skin.

Yellen pulled her eyes away. She felt numb, dead, and depressed. She'd seen plenty of corpses in the war, but after seeing Trun-Ca's corpse, her culpability was really hitting her. Worse yet, for the first time in her Jinn life, she was alone. She was no longer a soldier and no longer a lover. Simhonit had whispered in her ear to come see her in the dream world, but she'd never had much ability for dream travel, certainly not enough for such risk.

Perhaps she deserved a solitary road, the better to reflect on her past and future. Perhaps she was making a big mistake. Perhaps for the first time in a long time, she was making her own way in life instead of just following orders.

She intended to see Boudi-Ca safely through the Bolgia. In fact, she was entertaining a notion of asking for an invitation to Lydiah's mysterious hideaway destination, there to continue Boudi-Ca's blades training. Boudi-Ca was a worthy quest for redemption. They needed to survive the Bolgia pits first.

Yellen advanced down the passage after Golda, who surged ahead again with long strides through another laboratory room and into a far hallway. The hallway bent and entered another prison common room. The room was shaped like a cross with ceiling-height iron cages lining the walls in each of the four candlelit wings. Two freshly dead devils lay on the floor with their acidic blood running and smoking. At the end of one wing, two Jinni were dressing themselves. The Jinni stood over two more bodies.

Golda gestured. "Are those your friends, Lieutenant?"

"Yes. Let's join them," Yellen answered. She advanced ahead of Golda. She recognized the two Jinni, despite their newly shaved heads. One was Mistress Changeh, and the other was Mistress Na'armeh. Na'armeh hefted her sword, as if wanting to re-play the pitched ambush in the feeding rooms at the Smokeless Flames monastery. Changeh stepped forward and brandished her whip with a curl of suppressed fury on her lips.

"Well, look. It's the lapdog Lieutenant and Councilor Lydiah, the Hell's Court bitch who sucks devil cock and betrays the Flames every chance she can get."

"You can call me Councilor," Lydiah said. "I don't respond to the word bitch, except from my husband."

"'Former ambassador' has a nice ring to it." Na'armeh spat on the floor. "I like bitch, though, and I really, really need a sweet bitch."

"You can call me Ambassador." Lydiah smiled thinly. "If we escape, I'm putting that at the top of my curriculum vitae, Na'armeh. I see the devils haven't broken your spirit like those others. I'm glad. I'd rather you loathe me than feel nothing."

Na'armeh snorted. "Aye, I loathe you both just like Changeh, but I'm in no shape or form to take revenge by gutting anyone, even with my fledgling dead and cut to pieces by the devils. Simhonit explained the situation. We need all of our arms to survive this and escape."

"We need your tracker," Mistress Changeh added. The Asian mistress gestured at Boudi-Ca in Golda's arms. "And who is this young, tortured beauty?"

"She's my fledgling," Lydiah answered. "I know you hunger, but don't even think about molesting my Boudi-Ca. I'll have your head."

"She's my ex-girlfriend," Golda growled. "She doesn't belong to Lydiah."

"She's a very talented blade fledgling, who has suffered as much as any of us from the devils." Yellen scrunched her nostrils at the foul odor on the dungeon air. She gazed at the two battered, gashed bodies on the floor. The faces of both women were melted into goo, and their throats were cut. Smoking rivulets of red-pink liquid ran towards the floor drain in the nearest empty cage. One looked like the Sister who had called herself the Weasel. Na'armeh and Changeh had evidently stolen every piece of Weasel's clothing. "What happened to them, Na'armeh?"

Na'armeh shrugged. "They weren't completely dead, but Simhonit didn't want to carry them up to Mer. The devils had a jar of acid on hand. We needed to erase their identities and make sure they were dead, so there can be no investigation or connections. So now that business is done. We have weapons, and we have your tracker. We need to go through that door there, and quickly."

"We have keys?"

"Simhonit gave them to me," Na'armeh answered. She jingled the keys in her hand.

"I have the keys from the registry room as well," Lydiah added. "So let's go."

"We need to feed." Changeh hefted her whip. "Na'armeh and I are desperate, so if we find another devil, we might want him alive. Watch the acid when you pass."

Na'armeh turned and strode to a silver-grey door with relief metalworking of a serpent crowned with stars. Yellen stepped past the body of poor Weasel, and Lydiah brushed past her in turn. Lydiah reached to run her manicured fingers over the old, tarnished door.

"I remember this door. It's one of a beaucoup de portes made by a Ukraine metalsmith over two centuries ago on the centennial. Thirty-three doors were made for thirty-three new entrances when the Bolgia pits were being renovated. I went to the ceremony to commemorate the doors with Fennel. It was one of our first official public appearances together after the Ukraine revolution. Might this one be trapped like the other one we passed?"

"I inspected it and didn't find anything," Na'armeh said. She turned a key in the lock, and the door creaked open on its ancient hinges. "So you know your way through, Lydiah, or are we following the tracker?"

"I might recognize some hallways," Lydiah answered. "I've never visited this way through the devil sections."

"I can see everything." Golda stepped forward gamely with Boudi-Ca in her arms. "I know the direction we're facing, and I know the direction we need to go. First we're going to find healing for Boudi-Ca in the pits, so hopefully she can walk."

Lydiah nodded. "The physician should be in the next level of the pits. It's the level reserved for important people who might have important visitors. I didn't see his name in the Pit Master's register, but his name is Master Mengele. He's a Denmark physician, and he was a close colleague of my husband until he botched a surgery on Kaiser Wilhelm while my husband was assisting. The blame was either on Mengele or my husband, and you can imagine whose story held more weight in the Court. In the end, my husband spoke for his life, and the devils agreed. Mengele lives down here now as a museum piece of medical history. We could free him, and he might help Boudi-Ca."

"Yes, well." Golda cleared her throat. "This Djinnus sounds like a fine helper, but peoples' names aren't written on the tapestry, Lydiah. Germans don't have a national flag on their track, either. I've never met him, so—"

"I thought you were supposed to be a great tracker, a student of Masad? I guess you can't see everything then, can you?" Lydiah sighed. "Fine. The devils will be coming. We need to get deeper into the old underpasses that will lead us east."

"And then what?" Changeh interjected. "We're trying to go through the Bolgia underpasses into the Great Blue Hole mines, right? And if we make it out of the mines, what then? I'll likely head for Cocytus. I have a few friends there who work in the smithies of Oya."

"If you even live to see the mines, you should be pleased," Lydiah answered. "The Beast is worse than the devils and my husband put together."

Yellen tightened her grip on her sword and looked over her shoulder. They needed to be moving in that moment, not discussing strategy. Such was the weakness of a group lacking a real leader that everyone could accept. She thought of Henne. In that moment, while she was fighting for her life, Henne was on a comfortable, pampered honeymoon with her man. Yellen edged forward and caught Lydiah's eyes.

"I know where we might find a Nanka near the Great Blue Hole mines."

"Yes. We could commandeer a prisoner transport," Lydiah mused. "It's an interesting idea, but risky. The Court flies a few condemned humans from Mer to the mines about once a week. We need to avoid all confrontations though, for reasons that are probably not known to any of you. My husband didn't just happen to find Boudi-Ca killing Breanarachelle. He traveled backwards in time using his Ebon Timepiece."

Nefra took a deep breath. "I was actually thinking of a remote tower on the Carthago promontory. The Carthago is a high rim country between Haawiyah and Erebus, and the tower overlooks the Great Blue Hole mines. My ex-girlfriend is there alone with her husband on their honey moon. She said they were flying up. We'd have to traverse around the cliffs through the forest to reach it, but we could maybe take their Nanka. Right now, we need to move. Go, Golda. If you can't find Lydiah's physician, then we still need a few male prisoners for Changeh, Boudi-Ca, and Na'armeh. Let me take over and carry Boudi-Ca."

"No," Golda said. "We need your sword arm more."

"Golda is a cat, but she has horse sense," Lydiah said. "At least that's one thing to her credit."

"For feeding, there may be a few strong Gypsy men down here." Golda pushed forward through the open centennial door and paced into a dark arched corridor. "Maybe there are a few former residents from Allyssia's city, as well. I have many old friends whose lives were ruined by your actions, Lydiah. I don't know if I'll remember their threads, but maybe some are still imprisoned in here."

"Credit retracted."

Yellen followed through the open doorway and into the corridor, which gave onto another stairway leading down. She hoped the rescue party didn't implode. She was well aware of the tension between Golda and Lydiah, just as Na'armeh and Changeh had made their own simmering venoms known. When the stairs ended, Lydiah summoned a tenebris lux, but the lux faded and dimmed as soon as it sparked, and the hallway fell again into inky darkness.

"Anti-magic," Lydiah murmured. "The devils think of everything."

Golda led the way down the dark arched passage with Boudi-Ca in her arms. A feeble light glowed ahead, and soon the tracker paused at a junction where a single oil lamp flickered. The lamp revealed the niches of old tombs in the sides of the passage. In each niche, withered skeletons lay with their necks still chained to the stone. The prisoners had once been alive, but no longer. They were only piles of bone stretched with dry husks of flesh.

Yellen went to the oil lamp and liberated it from its fastenings. She held the lamp aloft for Golda's benefit. They continued on. The passage descended into darkness again, down two more sets of wide stairs, and then into a maze of passageways. The level was dimly lit with a small burning lamp only at each intersection. Ancient doors between the intersections marked individual prisons. An engraved number was carved into the stone beside each door.

Golda slowed. "The devils are already coming. They're somewhere above us. I see several of them, maybe a dozen, but my sight in the proprietary weave has turned difficult. Everything down here is heavy and oppressive. I want to curl up and hide, not open my mind wider to all of this death and misery."

"Is my husband among the devils?" Lydiah's voice held a tone of urgency. She fingered the leather satchel that rode on her hip.

Golda's eyes fluttered half-closed as she concentrated, and her wild, tangled hair threw her face into shadow. "No. I might have a powerful healer though, and she's located nearby to the Gypsies."

Lydiah frowned. "If you can find someone with a skill for healing, then why can't you find my adorably twisted, psychopathic Denmark physician? That makes no sense."

Golda continued forward as if in a trance and didn't speak further. Yellen followed with her blade at the ready. She tried to measure how long they'd been descending, and how long it would take the devils to catch up with them. She guessed they had fifteen minutes, maybe twenty. Golda turned a corner, then another. The tracker stopped in front of a cell and nodded impassively.

"There's someone in here who might help Boudi-Ca."

Na'armeh stepped towards the door, but Lydiah reached the door first with her own key ring. She quickly tested key after key until one turned, and the door swung open. The cell was pitch dark except for a pale golden glow. The glow hovered over a large pile of dusty rags in the corner. The pile of rags stirred, revealing the living face of a woman. The prisoner's face lifted. She squinted and brushed dust from her face, as if unsure whether she was seeing a truth or an illusion.

"Who are you there?" The prisoner's voice began as a whispered croak, then strengthened. "Are you real? You people aren't devils, but I can feel your wickedness and sins."

"Ambassador Octavia?" Lydiah stepped further into the cell. "Octavia, surely you remember me. We met in three or four meetings, trying to negotiate the disputes in Meristyian before the war broke out. I'm Ambassador Lydiah. You've been imprisoned for far too long. I fought against this, but you know the devils. I told them—the Ambassador for Heaven is a good friend of Hell. Of course, they don't always listen to me. On behalf of Allyssia, I'd like to formally apologize. Please rise, and be free with my blessing."

"I don't have my wings." Octavia's voice strengthened further, and her halo glowed a little brighter. "I can't return to Heaven, or so I'm told. Where am I going to go?"

"You're going to go with us," Lydiah answered. "I'm going to have to insist, and I might also add that we're in a hurry, so I have a simple request to make in return—"

"Natasa?" Octavia stood upright, unfolding her long pale legs from under her skeletal torso. She wobbled forward like a wounded giant, and a ghastly pall fell over her face for a moment before an inner strength glowed, and a light burned again feebly in her eyes. "It's you, Golda. You've changed in these centuries. You're so much stronger."

"Yes, I suppose." All eyes turned to Golda, who carefully lowered Boudi-Ca to the dungeon floor. Golda rose and stood at full height, but she was several inches shorter than Octavia, who towered over the group. Octavia's faint halo seemed to scrape the ceiling. "I'm sorry, Octavia. I might know you, but I've forgotten."

Octavia nodded slowly. "You've been through much to be standing here, old friend, just as I have. I was once known as Octavia the Younger on Earth, the sister of Gaius Octavius, Emperor of Egypt. I'm your old countrywoman, Natasa, and I was also your official guardian for thirty years or more in Heaven. The guardianship ended when I was transferred to another post in the Conclave, and you were assigned to someone else. I'm sorry. I failed you, and you were cast into Hell. I wasn't at your formal interview, and for a long time, I felt responsible. When I was eventually promoted to junior ambassador and visited Haawiyah, I pulled all sorts of strings to travel and find your owner in Vegasis, but—"

"Vegasis is beautiful in the springtime," Lydiah interrupted. "So apparently you know Golda. Lying at her feet is my fledgling, Boudi-Ca. This is Lieutenant Nefra, and this is Sergeant Na'armeh. We really have no time to chat and catch up with old times, Octavia. The devils are coming for us any minute."

"Yes," Na'armeh added. "This isn't a gods-damned diplomatic mission. This is a prison break. Get on with it already, or this group is splitting."

"We have wounded," Golda said. "Octavia, can you help my friend? I know Mimos are great healers. If you can help Boudi-Ca, then please relieve yourself of any debt you feel towards me for things that happened. I'll be in your debt instead."

"Let me see her then." Octavia ambled forward, knelt, and passed her large, bony hands over Boudi-Ca's legs for long moments. The elder Mimo̧ pressed and held fast. Boudi-Ca groaned in pain and made panting sounds like a small animal.

"Give me the keys. I'll get the men." Golda grabbed at the keys in Lydiah's hand. The two glared at each other for long moments before Lydiah surrendered, and Golda drifted away with the keys down the dimly lit hallway. Na'armeh and Changeh followed the tracker.

Yellen hefted her blade in one hand and the oil lamp in the other. She took a few subtle steps to the left of Octavia until she had an angle to watch the corridor behind them. She guessed they had ten minutes left, even as her depression and unease settled even heavier on her soul. Lesbianism and assaulting devils were bad enough, but there was one crime held by the devils as the worst among all others. The crime was treason against Lord Hades, which included aiding the enemy, especially the agents of Heaven.

She vaguely remembered the name Octavia, and she remembered that Heaven's ambassador had been arrested and imprisoned when the war had broken out between Heaven and Hell a few years previously. Octavia was a war prisoner like most of the Mimo̧s in the Bolgia pits.

Yellen watched Octavia's lips mutter in a silent prayer, working her divine healing magic. She didn't want to face the devils again. She wanted to run like a jackal into the underpasses and hope the Beast wasn't particularly hungry that afternoon. A door creaked far down the hallway, and male voices echoed through the darkness, followed shortly by a loud moan of male pleasure. Octavia finally removed her hands from Boudi-Ca.

"Rise, child. Rise. You'll live to see the light."

"Thank you so much. Most of my pain has gone away." Boudi-Ca sniffed and rubbed her damp eyes. The Mimo̧ girl levered herself onto her feet. She gathered the dirty flounced sleeves of Golda's shirt and tied them around her waist to form a makeshift skirt. "It still hurts a little, though. I'm so tired of pain. All I ever wanted was love, and all I ever get is pain. I'm ready to just give up."

"No," Octavia said. "When the darkness seems to be greatest, that is when we must have the most faith. The devil magic in this place tries to destroy the spirit with hopelessness, but I've learned ways to let the Lord's light through with grace."

"Light is beautiful, just like my fledgling," Lydiah said. "So let's go then. You need to come with us, Octavia. We may need more healing."

Octavia pressed her hands together and put her fingers to her lips. "You need me again already. I'm not done healing yet. Boudi-Ca is suffering from a horrible curse. You are cursed as well, Ambassador Lydiah. Everyone here is cursed. This is the most horribly cursed group of people I've ever seen in my life."

Lydiah's eyes gleamed silvery in the gloom. "You can remove curses? You can heal my curse, the one Allyssia placed upon me? Please say you can, and I'll promise to never to fuck my sweet fledgling again, or may Lord Tuhan smite me where the light doesn't shine."

"We need to move," Yellen interjected. She wanted to grab everyone and push them bodily down the hallway. Anything that wasn't mandatory at that moment was a precious waste of time and energy.

For the first time, Octavia's lips formed a smile, a look of serene benevolence. "I can't heal a divine curse, Ambassador, and powerful are the curses on you and Boudi-Ca. Lieutenant Nefra's curse is much weaker."

Yellen stiffened when Octavia pressed a big hand over her forehead. She felt burning hot for a second. Her head went light, and the weight went completely off of her shoulders. For the first time in a long time, she felt free, free like she'd felt when she'd flown into Mer on the back of a Nanka weeks previously, expecting a long, pleasurable vacation. "Whatever you did, thank you, and bless Lord Tuhan."

"Was that your magic on her, Lydiah?" Octavia shook her head. "Tsk, tsk. You're a sneaky one. I remember you, yes. I remember your serpent tongue. Thank the good Lord your evil sorcery won't work on an Mimọ soul, or we might have had more problems."

"So we're going then. Come along, fledgling." Lydiah turned on her heel and stalked down the hallway. Her tenebris lux drifted over her head, shining on her flowing white-blonde hair in the half-dark.

Yellen followed. What sort of curse had she suffered from Lydiah? She'd been under a curse of mind control, surely. Her doubts about the mission suddenly came back to the fore and hit her all at once. What was she even doing in the pits? Her abiding distrust of Lydiah resurfaced and multiplied ten-fold.

She didn't need to escort Lydiah and Boudi-Ca all the way to the Great Blue Hole mines, much less fight on point against the fabled, ageless Beast in the deep. If she'd simply gone back with Simhonit, she could have rekindled her old flame with Sim and waited on Befanah to get her an official Nanka flight out of Mer. The party rejoined at the end of the corridor. Golda stepped forward with two strong-looking nude human men.

"This is Agron Reik, and this is Johns," Golda offered. "They'll come with us. For the moment they're empty, and Na'armeh and Changeh have fed."

"That was a small price to pay for freedom," Agron muttered grimly. "Thank you, Golda. I was right to trust your integrity all along. The Hell's Court devils are the real scum in the Underworld, not the Jinni. I have to ask you something. Is my wife—"

"Priebus is free," Golda answered. "Elder Tahany paid the bribe, and Priebus is well on her way to Erebus with the Akhen family."

A pained smile of joy came over Agron' face, and he wiped a tear from his eye. "I thank the goddess Allyssia for that, and the Mimos in Heaven, and whoever else stands for justice and love in the Underworld. I have to get out of this cursed place now. I have to see my wife's smile again. Find me a good sword, and I'll fight like a mad dog against the devils for my life. I don't care if your presence played a role in what happened in the forest, Golda. Bygones will be bygones. You're still a friend of the Gypsies."

"Indeed," Lydiah said with an annoyed tone. "And it's curious how Golda's friends are multiplying so quickly amongst us."

"Enough!" Yellen said. "Golda, get us out of here. Now."

"Right away, Lieutenant. It's so wonderful to see you back on your feet, Boudi-Ca." Golda stepped forward to hug Boudi-Ca and press a quick kiss. A small, surprised smile crept over the fledgling's lips. Octavia seized Golda's shoulder.

"Oh, my good Lord in Heaven. The girl just got back on her feet, and you're already putting your tongue down her throat? I'm well aware of the unthinkable levels of lust in this realm, but I expected better from you, Golda. I'll try to help one more of you, please. I just need a moment more."

Chapter 33.

Candlelight flickered inside the cubiculum. Natasa peeked through the curtain. Her husband's hairy ass was pumping between Sophistra's thighs. Sophistra was a senator's daughter in the bloom of her pubescence, known for her sweet voice that lured men and harmonized with the lyre. In that moment, the girl was moaning like a goat.

Natasa suppressed a hollow feeling that inspired vomit. For years, she'd elevated her husband's political status as well as his cock, and her efforts had succeeded beyond her wildest dreams. She hadn't given her life to Natat so he could prong the honeyed amphora of every young girl who batted her eyelashes at him.

Natasa retreated from the archway. She leaned and whispered in her Greek servant's ear. "Call my husband to the vestibule, Khonia. Tell him I'm here to surprise him. When he comes to see me, put on your hood, go into the dormitorium, and dump the basket of serpents on Sophistra. Escape through the rear of the domus and meet me in the driveway."

Khonia bowed. "As you command, Domina."

Natasa stalked back through the hallways of the country villa to the vestibule. She hugged herself against the cool of the night. She jumped when a pair of dark forms skittered around a column. They were only the grey Egyptians that had dropped in a litter at the country villa the previous summer. They'd stayed to prey on the mice and sip bowls of goat milk.

Natasa admonished herself for her nervousness. She'd never before plotted against her husband, but she was no girl-child to Egyptian politics. The cats swirled and scratched their cheeks on her legs. She hoped the cats would chase the serpents from the villa and not vice versa. She heard her husband's raised voice and hurried footsteps.

"What insult is this?" Theoph wrapped a linen around his muscled waist as he entered the vestibule. "You came all the way out to our country villa to bother me about Sophistra? I'll give you a mirror and show you a hypocrite."

"It doesn't suit the ruler of Egypt to chase after young girls, my husband. Our daughter will be Pope Sergius' concubine. Soon we will whisper in the ears of Lord Tuhan himself. You're lowering us both with your indulgence. Take a mistress if you need one, but not a fish-eyed senator's niece who fucks for politics."

"You're joking, Natasa. I know you've fucked Sergius yourself, and now he wants our daughter, so you're giving him Marozia. Political schemes and power have always meant everything to you. At least I fuck for love."

"Love?" Natasa snortled, but she stilled at the sounds of the planned disturbance. Sophistra's shrieks were loud down the quiet villa hallways. "It sounds like your kitten is frightened, Theoph. Perhaps you should go to see what's the matter."

"By the gods, Natasa. What have you done?"

Natasa watched her husband disappear back into the atrium. She pivoted and strode out of the villa into the night. When she reached the carriage, Khonia was just emerging from the overgrown gardens.

"It's done, Domina," Khonia said breathlessly. "I pretended the basket was a gift. I dumped the snakes on her. Sophistra jumped from the bed screaming. The snakes were hissing and biting her."

"I feel sorry for the girl, but she got what she deserves for insulting me. Do you believe in love, Khonia?"

"Yes, Domina." Khonia bit her lip, and her dark Greek eyes went sultry and limpid. "When Cupid's arrow strikes my breast, it elevates me. Love is divine."

"I don't believe love exists. If we think rationally about its purposes, we can see that love is just an animal impulse."

The scene shifted. She was floating. Natasa looked down at the crowd around her Egyptian deathbed. Theoph was there with his bald patch, and so was young Marozia, and Sergius himself with a cadre of white-robed priests, whispering a low prayer to the Lord and savior.

Natasa gazed down with wonderment at her sweaty, receding corpse. Her human body looked ugly from that flat clinical angle—paler and more wrinkled than the Egyptian linens. A profound peace crept over her soul, soothing every muscle and bone as she rose. She felt no more pain. Her teeth and belly no longer ached.

The scene disappeared again, and she floated to where her feet found curious purchase. She clambered up from the human bustle and sweaty toil of Egypt into a wide-open sky on a wide white stairway. After hours of climbing—or perhaps seconds—she reached a mother-of-pearl gate that shone in the bright sunlight. An old man in a white robe stood with a shimmering halo above his grey hair.

"Natasa of Egypt, wife of Natat!" The man seemed pleased. "We've been expecting you!"

"You know me?" Natasa took a deep breath of the sanctified air. "So there really is a Heaven. I'm relieved that Lord Tuhan recognized my charity, piety, and devotion to the Christian church."

The man winked. "I wouldn't be so sure of your status yet, but you're granted a special interview to plead your case. Come with me, please. My name is Petrus."

Natasa followed. She'd worried for years as old age had crept over her that such a thing could be true—that her soul would face judgment before entering Heaven. She'd committed many sins in her life—fornication, adultery, agnostic prayers to Venus and Ceres for romance and prosperity, the occasional unnatural act with Theoph, and a few acts of violence, like with Sophistra.

She needed to petition well. Her soul depended on it. She needed to argue with the same oratory that she'd shown in front of the senate, when she'd been called to explain why Sophistra had died by snakebite. Her situation in Heaven was worse. The arch-Mimọ wouldn't accept bribes.

Petrus took her hand and carried her mystically through a thin grey space. They entered a large square room that was filled with the brightest light, like sunlight shining on an ivory jewel case, so bright that it was hard to look at the two shrunken male Mimọs that waited.

"I am RayLewis," said the Mimọ on the left.

"I am DonaldJohn," said the other.

Natasa stared suspiciously at the two shining men. She didn't like them at all. Surely they weren't to be her judges. They were dwarves—malformed creatures of inauspicious birth, the kind who were spat upon in the streets of Egypt for lacking the stature of a real man. Worse yet, the dwarves were dark-skinned foreigners. The Mimọ named DonaldJohn held up a tablet. He examined it.

"You are Natasa of Egypt, wife of Natat, the Egyptian Consul?"

"I am," she replied.

"Do you affirm that you owned a female slave?"

"We never called her that, but if you wish. The rulers of Egypt have owned slaves since antiquity, little man. The wisdom of the Biblia gives us guidance in how we must treat them. What's wrong with slaves?"

"Nothing, by the good word of Lord Tuhan," DonaldJohn answered. "Unless a Domina orders her slave girl to murder a young woman, causing her to die from poisonous serpent bites."

"I didn't know those serpents were poisonous. I only meant to scare Sophistra. I asked Khonia to procure the serpents in good faith. You should interrogate her, not me. The Greeks are well known in history for making mistakes."

"Lies," DonaldJohn continued. "You think to deceive us? As the church teaches, a woman's virtue is humility and obedience to her husband's wishes. It's unacceptable to arrange the murder of your husband's lover. You should have turned the other cheek."

"You mean my other ass cheek, since my husband wasn't fucking me? Yes, accusations of murder were whispered by my husband's tongue and others, but one thing is true. I did not kill Sophistra. If Lord Tuhan himself did not send asps into the cubiculum of my country villa, then it must have been the Fates."

RayLewis scowled. "Those old crones have no authority over our great Lord Tuhan. You dare blaspheme in this holy place?"

Natasa felt faint, and her ethereal body burned with a curious, heavy heat. "I've been a loyal supporter of the Christian faith. I've attended the church and prayed to Lord Tuhan. I'm a wealthy, respectable woman of Egypt. I deserve to be in Heaven."

RayLewis examined his tablet and arched his eyebrow. "That is not your only sin. The Conclave has recorded several unnatural lustful activities."

"What desirable Egyptian woman hasn't slept with a few men out of wedlock, and what self-respecting man doesn't indulge in his wife's ass?"

"Your sin is with women," DonaldJohn interjected. "You pleasured and scissored with your slave girl Khonia in your bed when your husband left. This is unacceptable."

Natasa raised her hands in supplication. "You little men are the real perverts aren't you—watching over me in my private moments? Who are you to pass judgments on certain forms of love, as if one sort is acceptable over another? Cupid and Venus would like to have words with you."

"This is not our judgment," RayLewis said. "It's yours."

"Then I'd like to speak with a female arch-Mimo, please."

DonaldJohn laughed, and when he laughed, white flames forked from his tongue. "We have no women in the Judgments Conclave. Your time is over, Natasa. This was only a formality. You're the source of the Pornocracy in Egypt—the mother of the corruption."

"I'm the mother two daughters."

"Precisely," the dwarf retorted. "Now we only have to extricate Pope Sergius from the corruption of your Marozia, who is a wicked Jinn operating under orders from Hell. You won't need to worry about that. You'll be too busy suffering for your sins."

"All men have their price. What do you want? I'll deliver fine wines and willing young concubines to you. You'll drive the finest gilded chariots over Heaven's roads, and stacks of gold aurei will be yours. Artisans will immortalize your image, and statues will be erected in your name. Those will be small statues of course."

RayLewis smirked. "The Earth is better for your death, Natasa. We can't let your stain to spread to Heaven."

Natasa gasped. The floor underneath her gave way into a blank greyness, and she fell into it. Her fall went on and on, and the bright light of Heaven dimmed and folded into the darkness above. When she hit the bottom of the darkness, every inch of her body felt the impact. She cried out in agony, such was the unbearable and unequalled sensation of pain. She felt like her bones had all shattered, but her skin showed only bruises and cuts. She'd never felt such suffering, but she collected herself up, sobbing, and wiped tears and dust from her eyes.

Her body felt queerly heavy, like a bag of ill-gotten coins. She looked down at her body with a slow shock. She was herself, but she wasn't. Her breasts were no longer the sagging, over-handled bags that Natat had ignored. They were the proud freckled half-globes from decades ago. Her stomach showed no birth-wrinkles or pallor's of sickness, and her thighs were smooth, shapely spindles. The skin of her arms was unblemished and stretched over graceful bones. She was pretty and nubile again from head to toe.

Natasa squinted through the gloom. She could see a small throng of souls limping and crawling into a crowd that formed at a low broken stone wall. Beyond the wall, a line of horses and wagons was just visible in the blowing dust and wind. Each wagon bore a large cage, and the humans were filing towards the cages with the assistance of foul, frog-nosed devils.

The wagon-cages were rigged by iron chains to a yoke, and the yoke was fastened to sturdy black horses with tooled leather harnesses and black feathered plumes. Golda opened her eyes. The dark world disappeared, replaced by the dungeons of Mer again. Lydiah's furious face loomed in the dungeon darkness. "Are you there?"

"Yes. How long was I gone?"

"Just a minute," Octavia answered. "The mental realm moves much faster. So I finally know what happened. Those were confusing days for Heaven. They were dealing with bureaucracy and intercultural issues. It's curious what RayLewis said about the Fates. If your presence down in this realm is a mistake made by Heaven, then I wonder who has jurisdiction over your soul. Perhaps no one."

Golda rubbed her forehead. "I appreciate you showing me those memories, but what was the point?"

Octavia shrugged. "Are you a better soul now, or are you even more corrupted and sinful from your long stay in Hell? I just want you to ask yourself that question."

"Apparently I was an arrogant, self-important wealthy woman in those old days. I reminded myself of Lydiah. Since then I've suffered and struggled for centuries. I've hurt, but I've learned so much. I was an addicted, whoring bliss-kitten on a leash, and then Allyssia set me free. Now I'm an animal in this world, trying to survive. I'm better for that."

Octavia shook her head. "Animals aren't better, Natasa. They are animals, and they act only on animal impulses, like you just showed. The inner beast needs to be tamed and suppressed at every turn."

"That just doesn't work. In a world where I've been chained, abused, humiliated, and recently hunted, I've learned a lot more compassion for myself and others. I've learned a higher appreciation for Love amidst so much suffering. You can't love if you don't live, and you don't live if you're trying to suppress everything. Love is divine. Love elevates us."

"You certainly need elevating, but by the hand of Lord Tuhan," Octavia countered. "You could start by finding yourself a robe or blouse to cover up your animal assets."

"Boudi-Ca is wearing my blouse right now. Pardon my tits."

A canine howl echoed through the dark hallways, and then another. Golda turned away from Octavia and forced her mind back to the tapestry. The devils were close, and they had Hell hounds with them. The emotions from her memories were simmering and raw in her belly, but she needed to ignore them and focus. She needed to find the right path through the oppressive weave of the tapestry. One bad direction could easily stop at a dead end or a sealed passageway, dooming the group.

She found a straight passage south and quickened her pace, looking over her shoulder as she went. Boudi-Ca was lagging at the back with a mask of pain on her face. The Mimǫ girl was game, but she was limping and vulnerable. Golda turned into a low corridor with no more cell doors.

The tapestry showed the way down to the next level. She was close, and she'd completed all of her objectives in the Bolgia pits. She'd found a healer for Boudi-Ca and an unexpected ally in Octavia, almost as if the Fates themselves had willed it, or if not the Fates, then at least whatever divine forces she had at her back. She also had allies in Agron and Johns as soon as she could find weapons for them. The Gypsy men were scarcely matches for the pain-loving Hell's Court devils, but they were still among the best of the human breed.

She'd also scored points with Boudi-Ca and Lieutenant Nefra. She needed every edge she could get. Even if she could get the group away from the devils, she still faced Lydiah. Lydiah was powerful, without any shred of honor, and would never surrender Boudi-Ca voluntarily. Golda licked her lips. She always trusted her instincts, and her instincts still told her that if she wanted to get Boudi, she needed to betray Lydiah at the correct moment. Otherwise, her own death was possible, if not inevitable.

The tunnel ended at a bend, and her heart went cold. Where she thought she'd find a doorway down, she saw only a blank wall. She'd mistaken the weave at that place. She could see humans in the weave beyond the wall, but the humans weren't prisoners. They were the slaves in someone's deep pit. A private party had dug deep into the Bolgia, then sealed over the breakthrough with a wall of stone masonry.

"Where in the hells are we going?" Lydiah gestured at the wall.

"I made a small mistake. This way." Golda reversed course and returned to the previous fork. She tried to focus. She was only barely ahead of the devils, but she was almost out of the downtown Merian area and the domain of Hell's Court. The masonry was noticeably less maintained, and the tunnels were less well-traveled. She took the westerly route at the fork, even as the howls of the hounds grew louder.

"I'm sorry I'm so slow," Boudi-Ca sobbed from behind. "My feet are still hurting."

"We're almost there. Let me know if you need to be carried." Golda grimaced and willed Boudi-Ca to keep moving. The devils were very close, and worse yet, behind the first group of devils was another larger group, a real war party with a tracker. She could see the route down however, and she could smell the lower depths rising from the chamber ahead.

She hurried under an ancient carved archway and through a promising pair of open double doors. The room beyond was some sort of ritual chamber with a stone altar presiding over a wide black hole in the floor. Golda felt her belly clench. The way ahead was wide open to the lower levels. Unfortunately, the black ten-meter shaft plummeted vertically downwards into the rock. She stopped at the edge as the others joined her. Nefra lifted the oil lamp to show little in the way of handholds, just sheer carved stone.

Lydiah raised her hands to her forehead in exasperation. "Well done, Golda. Unless we transform into vampire bats, we aren't going this way." As Lydiah spoke, the howls came loud and close from the corridor. Nefra moved to the doors, accompanied by Na'armeh. They shouldered them closed and threw the ancient bolt.

"This won't hold," Nefra said matter-of-factly. "How many, Golda?"

"There are two hounds and maybe seven devils. That's the advance guard. Right behind them comes another party of eighteen or twenty, and more hounds. Can we cast a ward on the doors, or is the magic still dampened?"

"I feel we are outside of the anti-magic zone here," Lydiah said. She snapped her fingers, and a low tenebris lux flared over her head. "Yet there is no point in casting a ward. We might only hold out here for a while until they find a sorcerer to counter whatever spell I might cast. I remember this place. This is the chamber of Amargol. In ancient days, a devil sorcerer sought to dig the deepest pit in Mer. Here is where he made his slaves toil for five decades and more."

"So strange, digging a big hole for your own ego." Octavia gazed down at the pit from on high. "Normally men build big towers."

"Good for you, Octavia. You made a cock joke. Now I'm not the only hypocrite amongst us." Lydiah rolled her eyes. "Amargol eventually broke into the deep volcanic passages under the Bolgia, the same passages that I hoped would lead us to freedom. In more recent centuries, this pit has been used to feed the Beast. Hell's Court can't be bothered with imprisoning every petty law-breaker in Mer, and some souls aren't even fit to work in the Great Blue Hole or die to the fighters in the Coliseum. If a crime is clear and isn't worth a judge's time, the devils sometimes just strip the prisoner right here and throw them into this ritual pit for the Beast to eat, far down in the black tunnels below."

"Come beasts or devils, I want to die down here as a man instead of a naked prisoner." Agron strode to the piles of refuse that littered the edges of the chamber. He fished and drew a blade. "This will do the trick."

"An ogre blade." Na'armeh advanced and dragged a hooked sword from the rubbish. She examined it with both hands. "This thing can cleave a devil skull if I can wield it. I'll be happy if I can take just one devil to the void with me."

"Well spoken," Johns said. The Gypsy hefted an old helm and planted it on his head. He sifted again among the refuse and withdrew an old studded cudgel.

"You're all ready to fight the devils then, and that's just excellent." Lydiah's voice dripped with sarcasm. "Because we can't be trapped here. We have to open the doors."

Nefra nodded. "Precisely. We have no choice. If we can take the advance guard—"

"It's better than sitting in this trap," Lydiah finished. "We can't wait for the devils to amass a horde on the other side of those doors. I think I remember the way down, now. We needed to go west first in order to go east. The next lower level holds the most dangerous prisoners in the Bolgia pits, so the entrance is hidden. I'll stand to one side of the doors with you and my fledgling, Nefra. Everyone else can take the other side. We'll have them in a vise. Everyone needs to step up now to compensate for Golda's failure."

"The doors are opening in sixty seconds," Nefra said tersely.

"So are we dying already, then?" Boudi-Ca sniffed. Lydiah whispered quiet words in Boudi-Ca's ear, and the fledgling joined Agron and Johns at the trash heaps, where the men were going through old, dusty clothes. Boudi-Ca pulled an old blade from the mess of vestments and gear that had apparently belonged to the Beast's many victims over the centuries.

Golda stripped her boots and pants. She needed to be ready to shift if needed. She ignored Octavia's look of disdain, as well as the accusing, angry looks of Changeh and Na'armeh. She'd kept her mind open for a long time to the horror of the Bolgia pits. She was so overwhelmed by horrible emotions that she could hardly feel the added mantle of guilt and culpability that Lydiah had thrown over her shoulders.

She bent and stowed her folded clothes next to the ancient altar. She eyed the wide black hole in the floor, wishing there were some solution that would allow the group to pass down. She could see no ropes or ladders among the junk, and even less hope. The dread of the Bolgia pits gripped her even more heavily when the growls and thumps sounded on the far side of the door, followed by barely audible male voices.

More thumps came, and the doors shivered. Golda took her place among the others. She weighed her stolen Gypsy sword in her hand. She'd dedicated her life to saving Boudi-Ca from Mer, and she had no intention of giving up in the last moments. She refused to accept failure.

"Embrace the pain," Lydiah said. "Even if you get a hook, don't let the pain and fear distract you. A devil can be killed, and my fledgling is proof of that. She wanted to kill all of the devils, and now she has her chance. Open the doors, Nefra."

Nefra threw the bolt and swung the doors open. The snout of a hound pushed through, and then a huge body. The Hell's Court hound was as large as a human on four legs, with glowing red eyes. Its maw opened, and a gout of flame spat at Nefra, who narrowly dodged to the side. A burning smell filled the air.

Golda pushed forward to attack the hound's flank, narrowly missing the swinging door. She was suddenly out of position and exposed to the onslaught of the devils. They came swarming through the doorway from the darkness, and a hook found her bicep even as she slashed and caught the hound with a crippling blow.

She was crippled in turn when the hook pulled taut. She hauled back against the sudden tension, and the devil followed her, tethered by the cord to her flesh. His cruel lips split into a confident grin as he reeled her in. He wore a black robe, and his head was shaved bald. Steel piercings festooned his ears.

Golda swung, but her sword arm was thrown and compromised. The devil raised a curved sickle to finish her. He swung. She dropped her blade and changed. The sickle skimmed past her head, which turned furred. Golda roared. Her change dislodged the hook, just as she'd hoped. She leapt and tore into the devil's thigh, ripping it from under him. The devil moaned with pleasure. Agron boldly joined the attack. The devil was broadsided and toppled, but another devil replaced the first. Agron cried out in pain.

Golda winced as her own pain washed through her mouth and tongue. The devil blood was smoking on her cat lips, burning her like acid. She backpedaled, but she leapt forward again to defend Agron, who in turned was reeled in with a hook. She lunged and bit again, and she regretted her use of shifted form. She was stronger and more resistant to magic as a feline, but she hadn't realized the true caustic strength of the devil fluids.

She ignored the pain and shifted back into her human form, grasping her fallen sword hilt as she rose. She had no time to press the attack against the devil who assailed Agron. Her own devil was on her back again, and she parried at the last moment. He swung his hook, and it failed to bite, only raking her shoulder painfully. The devil's baleful yellow eyes were alight with the pleasure of combat, and his froglike mouth grinned wider. She felt blood trickling down her back.

The devil's grin vanished when a bright light struck him, knocking his bald head sideways. The devil toppled to the stone floor. Octavia uttered more holy syllables, and another bolt piled into the devil. Golda lunged and speared the devil, even as his sickle caught her arm, flooding her with more pain to the shoulder.

She groaned, and the devil moaned with her. He tripped her, and she fell. Her thigh hit the raging hard cock between his legs. She locked his arm and cut his throat with her sword. She grabbed him to roll him into the pit, which was only a few meters away, but the skin of her neck pricked with imminent danger.

A Hell hound had noticed her vulnerable position on the floor amidst the combat and chaos. The beast lunged at her. She shifted into cat form instantly and braced her hind paws to meet the onslaught. She twisted to minimize the vicious bite to her shoulder. Her own bite missed, but she managed to tangle the hound's claws. The hound yelped when Octavia's bright holy bolt found its flank. It twisted sideways.

Golda pressed the advantage, levering her hind paws on the shuddering, bleeding devil underneath her. She pushed, and the hound skittered backwards. Another holy bolt sent it further towards the edge of the pit. Golda roared and thrust. The hound slipped over. Its howl echoed down the pit, and then it was gone. She shifted again to human form, the better to grab the fallen devil. Octavia hurried to assist, and together they sent the devil over the edge to follow the hound.

Golda retrieved her sword again and surveyed the scene. Boudi-Ca was defending Lydiah on the left with an old, shaky sword. The blonde fledgling skillfully turned back the harrying attacks of a devil, while Lydiah occupied the other Hell hound with well-timed kin-hexes. Meanwhile, Lydiah's lux swooped through the air in the shape of a glowing bird. The bird attacked and blinded the devil, allowing Boudi-Ca a timely advantage. Boudi-Ca flashed behind the devil and struck a decisive blow. To the right, Agron still struggled against a devil, who had pressed the Gypsy leader to his knees.

Johns was down, and so was Changeh along with two devils while Na'armeh and Nefra stood back-to-back to fight the rest of the assailants. Golda dashed forward on the attack. Her morale felt buoyed by Octavia's towering presence by her side. She backstabbed the devil that locked Agron. He groaned his appreciation for the pain, even while bleeding. He fell face-forward to the floor. Agron slumped and fell alongside.

Golda pushed on, only to find Boudi-Ca instantly beside her. The fledgling had finished her devil, then flashed across the room to flank-attack the devil that faced Nefra. The devil whirled with a vicious cut that narrowly missed Boudi's face, even while Nefra pressed the attack. The devil groaned, and his face lifted with divine ecstasy as three blades hacked and stabbed him.

Finally he went down, and the final devil followed him.

Golda limped quickly towards the altar and her pile of clothing. She needed her boots. The devil blood on the floor was smoking and burning her toes and soles. The battle was over, and everyone in the room was wounded and bleeding, except for Boudi-Ca and Lydiah. Na'armeh moaned and whimpered from where she had fallen along with Changeh, Johns, and Agron onto the hard stones. Na'armeh clutched at her thigh, where a devil hook was deeply embedded. Agron echoed her efforts, grabbing weakly at a deep hook in his bicep.

"By the gods," Agron breathed. "It's too much blood. I'm going to the void."

"Not yet." Octavia knelt at the side of Agron, clutched his arm, and began her healing magic. Golda sniffed. The odors of acrid blood were thick on the air, and the blood would thicken further if they didn't leave immediately. She re-opened her mind to the weave. The second wave of devils was closing the distance quickly.

"We need to move," Nefra said. "There is no time to lick our wounds. We did well thanks to Boudi-Ca, but the larger group is still coming. Is that right, Golda?"

"Yes. We only have a few minutes." Golda drew on her pants. She grabbed her boots and wrestled her burning feet back into them. She laved her mouth, trying to assuage the pain there as well. She could feel Boudi's eyes on her body, and her heart lifted again from the chains of the depression that weighed it. From the look in the fledgling's smoldering umber-silver eyes, there was real hope. "The way down is to the west then, Lydiah? I was trying to go east towards the forest and the mines."

"Yes. I think the stairs are through some old tombs." Lydiah stepped past Agron and Octavia to where Changeh lay half-conscious and bleeding. "And if we are leaving immediately, we have no time for this silly healing."

"My stomach and my leg." Changeh whimpered and sobbed where she lay clutching at her leg, which was gashed and bleeding up its length. "I need the healing next. Please."

Lydiah grabbed Changeh's torn leg and dragged her across the floor towards the pit. "Who is the bitch now, bitch?"

"No! No, please!" Changeh groaned. "I just need healing! Oh gods the pain—"

With a final heave, Lydiah dragged Changeh to the edge. Lydiah aimed a ferocious kick. Changeh grunted and flopped over the edge. Her anguished, strangled shriek echoed down the pit shaft.

Golda stepped quickly behind Lydiah. She felt a sudden heat prick her skin, but no more fear. She was totally focused in that moment. She summoned all of her love for Boudi, all of the passion that she'd felt for so many moons.

"That takes care of that," Lydiah said, turning with a satisfied smile. "And you, Na'armeh? Are you getting up, or—"

Golda stepped forward and shoved with all of her strength. She caught Lydiah square in the chest. Lydiah rocked backwards. Golda pushed again, throwing her weight and strength forward. Lydiah snapped a quick hex, but the force of the spell only served to tip the momentum further. Horror came over Lydiah's face when her feet stepped on air. She grabbed for the edge as she fell, but her shoulders were too far over. Lydiah dropped with a prolonged shriek into the black void.

"No!" Boudi-Ca yelled with a voice that sounded more anguished than any pains of mere flesh. The fledgling leapt to the edge of the pit. "Mistress!"

Chapter 34.

Boudi-Ca whirled and leveled her sword at Golda's throat. The tracker edged away from her, but she edged forward in turn. Her hand trembled with a desire to spear Golda, ending the rebel who had ended her Mistress. She could see Golda's silver-blue eyes in the sudden gloom. Lydiah's bright tenebris lux had followed her down into the pit, and the only illuminations left in the room were Octavia's halo and Golda's lux, which threw her face into shadow under the sweep of her mane.

"Why did you do that?" Boudi-Ca managed. "I was starting to think you were nice, but instead—"

"She tried to kill me first," Golda countered. "She tried to control me with a mind spell, and then she tried to strangle me—"

"I don't believe you. My Mistress says you tell lies. You're an animal, but you're more of a rodent than a cat. You're a—"

"Hero!" Na'armeh chortled. Na'armeh's body was washed with blood and cuts, but she tottered unsteadily to her feet with Octavia's help. "Golda is a gods-damned hero. I hope the Beast consumes every little morsel of Lydiah's pathetic, broken corpse. Now put that damned sword down, fledgling. If you kill our tracker, you'll be the next into that pit, even if you killed half those devils yourself."

"Indeed," Nefra said cautiously. "Please, Boudi-Ca. You and Golda are both very important to this group."

"Yes," Octavia added. "Listen to wisdom and let go of your anger. Save your energy for the devils."

Boudi-Ca lowered her sword. She didn't have the emotional strength to kill Golda. Besides, Golda had been nice to her. Golda had carried her through the darkness. Golda had kissed her on the lips, which was more than Lydiah was willing to give her. Golda even cared about her, and perhaps she could use that, at least until the time was right for any proper vengeance.

A low, uncanny roar came from the pit then—a hollow, echoing roar that resonated through the hallways of the Bolgia. The very floor seemed to shudder. Boudi-Ca turned to the edge of the pit. She had the urge to call out, but she resisted. The roar came again. The floor seemed to shudder like a mountain shrugging off an earthquake.

"What was that sound? Is my Mistress still alive?"

"Please, fledgling," Nefra said quietly. "We need to go. We need to run. Perhaps that was just the wind. The bowels of Haawiyah sigh sometimes with foul gases. Or perhaps it was just a minor volcanic quake."

"Oh, right," Na'armeh said. "I'm sure that wasn't the Beast, who is now wide awake and hungry to feed on all of our flesh."

Nefra cleared her throat. "In any case, we need to leave before the rest of the devils show up to finish us. Come, Boudi-Ca. We need to mourn our friends who have fallen, but mid-battle is not the time for it."

Boudi-Ca nodded at Golda, as if with a silent peace offering. She was tired, so tired of fighting the pain, the fear, and everything. Lydiah had sacrificed everything so she could live. She couldn't let that sacrifice go to waste. "I still hunger. Octavia's healing helped me, but I still haven't fed."

"I'll find you something in the next level," Golda said quickly.

"Lydiah's satchel." Na'armeh ambled across the room at surprising speed for her wounds. The leather satchel sat in the corner behind the door. She snatched it up and grinned grimly. "This feels like something nice. I'll hold onto it for safekeeping."

Boudi-Ca fell in behind Golda and Agron. She didn't like Na'armeh taking Lydiah's satchel, but she wasn't going to argue in that moment. She followed the other Jinni past the body of the Gypsy named Johns, whose bloody face was frozen in either unconsciousness or death. Boudi-Ca looked away. She imagined Lydiah at the bottom of that bottomless pit, contorted in agony, also breathing her last breath.

For an hour all too brief, she'd felt Lydiah's love and protection. She'd finally gotten the full attention of the Mistress, yet she couldn't keep even that. Every time she desired something, it was torn away from her. She had a sudden, powerful desire for a pastry, and her mouth wetted with the thought of a sweet, honeyed morsel. She desperately needed a pastry to make her feel better.

She needed nectar as well. If she only had nectar, her pain would go away. She wanted nectar, an entire box of it, and a hot bath with a handsome slave boy. She winced and pressed her feet to move faster, but every step sent dull pains through her feet and calves. She was lagging. Golda had accelerated to almost a run down the dark dungeon corridor.

Golda looked over her shoulder and slowed. Boudi-Ca pushed a little harder. The tracker wouldn't leave her behind. At least Golda actually wanted her, instead of considering her some sort of curse that needed to be lifted. Lieutenant Nefra seemed to care for her too, and so did Ambassador Octavia. Perhaps, even though she felt alone, she wasn't alone among those other women, who also held the devils as the enemy.

The group moved quietly through the darkness for several minutes. A low passage opened into a wider hallway with ancient doors lining each side. A painted vase decorated each sealed doorway. Some vases sprouted dead vines and stems, as if from flowers that had long since withered. Golda led the way through an archway and down a long flight of stairs. Soon the stairs doubled back, heading still deeper into the depths.

The stairs gave onto a hallway into the next lower level. A decrepit archway led into a high square chamber. A long desk with chairs sat against one wall. A rack of weapons sat next to the desk. Golda paused and summoned a stronger lux. The tracker went to the desk and held up a ring of keys.

"This is the registry room for this level. I was hoping we were leaving Mer, but instead we're leaving the old tombs and re-entering another section with prisoners. I can still see the big force of devils in tapestry. They seem to be delaying for a moment where we had that battle. We've opened up a bit of space."

"Maybe they think they have us trapped," Nefra offered. "I'm more and more worried about our intended exit. Once they realize what we're up to and where we're headed, they could arrive there before us on horses."

Golda nodded. "A good point. Let's hope there is more than one exit in the Great Blue Hole mines, and let's hope we find the exits before the devils can block them off, if they care to try so hard. How are your feet, Boudi-Ca?"

"My feet hurt, and I hunger so much. I feel really weak."

"Sit on the desk," Octavia said. "I'll look at your feet again."

"No," Golda answered. "We'll rest when we find more men. Agron is empty, and Boudi-Ca needs to feed. We need her sword arm, and feeding will heal her. Boudi-Ca, you can't heal yourself?"

"No. Can I?"

Golda sighed. "I pray to the Lady your skills will return, and Lydiah hasn't ruined you. More weapons are here if anyone needs them."

"I might look for an upgrade," Na'armeh muttered. "This ogre blade was too slow, and a few extra weapons might be handy if we unlock more prisoners to help us. Lydiah said the prisoners down here are extra dangerous. I like the sound of that. We need replacements."

Na'armeh tossed her heavy ogre blade on the low desk, along with Lydiah's satchel, and examined the devil weapons. She drew two curved daggers, a poniard, and a bec de corbin. Agron hefted the ogre blade and tested its weight. Nefra slid the leather satchel off the desk and opened it.

"I figured we'd split the coins," Na'armeh said quickly. "There are a couple hundred aurei in there, some bags of nectar, and an old beat-up book filled with papers of some sort. I don't know what the book is about. I'm not a sorceress, and the book might be cursed for all I know."

Nefra's eyebrow arched in the low light over her head. Nefra had cast a tenebris lux to join with Golda's. She handed the satchel back to Na'armeh. "I'd be more worried about stealing a pile of gold from Archduke Fennel, especially if it was a windfall from killing his wife. I'm starting to agree with Octavia. This whole group is cursed, and things are going from bad to worse."

Na'armeh smiled. "You're such a law-abiding citizen, Lieutenant. Will you split the loot then, Golda? Or are the coins all mine?"

"I only want Boudi-Ca. The coins are yours, unless Agron wants a Share. He's a free Gypsy of his own accord. He isn't a slave boy."

"I'm more interested in seeing daylight and my wife again," Agron said. "Although when we're free and going our separate ways, then perhaps the coins should go separate ways as well. It's a certain condemnation if the coins are found all in one lump in the bag they were stolen in. I'd give half my Share to Johns' wife, Marissa. He went to the void because he bravely helped defend our family against the devils, and now she will never see him again in this world, much less give him a proper burial."

Na'armeh shrugged. "We'll see, Gypsy. A sword speaks louder than words, and we Jinni aren't much for human sympathy, if you know what I mean. Shall we go?"

"I wonder if we can barricade this door on the far side." Nefra examined the heavy desk. "I don't even know if we can move this through, but it's worth an attempt."

"An excellent suggestion, Lieutenant," Octavia said. "Let's pray this will hold them." The towering elder Mimọ stepped forward and gripped the edge of the heavy desk in her large hands. She heaved it towards the door. Nefra stepped forward to assist alongside Agron. Golda tested the key ring on the door. Double locks soon clicked, and the door swung open.

Boudi-Ca watched the efforts to move the desk into the hallway beyond. Her belly felt tense and queer from Golda's direct assertion concerning her. She still wasn't sure how Golda 'wanted' her, but the thought secretly stoked her with a renewed inner conflict. Golda's desire was evidently strong enough to risk life and limb, as well as commit murder.

Meanwhile, Lydiah's death was starting to feel like a blessing as well as a tragedy. For the first time in her memory, she was free, and she was also with other women like herself. Those were the reasons why she'd wanted to join the Smokeless Flames in the first place. On the other hand, she was in a desperate situation. She didn't know where she was going, and only Golda seemed to offer her a road to take.

Of course, that was exactly what Golda wanted. Boudi-Ca bit her lip. She'd felt Golda's love first hand, but the Djinnus in Mer had taught her that everyone had an ulterior motive, typically based on lust and the desire to fuck someone. She slipped through the door at Lieutenant Nefra's beck, and she tried to help press the massive desk into position against the closed door, effectively preventing anything but a very powerful force from breaking the door open.

"So how far are we actually going?"

"It depends on the lay of the passages, I'd imagine," Nefra answered. "As the crow flies, we might walk three days from downtown Mer to reach the Great Blue Hole—"

"Two, or even one and a half at a good pace," Golda interrupted.

"Or we might be down here a week if we're lost and wandering," Nefra finished. "Thankfully we have a great tracker with us, one of the best in all the realms. I have faith in her to lead us."

Golda smiled grimly and pressed ahead into the barrel-vaulted passageway with her dim tenebris lux over her head. After a hundred meters more, past the openings of dark and abandoned storage rooms, the passage reached a fork.

Golda elected the low road, which descended a long ramp to a bend, and then into another passage lined with the cell doors of more Hell's Court prisoners. Boudi-Ca groaned quietly at the pain in her feet, which seemed worse going downhill. Meanwhile her Hunger was ravenous in her belly, and she was feeling faint. She struggled to match Golda's long lope. She tried to move her focus away from her pain and back to Golda's comment that she'd been ruined. She didn't feel ruined. She'd killed more of the devils than anyone else, not to mention Breanarachelle. At the thought of

Breanarachelle, pastries filled her head again.

She needed pastries and nectar. She wanted pastries and nectar, a whole plate of pastries and nectar all piled together in glorious sugary splendor. She could imagine the wonderful flavors—the honey, the sugar powder, and the nectar that made her body warm and swell with pleasure from her throat to the tips of her toes, and especially in her sex.

She focused on the thoughts of pastries. The intense desire seemed to strengthen her inside, ameliorating the pain slightly. She followed the group down another long hallway and another low junction. She was so lost in fantasies that she almost ran into Na'armeh when the group stopped, and Golda tested her key ring at a cell door. The redheaded tracker tried one key after another.

"The others in these cells are mostly wasted husks," Golda said as she worked. "Many of them are half-dead, unfed Jinni with scarcely a knot left in the tapestry. There is no point to opening these doors just to look at piles of skin and bones. I'm depressed enough as it is."

Nefra's worn hand slid to the hilt of her sword. "And this one, then?"

"This prisoner in here seems unusually alive. He's a strong soul, and he hasn't folded his hand, as the werewolves say in their card games. He has some life and hope left."

"These must be the oubliettes," Nefra said. "This is the lowest level of the Hell's Court pits, where they send the worst prisoners, the ones condemned to imprisonment forever."

A key finally clicked and turned. Golda opened the heavy door to a small, cramped cell. The cell was some three meters square and cut from the under-stones of Haawiyah, with no masonry past the cemented frame of the doorway. A gaunt male curled in the dirty corner. Golda stepped forward cautiously. "Hello? You there."

Na'armeh stepped forward and gave the male a swift kick in the ankle. "Wake up, prisoner!"

The male stirred. He blinked and squinted against the lights of the tenebris luces. His eyes were in a distant place, and he slowly focused on Golda's knee. His eyes ran up her leg, as if realizing she was real. Behind his beard and long hair, the man was handsome, except for the horrible scar that was his missing nose. His eyes shimmered in their deep sockets, revealing him to be an Djinnus.

"What goes? Is this flesh, or a trick of the dream world?"

"This is real," Golda answered. "We're here to rescue you, and we need your help in return."

"By the gods," the man said. He grabbed his face, as if assuring himself of his material form. "I'd almost forgotten this place existed. Yes, I was having a quite pleasant day with my lovers, high in my wizard tower, and I have little desire to return to this terrible dark place. You're setting me free, say you? Nay, I was already free."

"Who are you?" Golda persisted.

"My name is Wilhelm." The male sighed. "Baron Wilhelm the Great. So you won't just leave me alone and go about your way?"

"No." Na'armeh kicked him again. "Get your ass up and service Lydiah's fledgling like a man."

"Fine then, I could be convinced that flesh and blood Jinni have their merits." Wilhelm squinted and surveyed Golda's figure again from head to toe. "You're quite a nice bit of jam, and I confess a leaning for ample teats. I also confess this cock hasn't had a proper wank in forever. What year is it? Are we sometime in the early nineteen hundreds?"

"No," Golda answered. "That was a century ago. So what are your skills?"

"By the gods, time flies when you're living in dreams. I'm a wizard. I was caught with my hands in a certain place where they shouldn't have been, namely between the delicate spindles of Marie Antoinette, who hired me for a drop of spying in the Ukraine Quarter. King Shulamit tossed some coins at Hell's Court, and he railroaded me into this place to get rid of me. The Ukraine are arrogant wankers like that." The man rose to his feet unsteadily and surveyed Golda. He stretched out his arm as if to greet her, but his hands were missing, to match his nose. He looked down at his stump with mild confusion. "Have you seen my hands, by the way? I'd quite forgotten this bloody complication."

"Excellent," Na'armeh interjected. "I'm carrying extra weapons for a handless wizard. You can really pick them, Golda."

"He has more strength in the weave than anyone else we've passed since the uppermost level," Golda countered.

"Perhaps you're mistaking his strength for his odor," Octavia said. "I'll be waiting outside the door."

Wilhelm managed a crooked grin. "No, I'm quite strong, you see. I've mastered the ancient Taoist art of conservation of my seed. Without my hands, wanking was almost impossible unless I wanted to fuck the stones, so I turned my sexual energy into the dream world. I prayed to Allyssia for guidance, and she sent me a girl in red. The girl made my inner serpent rise. My sex-obsessed mind gradually opened towards higher things. Yes, I have dreams, but my dreams are real. I meet other dream travelers sometimes. I have hands in my dreams. I have friends. I have girlfriends. I don't need any hands or friends in this place, but I'd still rather get frigged than kicked, mind you, so be on with it or sod off."

Boudi-Ca eyed the scraggly, bearded, noseless Djinnus. Golda could hardly have picked a more disgusting male specimen for her to fuck. Her gaze drifted lower nonetheless, and she riveted on the impressive bulge in the drawstring pantaloons that hung in threadbare tatters from Wilhelm's bony hips.

Her need urged her to shoulder past Na'armeh. She seized the wizard's cock, and he moaned his appreciation. She pushed him hard against the wall, and the buffeting seemed to awaken him further. She dropped her skirt and attacked him like a predator. She seized his dirty, cracked mouth with her own. She took command of his cock, lifted her hips, and took him deep into her already-wet sex.

The intense pleasure forced a whimper of aching need from her lips. She ground down on the wizard's cock, almost jumping on his shaft, until he lowered himself to her height and measured up with her angle. She seized him around his neck and applied her Jinn pressure. Wilhelm groaned, and she moaned in sympathy. She could feel his filthy cock twitching and jumping against her most sensitive inner flesh.

Boudi-Ca closed her eyes. A plate of pastries drifted into her mind. She pressed her lips to the wizard's neck. She imagined his dirty, dusty flesh was really a delicious dry oat cake. She entered a queer and needy pastry-trance. She nibbled, sucked, and bit. Her mind drifted back to Breanarachelle yet again, and the moments of unthinkable bliss and pleasure from being filled. If she only had pastries, her life would be almost perfect. She thrust like an animal with her hips, greedily wanting to get filled up and stuffed from her toes to her throat.

The wizard's cock, she imagined, was like a pastry applicator, and she was an empty pastry needing cream desperately. The sugary member twitched again inside her, and she applied all of her mystical suction. The wizard finally heaved. His super-abundant Djinnus seed flooded hotly into her deepest depths, and with it came a wave of the most wonderful pleasure.

Boudi-Ca took a deep breath and slid off of the wizard. When she turned, all the women were staring silently at her, except for Octavia, who lurked behind the others with her eyes averted. Golda's smoky silver-blue eyes were alive with desire, and Lieutenant Nefra's eyes also smoldered with a deep, lusty light. Nefra's long fingers gently caressed the hilt of her sword as if absentmindedly.

"Damn," Na'armeh finally muttered. "I'll say it if no one else will. You're one amazing piece of fledgling ass, Boudi-Ca. Lydiah was a psychotic bitch, but by the balls of Cerberus, she was a damned lucky—"

"Please spare us your oratory of lust," Octavia interrupted. "Boudi-Ca is cursed. She needs divine healing that only Lord Tuhan can provide. If she feels better now as a Jinn, can we please continue? More and more I think of my freedom from this place, and more and more I feel a desperation to see the Lord's light in Heaven again. The devils took my wings, but they haven't taken my soul yet."

"I'll be staying here," Wilhelm said. "He looked down at the stumps that had once been his hands. I'm going back to sleep. I have no need to escape from anything."

Na'armeh extended a blade and pressed its tip to the wizard's neck. "No. You're coming with us. Our human friend Agron isn't enough cock, and we have four Jinni who need to feed. We still have a long journey ahead of us."

"I'm suddenly more inspired to be free," Wilhelm said. "I'll agree at sword-point to accompany you fine Jinni and lend my assistance. A bit of earthly indulgence never hurts, and then I can return to dreaming. Perhaps I can find a nice hollow tree—or something."

"What can you do for us?" Nefra said. "Aside from feeding us?"

"I'm among the greatest of mages in all of the realms." The wizard's voice changed from sniveling to sonorous. "In fact, I am a legend. I can rain heavenly meteors down upon the heads of my foes. My empowered fire bolts can melt giants into ash, and my frost strikes can lay entire ogre villages to waste. I've slain several dragons, of course. I've also saved several princesses from captivity. Needless to say, those princesses were grateful and pleased to repay me. The last one was a dulcet brunette with the gentlest, most submissive demeanor that you've ever seen. She lives as my princess wife now in my wizard tower."

Nefra's brow arched with skepticism. "Well. At least we have a replacement mage, since Golda killed our last one. We could have used magic to seal that door as well as the heavy desk."

"This Djinnus is as mad as a hatter." Na'armeh grabbed Golda's hand and seized the keys. "I'm going to open a few more of these cells. Hells, why aren't we opening all of them? We can cover our tracks by giving the devils a real mess on their hands."

"That might not be advisable," Nefra said.

"Yes, this is supposed to be a stealth mission," Golda added. "And I don't think you're going to like what you find."

Boudi-Ca re-tied Golda's shirt into her makeshift skirt. She watched Nefra and Golda follow Na'armeh from the small cell. Her belly felt much warmer and happier in that moment. Her mind was clearer, and she no longer wanted pastries so much. With the exit of the others, the room went almost black, and she summoned a quick tenebris lux over her head. She offered a polite smile to Wilhelm.

"Are you coming, great wizard?"

Wilhelm shrugged, waving his arm stumps. "I can't seem to distinguish between dreams and the real, but in the dream world you have to trust your feelings about things. I have a bad feeling. Maybe it's only because I despoiled your virginity, fledgling Boudi-Ca."

"You didn't despoil me. I pretty much threw myself on you."

"There is more to the story of my affair with Marie Antoinette. She told me no, but I was sure that my spell of sonic vibration would butter up her bacon if she only gave it half a chance. My spell was a bit strong and gave her horrible cramps. She was screaming and kicking at me, and those Ukraine bastards beat me senseless and dragged me down to see the bloody devils." The wizard sighed and trudged forward. "Mayhaps I can redeem myself. I suppose you have a big, bad dragon that needs killing? Yes, of course. So if I slay your dragon with my magic and save you from certain death, will you agree to marry me, princess Boudi-Ca?"

"No. I really don't think so."

<h1 style="text-align:center">Chapter 35.</h1>

"This isn't a great idea." Yellen followed Na'armeh to the next door. "The wizard seems to be under control, but these prisoners are dangerous killers. We have no idea what we might unleash. We need to keep moving, and quickly."

Yellen watched Na'armeh test the keys in the door lock. Again the group had devolved into disorganization, and with Lydiah gone, she was trying to step up. Technically she was a ranking officer over Na'armeh. Na'armeh pulled the door open and gazed into the cell with a slow look of revulsion.

"No. That's just disgusting. Those fuck-sick devils—"

"Oh, my Lord." Octavia averted her eyes yet again. "Bless that poor soul."

"Horrible," Agron added. "I wish I hadn't seen that."

"I told you," Golda said. "The wizard is lucky to only be missing a few pieces. Try the fifth door down on the far side, Na'armeh. That one still has some warmth and life."

"Which one?"

"Just give me the damned keys back." Golda grabbed the keys, and Na'armeh surrendered them reluctantly. Yellen smiled. She found herself liking Golda. Golda was a shifty rogue, but she was a righteous, bold, and noble spirit. Golda was a redhead like Kiree and Henne, but her character was the opposite. If any vulnerable femininity lurked beneath the tracker's intense, guarded exterior, she kept it well hidden.

Golda led the group further down the hallway. She pushed a key quickly into a lock and swung another ancient door open. Yellen looked past Golda's shoulder. She saw nothing in the room, but the tracker stared low and ahead, as if glimpsing something beyond normal vision.

"It's empty." Na'armeh shook her head. "You're the worst tracker I've ever met."

"Come out." Golda gestured, as if to a pet. "We aren't devils. We mean you no harm." In that moment, a clang and clatter echoed from far away through the old dungeon stones. Another clang came, followed by a tapping. A rustle sounded in the room, and a small figure appeared in the doorway, as if undissolving from invisibility. The little being was smaller than a halfling, with pointy ears, bristly brows over wide, owl-like eyes, and an elfin nose. The creature wore dusty, threadbare linen pants and a matching maroon waistcoat with tarnished brass buttons.

"What's that, what's that?" The creature covered its mouth with its small hand.

"It sounds like the devils are at the barricaded door." Yellen felt a small chill run through her shoulder blades. The winnowed group couldn't afford to fight the devils again, even with Boudi-Ca's skills. "We have no more time for interviewing prisoners. We need to keep moving."

Golda nodded. "Yes. I'm following the devils in the tapestry. They're trying to get past that door now. What's your name, brownie? Would you like to try to escape from this place?"

"I'm Dingbie." The brownie stepped forward and poked its head further from the cell. It glanced cautiously from right to left. "You're setting me free, Miss?"

"Yes," Golda said. "We're escaping from the Bolgia pits. We're all in this together, and we have a weapon for you. Na'armeh?"

"Gods," Na'armeh said. She extricated the small poniard from her selection of weapons. "We have a no-handed wizard and a little Kishi girl-child to help us against the devils, and they're our replacements for

Lydiah, Changeh, and our dead Gypsy friend. Simhonit would be laughing right now if she could see this."

"I'm a boy I'll have you know." Dingbie snatched the poniard from Na'armeh's extended fingers. He held it in both hands like a treasure. His large eyes flitted up over the generous swells of Golda's breasts, which were higher than his head. "And what's your name, kinder Miss?"

"Golda," the tracker answered. "I don't care what you did to earn your prison sentence, but I hope you can help."

"Oh, you have a giant!" Dingbie's eyes went wide when he stepped from the cell and gazed up at Octavia. "And she glows!"

"Yes." Golda smiled. "We have a giant. So let's go."

Yellen drifted to the rear of the group, which forged down the hallway and around a bend. The devils were still working on the door to the lower level. The battering sounds echoed from far away down the dark, oppressive Bolgia pit corridors, punctuated by the occasional squeals of protesting metal.

Yellen drummed her fingers nervously on her sword hilt. She had to admit for the first time, without Lydiah's skills, a possibility for operation failure. She shouldn't have been in the Bolgia pits in the first place. She'd had chances to escape from the purgation unscathed, but she'd simply missed them. Lydiah's stealthy curse had coerced her into bad decisions, and then Lydiah had gone to her death, making things still worse. She wished she was with Henne. She wished she was with Simhonit. She could have done so many things differently, and everything had slipped from her fingers.

The tunnel broke into a junction, and Golda elected an ancient staircase. Yellen still followed in the rear. The stair gave onto another hallway, which was completely silent except for the hurried feet of the party. They passed door after sealed door, apparently the homes of dozens more doomed prisoners of Hell's Court. Yellen glanced over her shoulder yet again, even though it was pointless. The corridors had gone silent.

Had the devils broken through the barricade, or had they ceased their efforts and given up the chase? Only Golda knew the answer, and the tracker's fast, pressured pace spoke volumes.

The tunnel dropped onto another steep set of stone steps. The steps descended to yet another level, where they joined a wider corridor. The corridor was impressively arched, with its ceiling supported by dusty caryatid columns sculpted by slaves in ancient, forgotten days. Golda strode forward through a low archway at the end. A set of curved radial steps gave into a massive natural stone passage. The curved ceiling of the volcanic passage was crumbled in many places, and a small rivulet of water carved a path through a thick bed of crushed dust and pebbles. A suffocating odor of sulfur hung heavy in the air.

Golda followed along the side of the stream for what seemed like an hour, until finally a great archway loomed. The arch was a medieval affair of bricks and masonry that appeared more recent and well-patched than the Greek architectural elements in the previous passages. Golda stopped, as if to examine the script along the columns that supported the rising sculpted curves. "If I ever knew the English language, I don't anymore. How are you feeling, Boudi-Ca?"

"I'm better than I thought I'd be. How are you?"

Golda lowered her head. "I'm tired. I really to rest and feed."

"For you I'm ready to go again, my fair busty beauty," Wilhelm declared. "My seed is omnipotent, just like my spells." The wizard straightened and pushed his arm stumps at the rags that wrapped his frail hips, as if attempting to look regal.

Octavia uttered a low grumble. She approached the archway and studied the script more closely in the light of her halo. "This is the border of the city of Mer," she intoned. "This is the domain of the great Lord Hades and Lady Allyssia. All trespassers and enemies must turn back, or face the wrath of the lovers of pain."

"The lovers of pain are the algolagnites," Yellen added. "Those are the devil wardens of Hell's Court. We must be directly under the walls of Mer then. This is progress."

"We're going to pass under the forest next, correct?" Agron hefted his ogre blade to rest on his sturdy shoulder. "After that, we'll seek to come up through the Great Blue Hole mines, assuming we can escape from the devils that are still chasing us?"

"The devils are no more." Golda's tone was terse, and her face was shadowed under her wild hair. Her full lips were pressed into a grim line. "They've given up the chase."

Yellen felt her heart leap with sudden relief. She hadn't expected such a turn of events. Perhaps the operation had better chances, or then again, perhaps not. "If we've escaped from the wrath of the devils, then why are you so worried, Golda?"

Golda gestured at the wall of darkness beyond the grand medieval arch. "A big, horrible creature is waiting for us at the end of that tunnel, and I don't see any way to go around it. I'm guessing it's some sort of guardian."

"It's the Beast," Na'armeh muttered. "They say it has three heads, and it was born in the time of Babylon. It's ancient as sin and nigh as unkillable."

Octavia's eyes continued to scan the English script on the archway. "Sin is certainly killable, you poor deluded Jinn. I used to fight sin as my full-time job when I was with the Conclave Sin-Watch Conclave in Heaven."

"Well this isn't your goddamned Heaven, Ambassador. Take your perfect world and stand it on its head until your sky is black, and your gutters are drowning in filth and fuck. That's Mer. Any Jinn will take a donkey to bed if she can't find a man, and you're going to fight that? Good luck."

"If filth is all you know, then all you know is filth," Agron countered.

"You might want to keep your voices lower," Golda warned. "There is nothing to stop the beast from coming this way and attacking us where we stand."

"We could try stealth," Yellen offered. "We could extinguish our tenebris luces, and one of our stealthy sorts could distract the beast with stones or other noises while the rest of us make a run for the far passageway."

"My halo will be obvious," Octavia said. "I'm not much built for running or sneaking."

"Well, we need a good plan, so let's think of one." Yellen stepped away from the group and paced. She needed to think, and her fatigue and depression were affecting her judgment. Her initial suggestion had been thickheaded. She wished she knew the group better. She couldn't strategize if she had little idea of the individual assets on hand.

Octavia had once held real power, but the Mimọ ambassador for Heaven seemed a shell of her former self as a political negotiator between Lord Tuhan and Lord Hades. Apparently Octavia had also failed in her job, or else the recent conflicts with Heaven wouldn't have escalated for the first time in centuries. The towering Mimọ's voluminous dusty robe was adorned with long slits down her shoulder blades. The slits had once allowed Octavia's proud Mimọ wings to flare, but her wings were long gone. The back of her Mimọ robe was dark with rust-colored blood stains down to her bony elephantine buttocks.

"How bad can this beast really be," Octavia finally said. "Is it bigger than me? I have my holy bolts. You are all skilled with swords. I can be your distraction. I'll just walk up and grab one of its heads like I grabbed that desk, and the rest of you can kill it. I have no fear of sin. I have no fear of evil. If anything, this Beast should be afraid of me, not the contrary."

"Is this Beast a dragon?" Wilhelm raised his bearded chin proudly. "I have fought many dragons, and they have all succumbed before me. My spells will rain fire on this monster, and if Boudi-Ca won't marry me, then she should at least give me a kiss on the lips."

Boudi-Ca shrugged. "Fine. If you kill this Beast, then I'll kiss you."

The wizard's grin split his beard from ear to ear. "Let's sally forth, then."

"Wait. There is something I haven't mentioned yet." Golda looked towards the sandy tunnel floor, as if unwanting to say the words. "The Beast is apparently saving Lydiah for tomorrow's meal. The Beast has her. Her thread is weak in the tapestry, as if she's near death. If we slay the Beast, we can likely heal her."

"Or we can just kill her again," Na'armeh said. "I'll even help this time."

Golda eyed Na'armeh. "I might have to accept that offer."

"Why do you need to kill my Mistress so badly, Golda?" Boudi-Ca looked agitated. Her pale silver-umber eyes glowed with a simmering passion, a pain of lost innocence. "So you can have me? Well guess what – that's no way to get someone. Why don't you try being my real friend? If you kill my Mistress this time, just forget it. I'll go my own way, and I'll never want to see you ever again."

Golda sighed. "That's exactly the sort of no-win situation I was hoping to avoid. Boudi-Ca, you used to be different. Lydiah took all of your memories away with black nectar, and she molded you into a pretty doll like the rest of the Hell's high society Jinni. Lydiah ruined Lady Allyssia's beautiful city, and then she took your life as some sort of twisted trophy. Where is your best friend? Where is Tajee? Do you even remember him?"

"No." Boudi-Ca frowned. "Wait, yes. He's one of the boys at our château in the north country. We keep him in a cage."

"Good to know. Well, it would pain your soul if you knew the truth of everything horrible that Lydiah has done to you and Tajee."

"If she's done anything so horrible, then I don't remember it."

"Exactly." Golda's jaw clenched. "So let's just fight this beast. Maybe I'll die trying. If we win, then Lydiah needs to die again, and we need to kill her when she's weak. I'm sorry, Boudi-Ca." Golda drew her sword from her sheath, wheeled, and advanced grimly down the passage.

"Wait, please," Boudi-Ca said quickly. "Maybe my Mistress can help us. If she helps us, will you forgive her?"

"No."

"Still an excellent thought." Yellen summoned a bird quickly and directed it to Lydiah, relieved that Golda had come to her senses and was returning. "Please wait, Golda. I'll handle this."

We are here, Lydiah. What is your status? How can we defeat the Beast?

Yellen paced again. Silence reigned in the hallway for long minutes. Agron fidgeted with his ogre blade next to Wilhelm the Great, while Dingbie the brownie ran the Sharpness of his poniard along his little nostrils. The pointy-eared Kishi looked vanishingly small alongside Octavia's robed leg. Dingbie balanced his poniard on his fingertip and spun it with remarkable deftness, apparently unphased by an imminent battle to the death.

Yellen tapped her fingers on her sword hilt. No answer from Lydiah was forthcoming for long minutes. She finally shook her head. "Lydiah must be unconscious or half-eaten by the beast. She's an elder Jinn. She could survive for a long while with a loss of blood and limbs."

"Then my plan is still the best one," Octavia declared. "I'm not afraid to face this evil. Is everyone ready?"

Octavia beckoned and turned down the hallway. Octavia's halo nearly brushed the top of the archway. She strode proudly with a sudden purpose, appearing more regal, defiant, and holy instead of stooped and fatigued. The wizard trailed in her wake, and the rest of the group followed behind.

Yellen strode close behind Golda. She intended to defend Golda and shield her if necessary. Flames operating protocol dictated that the tracker always had to be defended, even more so than the mage. The tracker in any field operation was the greatest asset, without which the group was blind to enemy movements.

The high-ceilinged hallway past the arch gave onto a wide set of worn, broken steps leading down to a sunken, circular plaza. An enormous form stirred in the blackness. The form rose up with a low growl that boomed through the room. The Beast approached into the light of the tenebris luces.

Yellen felt her throat clutch, and a chill ran up the back of her neck. The Beast wasn't just large. The creature was enormous, as large as a house with three chimneys, and each chimney was a monstrous dragon-like head. The Beast's legs were like tree trunks, and when the creature stomped across the floor, the very bedrock of Haawiyah seemed to quake.

"Run away?" Golda growled. The tracker slipped left along the wall, and Yellen joined her. Yellen hefted her blade, but she could see no apparent weakness to the creature, no soft spot amongst the massive black scales and claws. The beast picked up speed. Octavia stood half its height, but she stood firm and leveled a stern voice. Holy bolts flew from her fingertips and pummeled the creature.

The Beast roared in pain, and for a moment it stepped back, but then it surged forward again. Its center head lunged and swallowed Octavia's head and shoulders. Agron charged the Beast's right foot, and Yellen finally sprinted forward to mount an insane effort with the brave Reik patriarch. She felt Golda close behind her. If she could drive her blade deep into the creature's kneecap, at least they might escape with their lives.

Octavia's muffled shriek was eerie in the Beast's gullet. The Beast thrust forward again, gulped, and chewed, but was unable to swallow the Mimo ambassador whole. Wilhelm the Great stepped forward then. The wizard raised his voice with commanding syllables, but no fire could be seen, no flames or fountains of frost. The beast surrendered Octavia, who collapsed into a motionless heap. Another horrible head snapped forward and grabbed the wizard.

Yellen arrived at the tree trunk leg, but not before Agron and Na'armeh. The Gypsy swung a tremendous blow at the beast's ankle. The ogre blade clanged away without penetrating. Na'armeh leveled her own attempt with the bec de corbin. The spiked beak of the long weapon sank deep. The Beast roared and stepped back, trying to find an angle to counterattack, even as the great creature's left head lifted the frail wizard into the air and swallowed him.

Yellen gave her effort at the creature's other leg. Her blade wasn't the best puncturing weapon like Na'armeh's bec de corbin, and the Beast's leg was moving and flexing. She tried to stay left under the beast's body, the better to avoid the heads. Her sword point clanged across the leg, scarcely denting the scales. The beast pivoted and took another step back, and she found herself under its belly. She shifted her grip with more leverage and stabbed upwards. Her sword penetrated with the awkward angle but only barely. The Beast's belly was like a heavy sheet of scaled armor, giving slightly under the impact, but resisting penetration.

Na'armeh screamed then and left her feet, the next victim of the heads. Nefra struck upwards again, realizing she'd been joined by Agron and Golda, who both skittered with agility between the beast's legs while searching for points of attack.

Yellen stabbed yet again, attempting the soft flesh between the belly and the hind leg, but again her efforts to thrust overhead were feeble. She skittered away, looking for a tail or a way to mount the beast's back to access its necks. Agron grunted. A leg had pummeled him, and he flew off his feet. He scrambled to roll away, but the Beast's enormous foot stepped on the Gypsy's legs. Agron groaned in mortal agony. The beast shifted and stomped again. Agron went silent like a crushed bug.

Yellen skated away from the legs towards the rear of the beast, attempting to gain space, the better to re-assess the desperate situation. She was close to the exit tunnel towards the Great Blue Hole. She glimpsed a figure in the darkness. Lydiah was standing on her feet in the gloom, surveying the battle.

Yellen felt her chest burn suddenly from the pain of her war wound. She saw Golda moving away, not towards the exit but towards Boudi-Ca, who stood motionless not far from the entry archway. Dingbie the brownie was nowhere to be seen.

She felt her skin prick with the feeling that she only ever felt in the presence of a superior opponent. Something wasn't right. In fact, everything was wrong. The beast finished Agron and turned its heads. Its dog-like eyes glowed with unholy fire as it charged. Yellen raised her blade. She stabbed upwards when the Beast lunged. Her sword entered its gullet and soft tissues, but the beast's horrible jaws still closed over her. Pain shattered through her soul as the enormous teeth crushed her spine and pelvis. She squirmed and screamed into the wet, stinking maw.

Chapter 36.

"We need to run. Come with me!" Golda beckoned to Boudi-Ca. She was on the verge of shifting into her cat form and fleeing, but she held herself together. Boudi-Ca wasn't moving. The fledgling's eyes were wide and horrified.

"I—I can't," Boudi-Ca stuttered.

"Come! We'll run back up the passageway. If the Beast catches us, I'll shift into cat form, and you just need to keep flashing." Golda grabbed Boudi's hand, but the fledgling resisted her effort. Boudi-Ca looked glassy-eyed.

"Octavia healed my memories a few minutes ago. She held onto my shoulder while Nefra was waiting for Lydiah's bird in the hallway. She worked the same magic that she worked with you, Golda, and a lot of my memories came back. I remember Allyssia's beautiful city, and I remember how much I loved you back then. I remember I wasn't happy because I didn't think you loved me back."

"It was a mistake I'm trying to fix." Golda winced at the crunching sounds as the Beast tore Nefra apart. She was faster than the huge creature in cat form, but she had only seconds left before the Beast came for her next. "I wasn't ready for you, but that's no excuse. I do love you, and that's why I came to save you. That's why I was in the forest outside of Mer for going on six moons."

I can't move now though. I can't help you."

"Why not?"

"My Mistress sent me a—a messenger bird." Boudi-Ca's chin was trembling with emotion. "She told me to not move, and everything will be fine. I really think I should follow her orders. I don't want to be stomped and eaten by that creature."

Golda looked over her shoulder. With the extinction of Nefra's lux, the sunken plaza darkened considerably into gloom, a darkness like a harbinger of doom. The Beast's heads swung around, and then it was thumping towards her across the plaza.

The Beast's three heads swayed as it ran. It snorted sulfur, and blood dripped across the floor from its teeth. Golda raised her sword and braced to be eaten. She couldn't bring herself to leave Boudi's side, not after everything she'd gone through, not after all of her efforts and sacrifice. She willed the creature to stop. She used the same telepathic animal connection that she'd used many times with her jackal mentor, Masad.

Please. I can't die yet. Please don't eat me.

The Beast lumbered to a stop, as if considering. Its center head reared back, turned slightly, and peered at her through the darkness with its burning red eyes.

You ssspeak to me. No one ever ssspeaks to me.

Golda lowered her sword slowly. I am a beast too. I know how it feels to be lonely. I know how it feels to be hungry. You have plenty of food now, don't you? You don't need to eat any more. It's nicer just to be lazy and sleep.

Lydiah wantsss me to eat you. More voices came from the beast. The other heads swung around, massive and drooling, and each spoke with a separate tone. Yesss, her voice is in our headsss. She wantsss us to do thisss favor.

The wizardress is a bad woman. She controls people.

The Beast growled. Lydiah is our friend. She feedsss us. We remember her ssscent. Oh yesss, we remember the sssweet pleasures of Babylon.

I want to be your friend too. You have enough to eat. Please. I need to live.

Yesss. You are a friend too, and we need to eat. We need to go back to sssleep. The Beast receded and turned to look at Lydiah. A low, menacing growl filled the chamber, then the Beast's left head drooped and grabbed the broken body of Na'armeh, who represented the nearest edible morsel. Bones crunched and blood dripped. The Beast settled on the floor and began to chew, chomp, and swallow.

"What in the hells? You haven't finished killing them yet." Lydiah's voice quavered as she slowly crossed the room. A low lux sparked, revealing Lydiah's white-blonde hair. She appeared like a disheveled ghost. One of her diamond earrings was missing, and her short black skirt was covered with dust and dirt. Her borrowed military blouse was missing most of its buttons. Her half-bared breasts hung loose and bruised.

"Apparently we're at an impasse yet again." Golda tried to smirk, but she felt a loathing so strong that she wanted to vomit. She didn't have the energy for so much rage. "You did this then? You told the Beast to kill all of us, even Lieutenant Nefra?"

Lydiah limped painstakingly across the remaining distance. She walked hunched with a limp. Her face was disfigured and purpled with blunt trauma. Her left arm hung weakly at her side, while her right hand still held her whip. Her mouth was taut, with no visible emotion. "Of course. Octavia was a sworn enemy of Hell. Lieutenant Nefra was too unpredictable, a loose end. She served the Flames well. I hope Allyssia blesses Nefra's soul on the way to the void. Perhaps you can console her when you arrive there shortly, Golda."

"I'll leave that to you."

Lydiah hefted her narcabyss whip, as if considering. "On the other hand, I could still use your services, and I'll agree to another agreement for our mutual benefit. This time I have an additional condition. I want you weaponless while you lead me and my fledgling through the rest of the mines and into the daylight. I want you to drop your sword."

Golda surveyed her options. She was hardly weaponless without a sword.

In fact, she was much stronger against Lydiah's magic and whip while in cat form, but perhaps Lydiah didn't know that. Perhaps Lydiah was only judging her from her poor performance against the devils. She tossed her weapon to the stones. "Fine."

Lydiah's bruised lips formed a wicked smile. "You may think you are strong, but protecting Boudi-Ca means everything to you. She is your real weakness. Where is my satchel, fledgling?"

"Sergeant Na'armeh had it," Boudi-Ca answered. "I think she dropped it over on the stair steps, but I don't see it now."

"Gods be damned. Well go and get it."

"I can't, Mistress," Boudi-Ca protested. "It was sitting right there, and now it's gone."

Golda hitched when Lydiah's narcabyss whip hit her chest, taking her breath away. She'd taken her eyes off of Lydiah to look at Boudi, and Lydiah had used the misdirection to strike her by surprise. The whip drew back, and came again to snap around her left leg. Golda moved energy to shift and surge away, but her feline hindquarters faltered.

The whip yanked her leg, and her knee and hip hit the floor. When the whip drew loose and came down on her head, panic overwhelmed her furred abdomen. She planted on the ancient dust and grit. She scrabbled to escape, but Lydiah's whip came down a fourth time and a fifth.

Golda groaned and slowly slipped back into her human form, as if her flesh and muscles had surrendered against her will to Lydiah. She'd been tricked once again by Boudi's horrible overseer. Lydiah bent awkwardly, reached down, and grasped the abandoned Gypsy sword. Lydiah closed the distance.

"It's time to end this, you pathetic creature. Boudi-Ca belongs to me. She will always belong to me. You will never have her."

Golda shoved with her knee, enough to shift onto her back. She was able to lift one half-numbed arm, her last working appendage. Lydiah edged the sword past her arm, seeking her exposed throat. Behind Lydiah, however, a low glow had risen from the darkness. Octavia was rising to her feet. The elder Mimọ was stained with blood from head to toe. Her towering body was every inch as bent, scarred, and broken as Lydiah. Another low, menacing growl came from the Beast, which rose up on its massive claws, echoing Octavia's resurrection.

Golda hitched when Lydiah lurched forward, grazing her throat with the tip of the sword. Lydiah gasped under the impact of Octavia's holy bolt, which had arrived just in time. Lydiah tripped and fell face first onto the stones. Another holy bolt followed, piling into Lydiah, and the smell of smoke and singed flesh rose from her burnt robe.

"Wickedness and treachery!" Octavia lurched forward. "You must...be... expunged from existence, you evil...disgusting Jinn."

"Stop! Please stop!" Boudi-Ca raised her sword at the ready, hesitating on the tips of her toes, as if wanting to assault Octavia, but unwilling to kill the elder Mimọ. The Beast showed no such qualms. With one thunderous bound, it seized the towering Mimọ ambassador again in its enormous maw. Octavia's cry went muffled and silent as she crumpled. The Beast drove Octavia back down to the floor with a heavy crack and scrape of monstrous claws. Golda heard the Beast's voice again in her head.

Thisss one is deliciousss. Very sssweet when she bleedsss and squirmsss.

Boudi-Ca bent over Lydiah. "Mistress? Mistress? Wake up."

Golda worked feverishly to massage life back into her numb limbs. Thankfully Lydiah wasn't moving or responding to Boudi's overtures, at least not yet. "Boudi, your Mistress is evil. Please stop trying to wake her, and let's leave this place. If Lydiah hadn't ruined your Mimọ heart, you could have healed her, but you can't. It's a perfect reward for everything she has done."

Boudi-Ca sniffed, as if crying. She summoned a tenebris lux to replace Lydiah's lux, which had winked out. Boudi-Ca gripped Lydiah's burnt shoulder. "I'm trying to heal her like I remember, but it isn't working. I think she's dying!"

Golda snorted. "I'm sure all of the dead people in this room would be happy to see that, if any of them were still alive. Please, Boudi. We need to leave."

Golda willed more energy into her limbs, enough energy to shift into cat form again, which further dispelled the numbness. The Beast turned its six red eyes in her direction. It rose from Octaviah's broken form and lumbered across the floor. Golda wrenched herself lamely onto four legs and limped away, grateful that even Boudi-Ca had the sense to skitter from Lydiah when the Beast approached.

The Beast's three heads rose, and an earth-shaking wail rose in the cavern. One head lowered and licked Lydiah's leg. Another head darted down to swallow Boudi. Boudi-Ca flashed away in the nick of time. She re-appeared ten meters to the side, where she looked shaken, terrified, and pale.

"Fine! I want to leave now!" Boudi-Ca sprinted for the far passageway, and Golda urged her own clumsy, half-numb cat paws to propel her forward. The Beast gave quick chase, but the enormous creature slowed when Boudi-Ca flashed again, opening up still more space. Boudi's lux darted and spiraled after her like a will-o-wisp.

Tired. We are too tired to chassse this little creature.

Golda managed a grim smile as she picked up the pace away from the Beast's tree trunk legs. You have enough to eat. I would suggest the evil wizardress next.

Lydiah isss our old friend.

Golda pushed her cat legs harder to turn over. She finally rejoined Boudi-Ca at the far passage. She surged back onto her human feet, just as hope surged again in her breast, a warm hope risen from almost-extinguished ashes. She was weaponless and shaken, but she was once again headed in the right direction. The Beast had receded into its dark lair and was nowhere to be seen. She walked with Boudi-Ca along the passage for a long minute, then two as it sloped upwards towards the Great Blue Hole mines.

Golda felt happiness grow from her hope, along with a rare appreciation towards the Mimos of Heaven. She was thankful that Octavia had made a last effort to turn the skirmish against Lydiah's treachery. She said nothing to Boudi-Ca for fear of breaking the spell and the silence. They only needed to keep moving farther towards freedom. Golda opened her mind wider to the tapestry. She became aware of the presence of Dingbie, who was waiting for them just ahead. The little Kishi had cloaked himself with either stealth or a concealment spell.

Dingbie detached himself from the shadows of the cavern wall when they approached his position. He held his poniard in one hand and a bag slung over his shoulder. The bag appeared to be Lydiah's fine leather satchel.

"That was a big beast, yes, quite big!" Dingbie's owl-like eyes darted back up the passageway, and his lips turned an impish smile. "I'm glad you lived, kind miss."

"It's just us three then." Golda took a deep breath and allowed tension to drain a little more from her shoulders. She was exhausted, and her Hunger was surging in her belly, a dark undertone beneath her growing buoyance. "With a little help from the Fates, we'll soon all be free. Maybe the good side does win every now and then, or at least the meek."

Boudi-Ca frowned and pointed at Dingbie. "Isn't that my Mistress' bag?"

Dingbie blinked. "What? What's that? I thought it belonged to that one mean Jinn who called me a girl-child. She was your mistress? I didn't think you a slave girl, miss."

"Well at least you got that right."

The little brownie tilted his head. "Well I didn't have to stop and wait, did I? I could have taken these coins for myself, but no. Honor among thieves. That's an old Kishi saying, miss."

"Of course," Golda interjected. "So you're just a thief then, and not a vicious murderer or a crazed assassin. That's a relief to know, and you're welcome to keep traveling with us."

Dingbie reached for his forehead, as if to politely tip an invisible hat. "Quick fingers and a quick wit are the Kishi virtues miss, and to always remember a good deed done to us, or a bad one. I planned to give you the gold coins to repay you for my freedom, but I didn't know they were already spoken for."

Golda nodded. "You can give those coins to Boudi, if it pleases you. She has more use for them than I do."

Dingbie shrugged off the satchel. Boudi-Ca seized the bag and sifted through the contents. When Boudi's hand emerged, she held a small lambskin pouch. She quickly pressed it to her nose. An aromatic flowery smell filled the air. Golda sniffed. A tingle of pleasure and longing filled her head when she identified the fine scent of a violet-black varietal. She grabbed Boudi-Ca's hand, even as the fledgling tipped her head back and lifted the pouch to pour the powder out. Boudi-Ca snarled, an ugly sound coming from the fledgling's girlish throat.

"What are you doing, Golda? Let me go."

"No. You're not doing that anymore. It isn't good for you, and if you do it, I'm afraid I'll be doing it too. We need to stay focused. This isn't over. We still need to get past the Great Blue Hole mines and any Hell's Court devils that might be waiting for us outside."

"You're not my Mistress. You can't tell me what to do." Boudi-Ca lowered the little nectar bag nonetheless and returned her hand to the satchel. She extracted a leather-bound book. Her eyes widened as if in shocked recognition. She dropped the satchel and quickly leafed through the pages of the book in the light of her tenebris lux.

"Shall we be going then, miss?" Dingbie offered another nervous grin. "Good turns and all said, I'd still be grateful for an escort."

"This is my secret diary." Boudi's eyes flicked to and fro over the handwritten pages of the book. "This is everything I ever wrote about my Mistress and me. There is a lock of my hair in here, and one of my black silk hair ribbons, and one my punishment hooks. I think this is my blood. I told Breanarachelle that my Mistress had destroyed this evidence of us at our château in the North Country. I guess she didn't. My Mistress was collecting and saving everything, even while she was scolding me. She said the evidence needed to be destroyed."

Golda shrugged. "So Inanna was a hypocrite and a scheming, compulsive liar to the very end, and now she's dead. What did you expect? She was probably holding that book as leverage over you, and your blood was intended for some sort of evil control spell."

"No. She loves me." Boudi-Ca sniffed and wiped her eyes. She slid the book back inside the leather satchel. "I can feel it. She loves me, and I love her. Of all of her possessions, my Mistress only brought this book and some gold aurei to leave Mer. Now I'm abandoning her. I can't. I just can't. I have to try harder to heal her. Can you carry her, Golda, if the Beast will let us sneak in and get her?"

"No! I'm not carrying Lydiah. I'd rather bury her than carry her!"

Boudi-Ca turned and retraced her steps back down the passageway, quickening her pace as she went. Dingbie watched Boudi-Ca go with his eyes wide. "Where is she going, miss?"

"Boudi, the Beast just tried to eat you a minute ago!" Golda gritted her teeth as her tension returned to her shoulders tenfold. She wavered, and then followed Boudi. "Boudi, we can live happily at the werewolf stronghold until we can re-find the Lady. You'll be safe, and I love you more than Lydiah ever will. Please come back. We need to leave. Please leave with me!"

Chapter 37.

❦

Boudi-Ca picked up the pace towards the Beast's chamber. She held her sword firmly. She was worried that Golda might try to stop her with force. She could flash away if needed, but she preferred to save her energy. Golda was following only a few steps behind. The passage opened back up into the massive dome of the Beast's chamber, which had fallen into an inky gloom. Boudi-Ca descended the broken steps into the old sunken plaza. Her lux glowed dimly past the bloody remnants of Lieutenant Nefra to the hulk of the great Beast.

A queer, low moan echoed in the darkness. Boudi-Ca frowned and stepped closer, even as fear gripped her belly. She heard another muffled moan. The Beast's nearest head turned to glance at her, but without much menace. The moans weren't coming from the Beast. Boudi-Ca swallowed. She knew Lydiah's moans intimately, especially those moans that Fennel evoked in her, those soul-compressions of pleasure torn by cruel shreds of pain. Lydiah's pained moans in that moment came a little louder, followed by her breathless, panting voice.

"Yes. Come into me. Come, my lovely. Come for me."

The Beast grunted again and continued to work with its massive hips. Boudi-Ca dared to take a few steps closer. Lydiah's side-turned face was just visible beneath the Beast's scaly belly. The Beast heaved and lifted its three heads with a low, ululating sigh of pleasure. The creature lifted its bulk and lumbered away, where it settled on the floor again with a satisfied sigh. The Beast began to lick and chew anew on Octavia's corpse.

"By the gods," Golda muttered in a low tone. "I wish I hadn't seen that happen. Please, Boudi. This woman is a monster. Please come with me, quickly."

Lydiah dragged herself slowly to her feet. She stretched as if re-locating her bones. She composed the remaining tatters of her nightgown. She stepped forward and raised her hand. "No. Come to me instead, fledgling."

"Mistress, that was really sort of—"

Boudi-Ca gasped when the desirous kin-hex seized her from her feet. The hex yanked her forward so powerfully that she felt like her spine had snapped. She flew fifteen paces through the air and collided into Lydiah, hard enough to feel the warm wetness down the insides of Lydiah's thighs. Boudi-Ca twisted away from the ickiness, but Lydiah caught her from behind and wrapped her up with a tight one-armed hug. Lydiah chuckled.

"The pendulum has swung again, Golda."

Golda glared daggers at Lydiah. She edged towards her sword, which lay nearby on the floor next to Lydiah's whip. "So what next? You think you'll just walk out of here with Boudi-Ca? Your tricks and illusions aren't enough to kill me. Your Beast won't kill me. Boudi-Ca won't kill me. You have no one left to manipulate."

Lydiah executed another quick kin-hex. Her whip handle flew from the floor to her hand. "I think my fledgling and I will try for the tower that Lieutenant Nefra spoke of—her ex-girlfriend's honey moon retreat. My husband and I visited there a few years ago as a courtesy from Archduke Apollyon. I'll race you up to the Carthago promontory, Golda. The early bird gets Master Andros' Nanka."

Lydiah swung her whip low. Boudi-Ca shrank when the whip handle rubbed within inches of her crotch, but Lydiah wasn't thrusting obscenely at her nether petals. Instead, Lydiah muttered low, arcane syllables. The air crackled and congealed with tingling electricity. Boudi-Ca felt the space expand between her legs. An intense pressure thrummed, widening her thighs and pressuring the space under her buttocks.

A mane of glowing pink hair coalesced and ripped through the air in front of her, and she was suddenly elevated. Within a split second, she was straddling the saddle of an enormous glowing pink horse with Lydiah mounted right behind her. The magical horse darted into motion. It accelerated out of the Beast's chamber, and then began to climb the cavernous exit passage on silent hooves. A forlorn echoing whine came from the Beast in the darkness. A second, fainter growl sounded, accompanied by a fast patter of paws.

Boudi-Ca glanced over her shoulder. "Golda is still coming for me, Mistress."

Lydiah squeezed her more tightly and kissed her ear. "I doubt if she can go faster than us. Now stay silent, fledgling. I'm trying to remember the way out of this place, and I need to focus and maintain my pink horse spell. Once we leave the Bolgia and the mines, we'll be totally exposed. I see you found my satchel. I'm very pleased. Thank you so much, my love."

The pink horse flowed with speed up the tunnel, which soon gave into another cavern. Lydiah veered the horse into a side passage and on into a dark junction where an iron rail ran embedded in the floor. Old mining carts lined one wall, and an oil lamp flickered. A straight hallway with angled ceiling beams rose through a draft of fresher, less sulfuric air.

Lydiah turned the horse right and followed the rails to another junction, and within a few more minutes a light appeared. The pink horse trotted past a great heap of broken volcanic stones and through a dusty adit. A group of collared slaves paused with their mining picks to watch. The bedraggled, slack-jawed humans were filthy with dust and grit.

Dawn's chariot rolled low in the Haawiyah morning sky. A few more human slaves picked their way up the side of a wide bowl or caldera, which was crisscrossed with mining roads. Lydiah navigated upwards into the sunlight, accelerating to where the road crested the bowl. From the bowl's rim, a vast expanse of mining pits stretched in all directions. Old wooden watchtowers perched on the pit interstices. Work roads formed a spiderweb around vast honeycombs of stripped stone.

The pink horse accelerated around the rim road and joined another road, even as dark forms stirred and looked over the parapets of the closest watchtowers. The horse turned onto a third road, which curved up to a higher rim. The road rose for several minutes until a line of ancient trees became visible over an escarpment, stark in the morning sunlight. Odors of rotten forest and brittle brushes wafted to mingle with the smells of dust, sulfur, and slave toil. The pink horse darted onward and passed under another watchtower. Boudi-Ca felt her skin tingle, and not from the lips of her mistress.

"Mistress, the guards see us."

"Yes," Lydiah said in her ear. "I hadn't realized the watchtowers were so close together when we looked at them from the mine opening. I expect we can outrun the pit wardens and make for the forest. Hell's Court posts the laziest, dumbest devils out here in the Great Blue Hole. This is where we need a tracker, but I can't trust Golda. I have to say she's an impressive runner in her cat form, though."

The magical pink horse crested the highest rim of the mines and passed between two more watchtowers, where the dark forms of devils were scurrying down like a swarm of black ants. Dozens of Hell horses waited for the devils below. Lydiah pressed the pink horse harder up the rutted, over-traveled road. The road turned and leveled to traverse a bouldered thicket towards the forest, beyond which rose the distant high cliffs of the Erebus rim.

The pink horse slowed and came to a shuddering stop. A dark man stood in the middle of the road. Archduke Fennel was clad in a suit of polished black armor. His widow's peak and black hair made him appear raven-like in the morning sunlight. A cruel smile played on his thin lips. He held his bared sword-cane in one hand, and in the other he held an ebon-black obelisk some three hands high, tucked tightly against his armored chest. Alongside him stood a tanned Jinn with long dark hair. A curved sword hung at her shapely hip.

"Hello, my husband," Lydiah said loudly. "You're traveling through time again, I see. And you, Shadow. I hope you're staying well and healthy?"

"I am," Shadow answered. "Soon you will not be. We have you in a vise."

"So you came along with my husband and his Ebon Timepiece. You helped him prepare a trap for me in time."

"Yes," Shadow answered with a proud smile. "I told the Archduke my desire to bring you and your pathetic fledgling to justice, and thereby clear my name from failure in the purgation. The Archduke honored me with this duty. We arrived a few hours ago, and we arranged things with the Great Blue Hole devil wardens. They'll be swarming you and arresting you in a few moments, but you should really be negotiating with your husband, not me."

"Of course," Lydiah said. "I know you're stretched well beyond your personal limitations at this point, Shadow. So you're ready for me to kill you then?"

"Good luck with that." Shadow chortled confidently, but nonetheless she took a step back.

Lydiah cleared her throat. "Kill her, fledgling. I'll handle my husband."

"You won't handle anything," Fennel interjected. "You'll unsummon your horse and kneel at my feet, wife. You'll take your ebon collar. You'll deliver your fledgling back to Hell's Court. You'll beg for mercy from our Lord, my father."

Boudi-Ca gripped her sword hilt. She was absolutely terrified to go close to Fennel, but she steadied her nerves and flashed. She reversed her blade into Shadow's back. The attack was similar to the one she'd used against Breanarachelle, a quick strike to the side of her spine. Shadow screamed in pain, twisted, and toppled.

Anakh nothra. Ipsakh nothra.

Fennel's voice rose over the Great Blue Hole rim thicket. Smoky snakes congealed and darted forward from the ether. Boudi-Ca gasped as Fennel's magical snakes piled into her, faster than she could think to flash. Intense pain laced her insides. The pummeling forced a staccato of grunts from her lungs. She was knocked hard like a ragdoll onto the road stones.

Lydiah threw her whip, which curled and twisted around Fennel's legs, even as Fennel pivoted quickly and hurled his sword cane at his wife. The tip struck home in Lydiah's chest. Lydiah groaned in pain, and the pink horse underneath her flickered, dimmed, and sprang to life again, although more feebly. She wrenched the bloody cane from her chest. Boudi-Ca felt her belly clutch when Fennel turned back to her.

Anakh nothra—

Golda burst from the underbrush to take Fennel's legs out from under him. Fennel toppled over with his feet still hindered by Lydiah's whip. Golda reversed and pounced, flurrying and clawing for chinks in his armor. Lydiah urged her pink horse into motion again, veering left around Fennel to skirt the skirmish. Boudi-Ca rose unsteadily to her feet. Her rib bones felt broken, but she still clutched her sword. She tried to focus and find an opening to flash and attack Fennel, but her head swam.

Lydiah swept her from her feet and back into the uncanny glowing pink saddle, and then they were away into the fringe of the forest, even as the watchtower devils came in close pursuit with their herd of Hell horses. Boudi-Ca felt the leafy breeze blow past her face. She was in awe of the power of her Mistress, but she could feel a warm wetness of Lydiah's blood trickling horribly down her lower back.

"I love you, Mistress."

"I love you too, my fledgling." Lydiah's voice came quavering and pained. "I always wondered if you'd be the death of me."

The horse entered the dark forest and slowed to negotiate the trees. Boudi-Ca ducked and winced as the rough bark of low-hanging tree branches thrashed her. Lydiah groaned suddenly, and the horse flickered again. Boudi-Ca felt the saddle disappear under her buttocks. She tumbled head over heels through the detritus of the forest floor. Lydiah fell alongside her, wheezing and coughing. Lydiah's frontside was soaked in blood.

"Mistress?" Boudi-Ca felt tears coming to her eyes. "Mistress? Get up, please. We need to go. I wish I could heal you."

Lydiah gave a pained smile. "You've healed me, my love. You've healed me. You showed me feelings that I'd thought lost two hundred years ago when I lost Henry. Fennel drained everything good from me, and left only my dark side. You need to go on without me. You need to run and flash as fast as you can, and may Allyssia bless your footsteps."

"Surely the devils won't arrest you, right? They won't sentence you to death?"

"If they don't arrest me now, they will when your diary is published." Lydiah gave a coughing laugh, and blood dribbled from her lips. "I spent this last winter editing, then Vladimir made a copy. I delivered the sealed copy to my printer last week, and I sent him a bird before I entered the Bolgia pits. I ordered him to publish it. Everyone will know the truth of our love in a few months, and I'm proud of the truth. I'm proud of you, my fledgling."

The heavy hooves of Hell horses thumped through the forest. Tree branches snapped and cracked off of hardened devil armor. The devils had already caught up with them. The first devil hurled his net. Boudi-Ca twisted away. She flashed and struck the flank of the Hell horse. The horse screamed and bucked, sending the devil flying. Boudi-Ca kicked his ugly face as he fell and speared him through his exposed neck on the rebound.

The devils were a grim horde however, almost outnumbering the tree trunks. They carried cruel hooks and gaffes. Boudi-Ca felt her hollow belly go empty with despair. At her feet, Lydiah sighed and went white. The Mistress closed her eyes. Boudi-Ca curled her lip and darted forward to confront the next devil, but his long gaffe swung, forcing her to parry. The forest floor offered horrible footing. Another devil reined in behind her. A net flew. A hook snagged her shoulder.

~*~

Golda raked at Fennel's exposed face and head, the only flesh uncovered by his armor. He swatted her backwards, and she felt like her cat neck had snapped. She rolled with the punch nonetheless and surged forward to flurry again.

Fennel defended with his raised arm while his lips murmured another spell. Golda shrank from the draining force that assailed her psyche. A vortex pulled her down, as if the surface of the road was opening to swallow her whole, to suck her soul away into a distant, dark, and undesirable place. Fennel climbed back to his feet. His cruel face loomed above her, painted with an arrogant look of victory.

Golda threw all of her willpower against the devil sorcery. Even as her inner human soul was pulled down, she managed to hold onto her cat form and resist the magic. She emerged from the brink of the void and leapt to flurry again with her claws. Fennel was taken by surprise. She scored a deep gash to his face. He reeled and knocked her away bodily, dropping the Ebon Timepiece.

Golda quickly surveyed the scene. She'd distracted Fennel to buy Boudi-Ca time, and it was her turn to flee into the forest. A bright light suddenly burned across the morning landscape. The light flashed through the thicket and hit Fennel. The arch-devil groaned with a queer sound of mingled pleasure and pain. Another bolt of lightning streaked across the landscape, knocking the archduke back two more paces, even as he tried to bend and retrieve his Timepiece.

Golda blinked. A woman's voice sounded in her head then. It was a resonant, bell-like voice that she hadn't heard in five years or more—the voice of Allyssia.

Get the Ebon Timepiece please. Bring it to me.

Golda leapt and seized the Timepiece in her jaws. She turned and darted away, even as Fennel gave chase, evidently unscathed. She glimpsed a white figure at the verge of the forest, which seemed to recede even as she charged towards it through the thicket stones. She dodged around a boulder to evade a pair of mounted Great Blue Hole devils, one of which swung a hooked slave-capturing implement.

The attack was too high and slow. A dozen more Hell horses and grim, pitiless faces were streaming up from the mine rim. The devils had surely mounted a force of a hundred in the rim country that morning. The weave of the tapestry was an ugly nest of serpentine black threads. Golda ducked easily past another devil attack. She was too agile for the big horses amidst the scattered thicket boulders, and she was too fast for Fennel in his armor.

Strangely, the entire scene was pinwheeling around her as if in slow motion. She felt Sharp as a tack and fast as a rabbit.

She trotted unscathed into the forest and worked her jaw to get a better grip on the ancient magical artifact in her mouth. She could feel its power tingling in the sockets of her teeth. The familiar protective forest gloom closed around her and cloaked her. She was at the edge of the Bolgia rim country, a terrain she knew well from several moons of living with the Gypsies. She felt relieved for a moment until she heard Boudi's high-pitched scream, close through the old Haawiyah oaks.

A woman on a great white horse was waiting in the shelter of the forest. Artemisiah slung her bow over her shoulder. The avatar of the Love goddess nodded a greeting and reached low. "Give me the Timepiece. You've done very well, Mistress Golda. As always, you've exceeded my expectations."

Golda rose to human form even as her heart tore open from the continued sounds of Boudi's anguished shrieks of agony. Golda caught the Ebon Timepiece as it fell from her mouth and held it up for the virginal white huntress.

"How did I do well, my Lady? This is a complete disaster. We need to help Boudi. Please, will you help Boudi?"

"I hope I can," Artemisiah answered. "She is quite dear to me."

Golda blinked. "She's dear? If she's so dear, why did you wait more than three years after the fall of your city to show up down here?"

"I was waiting for you." The avatar of the goddess tipped her head apologetically.

"I was studying with Masad."

Artemisiah nodded. "Sometimes we put ourselves before love. Sometimes it's too late, and our love can't be saved. Sometimes everything is fine. Sometimes it's just a matter of time."

Artemisiah wheeled her horse and darted away with uncanny speed through the forest. Golda looked on with disbelief at the receding goddess, who was headed in the opposite direction from Boudi.

She slumped against the shelter of a tree trunk, even as she heard the hoof steps of the Hell horses filtering down through the forest. The devils were coming for her. She needed to shift and flee, but she needed a moment first. She was utterly exhausted. She'd given everything to chase Lydiah for a league or more, then to protect Boudi-Ca, apparently all for naught.

Heartbeat.

Boudi's cries had gone silent in the trees. The forest seemed to close in, and the gloomy, rotting foliage shifted oddly. Golda steadied herself and shook her head. She felt as if she might faint.

Heartbeat.

Golda looked down at the dead leaves and twigs under her feet. She opened her mind to track the devils in the weave, but the tapestry was slowly melting in her mind's eye like a tide, leaving a queer view of the red striations in the fateful underweave.

Heartbeat.

Golda opened her eyes. She levered her body up in the cool sand. She winced when her palm pressed against the hard edge of an old jawbone. The beach was littered with millions of old bones, all gleaming white in the pale sunlight. High above the Sea of Desire, green spider-lightning flickered in the Isandlwana atmospheres.

Boudi-Ca lay nearby. The Mimọ girl was still wrapped in her heavenly robes, pale and ethereal. The girl wore the magical Bliss-Trip Bonnet, which still looked damp from the perilous fall from Heaven. Golda pressed close and felt Boudi's chest. The girl was alive. Her chest moved slowly, straining against her chaste Mimọic straight corset.

Golda felt her heart beat harder, even as her Hunger quickened in her belly. The trip to Heaven had taken everything out of her. She was desperate to feed. She looked up at the sky and opened her mind wider to the tapestry. She could glimpse no Mimọ guardians, but she and Boudi-Ca weren't alone on those remote Isandlwana shores. A familiar thread was closing the distance, and another wasn't far behind. A feminine figure topped a low rise and approached. The interloper was Herpessenia-Ca, the younger daughter of Allyssia.

"Finally we found you." Herpessenia offered a faint smile with her fish-like, pointy little teeth. "You've got the girl, just as my mother promised."

Golda frowned. "Why are you here? This is kind of a surprise."

"I'm on a special mission," Herpessenia answered. "My Mother appointed me as an official ambassador for our city. She's sending me on a visit with my ex-husband under the sea. At first I was insulted, but I'm looking forward to Poseidon's court. Mother's city has gotten boring."

"Everything is relative."

Herpessenia sauntered close to Boudi, knelt down, and turned the girl's limp arm. Herpessenia smirked and examined a silver bracelet on Boudi's wrist. She tugged it with her fingers. "I've heard Mimọ girls taste like sugar, spice, and everything nice. They taste even better than a Seelie Kishi slave and best of all on a Sunday."

"What are you doing?" Golda licked the sea salt from her lips. She spat gritty sand. Her Hunger surged more in her belly, and her eyes drifted to Herpessenia's beauty. Herpessenia was wearing a diaphanous gown, a garment that showed all of her divine curves.

"I'm taking this Mimọ girl's magical time bracelet. It's part of my mission." Herpessenia made a bored face, as if overburdened by the chore. "Mother called it a wrist-watch. I don't even know what the wrist-watch is supposed to be watching. It's important, though. I'm supposed to drop it into the deepest depths of the Sea of Desire on my way to visit Poseidon."

"How could the Lady even know the Mimọ would be wearing such a thing?"

"I don't know." Herpessenia unfastened the bracelet and transferred it to her own pale wrist. "Are you feeling well, Golda? We've been looking for you for a quite a while, even though Mother told us where to go."

"I'll survive, and I can only hope the Mimọ girl will be fine. I'm desperate to feed though, and I need to get back to the city. Do you have a horse?"

Herpessenia shrugged. "It's in the forest. Have fun. I'm going for swim. Wish me luck."

Golda watched Herpessenia-Ca stride into the sea until the green waves crashed against her hips. The divine daughter dove into the waters and disappeared. Golda sighed. She wasn't surprised that Herpessenia wasn't interested in helping her any further.

She turned again to Boudi, even as her Hunger excavated more deeply into her belly. She'd expended everything on her long trip to Heaven with Mareinah. She was completely empty, and she had no emotional strength to mourn Mareinah's fate in that moment.

Golda tested her lips against the Mimọ girl's delicate mouth. She felt an intense yearning to sample the sweetness that Herpessenia had spoken of. Boudi-Ca was just a waif of an Mimọ, but she glowed with an unearthly beauty. Golda slid her hand over Boudi's abdomen and lower, pressing between the slender, yielding thighs. She fell into a trance and ignored the feeling of trespassing in a holy sanctum. She sealed Boudi's lips with her own. She was only vaguely aware when Ayelet approached on horseback over the sands.

"What are you doing to that poor girl, Golda?" Ayelet dismounted. "Leave her alone. By the gods, she's beautiful though."

Golda clenched her jaw and used all of her will to break the kiss. She shook her head, trying to clear her dull senses. "I need to feed desperately, but you're right. I've been on a wild journey. I'm not in my right mind."

"That's understandable, chérie. You're gaining more self-control as you grow. I apologize if I never had enough patience with your impatience." Ayelet cleared her throat. "We need to get off of these sands right away and rendezvous with Mistress Ivanka. The Lady warned me that the Mimọs might send a rescue party. I can help you onto my horse. Once we get into the safety of the forests, you can take me or a willing Kishi if we can find one."

"You don't do your fledglings. It's one of your rules."

"Lady Allyssia has told me some interesting things as of late." The crow's feet furrows deepened around Ayelet's hazel eyes, and her gaze went far away. "I say screw the rules. I say live and love who you want while there's still time. Love should never, ever be subjected to rules and regulations. I want to live my life to the fullest while I'm still alive, at least until I'm spending every hour training this girl in blades and love taking."

Golda tilted her head and looked down again at the Mimọ girl. "I can't imagine a sword in Boudi's hand. She's too weak. She's innocent. She's meek."

Ayelet smiled. "I'm not worried. Muscles don't count for so much in the desire-realm, as you well know. The Lady assures me that Boudi-Ca will be a great fledgling, and one day she'll be one of the finest blade mistresses in all of the realms. I have every reason to believe."

###

~*~

About the Author

Arnett Hartwell, Born in London, UK in 1955. His parents are Ed and Liz Hartwell. Arnett studied Communications at the School of Oriental and African Studies. He overcame wrongful conviction early in his life, alcoholism, and smoking Kush (not really, he is working on giving up kush) (No that's not true either; he loves kush and is not giving that up). He worked in sales at Montanaro Asset Management. Where he challenged upper management to create a lounge area for all the employees. Arnett is Kind, honest, Loyal, funny. He is always telling great stories. And never afraid to stand up to injustice, big or small. He is most known for twerking with a coworker at an office party.

We developed each manuscript through hundreds of hours of effort and many revisions to deliver the finished, polished work. Any form of patronage and support is appreciated.

Deviant: Boudi-Ca Chronicles Book 1

In an Underworld city ruled by a Love Ifreeta, (powerful Djinn) Boudi-Ca is adopted by a Jinni who sees potential in encouraging her rebellious urges. Boudi-Ca must re-evaluate her sense of self in a society where the patriarchy is turned on its head. The women are powerful, magical, and dominant.

Dreams: Boudi-Ca Chronicles Book 2

In the second book of the Deviant Dreams Deliver trilogy, the storm clouds continue to thicken around the Lady's little city. The pleasurable life of every New Order jinni is once again in jeopardy